WELCOME TO THE DARK AGES

Morgan and Merlin's Excellent Adventures: Book One

By
MALORY

TABLE OF CONTENTS

For Dad,

I'm sorry you didn't get chance to read this.

PROLOGUE

It had been too long since Merlin had focused on his own cultivation.

He saw that now.

Not that he had been lazy during the preceding centuries. Far from it. There had, quite simply, been too much to be done. Too many wars that needed his presence to tip the scales. Too many apprentices requiring personal guidance. Too many demons to be dispatched back to whence they came.

Amongst all that hurly-burly, when was the last time he had genuinely focused on cultivating his Qi?

Well, it was now far too late for 'what ifs.'

Time was an unforgiving mistress whose forbearance with his frivolity had run out.

Even so close to the end, he still had thought he could force the necessary breakthrough. Sensing the stalking approach of his death, he had withdrawn from Court life and dedicated his focus to cultivation. Closeted up in his tower for these last few months, he had thought he was close enough to the threshold to make up for the centuries of neglect.

But, alas, no inspiration had arrived. So here he was, seconds from death.

Strangely, the fear he had anticipated would arrive at this moment was not there. Yes, there were things he had left undone: intricate plans would now crumble; allies would fall; foes would rise.

But he left this realm a better place than it would otherwise have been. And that would have to be enough.

He just wished –

CHAPTER 1 - IN WHICH A LEGENDARY WIZARD FAILS TO FIND MY ARSE INTERESTING

"There's still time to run, you know?"

Wulfnoð glanced up at his father and mutely shook his head. The older man had been towards the centre of the shield wall for much of the day, and his exhaustion showed. Three times the blue-painted warriors from over the river had charged down at them. On each occasion, their line had held and they'd forced the attackers back up the hill.

No one thought it would happen again.

"Someone needs to let the village know we've fallen. You could buy your mother half a day's head start if you were quick . . ."

He knew his father, Æbbe, did not mean anything by it, but his words cut Wulfnoð to the quick. As the youngest member of the fyrd that were raised in response to talk of raids across the border, he had been kept in reserve during the battle thus far. Only the day's heavy losses had brought him so close to the front of the line. With the end in sight, his father had sought him out.

In frustration, Wulfnoð crashed his borrowed sword against his too-large shield, startling the older man. "Stop treating me like a child! You were years younger than me when you first stood in a wall."

Æbbe smiled sadly. He'd been barely into his teens when his own father had dragged him along on raids. There had been little of glory in what had been done in those days, and he had wanted something so much more than dark slaughter under a moonless sky for his boy.

But, as in all things, there was no second-guessing fate.

There had seemed little danger in the boy tagging along with the fyrd to repel an opportunistic raid. It had been years since those from across the river had done anything more than indulge in mild banditry. When they set out the week before, Æbbe had expected nothing more than a chance to give his son a taste of the boredom that came with warfare to dispel any romantic notions he had of the heroism of the warriors he so looked up to. Few such starry-eyed ideals survived days of marching, or sleeping countless nights in the mud and rain, before returning home without seeing hide nor hair of the enemy.

The tales of a minor incursion, however, had somewhat underestimated the scale of the force arrayed against them.

Æbbe was not a stupid man, but he could not count high enough to describe the numbers of the invaders that had swarmed down the hill that morning. That their line had held at all through the day's clashes spoke less to the stoutness of the fyrd, and more as to their recognition that to break was to ensure death reached them even faster.

He considered his boy; big for his age, but with no beard yet showing on his chin. His hair had the dusty brown blonde that spoke of the years of intermarriage between his people and those they now fought. Although, he supposed 'marriage' did not accurately describe the regular stealing of young women in which the various tribes engaged. He hoped his wife had her wits about her to ensure their family's safety when these invaders swept outwards towards their village.

Wulfnoð clearly thought he had been kept from the front lines due to some misguided wish to protect him. The truth was more mundane. No one wanted a child at their shoulder in the shield wall if there were any other options. Brave he may be, but bravery only goes so far when your survival depends on the strength of the man beside you.

Now the final battle was upon them, there was no longer that luxury. Æbbe had not sought him out because he wanted to encourage him to run; rather, it was so that no one else had to have a weak shield-mate when that last clash came. He was comfortable, as far as anyone could be, with their impending deaths. That was the way of fate, after all. But he did not want any of his friends to fall because his son could not hold the line.

He did not want that to be his last sight in this world.

"I meant no disrespect, Wulf." He held his son's eyes and smiled broadly. "You are certainly no child, and I am proud to share this day with you." In his peripheral vision, he could see the force at the top of the hill begin to form up.

Whoever was in charge up there seemed to know their business. For as long as Æbbe could remember, clashes with those from across the river had been chaotic affairs. The ones painted in blue would charge, madly, towards them, and should their shield wall hold, they would push the attackers backwards until they broke. Or, much more rarely, the frenzied attack would breach their line, and things would descend into a melee.

Today had not worked out like that.

For a start, whoever was leading this invasion had somehow persuaded enough horses to cross the river to field a significant cavalry force. That accounted for the fyrd finding itself trapped within a tight square at the base of the hill. Although no horse would charge into a forest of shields and spears, no running man could hope to outpace pursuit on flat ground. So, they had been forced to cluster up into a tight group.

It was the worst possible formation for when the opposing force had archers. Oh, and a wizard.

Æbbe could not remember the last time he had faced a wizard on the field of battle. Thirty? Forty years? He had assumed the people from across the river had lost the knowledge to produce them. That or they were all too afraid of Merlin to risk making themselves known.

But, there he was throwing balls of flame into what remained of the fyrd. Wooden shields could keep a man safe from inexpertly launched arrows. Fireballs, not so much.

He pressed his hand down on his son's shoulder and turned to face the attackers. Æbbe knew how this would go. There would be a final volley from the archers, a last ball of flame from the wizard, and this would make the fyrd take refuge behind their shields. As that was launched, a mass of warriors would hurtle down the hill to crash against their front row.

If they were lucky, the shield wall would hold, as it had three times already today. But if, as Æbbe knew it would, the line buckled, then those horsemen would immediately sweep down upon them and into the gap. He mentally rehearsed the movement of his shield arm to protect his boy from a downward swing from a mounted foe.

He might be able to buy him the time to retreat and -

But, no. The commander of that force would not want any word of quite how extensive this raid was to leak out. So, there would be no surrender; not that Æbbe felt anyone would wish to seek it. Tales of the grisly fate of those captured by the blue-painted ones were used to keep children up at night. Æbbe was fairly sure similar stories were probably told on the other side too, but no one was going to risk that theory.

"Arrows!" The shout went up, and Wulfnoð, as he had been taught, raised his shield to slot it in against his father's and the man to his other side. Seconds later, they felt repeated impacts and searing heat as a fireball followed the arrows.

There was just a moment for Wulfnoð and Æbbe to meet each other's eyes for a final time before a horde of blue-painted warriors surged into their shields, and their line, inevitably, broke.

**

I don't know if you've ever had your soul forced inside the dead body of a dark-age warrior?

I'm going to assume not because, if you had, I would like to think you might have left the rest of us some tips. Because, as an experience, it is a lot.

One minute, I am looking onrushing death straight in the face, and the next, I'm lying on a battlefield, surrounded by mangled corpses – are some of them on fire? - and a crow is trying to peck out my eye.

Don't move.

"Sure, disembodied voice. Now is just the time for a game of Sleeping Lions. I have another eye, after all. I wouldn't want to spoil the fun."

If you move, they will see you still live, and then they will kill you.

"If I **don't** move, I'm going to lose an eye and scream like a banshee. I imagine that will also let them know I am alive, and then they will kill me. I just will see it coming fifty per cent less well."

I am beginning to regret my choice—one moment.

I hear a caw of pain – when did I get so good at interpreting the vocal stylings of birds? – and then there was the unmistakable smell of roast chicken. In which I guess I was mistaken as, presumably, my unseen friend had just flash-fried the crow.

As someone who has spent most of their . . . I guess my previous 'life' in a state of crippling anxiety, I was enjoying how chilled I seemed to be in my new body. Reincarnated? No problem. Unseen voices flinging magic spells at birds? Bring it on. Apparently, all those years of SSRIs could have been avoided by simply moving my soul into someone else's noggin. Who knew?

Speaking of which, as I fumbled around inside my new skull for a moment, I stumbled upon the memories of the body I was now inhabiting. I seemed to be called Wulfnoð. Well, that was a hard 'no'. I have this thing about my name being composed of letters I can pronounce. Picky, I know.

I also seemed to be a boy.

I turn my head and feel a little burst of sorrow at seeing the man lying next to me. That was a bit unnerving. Did that mean Wulfnoð was still in here somewhere with me? That would be weird. Weirder. Actually, that aspect of weirdness could take a ticket and get in line. Of all the weird things about today, a bit of Wulfnoð's soul still being in this body was not going to feature in the top ten.

Anyway, the memories I had access to told me that the body I was looking at was Wulfnoð's father, Æbbe. This dude was extremely dead. From how his shield was lying partly over my body, it did not take a huge leap of deductive reasoning to recognise he had sacrificed his life to protect his son.

He was a good man. Even at the end, he chose his son rather than his own life.

"I'm sure Wulfnoð was very touched for the few more seconds of life that bought him."

It did not buy the boy any more time at all. Instead, Æbbe's sacrifice allowed me to pluck you from your own impending death and move your soul here to replace his just as it fled.

I did not immediately have anything to say about that.

Wulfnoð's memories overwhelm me for a moment. He seems to have had a pretty good life, as far as my understanding of sixth-century England went. Was this even England? The people in Wulfnoð's memory all looked pretty Anglo-Saxon, and there were all those weird letters too. There was a mother who seemed to care quite a lot about me. Wulfnoð. I need to keep that clear in my head, or that way madness lay. He had a bunch of siblings that hated each other with exactly the right amount of red-hot heat to suggest they were extremely close.

And then there was Æbbe, who he adored.

Yeah, mooching about in these memories is going to make me sad. The last thing I need right now, on top of everything else, is to realise I have possessed the body of an illiterate barbarian from the beginning of history who had a deeper emotional bond with his family than I did with my own.

That was the sort of wound that could fester.

A group of faces from my own life seek to swim upwards in my memory. I drown them with the ruthless efficiency of the owner of a cattery two months after a un-neutered tom got loose.

Goodness. That was a bleak metaphor. Moving swiftly on. "I'm going to need a bit of a catch-up here about what's going on, oh voice with the skill to cremate crows with the power of thought. Who are you, and what do you want with my dead arse?"

I am more than happy to enlighten you, my dear. But, to reassure you, there is absolutely nothing about your arse that interests me. My name is Merlin, and I am going to need you to help me save the world.

CHAPTER 2 — IN WHICH A LECTURE ON CULTIVATION IS GIVEN

It's much harder to commune surreptitiously with the spirit of a legendary mage than you might think. Especially when you're lying in the middle of a muddy battlefield surrounded by the slowly decomposing bodies of what used to be your friends and family.

Of course, I didn't personally know these guys from Adam, but it was hardly the lack of familiarity which made all this feel a bit awkward.

"Merlin? As in Arthur's Merlin?"

I prefer to think of it more like he is Merlin's Arthur, but I guess that's by the by. At the very least, you've heard of me and understand who I am. That will save us lots of time.

"Sure. For clarity, are you the kindly old duffer, like in the Disney cartoon version, or the hot, young dude from the BBC show?"

I understand all the words you have just used in that sentence, my dear, but appear to be missing some vital context. For the sake of argument, let me just say that I am the recently deceased Merlin, worried he has passed from the world at a critical juncture.

"And you decided that the first move in your afterlife should be to portal the soul of a dying woman into the body of a Conan the Barbarian lookalike and — what? — see where that leads? Different strokes for different folks, I guess."

If I could have a moment to explain the highly delicate nature of what is occurring across the realms -

"I think my still-breathing corpse is about to be looted, by the way."

For goodness' sake — hang on. I should be able to . . . Yes. Okay. That should stop time long enough for us to talk properly.

At his words, the Smurf-looking dude bending over me stopped moving. But he didn't just stop moving like he was startled that the body beneath him was still alive, it was more like he suddenly became an image on a bad VHS tape and someone had pressed 'pause'. Even down to him flickering like he was stuck between frames.

I reached up and touched the hand he had been using to take the pouch on my belt. Even though it was blipping in and out, it was still completely solid and real. I scrabbled to my feet from under him and looked around the rest of the battlefield.

Everything, the other soldiers, the horses, even the birds in the sky, looked as if they had been turned into a slightly blurry two-dimensional picture.

It was too good an opportunity to miss.

What are you doing?

I carried on repositioning my prospective looter's hand on the crotch of one of the other guys ransacking corpses. I had already moved the lip of a broken shield underneath the descending foot of another soldier so that, when time restarted, it would ping upwards in the best tradition of rakes and Wily-E-Coyote.

"Are you kidding me? This is like one of those superpowers you fantasise about having as a kid. You know, so you can stop time and then mess with everyone so they totally freak out when time restarts. Don't tell me you haven't pulled something like this around the Round Table: I'm sure Lancelot would be an absolute monster for it. Now, where's a bucket of water when you need one?"

If I can just draw us back to the issue of the end of the world for a moment . . .

I sighed, empathising with how Bilbo felt when Gandalf wouldn't just let him get on with enjoying reading his books and eating his breakfast. "What you need to understand here, Merlin, is that I'm dead. I died. It's over. Croaked it. Kaput. My watch is ended. Sure, I probably would have liked a few more decades to really try to nail down adulting, but I can make my peace with this being all she wrote. Now, here you are trying to get me back on the whole 'life' merry-go-round, and I'm not seeing it as the wonderful opportunity you clearly do."

I looked around, trying to find a focus for my monologue, but the wizard remained resolutely incorporeal. "Out of the two of us, I think I'm the one having the more mature response to the whole 'end-of-life', thing. Here I am, just rolling with the whole Isekai vibe you're pulling on me. Whereas you're mithering about how important you were and wondering if the world can cope without you in it. It sounds like Merlin might have quite the high opinion of himself . . . Mate, look at it this way. We're both in the same dead boat. And that particular nautical vessel doesn't have any skin in the game over the ending of the world."

You can pretend you feel no sorrow for your passing, but we both know your heart is not as callous as you seek to suggest. I could feel your ambivalence at your moment of death. Yes, there was considerable relief for the cessation of considerable pain, but there was regret and sorrow intertwined with that too.

"Maybe. But saving the world? It's not like I was a 'do-the-right-thing' girl in my own timeline. On my best day, I'd not have been your go-to person for a quest more significant than a hunt for a properly brewed cup of tea. And that was when I was me! The heart that I've got right now is from some dude called Wulfnoð, who has just seen his dad killed, and his friends hacked down around him. I'm not sure his blood-pumper is filled with sunshine and rainbows for the continuing existence of the universe either."

Wulfnoð was an honourable boy. Just as you are an honourable woman. You both had great potential as cultivators. Indeed, you may have made the very heavens tremble in other worlds and at different times. I say to you that had he not fallen this day, I would have sought to use him in the way I now appeal to you.

"Merlin, mate. You're not hearing me. The boy's dead. I'm dead. You're dead. There's a theme here. What does it matter to us if the world ends? We're dead already!"

Because if you do not help me avoid the upcoming cataclysm, your whole timeline will be wiped out.

"That's not the dealbreaker you seem to think it is. I'm dead. What do I care if people are robbed of Dave Filoni's next outrage? In fact, if you'd offered me the end-of-the-world or another seven hours of Ashoka, I'd need to take a moment. We could be doing people a favour."

You might profess not to care — I do not believe you, by the way. The occupational hazard of being, well, me, is that I can see the truth in most things — but even if you do not care about the world in general, I think you'd hesitate to condemn your sister to never coming into existence.

Man, wizards. They sure know which buttons to press.

15

***

We'd walked a distance away from the battlefield. I say 'we', but I guess I mean that I walked, and the disembodied voice of Merlin continued to lecture me from inside my head. Fortunately, years of conversations with my mother prepared me well for such a situation.

I should say it was quite a thing to walk through a time-frozen landscape. You take so many things for granted when walking in the 'real' world that suddenly do not happen when time stops.

For example, let me talk to you about blades of grass.

In a timeless universe, these bloody lethal spikes of death do not gently collapse under your feet. No sir. They stay perfectly solid and rigid and shred the seemingly solid leather boots your new body is wearing. I wondered if people who put up the 'Do not walk on the grass' signs are time-travelling altruists anxious to save humanity.

When Merlin judged we were far enough from the army, he released his hold on time, and I felt the world flow back into existence. I cocked an ear, hopefully, to see if the sound of shield-hitting-nose could be heard, but — as with so many things lately — I was to be disappointed.

In the end, I just couldn't take it anymore. "Okay. I get it. No need to keep belabouring the point. You believe you've died at the wrong moment in time, and because of this the whole world will turn out differently. Let's take that and bank it. Merlin is gone, the world is screwed. We're on the same page."

A thought occurred to me. "Aren't you supposed to be walled up for all time by the Lady in the Lake? I mean, that's not much better than death, I get it, but I don't think I've ever read that you just straight up died?"

There was what I assume to have been an awkward silence. Not having had much experience with legendary wizards, it was difficult to judge the etiquette.

What do you know about cultivation?

The non sequitur took me by surprise. That, and the fact that word took me back fifteen years to an ex-boyfriend's flat, and a pile of comics that he would defend to the death, were highbrow art and not low-key porn. "Some. I've read a few of the more well-known titles. The idea is that you get stronger by improving yourself. Like, inside and out? So, to mix genres, it's not just hacking down orcs for XP like in Warcraft. It's about understanding yourself better and meditating on your experiences. So, quality, not quantity. Oh. And there's pills. Lots and lots of pills."

That explanation is . . . not totally without merit.

"Don't burst a blood vessel with all the praise, mate. You know, I had teachers like you, Merlin. You should try turning that frown upside down once in a while."

What I mean is you appear to grasp something of the essence of what I wish to explain which pleases me greatly. I was a cultivator for many centuries – making myself 'better' in your words. By improving myself, I significantly improved my lifespan and hence was able to increase my impact on the world.

There was a pause, and I worried we'd somehow been cut off. Was bad phone signal a thing in the sixth century?

I am sorry to say I became a touch blasé about my progress. It had all come so easily to me that I did not, for a moment, think that I would fail to keep moving through the realms. After all, I had opened my meridians before I lost my first milk tooth. My dantian was full, and I had forced open my eight further meridians, before my twentieth birthday. I mastered all elemental affinities before my thirtieth year . . .

I'm going to be honest, I started to tune out a little here. I kind of felt like Merlin had invited me around for dinner and was now showing me all his holiday photographs. Whilst these accomplishments obviously meant an awful lot to him, it was just a lot of words I did not really understand. Like waxing lyrical about how beautifully the light hit the Acropolis at sunset. Sure, sounds great, but can I get another beer?

… and so I never truly focused on forming my Qi core.

The pause in his lecture sounded like a response was required. "I feel you, mate. The number of times I found myself at McDonald's rather than at spin class. Focusing on that core is hard when life gets in the way."

I don't know if it should be possible for a disembodied voice to express quite so much frustration, but the Merlin gave it a good go. *What I am trying to explain is that I became too focused on what I could achieve in the material world and neglected my spiritual journey. I thought I was doing the right thing, but now I sense the world will not progress as intended because of my failure.*

"So where do I come in?"

If, through my own selfishness, I have allowed a hole to appear in the fabric of the world, it is surely my final duty to ensure it is repaired. Thus, at the moment of my death, I sought to leave a part of myself behind to begin that work. Across time, I have searched for anyone with the potential to replace me and perform my role in this realm.

"And the best you could come up with was me? Dude, that's a crushingly low bar."

Far from it, my dear. I have been searching across time for millennia. However, each and every time I identified a potential successor, something – or more likely someone – has ensured the focus of my search became unavailable to me.

"By double booking them to play the Roxy?"

By murdering them. In all the realms to which I have access, across all of time, thousands upon thousands of potentials have been snuffed out at the moment I sought to approach them. Imagine my despair when I found myself down to the last two possible beings in all of creation with the potential to take up my mantle. And then, just as I reached out to them both, at the same moment, they were wiped out. One in a battle where the odds, surprisingly, turned against him. And the other –

"Let me guess. Did she fall in front of an articulated lorry?"

CHAPTER 3 — IN WHICH I COMMIT AN ACT OF WANTON ANIMAL CRUELTY

"That's some serious Jessica Fletcher energy you've got going on there, Merlin. Ever thought that, maybe, if you left these people alone, they wouldn't all end up horribly murdered?"

Silence.

Was it possible I had finally exhausted Merlin's last nerve? It said nothing good about my personality that spending such a short time with a mythical being capable of travelling across the aeons of space and time, I had already managed to bludgeon them into speechlessness. Maybe every single one of my exes was right after all?

I was just packing that wonderful thought away into the mental box marked 'not enough therapy in the world' when a low growl caught my attention. I spun around to see a disconcertingly large wolf enter the clearing. Not, I should be clear, that there would be a size of wolf that I would find concerting. Concerting: was that even a word? What was the opposite of disconcerting?

As with most moments of stress in my life, the verbal diarrhoea had begun.

"Any chance you have another one of the crow-cooking firebolts handy, Big M?"

Silence.

The wolf stalked towards me. Despite a number of relationships that had ended in a less-than-amicable way, I had never truly appreciated the majesty of being genuinely 'stalked'. I can absolutely confirm this wolf did it with style. With each step, sway and undulation of its body, it well and truly stalked the shit out of me.

Backing away as fast as my legs could carry me, I searched Wulfnoð's memories to see if there were any gems of wisdom to be gleaned there. It seemed the key to survival in such a situation as this was . . . to never be alone in the woods with a wolf of this size. In his extensive experience of such things, having at least six or seven warriors, each armed with a iron-tipped spear, was pretty much the minimum expectation for making it out of this situation alive.

Cheers for that, Wulfnoð. Never let it be said you don't have my back.

I felt myself press against a tree. I was right at the edge of the clearing. I briefly considered running, but I didn't think there were all those fairy stories about deep forests, young women and wolves because that was a viable survival scenario. "Good wolf. Nice wolf. Tell you what, there's a whole battlefield of dead bodies over there. Give it a few hours, and it'll be a veritable smorgasbord for a growing wolf. You don't want to fill yourself up on this stringy body. I barely want to bother with it, truth be told. But it's the only one I've got at the moment."

If my words had any impact on the Big Bad Wolf, it didn't stop it from getting closer.

There was a moment — a decent one, to be honest — where I basically just shrugged. I wasn't sold on being reincarnated or Isekai'd or portalled or whatever the fuck you want to call this. I didn't wake up this morning and have 'get eaten by a wolf' on my dance card, but I'm a broadminded girl and I've always been open to new experiences. I meant what I'd said to Merlin about being pretty much done with it all.

But then there had been the whole *condemn your sister to never coming into existence plot twist and I needed some time to properly digest that. I'd run my race and had few regrets at punching my ticket out. Well, to be fair, I'd started running my race, got distracted by all the fun things there were to do rather than running and ended up in a blissful heap on the side of the road. But Zizzie? Nope. I wasn't ready to call time for her. Yet.*

Punch it on the nose.

All my life, I've suffered from intrusive thoughts. You know, the little voice in your head that tells you to do things you really shouldn't: push your boss down the stairs, tell her she looks fat in that dress, step into the middle of the road.

For the most part, until recently, I've kept them at bay. But now, as I circled around, trying to keep a safe distance from the last sight Red Riding Hood's grandma ever saw, I was wondering how often that little voice was, in reality, an ancient wizard seeking to teach me some sort of lesson about life, the universe and Qi.

Fill your fist with energy and punch it on the nose.

"You know you sound like an absolute mentalist when you say things like that. No sane person punches a wolf on the nose. That's very close to the bit with all the teeth."

It's going to leap . . .

I threw myself to the left as the wolf suddenly bounded forward. Its jaws snapped inches from where my head had been, and I crashed with no elegance whatsoever to the ground. Hurriedly, I dragged myself back to my feet, just as the wolf turned to follow me, snuffling as it did so. I may have been anthropomorphising the whole thing a little, but I couldn't help but imagine it grinning at my pathetic show of defiance.

This is an entirely mundane animal. If it had the faintest idea of your cultivation potential it would not dare to be within a hundred miles. Direct some Qi into your hands and kill it, we have more important things to discuss.

"I don't know what you're talking about!"

There are several different schools of thought about how best to impart knowledge. Socrates, of course, pioneered the question-and-answer system. On the other hand, many favour the more direct, didactic approach. I, it will not surprise you to learn, subscribe to my own individual method.

"Which is?" The wolf and I had completed one entire circuit of the clearing and I sensed it was about to attack again.

What doesn't kill the apprentice makes them stronger. I have given you the solution to your problem. It is now up to you.

With a sudden burst of speed, the wolf lunged towards me. Instinctively, I raised my arms, attempting to shield my face, and its teeth sliced into my forearm. I kicked out, desperately trying to push it away. As the wolf was clearly still in 'playing with its food' mode, it backed away from my kick and looked at me, tilting its head as if to say, "is that the best you got?"

I scanned my surroundings frantically. There was literally nowhere for me to go, other than back towards the army. Proper frying pan and fire stuff. Cursing Merlin with every word I knew, I kept moving, trying not to turn my back to the wolf. It snarled and leaped again, with me diving to the right this time — got to keep things

19

fresh— my heart racing. I could feel pain throbbing through my arm, but fear and adrenaline kept me moving.

I knew I couldn't outlast it. Wolves are built for sustained effort, and I was — at least my old body was — built for eating cake and judging the sex lives of celebrities. I was already feeling the strain of the whole 'death of body and spirit' thing and the blood loss was a bitch. I need to end this quickly. I stooped and picked up a sizable rock. As the wolf approached for another pass, I swung with all my might, aiming for its head.

The impact barely registered — seriously, it's not even stunned — and it snapped and growled back at me. As it did so, I felt drool spatter my face. I recognise that was not the worst thing I had experienced in the last day or so, but this was my final straw for some reason.

My hands were suddenly hot. Not 'tried-to-pull-the-baking-tray-straight-from-the-oven' hot, more like they had suddenly filled with magic and turned into two orbs of pulsing light. Which was a pretty good description of what was at the end of my arms. Although, right now, it helped a bit to think of them as Wulfnoð's arms.

The wolf bowled back into me and pinned me to the ground under its weight. In a panic, I grabbed its head to keep its teeth away from snapping around my head like a bear trap. The snarling was utterly disconcerting, quite apart from the approaching likelihood of being devoured.

In desperation, I slipped my glowing hands between its jaws to prevent them from chomping down on me. Blood flowed from bites there, as well as from my earlier arm wound. And with that, I was absolutely done with all this. I hadn't been able to do much about a truck mowing me down on the main road, but I was not having 'eaten by a wolf' on my tombstone.

Without really knowing what I was doing, it occurred to me to try to pull the wolf's jaws apart. I could hear it yelp in pain as its mouth was forced wide open. And then a bit more open. And then a bit more. And then I ripped the whole animal in two with a final heave.

If I had found getting some of the animal's drool on my arm to be pretty offensive, it was as to nothing to my response to the tsunami of blood, bodily fluids and crap that covered me from the dismembered carcass. I quickly added my own pool of vomit to the wonderful fragrance that now infected the air around me.

That was . . . quite something.

"Can't talk, Merlin, being sick."

Yes, that can often be a side-effect of a cultivator's first use of their Qi.

"I think it's more the smell of everything that should be inside a wolf suddenly being on the outside of me, to be honest. But sure, if you want. The Qi thing too."

You should see if you can gather the essence from that beast. It will make you feel better.

"And after I do that, I'll percolate the doodad on the thingymajig."

Sorry, my language skill must have failed for a moment. That sounded like gibberish. Can you repeat it?

"Mate, I really don't have a clue what I'm doing here. It's been no time at all since I died, I'm suddenly in the body of a young boy, talking to Merlin, having just ripped a sodding wolf into two pieces. And I have no one around who will appreciate the joke I want to make."

You can tell me the joke.

"Don't patronise me, Big M. I know your deal is all about the Qi and the essence and the saving the world from shadowy forces that are killing potentials."

I can do all that and still appreciate a good joke.

"Really?"

Really.

"Okay. Well, you see that wolf?"

I do.

"He tried to bite off more than he could chew."

I'm ready for you to tell me the joke now.

"Fuck you, Merlin."

CHAPTER 4 – IN WHICH THE ACT OF ABSORBING ESSENCE IS MADE UNNECESSARILY SEXUAL

It took quite some time, but I eventually grasped what Merlin meant about gathering the essence from the body of the wolf. If I did something funny with my eyes – like doing one of the Magic Eye books that were popular when I was a kid – I could see these ugly red glowing blobs floating above both halves of the animal.

The effect was creepy as all hell, especially with the sun starting to fall. Apparently, what I needed to do, according to Merlin, was pull that red light into my body and then . . . well, the way he put it, I needed to think about it for a bit.

"Mate, I've spent many a long hour pondering my choice to put things in my body that were probably a bad idea. Like Tom Barnes, the first year of uni."

I sense there is some sort of underlying sexual innuendo here rather than it being a statement of fact. Should I be laughing?

If I was going to remain sane in this new world, Merlin would have to develop a sense of humour, or I would need some new friends. Speaking of which . . .

"Should we be worried about the army coming this way? Do you know which way they will be heading?"

I would rather you focus on gathering this essence rather than worrying about the world's trials. Remember, the reason why I am in this predicament is ignoring opportunities like these in order to run off and save people.

I sensed Merlin had issues about our situation that he probably needed to work through himself. I tried to move the conversation back to safer ground.

"What happened with my hands back there? You said I should push my Qi into them?"

Cultivators, even ones as newly awakened to the path as you, can have a significant level of control over their Qi. Moving energy to your fists to temporarily increase your strength is one of the earliest usages most talented children learn.

Ignoring what I sensed was a touch of passive-aggression there, I pressed onwards. "But I didn't move it on purpose. My hands were suddenly hot and I was strong enough to rip that wolf in half."

I may have . . . given things a bit of a nudge.

"How?"

When I pulled you into this realm, I needed to anchor this fragment of my spirit to yours. That gives me some — limited — access to your Qi. Not enough to do anything impressive, but I can certainly, for example, manifest a small fireball, or briefly pause time, or guide a small amount of energy to where it is needed in your body.

"Apropos of nothing, I have always thought 'The Host' was a far better novel than 'Twilight'."

Ah. I do recognise that reference, my dear. No. Nothing like that, I assure you. On the three occasions, I have used your Qi thus far, it has been for an outcome you desired. I merely facilitated your wish. And even doing that has left me significantly exhausted. Please, believe me, I will not be taking control of your Qi against your will.

I was pretty sure Eddie Brock may have had similar conversations. But that was a problem for another day.

"So, what's the deal with" — I gestured towards the two red spheres still floating in the air above the pieces of the wolf — "absorbing this stuff?"

Cultivators can increase their amount of available Qi by, over many years, meditating and reflecting upon the nature of life and existence. Slowly, but surely, each cycle accumulates more and more energy, and those that choose that path can progress in that way. On the other hand . . ."

"Oh, let me guess, you can kill loads of things and drain the Qi out of them until you're King of Qi hill. I'm going to call that The Highlander approach."

It is an awful lot more complicated than that, and it is important to combine both approaches to cultivation. But yes, one of the quickest ways for you to . . . the only words I can find in your vocabulary to adequately explain the process are 'level up'. Does that make sense?

"Mate, ask the continent of Tamriel if that makes sense. I'm all about the level up."

I didn't think the silence that followed was one of awe.

***

Merlin had said I needed to "breathe the essence in". Which sounded gross when he put it like that, but then again, I was covered in crusted wolf guts, so who was I to judge?

We'd been trying for hours — and I was getting dangerously close to hyperventilation — when the sphere on the right-hand side twitched and then flew straight into my mouth. I gagged and then swallowed the unexpected red energy down. "Yep," I thought. "Exactly like Tom Barnes."

You need to visualise what happens next.

I closed my eyes and mentally tracked the journey of the wolf's Qi into my body. The only way I could make sense of it was that it was like a blob of red paint being poured onto a pristine blank canvas. I knew — I have no idea how, but I did — that this sheet of white represented my spirit. The red paint, the absorbed wolf's Qi I presumed, had simply plonked itself down in the middle of my canvas.

I wasn't quite sure what I was supposed to be doing next.

Then, as if out of nowhere, the redness was surrounded by a small pool of liquid that I instinctively knew was my Qi. It was purple, which had always been my favourite colour in my paintings, and within a few seconds, it had completely overwhelmed and mixed in with the redness, seemingly absorbing it into a slightly bigger blob.

Then I was back in the real world, looking at a second orb of red floating above a wolf's carcass. I sucked that one down much easier this time. It hit the blank canvas with a Pollockseque splat, and was assimilated much quicker in the same way. To my untutored eye, my pool of purple liquid felt more substantial than it had before pulling in the wolf's red light.

Interesting. How did your mind make sense of that process?

23

I explained the painting metaphor: that the red colour was absorbed into the purple liquid.

Well, isn't that quaint, my dear? For me, it was like adding tiny drops of water to a giant ocean. As the end approached, I just couldn't find enough water to pour into it to make it overflow. Without that breakthrough, I died.

I didn't know what to say to that.

Although I think we are going to need to seek to progress more from violence than prayer, it would help if you spent time meditating on what you did to the wolf. Think about the sensation of Qi being channelled into your hands and how you then pulled the wolf's essence inside you. Take your time. You've accomplished more in an afternoon than most people achieve in their lifetime – if that doesn't prove you were the right person to put my faith in, nothing will.

But I wasn't really listening. A voice, not Merlin's, was whispering in my mind. It was getting quite crowded in here.

"That army. Where will they be heading next?"

It's an invasion force. They'll follow the route of the fyrd back to the various villages. Why?

I was suddenly overcome with images of a woman with kind eyes stroking my hair. Brothers and sisters playing with me in the fields. A house. Friends. A lost father whose last action was to keep me alive.

"They're heading to Wulfnoð's village. We have to stop them."

Stop them? It's an army, my dear. You may have a newfound talent for disposing of wildlife, but don't think for one moment you are ready to confront even a small group of people, let alone armed ones. Please don't fall into my trap. If we're going to achieve anything, we cannot be distracted by minutiae.

An image of my sister's face suddenly replaced those of Wulfnoð's family. I'd never had much truck with having a conscience during my life, but there had been moments when the horror of explaining my actions to Zizzie had stopped me from straying too far off reservation. If the whole point of staying alive was in order to keep her existing, I was damned if I was going to do things I'd be embarrassed to tell her.

"If you want me to ever speak to you again, do not describe people in danger as 'minutiae'. We don't have to fight the army, but we need to warn Wulfnoð's family what's coming."

I started to run before realising I had no idea where I was going. 'Merlin, which way?'

There was a pause before the wizard replied. *So be it.*

And we blinked out of existence.

CHAPTER 5 - IN WHICH I GLOW UP

"We'll need a signal if you plan to do that again. I'm thinking something like "Mr Scott, beam us up" What do you think?"

Noted. Can we make this as quick as possible, please? The outriders from the invasion force will be here shortly.

"Dude, you can stop time. Do we need to be worried about hurrying up?"

My dear, I don't really know how else to put this in ways you will understand. I am not what I was before. At the moment of my death, most of what constituted 'me' - the 'me' with almost limitless power and capacity for such shenanigans - moved onwards to whatever lies beyond. What has been left behind has much of my wisdom, to be sure, but my ability to influence this world is finite and undoubtedly limited in scope. As we discussed, I can make use of your Qi to a certain extent, but I have already, in our short acquaintance, done more at your request than I had ever planned for. You need understand there will soon come a time when I have nothing left to give.

"You can just ask me to stop bugging you, you know. No need to go all Mufasa on me."

I had reappeared on the outskirts of what probably was a fairly impressive dark-age village. I mean, Fred Flintstone would probably have looked askance at the plumbing, but the huts had roofs on them, so score one for fledgling architecture.

I started to walk towards the biggest of the buildings and paused. "Any advice on how I play this? The benefit of all that collected wisdom would be much appreciated."

You can either pretend to be Wulfnoð to deliver the news of the impending assault or change your shape to something you are more comfortable in and spread the word that way.

"I can do that?"

If you pay heed to my advice, you will soon learn there is very little in this world that you are not able to achieve. A true cultivator has no limits to their power and ambition within this world. Indeed, the gods themselves will tremble should you reach the potential I feel exists inside you.

"When you were alive, Merlin, did people tend to glaze over when you said things like that?"

Initially. But I had them flayed alive, and their children fed to my dogs. Attention spans seemed to improve after that. There was a pause. *That was a joke.*

"Right. For future reference, shall we try to keep the humour a bit lighter? You know, let's function at the level of friendly banter rather than focusing on the hypothetical murdering of children?"

Everyone's a critic.

"Okay, so shapeshifting is a thing. That's a trip. So, am I able to make it so I look like my old self? I'm not sure I have it in me for some Freaky Friday shit with Wulfnoð's mum."

If you have a strong impression of how you would like to look, you can channel your Qi in such a way as to make alterations to your physical form.

25

"You keep saying 'channel your Qi' as if I'm supposed to understand what you mean."

I know. If only I had been able to spend some time with you dedicated to helping you train, rather than teleporting you around the countryside on urgent missions. It is almost like you might start to get the answers for which you are looking if you'd take even a smidgen of advice. Some may say that shutting up and hanging on the every word a legendary expert in cultivation would probably be a sensible course of action if you ever want to master the art yourself . . .

"Been holding that in for a while, big fella?"

Indeed. In the spirit of moving things along, on this occasion, I will have to provide significant guidance and support to the way your Qi goes about the reshaping. This will, as I have mentioned, reduce my long-term viability in this realm. However, I can see the merit in advancing your practice in this area, and I am willing to do it.

I sensed a 'thank you' was being fished for here. I wasn't biting. "And if, just hypothetically, I wanted to make improvements to the original me, would that be possible?"

All things are possible to a cultivator of sufficient capabilities. Hold an image in your head of how you would like to look, and I will do the rest. Please understand that we are going to need to spend considerable timing learning what 'the rest' entails. I do not want you relying on me as a . . . I think you would term it 'cheat code' over and over again. You need to learn these techniques yourself.

With that, I felt a warmth wash over me like my whole body had become wax. There was probably a more technical way to describe it, but it was like Merlin had basically turned me into human playdough. Hurriedly, I considered the image of 'me' I had in my head and, just as quickly, discarded it.

Don't judge, but having spent most of my life wishing that I looked differently than the face that peered back at me from the mirror, I suddenly was a touch leery about going back to that. Tell me someone who wouldn't want to make a few improvements if the most powerful wizard in the world offered them a makeover . .

.

It would help if you had a clear conception of how you wish to look in your head. I cannot work with vague thoughts of 'me only better.' It would be best if you hurried up and settled on an image; this is a highly intensive use of your limited Qi whilst you prevaricate.

Various celebrities ran through my head. After all, who would know? It was not like I was going to bump into Anne Hathaway in downtown Camelot.

My dear, if you want me to do this, it has to be now.

But then I remembered one of my favourite paintings: Dicksee's 'La Belle Dame sans Merci. I loved that picture: a print of it had hung in every place I had lived since I was sixteen. You'd know it if you saw it, it's the one with the woman on horseback leaning over to enchant a knight in armour that is walking at her side. Although Dicksee was not a pre-Raphaelite, he absolutely channels their vibe, so his Belle Dame has a flower crown atop her mass of cascading red hair, has porcelain skin that never saw a moment outside in its life and is wearing a floaty pink dress that I searched every charity shop up and down the county to try to re-enact.

Are you sure that's what you looked like? My memory suggests different.

"You're an old, dead wizard. Who cares what you think you remember? I know what I want to look like."

So be it. And my body shifted.

Have you ever had a massage from someone who took your knots as a personal insult? That is what Merlin's reshaping of Wulfnoð's body felt like. Everywhere. All over. All at once. I would have screamed long and hard if my lungs were not being squished around within a new ribcage and my neck was not being stretched like a chicken being prepared for the Sunday table.

I'm sure it only took a moment, but I genuinely had never felt agony like it. When the shaping was over, I dropped to the floor, panting.

"Did it work?"

Of course. I did mention I was the most powerful wizard in the world. Even this reduced echo can do a fundamental physical reshaping without – oh. Bugger.

I waited for a moment to catch my breath. But Merlin's voice did not return. 'Big M? You still there?'

Nothing.

Considering the last time my disembodied companion had vanished, a wolf attacked me; this did not feel like a good development. I went to stand and then noticed a further new and disturbing development.

My new body was not at all like Wulfnoð. And, whilst that had been kind of the point of the torture I had encouraged Merlin to put me through, neither of us had foreseen that this might lead to … sartorial challenges.

"Who in the heavens are you?"

I turned, naked as the day I was born, to see two women standing near me. They were carrying buckets filled with water, having clearly just returned from a nearby spring.

I immediately took advantage of hair that now tumbled down to my knees to cover up what remained of my modesty. These people had never heard of Cousin Itt, and thus an opportunity for some Addams Family based humour was missed.

Maybe there would be time later.

"Hi" I waved awkwardly, noting my new, extremely thin arms were the colour of milk. I was surprised the moon wasn't burning me. Damn you, Frank Dicksee. There isn't going to be enough aloe vera in the world.

"What's a Celt doing here?"

Ah. The red hair. That could be a problem …

I rallied magnificently. "Take me to your leader; I come with an urgent warning."

The two women looked at each other and then back at me. The older of them scratched her nose in contemplation. "I don't know about any 'leader', but Old Dudda would probably like to talk to a naked Celt. What do you think?"

The other shook her head. "He'd like to gawp, don't know if he'll be interested in talking. Mind you, he ain't been able to do anything with it for years, so she'd be safe with him. You speak true about a warning?"

I nodded, a deep red blush spreading across my face. You'd think you'd be less shy when it wasn't your own body on display. Turns out that's not true.

The women looked at each other and seemed to come to a decision. 'Better wake up Ealdgyð, then.' They started to walk away from me, then stopped to indicate for me to follow. "Come on, she'll be pissed enough as it is, might as well get it over with. Do you have a name, Celt?"

And that was an interesting question. Did I have a name? I wasn't Wulfnoð any longer, that was clear. But was a part of him still here? Something in me smiled in recognition of the two women guiding me through the wooden huts. There were visions of a beating from the younger one, Hild, for stealing food and of the other one laughing as I – as Wulfnoð – played at her feet. She was called Leofflæd.

She was my mother. Wulfnoð's mother.

I shook my head to clear it. This would be a good time for Merlin to explain exactly what relationship I had with the boy whose body I had possessed. Especially as it was not even his body anymore. But, no, that voice remained steadfastly silenced.

"Did you hear me, Celt? What should we call you?"

A plethora of names ran through my head. New body. New me. But I needed something that would help me fit in. I could use the title of the poem my body was based on. Belle? But that seemed to invite a future where I'd need to break an enchantment on a tea set, and there was already enough weirdness in my life.

Anglo-Saxon names wouldn't work – not with all the hair and the skin. They'd penned me as a Celt, so I needed to lean into that. What did I know about Arthurian legend that would help me blend in somewhat? Well, there was one name. And Merlin had suggested I was going to be his apprentice, hadn't he?

"Morgan. You can call me Morgan. Morgan Le Fay."

CHAPTER 6 – IN WHICH I MEET A STRONG, INDEPENDENT WOMAN

Ealdgyð was undoubtedly not amused to be woken up.

She likewise took exception to my nakedness, my Celticness, my name, and to … well, pretty much every single thing about me.

My only crumb of comfort was that, as the women accompanying me were not spared the whip of her tongue, this seemed to be her usual state of being rather than anything particularly personal.

I eventually managed to quell the flow of invective coming my way long enough to mention the rapidly approaching army. Ealdgyð paused shouting long enough to blink at me for a few seconds in silence.

"Don't be stupid, girl. The fyrd will meet with them long before they reach us."

"The fyrd has been defeated." I felt the older woman behind me sag a little at the knees at that. I half turned so that I could look at her. "I'm afraid there were no survivors." Considering I've been known to fall into a puddle of tears when I'd run out of cookies, I felt Leofflæd took that double body blow like a champ.

Ealdgyð was shouting at me again, so I turned back. "A cow raid defeats two hundred spearmen? I see tales of Celtish naivety are well made."

"I can only tell you what I saw. I come from a field of battle on which men painted blue were looting hundreds of corpses."

"Did truly no one escape? My son and husband –"

I did not turn around this time. I could hear the tears in her voice. I drew on Wulfnoð's memories to try to explain what had occurred as fully as possible. The woman deserved that. "The enemy forces were present in far greater numbers than a mere cow raid. As well as spearmen, I saw archers, horsemen, and even signs of a wizard. It looked to me that the presence of the horsemen pinned down your men, and despite holding bravely throughout the day, the shield wall eventually broke under the pressure."

"You watched them clash throughout the day?"

Shit. Ealdgyð was a sharp one. "I am adept at reading the signs of war." Bloody hell, I was properly embracing my role as a mysterious stranger. I'd be offering prophecies next.

The angry woman stared at me for a long moment as if deciding whether to believe me or have me drowned as a witch. It was not clear she cared much either way. Eventually, she broke the silence, her voice heavy with exhaustion. "An invasion. From those who have not crossed the river in such numbers for decades. For them to have driven horses across the water stands not within the prospect of belief—no more than they would have access to a wizard. And, on top of that, you speak of the slaughter of all our men. That's four times our doom you pronounce, fire hair."

"She says her name's Morgan." Hild's voice came from the back of the hut; she had moved to comfort the older woman.

"You came to us to spin your tale, Morgan. What would you have from us? What boon do you seek from a people to whom you bring such news?"

I feared a drowning was looming increasingly prominent in my future. "I followed the path of the fyrd back to you. The invaders will soon be doing the same. I came with a warning. I would have you run."

Her eyes flashed, and she glanced around at Hild and Leofflæd. "Thoughts?"

"I see no benefit for her in treachery. If the fyrd still lives, they will return soon. Our men are not so hopeless as to fall apart because the village is temporarily empty. We can soon return if all she says is a fantasy. But, if what the Celt says is true, she gives us a chance to escape capture or worse." Leofflæd spoke softly. Something in me urged me to turn and hug her tightly.

"I see no downside in taking to the hills." Hild chimed in.

Ealdgyð came to a decision. "We leave. Spread the word of what this one has shared. Put out the fires, gather up the children, take what provisions can be carried, and everyone is to head for the Dark Stone." She turned to glare at me. "And get the Celt some clothes. All that white skin will be like a beacon to our position. You do realise you are coming with us?"

"I wouldn't want to be a burden. It seems like you have a lot to organise. I'm happy to slip off on my merry way." I started to back away until I hit the solid body of Hild.

Ealdgyð's eyes were hard. "No burden. I want you close to hand in case this turns out to be a trick. It's been a while since there was a blood sacrifice at the Dark Stone. Might be the time for us to renew the tradition."

Awesome.

***

I might be being sexist here, but I couldn't help but feel a touch of feminist pride at the efficiency with which the village emptied into the surrounding hills and woods.

Having seen how my father coped with the challenges of taking us camping every summer, I could not help but draw some fairly uncharitable comparisons.

Ealdgyð, it turned out, was the wife of the village's headman, Hrothgar, and therefore had quite some pull. If I'd had my wits about me when we spoke, I'd have realised she'd likely lost someone close in the battle.

Wulfnoð's memories had Hrothgar fall in the first of the charges of the shield wall. He'd seemed a decent enough leader, but once it became clear how many men they were facing, there was not much to do but hunker down and pray for a miracle. The gods did not seem to be listening. All of Ealdgyð's sons had been with the fyrd, too. In one day, her entire family had been killed.

And yet, here she was, forcing slow-moving oxen into the trees whilst castigating scurrying women who 'need to set a fire up their arse.' The remaining people in the village needed her to lead them to safety, and she would carry that burden with her head held high.

This was a tough woman.

Of course, my appreciation for her strength would have been even more profound should she not be dragging me behind her, hands tied roughly together by a coil of rope.

On the plus side, though, they had found me some sort of rough tunic, so I was no longer flashing all and sundry. You win some; you lose some.

Basically, what I'm saying is that the evacuation was a bit more 'The Great Escape' than 'Dunkirk'.

In no time, the majority of the village had vanished into the woods on their way to the not-in-any-manner-ominously-named Dark Stone. Ealdgyð and I were the last two left at the tree line, looking down at now deserted huts.

We'd been doing that for some time - I kind of felt she was dragging out the tableaux a little - when she finally spoke. "If this was all a tale, you'll live to regret it." Even though we weren't moving, Ealdgyð tugged on the rope, and I stumbled forward. She kept doing that. I was beginning to suspect she didn't like me.

"If it helps, I'm pretty much regretting it already. Don't you people have some sort of code about how you treat visitors to your hearth? Like, you're not allowed to hurt them once they've eaten your food or something like that?"

Ealdgyð just carried on staring below.

Never knowingly turning down the opportunity to start a fight, I tried again. "I mean, my learning point from all this is basically that I should have carried on my merry way and let you be slaughtered. Are you sure that's what you want me to tell people on my travels? Did you know people share bad experiences with four or five others? Once this gets out, it could really hit your tourism numbers."

"You sure there were no survivors?" Ealdgyð's voice was steady, but I could sense its sorrow, locked down tight.

Okay. So, it was probably time to dial down the banter. "No, I'm afraid not. They killed all of them."

She nodded softly, then turned to look me in the eyes. I was utterly flummoxed to see that her own were filled with tears. "You ever lost anyone, Celt?"

I nodded back, suddenly not trusting myself to speak. It was one thing to chatter on to fill an awkward silence; it was quite another to intrude on such overwhelming grief. Ealdgyð regarded me steadily for a few moments as if sizing me up.

"Aye, you have done, haven't you? It's writ all over you. You're all bent out of shape around the pain. That doesn't help, does it?"

I shook my head.

Ealdgyð sighed and turned back to the empty village. "No. It certainly does not." We were silent for a good few minutes before she started to speak again. "There's five of my babies buried down there. Not one of them lasted that first night. I'd given up thinking I'd ever see one grow up to hold a spear. Then we had Stilwell, then Sinley and finally Brecc. One a year, each after another. It was a miracle. And they just flourished. Each the spit of their father, but with my fire. You should have seen them. Glorious they were. Thought they would be running the world in a few more seasons." She rubbed a hand across her face, displacing the tears. "Ah, well. No more of that."

More silence.

Then a voice. I was astonished to realise it was mine. "My sister's not dead. Not like that. At least not yet. But I haven't seen her in years. Growing up, she was really the only one that ever got 'me', or at least the 'me' I thought I was. But as we got older, I felt her step away. Not that I blamed her. You don't hug a skip-fire closer to yourself, do you? We didn't exactly drift apart, but it gets to be that there's so much water under the bridge you drown if you think on it. But it doesn't stop the space she used to fill from feeling empty."

"But she's still alive, you say?"

I nodded.

"Then I think we're talking about two different types of grief. You can still fix yours."

I had a pithy answer to that when a bunch of horns sounded, and a group of blue-painted spearmen appeared on the road beneath us.

CHAPTER 7 – IN WHICH HEADS ROLL

"Alright." Ealdgyð drew a knife and cut the rope around my hands. "I'm going to go down there to see what this is all about. See if I can buy everyone a bit more time to get clear. The Dark Stone, you hear me? That's where everyone needs to get to. There are enough old timers who'll know what to do from there."

I was a bit taken aback by this. There was absolutely no need for her to show herself to these raiders. The people in the village were free and away from the threat they posed. I couldn't see many circumstances where an army would bother scouring the forest for a few women and children. Particularly if all they found was an abandoned village. "There's no need to go back. We can still slip away."

For the first time in our short acquaintance, Ealdgyð smiled at me. I didn't like the sadness behind it. I much preferred her scowling. "That's not my path, Celt. Life is for living, not mourning." She tapped my hand, and it was like I was transported back to my grandmother's house. Me, sitting on her knee. Her smoking her fiftieth cig of the day and dispensing life advice. Although, I imagine Ealdgyð might be less casually racist about her next-door neighbours.

"Hrothgar always made a point of greeting visitors to the village personally. Kind of feels like the best way I can honour him is to do that in his stead. This isn't on you. You've given us more of a chance than we would have had otherwise. There's those that will be waking up tomorrow that have you to thank for it. That's not a small thing, and we haven't rightly given you thanks for it."

I waved her words away. "It's fine. But you're not making any sense. There's no point in going down there! Your people are going to need you after this. Especially with all the men wiped out. You can't just give up on them now."

Ealdgyð's smile didn't budge. "Don't think I don't recognise a kindred spirit when I see one, Celt. You understand me when I say my tale's all told. I haven't got any more verses in me after today. And that's okay. There's nothing left for me now. But at least I get to go out on my own terms." The smile vanished. "But that's where we're different, you hear me? You still have something to live for. You make amends with your sister. Your story has yet more in it."

Memories shuffled, and I was thrown from my grandmother's knee to shouting terrible things outside a window at 3am in the rain.

I heard what Ealdgyð was saying, but she was just the latest in a long line of people giving the same advice. But that was the problem, wasn't it? I was always more comfortable with burning bridges than building them.

And now I wasn't even in the same timeline.

I opened my mouth to speak, but no words came out. I don't really think there was anything more for us to say to each other.

Ealdgyð gave me a wink, turned and walked back towards the village.

I stood, frozen, on the dirt track leading into the trees. Every instinct told me to run as fast as possible into the trees and ensure I was well out of sight before anyone noticed me. But another part, and I'd like to think it was me, rather than any residual Wulfnoð or pressure from Merlin, needed to witness the woman's end.

Because I was sure that was what was going to happen. I watched as she Butch Cassidy'd her way down the hill.

And then the Sundance in me won out, and I crept downwards towards the village.

It took me longer than I'd have liked to get there. It sounds silly, but I still wasn't quite at home in my new body. Trying to achieve a degree of stealth with legs that are slightly longer than your brain remembers is harder than you'd think. More than once I nearly went arse over tit as I crept towards the huts.

By the time I got there, the scene that greeted me was pretty much as I had feared. Three horsemen, their mounts exhausted by the hard riding, were towering over the small woman. Two of them were in heavy armour, and one, well, let us say if he wasn't a wizard, I wanted my geek membership revoked. He had a long beard, was wearing flowing grey robes and gave off every impression that if I yelled 'oy, Gandalf,' he'd turn around. There were three or four blue-painted spearmen around them – scouts, I presume, as there was no sight or sound of the rest of the force.

From the expression on the invaders' faces, I did not think Ealdgyð was winning them over with her light and breezy personality.

"I'm rapidly losing patience with this conversation. I will ask you one final time. Where are the rest of the women, bitch?" The first of the horsemen growled out, his voice gravelly. I chose to designate him Dick #1.

"Bless your heart," Ealdgyð replied. "I'm sure I will be more than enough for the likes of you. From what I hear, those of you from over the river have cocks so small your women choose to lie with goats." She gestured towards one of the spearmen. "You have the look of someone whose mum liked a good goating. Bet you have to shave thrice a day."

The second horseman, Dick #2, snorted at that, earning himself a withering look from the wizard. I did not feel pseudo-Gandalf was particularly comfortable in this company.

"My army will be here before sun-up, and they have been promised a reward for their recent victory. Your menfolk lie rotting in a field, and we would not be human should we not want to bring comfort to the widows they have left behind. So, I ask you again. Where are the rest of the women?" Dick #1 was really leaning into his role of Lord High Wanker.

Ealdgyð stuck her chin up and did not answer.

"Why are we wasting our time?" Dick #2 chimed up. "The village is empty; they've obviously fled. Let's move on. These people breed like cockroaches; we can stop at the next village to … release some pressure."

Dick #1 was holding Ealdgyð's eyes. He kept licking his lips in a way that I'm sure he felt was intimidating. For me, it just looked like he lacked good chapstick.

After a few moments of silence, he shrugged. "If we must. But I don't want us getting too far away from the others. Make sure you share news of our disposition with your fellows." The last was directed to the wizard, who paused, then nodded his agreement.

The horsemen wheeled their mounts around to leave. "Oh, and Melehan, kill the bitch."

The wizard sighed as Dicks #1 and #2, and the accompanying spearmen, moved away and then looked at Ealdgyð with pity. "I'm sorry. These are very petty men. You must have expected this would be the outcome once you put yourself in their way."

Ealdgyð lifted her chin and shrugged right back. The woman had balls the size of watermelons.

"If it helps to know, it was a much harder battle than they'd anticipated. Your men fought well. They're so jumpy because we've fallen behind the rest of the invasion."

Ealdgyð didn't answer.

"It will be quick. You may want to close your eyes?"

In response, Ealdgyð smiled and made a hand gesture that I was interested to note appears to be pretty universal across timelines.

Melehan's hand glowed momentarily, the way mine had when I fought the wolf. However, rather than stay within his body, the light suddenly lashed out in a beam of energy. It crossed the gap between the two and, quite simply, blew Ealdgyð's head clear from her body.

The wizard waited for a moment until the headless corpse hit the ground. He appeared to say a few words under his breath, and then he turned his own horse around to follow the Dicks.

However, he then paused and turned in his saddle to look straight back at my hiding place. "I have no orders concerning you, so you get to walk away. A word of advice, though, a child could hide their Qi better. If you want to skulk around in the dark, get that bloody light under control."

And he kicked his horse to ride out of the village.

CHAPTER 8 – IN WHICH THE CONSEQUENCES OF MY DRINKING BECOME APPARENT

"There are cheerier places to spend time than in an abandoned sixth-century village next to the headless corpse of a woman on whom you were developing something of a mum crush. I'd probably even sneak Wolverhampton on a Saturday night slightly ahead of it on the list, and that's saying something.

If you know, you know.

Once the wizard had ridden out of sight, I went and sat down next to Ealdgyð's body. Her head had vanished into a dark corner somewhere, and I was not eager to play that little game of hide and seek before sunrise.

I rested my hand on her chest - oddly, there was no blood - and thought how unnecessary her sacrifice had been. Brave, no doubt, but there'd been no one left in the village to interest the Dicks. There has been no need to 'buy more time'. If we'd just kept running towards the trees when we saw them, Ealdgyð would still be alive.

But that was the point, wasn't it? As she said, everyone she loved was dead, and once she knew she'd discharged her last responsibilities and that all the women and the children in the village were safe, she'd wanted out, too.

We'd had a lot in common, Ealdgyð and me. Maybe I should have joined her in that last stand?

But no, that was the point she wanted to make to me, wasn't it? We weren't quite the same. She'd lost everyone that mattered to her in the world. But I still had someone.

And they were in danger unless I pulled my head out of my arse.

I felt tears running down my face.

The world was about as quiet as anything I had ever experienced in my life. I'd grown up in various cities, and my every moment - waking and otherwise - had been punctuated with noise.

Yet here, in this village, for the first time since I had been … was the verb 'Isekaid'? Whatever. For the first time since I'd ended up here, I found myself wholly alone with my thoughts.

And if that didn't tempt fate enough for Merlin to suddenly become chatty again, nothing would …

But no. Nothing. Not even crickets.

Just the dark. And the silence. And the headless corpse.

I don't know how many hours I sat there, just staring into the blackness.

Without Merlin, I had absolutely no idea what I was supposed to be doing. He'd brought me to this realm for a purpose, dangled the imminent danger to the wellbeing of my sister in front of me, and then fucked off wi thout leaving an instruction manual.

I was basically Luke if he'd been at home that morning on Tatooine when the stormtroopers showed up to shooting.

I idly patted my own version of Aunt Beru on her headless shoulder. There's a chance I might have become hysterical at this point.

During the next few hours, I must have fallen into a breathing exercise some therapist or other had recommended would help with my anxiety. I'm not sure they ever planned for me using it in my current circumstances, but at £50 an hour, I felt entitled to give it a whirl.

And then, suddenly, things were not so dark in the village. Because I appeared to be glowing with purple light.

Like, full-on ET chest glowing shit.

The shock utterly killed my calm buzz, and the purple glow stopped as soon as it had begun.

I sat frozen for a few minutes, worried the light show would draw the raiders back. But, no. Only the silence returned.

Remembering the Magic Eye trick Merlin had me do with the wolf, I looked around to see if anything was glowing in the village. Maybe Ealdgyð had some Qi I should seek to collect? But she looked the same with, as I was coming to think of them, 'wobbly eyes'. I assume the wizard who killed her had already absorbed anything there was to be sucked in.

Actually, did cultivators gather Qi from humans in the same way as they did with animals they killed?

That seemed a touch ethically questionable.

Thinking about that, I rubbed my nose and let out a shriek as I caught sight of my hand.

My veins were visible through my skin, shining with a soft purple light. I realised I was still all 'wobbly eyes', and the glowing stopped as soon as I looked at myself normally.

'Get that light under control,' the wizard had said. Is this how she had looked to him? Like an extra from Tron?

But, more to the point, how was I supposed to 'get it under control'?

I ruffled through my memory for the Xianxia books I was monologued at about for about six months. My ex was always going on about the heroes moving their Qi around their bodies to release new powers. So maybe that was the solution? I needed to 'cycle my Qi'.

'Big M, I'd appreciate some force ghost guidance about now …'

Silence.

'Anytime. You just feel free to pop up with the words of wisdom any second ...'

Nada.

Okay. So, Clarence wasn't going to come through in this situation. But how hard could it really be? I'd practically done it by accident once already.

Steeling myself for a mental training montage, I crossed my legs, closed my eyes and tried to clear my thoughts.

***

Have you ever tried to think about absolutely nothing? It's not as easy as people like to make out.

It turns out I have a lot of thoughts.

I was amazed the Stay Puft Marshmallow man didn't appear at one stage.

I shouldn't have been surprised, really. If I was any good being alone with my own company, there were a whole host of disastrous life choices I would probably have been able to avoid. In fact, there was a whole decade of my life where I'd used booze, drugs and mediocre sex precisely to stop me from having moments of quiet introspection.

But, in the end, the dark, the quiet, and the breathing did the trick, and I was able to let my mind drift away.

This time, I felt, rather than saw, the purple glow from my chest begin again. It wasn't so overwhelming this time, more like a soft glow than a torchlight. Without really knowing how, I could make it dim and then brighten if I concentrated.

It was pretty cool, actually. Then the air buzzed like a fridge, like a untuned radio resonating with the Qi swirling within me, and the light went out again.

I was kind of disappointed I didn't hear a <ding> from whatever superior beings were in charge of this goofy system. By fiddling with the brightness of the light, I'd clearly passed some sort of threshold.

'Okay, so there is light. What do I do with it now?'

My blank canvas appeared again behind my closed eyes, but this time with a drawing of me-as-Vitruvian-man sketched on it.

Okay, so perhaps this was my level-up reward.

Right on top of my belly button was a blob of purple paint.

I looked at it for a while, willing it to do something. But, like all blobs of paint I have encountered in my life, it is just there. Satisfied with its inherent blobby paintness.

I watched the paint dry for longer than was probably necessary before having a moment of inspiration. Merlin saw his Qi as water to be moved within the ocean, didn't he? So, I should try something like that. Feeling a touch self-conscious, I imagined a rigger brush. I gently touched this to the purple blob, which seemed to do the trick. The paint suddenly vibrated, and a faint warmth washed over my body, spreading from my belly.

It was a good feeling.

As a connoisseur of doing things to generate good feelings in my body, I'd score this as two boxes of Dairy Milk inhaled in pyjamas after a bad day. Maybe even half a cider if I was feeling generous.

Whichever, I wanted a bit more of that feeling. So, with each intake of breath, I flicked the paint outwards from that blob and into the veins of the drawing of me.

As the paint spread out, I could tell one channel that seemed to run from my big toe, up my inner thigh and then connected to my ribs, which seemed to need more vigour to the paint flicking than any others.

'You need to clear away your blockages', I could hear my ex droning on. 'All that booze, it's too much for your liver.' Well, look at me now, Tim. Fucking cycling my Qi through my meridians like a pro.

I don't know how long I did this for. This process was both comforting and unnerving, as I could sense, with each flick of the paint, the power of the purple glow growing, fluctuating, and surging.

As I continued to cycle my Qi, twelve glowing spots of purple popped up on Vitruvian-me, and I could see that my brush was guiding the paint to flow through an intricate network of my body. Yep, the spot near the liver was definitely the part of the picture that needed the most attention; much more effort was required to keep a harmonious cycle when the paint passed through that spot.

Goodness knows how long I sat in the village's mud, painting internal me purple. Time seemed to have lost its hold on me, just like when Merlin had stopped it on the battlefield. I could feel I was drenched with sweat, and despite not moving, my muscles felt like I was at the end of a serious workout session.

But whatever I had been doing seemed to be working as, without needing to flick the brush anymore, the movement of the paint synchronised up with my heartbeat, almost as if they had become one.

I did a little internal skip of joy. I was CRUSHING Qi cycling.

And then everything went to shit. I really do like to tempt fate. In another life, I would have been a detective going to work on my last day before retirement and expressing how glad I was there'd been no shootings of cops for the last decade.

The purple paint was suddenly bone dry and resisting any efforts to encourage it to flow again. I could feel my glow start to fade, and my heart began to pound in my chest in distress. I could sense this was a critical moment. I'd come so far, but I'd have missed an opportunity if I didn't get things moving again.

I visualised a palette next to the canvas and swirled the brush in the well where I always held some water. Once the brush was sopping wet, I touched it to the dry, crusty purple blob on my belly button and encouraged it to return to liquid. It resisted at first. Then, slowly but surely, the skin on the paint yielded and began to resume its flow.

As I had thought, restarting the paint seemed to have been a breakthrough in my understanding of Qi. Whereas before, it had just been the funny glow inside me, I could now sense that it was much more than that. That it had possibilities. That the boundaries between me and my Qi had become blurred.

As dawn approached, the purple light surrounding me flashed once more and then settled down under my skin. I checked with my 'wobbly eyes', but none of my Qi was leaking out. My body - and for the first time since being in this world, it really did feel like my body - hummed with newfound strength and vitality.

I don't think I'd felt this proud of myself in years.

Oh, my word, that was painful to watch. Like a baby deer trying to walk for the first time. On lava. With two legs. Missing its head. How can anyone make such a drama about pootling that tiny drop of Qi around their body? This was a mistake. I should have tried harder to keep the boy alive; maybe moved his soul into her body and took it from there? I'm never going to be able to get her where she needs to be quickly enough. The world's doomed.

'Merlin?'

Silence.

'You know I can hear you, right?'

My dear! It's good to be back! I drained my tank a bit too much there, but now you've completed a cycle of Qi – nicely done by the way, very impressive for a first go – it's meant you can hear me again. Obviously. That's fortunate, isn't it?

'Merlin?'

Yes, my dear.

'It's good to hear your voice.' And, unaccountably, I burst into tears.

CHAPTER 9 – IN WHICH WE LEARN FAR MORE ABOUT ARTHUR'S SEX LIFE THAN FEELS APPROPRIATE

"And stay out!"

He heard the water jug smash against the wall as he fled their bedchamber. The servants carefully hid their grins as his naked form ran past them. As masters go, Arthur was pretty liberal, but even he would draw the line at them smirking at the little prince.

Grabbing a helmet from the head of one of the guards, he moved it to protect his modesty, pausing long enough outside the room to consider a retort.

But no. Sometimes, an ignoble tactical retreat was far preferable to provoking further engagement. Let tempers cool for a week or two.

'See the quartermaster for a replacement,' he called back as he stalked away.

He was not wholly sure which of his recent indiscretions his wife had uncovered, but he was self-aware enough to realise she was probably justified in her annoyance. It was a sore enough topic that they had been married for three years with no heir on the way, without every servant possessing tits dropping kids left, right and centre.

Whichever wag had rechristened Tintagel Castle as 'Came-a-Lot' was not doing much for the state of his relationship.

His mind was, therefore, elsewhere when a meaty hand took him by the throat and crushed him against the stone wall. Arthur struggled for a moment before submitting. Meeting the eyes of the colossal man that had accosted him, he whispered through a tightened windpipe. "Good morning, father. How have I disappointed you today?"

Uther Pendragon, King of all the Britons, scowled at his only son. For a moment, he wondered how many of his current headaches would be resolved by tightening his hold on the neck of this naked man. Then, with a sigh, he relented and dropped him to the floor.

"I have been petitioned, again, to remove you from command in the field. Adragain's report describes you as being either drunk or a fool during your last engagement."

"And that simply shows the lack of imagination which we both know is Adragain's key flaw: I was most probably both. Although, for the sake of completeness, is there a particular aspect of my role where Sir AgainandAgain feels I have faltered, or is it just his usual bile?"

"He notes that through your inaction, the rebels from Nanstallon could flee to the moors when more decisive leadership would have led to their destruction. He falls short of accusing you of cowardice but not by much."

"Of course, let's not forget I am fucking the man's wife. He may not be an entirely dispassionate judge of my performance. She, on the other hand…"

It had always been like this. Almost from the moment of his birth, Arthur had set out to undermine all the prophecies made of him. Had not Merlin himself prophesied that his boy would be the one to finally break the Anglo-Saxon menace and unite the country under one banner?

Everything Uther had done in his life had been in the service of that prophecy. He had given up all his hopes when he had to bed that harridan, Igraine, to unite the tribes. Merlin had been clear his boy would need the spears that unholy marriage would gain him, and he had made that sacrifice.

But looking at the unclothed man sprawled at his feet, he wondered where he had gone wrong.

"Is that what you would have me tell my thegns? That they should have confidence in their commander because those who complain of him are the ones whose wives he's fucking!"

"I concede that explanation is unlikely to be a balm on troubled waters."

"And is there another?"

Arthur adjusted his borrowed helmet as he tried to find, while lying on a stone floor, a more dignified position from which to address his father.

"We approached Nanstallen from the east road, but the rebels were clearly well briefed as to our disposition. We'd fought several engagements whilst still more than a day's ride away: all inconclusive but bloody enough to have given me pause. I judged that to have continued to engage in skirmishes, particularly when our opposition seemed entirely too familiar with our route, would have been costly. I sent Sir Adragain to explore alternative approaches to the town. When he returned, having found a secret road that would lead us directly to our adversities, I ordered our retreat."

"Because?"

"Father, Sir Agragain has abandoned our cause. Our assault on Nanstallen was too well known, and I judged that unless you had planned to send me to my death," Arthur looked up into Uther's eyes and paused for him to respond. When no answer came, he pressed on. "Someone else was sharing information with our enemies. Of course, his wife has quite the collection of Saxon finery in her bedchamber, which is fairly suggestive. I refused to lead the army into an obvious trap set by a traitorous cuckold. Should that require my removal, so be it."

Uther closed his eyes for a moment, then nodded. "I had Agragain burned alive this morning. Your assessment of his betrayal was accurate. It had been going on for six months."

"So, your morning assault on my person was because …?"

"Arthur. You are Prince of the Britons. You have no legitimate heir, yet I'm beggaring my treasury on the upkeep of your bastards. 'Our cause' is to put you on the throne. Men are dying to make that prophecy a reality, and yet there is no line of succession for which to fight. Agragain is not the only thegn to think there is a brighter future elsewhere."

"I imagine the flammable ones might be thinking twice right now."

"Impregnate your wife, Arthur. If you can't rise to the occasion in your own bedchamber, see Merlin. He always came through when I needed something to help me through the night with your mother." Uther suppressed a shudder. "We need the spears that will come with Guinevere's swollen belly. If we don't have them before the summer, we will not be able to hold the Saxon advance and will have to fall back from Isca Dumnoniorum. Should that happen, there will no longer be enough of

Britain of which for me to be king. And certainly nothing left for you to unite. Do you understand?"

"Alternatively, Merlin could just come down out of his Tower and vaporise the lot of them. Who needs spears when your best friend can destroy armies with a word?"

Uther shook his head. He was not having this argument with Arthur again. Particularly not with him naked.

"Merlin has made it clear that, right now, he has to focus on his own advancement. We will not be seeing him on the battlefield again until he makes that breakthrough. Our lives have been made easy by his power, I would have us try to stand on our own two feet in this matter. Merlin is not to be disturbed because the Saxons are getting frisky." Uther put out his hand to help his son up.

"But he'll be happy for me to knock on the door to ask for a potion to help me land one on Ginny?"

Uther hauled him to his feet. "Whilst he may not have the time to slaughter more thousands in our name, I think you will find he is not above slipping you a pill or two. Merlin loves nothing better than to relieve his youth vicariously."

***

Arthur liked Merlin.

Of course, it was hard not to feel affection for someone who declared to everyone that you would be an all-powerful King. Especially when he then moved heaven and earth – at times literally – to make that happen.

So, he had found the last six months a challenge. He did not quite understand why the wizard had felt the need to so completely retire from court life and lock himself up in his Tower, but the ways of cultivators were many and strange and were quite beyond him.

Nevertheless, he had missed his advice, his support and – in the face of his father's constant disappointment – his complete lack of judgement around his life.

"Uther loves you," Merlin would tell him. "He just has hazarded so much on your success that it pains him to think you are not so committed."

"I know. I just would like to think I had some options in life that were not wholly to be viewed through the prism of how best to ensure I become this legendary warrior."

Even to his own mind, that sounded pretty weak.

So, he rebelled – but in more minor ways than his reputation might suggest. Yes, he had slept his way across Dumnonii, but he knew for a fact his father had done much the same. He had fought, with distinction, in all the major conflicts to which he could bring his sword during his thirty years. No one could accuse him of cowardice and expect anything other than a summary fiery execution. He was liked, genuinely, by nearly everyone to whom he came in contact – spurned wives and angry husbands aside.

He guessed his father was correct, though. Until he had a natural heir, questions would remain as to the viability of his line. And without the men Leodogran had promised once his most waspish daughter was with child, the Britons would likely struggle to withhold the Saxon press come the summer. Particularly if their all-powerful wizard was too busy to lend a hurricane or two.

So that was why he found himself at the base of Merlin's Tower, seeking a little something to make the idea of a night with Guinevere cause him to stand to attention.

When his knock found no answer, he turned to Bors, the biggest of his household guard. "Break it down for me; there's a good chap."

Bors raised two massive eyebrows. "Break down Merlin's door? Didn't he tell us not to bother him. Won't he be angry?"

"Absolutely. Probably completely blow his top. That's why you're knocking it down, not me. I fear Merlin is very much a 'throw a fireball at the messenger' personality, and, well, you're more expendable than me. The once and future king, and all that."

"There's only so many times you can play that card, my prince." Bors took several steps backwards to give himself room to charge.

"True. But if you're not going to use it when potentially annoying a supernaturally gifted wizard who expressly has forbidden people from knocking on his door, when are you?"

Bors' answer was lost by the sound of him crashing through the heavy oak door. And then any quips Arthur might have prepared rapidly faded from his mind.

Because there was a smell coming from the Tower that was somewhat too recognisable to soldiers who had spent as long on battlefields as the two of them.

"Bors, when was the last time anyone saw Merlin?"

"Six months, my prince."

"Figures. Go find my father immediately. You need to let him know that Britain is, permanently, lacking its wizard."

CHAPTER 10 – IN WHICH MERLIN DISPLAYS SURPRISING FAMILIARITY WITH DARK COMEDIES OF 1989

Merlin was overbearingly chipper as we made camp for the night. I guess it didn't take a wizard of legendary power to tell I was feeling a touch wrung out by recent experiences.

At my insistence, he'd guided me through the use of my Qi to help dig Ealdgyð a proper grave. He'd grumbled, at first, as to further wasting of our 'precious training time', but following a full and frank exchange of views – I'm not proud that I think I made him cry a little – we decided I was right.

It turned out that if I coated my hands in my Qi, they dove through the earth like every metaphor involving knives and butter you can come up with. I'd checked with him that burial was appropriate at this time in history. I thought it was, but then I was acutely aware that much of my historical knowledge was through 'Horrible Histories', and whilst their songs were bangers, it was sensible to check with a primary source.

Plant her or burn her: I doubt her spirit cares. She was alive, and now she's dead. Such is fate.
"What happened to your body?"

There was a pause. *As far as I know, it's still rotting in my tower—the perils of being utterly terrifying and asking for some 'me' time. The fact the realm seems moderately calm suggests no one has found me yet.*

We'd briefly experimented with my generating a fireball for a no-fuss cremation, but as Wizard-Kilgore had waxed rather too lyrical about the smell of burning Qi in the morning, burial it had been.

After laying her to rest, I used a Qi-enforced finger to sketch some words onto a cairn I placed above the mound. I wasn't sure what I'd written translated all that well into Anglo-Saxon but Merlin assured me it did.

So, we'd abandoned the village leaving a newly raised barrow complete with a giant gravestone. It read: **Ealdgyð: I am a Woman Phenomenally. Phenomenal Woman, that's me.**

Angelou works for all time periods, Merlin murmured as we slowly walked away.

As we walked, we discussed where to take the next stage of our journey. I'd initially wanted to wait for the women and children to return, but we had no way of knowing how long they'd seek to stay away. Likewise, trying to pursue them through the trees would be a foolish and frustrating endeavour. If Merlin knew what and where the 'Dark Stone' was – and I suspected he did – he wasn't letting on.

That led us to our second major disagreement of that early morning. "We need to warn the other villages about what's coming," I'd said. The look in the eyes of the Dicks was not one that I was going to forget easily.

My dear, even if I knew the direction their army would choose, I still would not help you." I started to interrupt, but he spoke over me. Disembodied voices do that a lot. *"I did not bring your soul to this realm in order to run hither and thither around isolated border villages. You're thinking too small about all this.*

"I don't think what was planned for the women in this village is 'too small.'

Neither do I. But what I can sense is coming will make a little raping and pillaging in the outlying regions pale into insignificance. What you see right now as a terrible outrage will become these people's daily experience unless we are strong enough to stop it. I need you to help me to forestall a cataclysm that will fall across the lands. Once the world knows I have … passed, then what occurred here will become minor compared to the destruction wrought by those that no longer have to fear my wrath.

"Big M, I like you, and from what I've read, you were quite the spell flinger, but I feel you're slightly over-egging the '*I am death, destroyer of worlds*' vibe. I mean, you threw a fireball at a crow yesterday, and you've still not stopped moaning about it. At this stage, you're coming across a bit Ross-playing-rugby-to-impress-Emily."

The road around me shimmered, and I was stood on a battlefield – directly in the middle of two rapidly converging armies. Before I could shout in alarm, time slowed and then stopped as Merlin spoke.

I may need to be careful with my use of Qi to affect the real world, but it is reasonably easy to pull your spirit back into my memories. This is the field of Carlion. The stories will tell that this was a great victory for Arthur and that I counselled mercy for the fleeing rebels. The truth was different.

I can't tell one group of mud-smeared warriors from another. There are no flags to be seen, just hundreds upon hundreds of angry, shouting men paused in the act of running towards each other. One side had a massive numerical advantage; even my limited tactical knowledge could tell you that.

Arthur was still a boy running from his nurse when this battle was fought. Despite my attempts to broker peace, many of the tribes would not accept Uther as the Pendragon. They did not recognise his marriage to Igraine as valid. And, most of all, they would not countenance Arthur as heir. My prophecy was clear, yet they still would not be satisfied. Six of them – the mightiest, of course - raised their armies and brought them to lay siege before Carlion Castle.

"And you tipped the scales? That's the point of showing me this? You showed up, and it made them realise it was better to surrender than to fight you?"

No. I killed them all.

Time restarted with a colossal lightning flash that struck inches from my feet. I looked up and saw a dark figure floating ten, fifteen feet above my head. Corporeal Merlin had some swagger, I can tell you that. Blue energy crackled the sky around him for a moment and then lashed out, cracking like a whip, to strike the larger force.

He did not speak. He did not give them a chance to change their minds. He just quickly, efficiently and with great precision slaughtered them all.

I watched, in horror, at the impact of those strikes on the press of humanity so close to me. People exploded. They melted. They were burned alive within suits of armour.

Fortunately, Merlin had clearly decided to pay the extra Qi for the entire 4D experience, and I was treated to every smell and sound of the massacre.

"How many?" My voice was strained even to my ears.

The six kings each brought thirty thousand spears to Carlion. None of them left the field alive. The realm is still recovering from the devastation this wrought upon the population.

The vision faded, thankfully, and I was back on the road we were following away from the village.

That was twenty-five years ago. That was the last time anyone, other than the odd raiding party, thought to push back against Uther's rule. But his time of passing draws closer, and I intended to be at Arthur's side when that occurred to ensure stability. Without me and the certainty of eradication I embody, I fear we will see Carlion repeated up and down the country.

"But that doesn't happen. I know about King Arthur. Excalibur. Guinevere. He's crowned and rules for years, and then there's the bust-up with Mordred, and he goes for a rest in Avalon."

And am I there for all that?

"Yes. Ah, I see what you mean."

I fear someone is seeking to alter history. I am not such a fool as to have allowed myself to pass from this realm easily. There is another's hand in my death. But, what is more, even should I have erred so grievously as to allow myself to have died of old age, this version of my spirit should have been able to identify an heir quickly. There should not have been any necessity for me to scrape the bottom of the barrel for the last two in this realm with any potential.

"Hey! And 'hey' on Wulfnoð's behalf too."

I am sorry, my dear. But that is the truth. Significant efforts have been made to break with settled history. I have been pushed from the board, and nearly all possible replacement pieces have been removed. It is hard to conceive the power required to seek to achieve this, and I do not know why. What I do know, though, is that someone must stand at Arthur's side when he takes the throne. If not, the realm will descend into chaos.

"And you think you can skill up my Qi use in time to keep everyone in line and stop a civil war?"

Goodness me, no. But I think with your Qi and my know-how, we can give the impression of ungodly power long enough for Arthur to get everything in hand. Hopefully, before anyone spots we're bluffing. Be under no illusions, my dear; we are not the main characters in this little story. Our job is to make sure Prince Arthur becomes King Arthur and that he has the time and space to unite the country against the Saxons. Lacking a body of my own to accomplish that, I need your help.

I felt a little deflated at that.

When I had been cycling my Qi, there had been a moment when I felt I was capable of anything: that I had taken the first step on a journey towards challenging the heavens. To hear that all Merlin saw in me was as part of a relatively low rent confidence trick did not quite fit the bill.

"So, we're basically going to 'Weekend at Bernie's' the Dark Age?"

Only if we change the entire plot so Bernie possesses Larry and Richard to ensure Vito becomes the Godfather. So, no. Not anything like that.

"Solid reference knowledge, there, Big M."

I try.

Hey, it was not like I had much else going on at the moment.

"Okay. I'm in. So, what's the first lesson?"

CHAPTER 11 – IN WHICH LEWD GRAFFITI IS INTRODUCED TO DARK AGE CORNWALL

orry, I set the bar a little high there. That's on me.

As I looked at the smoking remains of my hand, it struck me, once again, that Merlin was quite the master of the understatement.

"First of all, 'Ow!' Secondly, let's take a moment to remember this is a new body, and I would really rather not be blowing bits of it off straight away. I might need that hand for something. I'm having flashbacks of buying my first new car and driving it straight into a lamppost as I pulled away from the dealer. I mean, it'll grow back, right?"

Sure. Let me just … there you go.

There's a horrible little insect called the Jewel Wasp that preys on cockroaches. It paralyses its prey first and then injects in some mind-control venom which means the cockroach has to do everything the wasp wants. Then it buries itself into the body of its victim, takes control of it and marches it to its nest to lay lots of eggs inside it. The eggs then hatch and devour the body of the cockroach in, what I sense, might be a moment of blessed relief.

I take this diversion into natural history because that's kind of how it feels every time Merlin makes use of my Qi.

He'd explained that he was able to do so, to a limited extent, because of having so little power of his own.

Remember, I can divert the flow because I know where it needs to go. But it's you that is providing all the energy. You visualise cultivating as painting, right? Well, I am merely providing the paint-by-numbers template, but you're the one who is holding the brush, my dear. As I have said previously – and I do not especially enjoy repeating myself, my dear –, if you did not want to do it, I could do nothing to make you use your Qi in this manner. However, you would not know what to do without me pointing the way.

I thought back to the previous night in the village. "Can other cultivators do that? Gather up my Qi and guide it in that way?"

No. You'd immediately reject anyone else seeking control like I'm doing it. Your sense of Qi, and understand that I am dumbing this down considerably, it's what you might think of as your soul. You'd absolutely know if someone was trying to make you do something with your soul in a way you rejected. It's only because I have such little energy of my own that there's no incompatibility. I can't force you to do anything you don't want to.

Under Merlin's expert guidance, my Qi slowly rebuilt things. I felt his hand guide my brush, sketching the outline of my new hand. The purple paint coloured the torn tissue, repairing it at a pace that surpassed mortal comprehension.

The process was not without difficulty; the damage resisted removal, attempting to reject the restoration. But Merlin simply bullied his way through the obstacle forcing my Qi into resistant channels. Finally, the glow around the hand subsided; a mutilated mess had been fully restored.

As one of our first lessons, we'd been trying to see how much Qi my fists could hold. I'd been quite interested in learning how to throw energy bolts like Malehan, but apparently, that was a little further down the training montage road. So, we'd been playing around with stuffing energy into my fists to enhance my punching power. I'd thought I'd reached capacity, but Merlin had been sure I could squeeze in a bit more.

It turned out legendary wizards don't always know best.

"Can I be honest? I'm not sure I'm a punch-first-ask-questions-later sort of person. Is throwing hands really my best option?"

There was a pause. I wondered how regularly Merlin's apprentices questioned his training methods and how often that worked out for them. A vision of a mouse, a broom, and a flood came unbidden to my mind.

You are in somewhat of a unique position. Whilst you have absolutely no idea what you are doing, you are in the body of a boy whose whole culture was dedicated to body cultivation. Not that they would call it such, but that gives you distinct advantages. So, with his foundation and my knowledge, there is, in theory, the chance that ...

Merlin's voice faded away. "Big M, you okay?"

I'm sorry, my dear. I'm just a little overwhelmed by the scale of the challenge here. The approaching cataclysm would be difficult for me to overcome. Not impossible, but it would be something that would test my power and experience. And I don't have that. All I have is you, and I worry that's not going to be enough.

"Don't do yourself down. If saving the world does not work out, you have a second career lined up in motivational speaking. I cannot tell you how inspired I am right now."

There was no reply. If I did not know better, I'd imagine Merlin had gone outside for a cigarette and to give himself a talking-to.

Well, this sucks.

Don't get me wrong; I'd disappointed plenty of people in my time. It was kind of my thing. In fact, my specialist subject on Mastermind would be 'Failing to live up to Low Expectations', at which I would, ironically, manage an underwhelming score.

But on this occasion, I did not really feel I was getting a fair shake of the stick. I'd taken dying, being reincarnated to the dark age, being a boy, dealing with wolves and witnessing a murder like a champ. It did not really feel that Merlin was entirely giving credit where credit was due. Sure, I was not immediately assimilating everything I was being told about an ancient form of spiritual existence quite removed from my Western Christian upbringing but, to be fair, it took me several films to accept Daniel Craig as James Bond.

I'm a Roger Moore gal.

These things take time.

I could feel a darkness begin to settle on my mood, and that never led to anything good.

I stood up, dusting myself down - both physically and mentally - and looked for something to do to distract myself.

Trees. Rocks. And nothing else as far as my eyes could see. To be honest, it was taking me quite some time to come to terms with how desolate this part of the world seemed to be.

From my understanding of myth and legends, I should be somewhere down Cornwall way – or what would eventually become Cornwall. I had vague memories of family holidays to Bude when I was younger and thinking if there was a bright centre of the universe, we had chosen the chalet it was farthest from.

It would be fair to say, though, modern Cornwall was a veritable Las Vegas of colour and vibrancy compared to its 6th-century equivalent.

Finding nothing external to interest me, I turned inward and examined what I was choosing to describe as my artist's studio. Merlin kept trying to get me to call it something else, but if he was going to get in a strop about my learning potential, I wasn't going to pay him and his dantians and meridians much mind.

My blob of purple paint was still there, but since I completed my first cycle, I could see it was branching off to move steadily around my body in time with my heartbeat. Vitruvian me, with softly glowing veins highlighted against my skin, was looking pretty darn cool, I must say.

No matter how much Deputy Downer wanted to rain on my parade, I felt I had made decent progress considering the speed at which I had needed to come to terms with things. From memory, characters could spend tens of chapters trying to do what I'd mastered in a few hours, so I was feeling a touch unloved by my mentor.

I flexed the fingers of my new hand and considered where I had gone wrong. Merlin was sure I should have been able to pack more Qi there, but it didn't make sense to me to think about things in that way.

I wondered if it was to do with how we both visualised the movement of our Qi around our bodies. For Merlin, it was all about water. Every time he spoke to me and the way to cultivate, it was about 'flow' and 'waves', but that metaphor didn't work for me. When my hand exploded, I could see that there was no more capacity for added paint – in the same way that I'd know a brush couldn't hold any more without dripping.

But, for Merlin, the ocean could always hold more water … Those were two fundamentally different ways of viewing the experience. Perhaps I needed to plough my own furrow here.

I started pushing more and more of my Qi towards my new hand. Once I felt it reach the 'full' stage again, I stopped and looked at it. Both inside and out, it was glowing a fantastic purple colour.

Like, a full-on Grimace version of Danny Rand but without the lame Netflix tie-in.

I opened my fist and moved it slowly in front of me, leaving purple light trails in the air. This was very cool. I sensed that the movement had dropped the levels of Qi slightly, so I pushed some more in.

I moved my hand faster, like I was cleaning a window and kept pushing more of my paint outwards. A cloud of purple light was taking shape in front of me, with each pass of my hand adding to its solidity. Rather than causing my hand to explode, I seemed to be able to have some control over its release.

Wax on, wax off, indeed.

An idea occurred to me, and a smirk appeared on my face. I closed my hand back into a fist and extended my index finger, crooking it at the end. Miming holding an aerosol can in my hand, I depressed my finger and watched a cloud of purple paint spray outwards.

If Merlin had felt a bit disappointed with me when he left, I thought it would be as to nothing to his reaction at seeing me having learned how to Qi-tag.

And if there was one thing I knew how to do, it was to lean into expectations of failure.

As I passed an enjoyable twenty minutes, I wondered if, in thousands of years, people would seek to ascertain the meaning of the giant purple cock and balls I drew in the middle of this field.

CHAPTER 12 – IN WHICH MORGAN 3:16 MAKES AN APPEARANCE

It is a truth universally acknowledged that a single woman drawing a massive phallus in a field will be accosted by undesirable men. The little-known first draft of *Pride and Prejudice* there, but Lydia Bennet was an absolute fiend for a bit of taboo sketching and look at the trouble it got her into.

It was the smell of them that brought me out of my artistic reverie more than anything else. It was one thing to intellectually know people in the dark ages had wildly different hygiene standards, but quite another to be confronted by that much intense masculinity wafting your way. As a connoisseur of many a sweaty dance floor in my youth, I immediately categorised it as Lynx Cornwall.

"Morning, dearie," a grime-encrusted face was mooching my way. I somewhat regretted using up the designation of Dick #1, as that would have been the perfect title for this vision of loveliness. However, never one to dwell, I settled on calling this example of alpha-male, 'Tosser'.

Despite centuries of evolution, it was amazing that I could have come across this guy on any Saturday night. That either said very little good for mankind or, more likely, was a searing indictment of the places in which I had chosen to hang out.

Probably a little from column A, a little from column B, if I'm being honest.

"Whatcha doing?" asked a slightly less offensive specimen behind Tosser. He was every version of Wingman I'd ever come across. He was not quite bold enough to push himself forward, but he was entirely happy to join in once the fun began.

"Immortalising my boyfriend's junk for eternity. He's just popped out to sharpen his massive sword. You?"

Tosser's lips actually moved as he tried to parse the sentence. "Ain't no one else about. We looked."

Awesome. Because if there's one thing you want to be certain of when meeting two extremely strange men in an isolated field is that they've checked for witnesses.

"He likes you." Wingman was fully embracing his role. "Likes your hair."

"Thank you. Merlin grew it for me last night."

If I'd hoped dropping his name would have changed the dynamic of the situation, I was disappointed. Tosser and Wingman just leered blankly back at me. I sensed they were both possessed of a resting moron face.

"Be easier if you don't struggle. Me first. Then him. If you're still alive, then me again." Never let it be said that Tosser did not have a way with the ladies: that was quite some patter.

"As tempting as that offer is, I'm afraid I'm going to have to turn it down. You see, I'm a cultivator, and I, quite literally, will tear you a new one if you come anywhere near me." I turned inside to my artist's studio and quickly cycled my Qi into my fists.

It was at this stage I made two unwelcome discoveries.

Firstly, Tosser and Wingman clearly had absolutely no idea what a cultivator was. If I had thus hoped to send them running in fear from my presence, I was to be somewhat disappointed. That, however, paled into insignificance to my realisation that painting a giant cock and balls onto the ground apparently takes up a lot of Qi.

Like, pretty much all of it. There was barely the tiniest dollop of paint on my palette.

Tosser grinned and swaggered towards me. As he licked his lips, I was reminded of Jabba pulling Leia close to him in Return of the Jedi. Judging by the amount of drool, I might not quite be Carrie in a gold bikini, but I was undoubtedly the tastiest thing this guy had seen in a while.

I backed away whilst trying to come up with a plan. Both Tosser and Wingman were, for all their various hygiene problems, built like the proverbial shithouses. The wolf I had killed earlier would probably have thought twice about taking on either of them. Both … I was in trouble.

See this as an opportunity.

"Welcome back, Big M. Do you have any fireballs handy?"

Regrettably not. As discussed, I can shape the direction of your Qi, but I have so little of my own I doubt I could give him as much of a sunburn at the moment. You, however, are very close to a breakthrough.

"I think that's precisely what these guys have in mind." I was uncomfortably aware that Wingman was flanking me, leaving me with very little room to manoeuvre between the two of them.

You've reduced your available Qi down to critical levels, which is the perfect opportunity to force yourself through a threshold. As you become more powerful, reaching this state of spiritual exhaustion becomes harder and harder, so you should take advantage of it.

"Any chance of some pointers before, you know, my rape and murder?" Tosser feinted a dart forward, and I stepped back, almost falling into Wingman's grasp. I spun away, and we continued our slow circling. I was running out of time.

You should seek to perform a Qi-empowered fighting technique. If you enact it correctly, that should be enough to force a breakthrough at your low level.

"Excellent. I'll get right on that. One Qi-empowered fighting technique coming right up."

You have no idea what I'm talking about, do you?

"Not the faintest. But, please, take your time." Tosser grabbed at my arm, but I was able to twist free and lashed out with my foot to force him back. Wulfnoð's body was significantly more toned than my own back in the modern world, and I was satisfied by the wince of pain that flashed across his face when I connected with his shin.

"Bitch. You'll hurt for that."

"And there was me thinking this was all going so well. Merlin now would be a great time for some inspiration."

If my two assailants were perturbed by me speaking out loud to an invisible wizard, they did not let it impinge on their plans for the evening. Suddenly a series of images started cycling through my mind. They were all visions of me delivering different attacks – I assume Qi-empowered fighting technique – upon Tosser and Wingman. As I watched a truly kick-ass version of me perform them, I also seemed to instinctively know the names of each of them: [Falling Ice Tree], [Rising Tiger Moon], [Blade of Cyan Grass]. While they all reduced my attackers to blubbering wrecks, they also looked epically complicated to perform.

I watched myself going through these elaborate combinations, and I looked pretty awesome doing them, but they didn't seem like anything that I was likely to enact in the near future. There's an attack that Chun-Li does in Street Fighter 2 where she spins upside down and helicopters across the screen, kicking her opponent in the face as she goes: that looked easier to achieve than most of the moves Merlin was showing me.

"That's great, Big M. But is there not anything that actually follows the law of physics? I'm not sure I get many shots at this."

The images continued to flash past me, hundreds upon hundreds of possible techniques that I would have needed more flexibility than I'd ever been able to achieve, even at my most adventurous.

And then, suddenly, there was one that I sort of recognised.

Well, not quite. What Merlin was showing me was an elaborate kick, magical blast, and complicated body twist routine. Still, I definitely had seen something not a million miles away from it used before to good effect.

As Tosser moved towards me, I felt there was nothing to be lost in putting the technique into action. It was hardly going to make the current situation any worse.

I lashed out with my right foot and caught him square in his happy – or, I guess, not so happy – place. As he doubled over in pain, I replaced the magical blast in the middle of the technique by giving him the bird with both hands.

As if that was some sort of trigger, that seemed to be the signal for the last bits of my Qi to begin swirling around my body at great speed. As it did so, I half-turned, wrapped my right arm around Tosser's neck and tucked his near arm under my armpit. Then, as the swirling of my Qi reached a fever pitch, I jumped into the air, then fell on my arse, pulling his head downward to smack his jaw against my shoulder.

Three things then happened in pretty short order.

Firstly, as Tosser's chin connected with my shoulder, it shattered with a very satisfying crunching noise. Think stepping onto a floor of bubble wrap. In clogs. After a bad day.

Secondly, purple light bathed me, lighting up the surrounding field like a beacon, and I felt my palette of paint fill back up to the brim: there was much more there than there had been previously. I also felt the words [Unknown Technique created] resonate across my very soul.

Thirdly, and finally, Wingman made his first good decision in a decade and set off running as fast as he could away from me.

Well. That was unexpected.

"You're telling me. What happened?"

I think you took the essence of the [Dark Kestrel Strike] and perverted it into some sort of ungodly version which you appear to get to name. I don't think I've ever heard of someone with your lack of ... foundation crafting their own technique in such a fashion. You live and learn.

"Have you done it?"

Obviously.

"A few days after becoming a cultivator?"

No. It took many years of patient study and –

"So, I did it quicker than you and under less auspicious circumstances."

I would not put it like quite that –

53

"It doesn't matter how you'd put it. It's how I'm going to tell it. Yes, I just came up with it off the top of my head. I know, faster than Merlin, too. Who would I have thought it? Quite the prodigy, am I."

Have you quite finished?

"Probably not. How do I name the technique?"

Perhaps you should think about it first? Techniques are hugely influential in the way in which cultivators are viewed. We might be able to overcome any number of perception challenges if we can leverage an appropriately impressive -

[Can of Whoopass] technique named.

"Don't worry. I figured it out."

You could not help yourself, could you?

"And that's the bottom line. Because Morgan said so."

CHAPTER 13 – IN WHICH DICK JOKES AND MILITARY STRATEGY ARE EXPLORED

"You've been sat there without speaking for quite some time now. Do I assume you've died and I've to start making arrangements for my coronation? Oh, how the people will rejoice."

Uther took a breath and looked at the others in the chamber. Arthur had requested to deliver his urgent news in private - but in 'private' for the King meant there were any number of guards, servants and hangers-on that had just heard that Britain was, for the first time in generations, without a wizard.

"You're sure he's dead?"

"Am I sure he's dead?"

"Yes. He's Merlin. It's not like it would be wholly unheard of for him to be able to bounce back from grievous injury. Did you, I don't know, poke him with a stick, or something?"

"He's a rotting cadaver. I'm as optimistic as the next guy, but he's not shaking this one off. Not without limbs flying everywhere, anyway."

The crown on Uther's head was suddenly feeling heavier than it had in decades. When Merlin had made his prophecies regarding Arthur and the future of the war against the Anglo-Saxon invaders, they'd been exactly what he needed to give his life purpose.

Instead of being just another ageing Warlord slowly losing territory to a seemingly never-ending swarm from across the sea, he was given a vision of a British destiny where he played a crucial role in the survival of his culture.

Of his people.

With just a few words - and, of course, a series of devastating military successes - Merlin had given him a clear path to success and told him to walk it without fear or favour.

Merlin's overwhelming power would supply the stick and his job was to sire an heir and to prepare the ground, via the carrot of diplomacy, for Arthur to become the great man the realm needed.

As far as Uther could see - give or take Arthur's inability to impregnate his wife - he'd more than fulfilled his part of the deal. Come this campaign season, his son would finally have the spears he needed to push back on the invasion, maybe even as far as some of the lost Roman cities near the Thames.

With the Saxons broken, and with Merlin at his side, there would be a chance for his son to rule over a world that genuinely knew peace. What greater gift could a father ever hope to offer his child?

But now, all that was suddenly up in the air. Who could have expected that the old goat would up and die on them before any of the really meaty stuff could come to pass?

The critical question now was, did Merlin know he wouldn't be around to help Arthur's rise to power or had something gone, catastrophically, wrong?

Uther's key worry was that, having spent many a long evening discussing the kingdom's future with the wizard and making elaborate plans which had that Qi-botherer at their centre, he couldn't help but feel the topic of him not being there might have come up...

That left the rather distressing possibility that a plan had been put in place, six months ago, to take out the most powerful individual in this, or any other, land.

And he was only just finding out about it now.

That was more terrifying than any rampaging Saxon horde. The question is, did they have the capacity or the capability to do anything about it?

"Who else knows?"

"Bors was with me when I found the body. But he's pretty tight-lipped about most things. Considering he didn't mention a sucking chest wound for weeks after a skirmish because 'he doesn't like to make a fuss', I can't imagine this will slip out in idle conversation."

"Other than that?"

"Father, there's ten people in this room. There were twelve when I arrived, but two slipped away as soon as I gave you the news. I imagine the guards I stationed outside will have intercepted them and, even now, will be exploring which master they serve."

Arthur took the time to make eye contact with the remaining ten. "Some of those here I know, some I don't. I'm not wild about executing them because you don't understand that 'private' means 'for your ears only.' But if you think we have a shot at keeping this under wraps, my soul can stand the stain."

There was a tense silence. Then Uther exhaled a weary sigh. "No. It's hard enough to find reliable help without murdering the ones we have." He raised his voice so that all could hear him. "But, if any of you leak what you've heard tonight, please be assured that it will not be Prince Arthur that comes after you. He is far too merciful and honourable about such things. It will be Uther Pendragon that will visit you, your families, and anyone else I think might help make a constructive example as to the necessity for discretion in my court. Now, begone."

They watched the fastest exodus from a room occur since Guinevere placed a pair of women's undergarments on the table at a banquet and asked Arthur, "Which of your latest bitches do these belong to?"

"So, we are without our greatest asset on the eve of our most important push against the Saxons. What do you advise we do?" Uther's voice was low, the strain of an uncertain future weighing heavily on it.

Arthur went to answer, then paused. When he spoke, there was an authority to his voice that Uther rarely heard - though he knew it was the side of his son his men saw regularly.

"Merlin's not been a feature of court life for six months: there's no immediate issue for us in him not being about. There would obviously be a colossal hit to morale should his loss become known, but no one is expecting to see him until he makes his 'breakthrough', so we don't need to worry his absence is suspicious. We keep his Tower locked up and bemoan the strange and mysterious ways of cultivators should anyone question it."

Uther nodded. "Agreed."

"However, that does not change the fact that we can no longer call on him. For far too long, he's been critical to all of military strategy - even if just as a fallback option. No real need for a Plan B when he can swoop in and pull us out of the fire. We are going to need to make immediate changes to our military doctrine to avoid that being an issue. But that'll make us look less ambitious, less aggressive. That could be a problem."

Arthur paused, stood and began pacing the chamber. "But, we can play it as my growing maturity as a commander. Less concerned with dick measuring and more with sound planning and redundancy in the system. We can let it be known I'm trying to come out from your and Merlin's shadow. That I don't want to have to have you watching over me all the time."
Uther smiled as his son paced, wondering if he even needed to be here for this conversation.

"But there's more than just the day-to-day support he's given us. Fear of Merlin has kept most of the other surrounding kingdoms in line, but we now know - even if they don't - that there's no longer immediate doom coming their way if they step out of line. So, we need to bolster our conventional forces. Not just more spears, but grow the mounted contingent. Maybe throw in some mobile siege weaponry. We make our army the biggest swinging dick in the room, rather than wangling Merlin's around all the time."

"Sound thinking. With the unnecessarily phallic metaphor, of course."

"Of course. Have dick will quip. Then we need to subtly put the feelers out for any other cultivators in the realm; I know Merlin always said he sucked up all the Qi there was available, but you never know. We've got used to having his power for all manner of things, so it's going to be a loss in ways we've not thought of yet. Of course, we're not going to find anyone like him, but there might be a group we can put together that can fill some of the gap."

Arthur paused and shared a look with his father. "I'm sorry your friend is dead, by the way. I hadn't said that before. But we cannot overlook the fact", Arthur continued, "that there is likely to have been foul play here. If anyone is powerful enough to get rid of Merlin, we will be in for a rough time of it. We need to prepare for being on the receiving end of something nasty. I suggest pulling everything back from the borders - salt the fields, kill the oxen, and go for a full-on scorched earth approach. If the death of Merlin is the precursor for a Saxon push, let's give them nothing on the land for their troops."

Neither of them gave voice to the unspoken truth that gnawed at them that if the death of Merlin was the beginning of a Saxon push, they'd had a good six months to prepare.

As they discussed the possible direction of the coming campaign, Uther found himself repeatedly nodding at his son's words. There were times, he thought, he could see the future Merlin had sketched out so many years ago. When there was less of a focus on what he could bed, he could see the shape forming of a fine young man.

They spoke long into the evening, toasting their absent friend many times, and when the two men finally stood and clasped hands, each had a myriad of tasks to put into place.

Uther hesitated just before leaving. "I don't say this often enough, Arthur. But I can see what Merlin meant when he said you would be the man to bring order to the world."

Arthur, for once, was lost for words. He knew, intellectually, his father cared for him, but expressions of that love had not been regular in their relationship.

"Oh, and you've totally arranged for those ten servants to be executed, right?"

"Of course," Arthur nodded. "Surprised we didn't hear the screams."

CHAPTER 14 – IN WHICH I SEEK TO DEVELOP SOME CHILL

After some discussion, we'd simply left my stunned attacker in the field. Merlin was keen to see if I could heal and revive Tosser with my Qi and then work on refining my new attack technique on him. However, that felt dangerously close to crossing a line from self-defence into something the good people of Geneva had a whole convention over.

Also, I was increasingly distracted by the smoke columns that were popping up in the distance, dotting the landscape in a fairly macabre way. You know what they say? Red sky at night, shepherd's delight. Red sky in the morning, shepherds being raped and pillaged by an invading army.

Or something like that.

"Is there really nothing we can do?" I asked Merlin for what felt like the thousandth time.

My dear, unless you can convince every single one of them to engage in melee combat so you can use your adapted [Dark Kestrel strike]...

"[Can of Whoopass]"

I've told you, I'm not calling it that. There's a long and prestigious history to those who use the Kestrel techniques, and I'm not going to sully their culture in such a way.

"Counterpoint. You want my help, and I'm nothing if not stubborn. I once sang the entire score from Hamilton until my boyfriend bought me the shoes I wanted."

That doesn't sound too bad...

"Remember, I'm extremely white and from Birmingham."

Even so...

To be fair, he did quite well to last until the rap in 'Guns and Ships'. I could usually bring people to horrified acquiescence well before then.

As I was saying, there's very little to be done at your current power level. You cannot... I'm sorry, are you really this juvenile?

"Watch me engagin' em! Escapin' em! Enragin' em! I'm-"

As I was saying, you cannot just open a [Can of Whoopass] on them individually and hope the others wait in line for their turn.

"Sounds to me that someone neglected his study of the 2002 Royal Rumble."

There was a pause during which Merlin appeared to find hitherto unplumbed depths of patience.

What you - we - need to do is find a way to replicate several decades' worth of cultivation in short order so that you are remotely useful in the coming struggles. As you rejected the chance to practice some techniques on your would-be attacker, we now need to find another safe yet impactful method.

"For future reference, I draw a hard line on torture, okay?"

As long as you understand, that will make our path both more perilous and uncertain.

59

Truth be told, I wasn't one hundred per cent happy with this side of Merlin. There'd been a couple of occasions now where I wondered if my perception of him as Giles-to-my-Buffy might not entirely be the fitting metaphor. After all, my understanding of Merlin was coloured by hundreds of years of folk legends that led to Gandalf, Dumbledore, Disney's The Sword in the Stone and every other elderly, benign super wizard I'd ever read about. I needed to remember that just because everything I'd come across said he was a good guy, it didn't mean I needed to let my usually acute 'mad, bad and dangerous to know' guard down.

Obviously, whenever that particular alarm went off, I did my best to get into a toxic, co-dependent relationship with them. Merlin hadn't, as of yet, asked me to lend him money to pay off a bike loan, so he had that going for him.

Nevertheless, there was definitely something a bit off about his power-at-all-costs approach to things. I didn't want to cast aspersions at this early stage of our relationship, but if he asked me to start collecting infinity stones, I was most definitely out.

"There's got to be some sort of training we can do that walks the line between horrific torture of a helpless individual and taking on an entire army one-on-one."

There was an ethereal sigh.

There are countless approaches we can take, but cultivation - traditionally - takes time and effort. I don't have the time, and let's be clear, I doubt you can manage the effort. Although, and now I sensed Merlin was speaking to himself as much as to me, *you mastered that technique more efficiently than expected. The boy's body has clearly undergone significant tempering to allow you to cycle freely with such little experience. Maybe...*

I waited for that sentence to complete. When nothing seemed to be forthcoming, I passed the time by cycling a small amount of Qi into the palm of my hand.

I needed to know more about all this.

I understand, at least on some level, that the glowing purple ball I was holding was 'magic'.

And this magic came from within me.

The artist's studio I could visualise was the centre of that power, and I could use this magic, this Qi, in various ways. I could use it to make myself stronger - say 'hello' decimated wolf carcass - I could project it outside my body to deface the local landscape with witty graffiti and, in a complicated way I needed to think about more, I could combine it with 90s wrestling moves to defeat would-be rapists.

It had been an odd couple of days.

For me, this felt like quite an extraordinary level of personal growth, but whatever Merlin had planned clearly needed something more from me.

As I was pondering this, I realised I had returned to my internal artist's studio. It was the work of moments to conjure up a brush and encourage the flow of purple energy around my body. I sensed this was something I should try to do whenever possible - all the cultivation novels that had been pressed upon me highlighted the importance of this routine.

But it felt like there was much more I could do here than just encourage the paint to pass around my body. Checking that there was nothing to inhibit that gradual flow, I gently dipped the brush into the palette that appeared in the air.

Everything there was a version of purple - reminding me much of my wardrobe back home.

I carefully selected shades that resonated with the mindset I sought. Soft mauve and calming indigo mingled with darker violet, reflecting the imagery I wanted to achieve.

A canvas popped into being before me, replacing the Vitruvian version of me. Well, not replacing it. It was more like I'd opened another tab in my internal browser.

That metaphor didn't work for me. I'd spent long enough as a data entry admin drone never to want that sensation again. I concentrated and felt the infrastructure shift. Now rather than browser tabs, I felt the different sections of my internal landscape were represented by pages in a book.

A lovely, leather-bound journal with acres upon acres of unspoilt creamy parchment.

Christ, I'm such a book geek.

Without knowing quite what I wanted to achieve, I dipped my brush into the first of my purples and set to work. As it so often had in the past, the brush became a conduit for my emotions. Each line, each curve on the canvas, mirrored my internal ebb and flow.

As I painted, key memories from my life, good and bad, washed over me like waves crashing against a shore. Yet, as always, at the centre of that storm, I found peace while working on the canvas. I guess for the longest time, painting had been a form of meditation for me, trying to find some way to reconcile with the past and find peace.

Yet there was something more, I don't know, tangible about this method. Like the difference between shadowboxing and then actually being in the ring. With each layer of paint, I could feel the Qi responding, slowly aligning with the colours and the calm rhythm of my brush.

The once erratic and wild energies within me - what did Dad call me? His little helion? - began to find balance and structure. Like one grand high master cultivating motherfucker, I guided the flow of Qi with unwavering focus, tempering its intensity and directing it towards tranquillity.

I had been going for some time before I felt Merlin join me and begin to subtly direct my brush. At first, I resisted, but it was that sort of arrogance that had blighted my whole life. Just occasionally, it didn't hurt not to be a strong independent woman - especially when experimenting with magic forces beyond my understanding.

So, through gritted teeth, I let him direct the flow. Slightly. At least a tiny little bit.

Through the canvas, we painted a new narrative for this Dark Age version of me. It was a story of resilience, finding strength in vulnerability, and embracing the scarred past as an integral part of my journey.

It was precisely the sort of thing the Hallmark Channel would produce in a heartbeat.

I mean, it made me want to vomit, but perhaps there were worse things than schmaltz. Memories of finding a letter from my sister, a busy road, oncoming traffic and a little voice that just went "fuck it, why not?" at precisely the wrong time tugged at my mood but were quickly washed away under this balm of purple.

As we put the final touches on the painting, a new sense of calm enveloped me. I hadn't appreciated quite how much tension I was carrying until it melted away.

I have a cunning plan.

The change of vibe Merlin introduced here was so startling I completely missed the opportunity for Blackadder-based humour.

"Sorry, what?"

61

MALORY

I'm encouraged by your recent development. So, knowing your joy in all things 90s, we're going to try and Groundhog Day a training montage.

CHAPTER 15 – IN WHICH THERE IS THE DULLEST TRAINING MONTAGE OF ALL TIME

I'm going to be honest, what Merlin outlined to me as his 'cunning plan' was such colossal bullshit that I'm not sure I'm going to be able to narrate it sensibly with a straight face.

***

Despite your low starting position, my dear, you have achieved some rather impressive things in our brief time together. Now, most of these successes have needed me to, as we have discussed, direct your Qi into powering techniques of which you have no knowledge. But the fact remains, you have had the raw power to do them and - and this is absolutely not the case with many cultivators - the iron will to see things through.

"I've had my personality described in many ways over the years. I'm not sure anyone would ever have noted I had an *iron will.*"

Perhaps 'cussed, bloody-minded stubbornness' would be a better description?

I think I preferred 'iron will'.

With that in mind, it seems logical to me that – given sufficient time to train – it is not inconceivable you would have eventually been able to walk that cultivation journey yourself.

"Mate, literally every conversation we've had since you brought me here has been that we have 'no time, no time, no time' like some sort of amphetamine-fuelled White Rabbit. Are you now saying that was bollocks?"

Not quite. But it occurs that these things are not quite as cut and dry as I may have suggested initially. Few things are entirely black and white in the world of cultivation. Indeed, I have reflected that we do indeed have a very limited window of opportunity where there is potential for you to make huge gains in developing a sensible foundation.

"There's more than a whiff of second-hand car salesman about your patter here, Big M. What are you getting at?"

I'm saying that I know of a spell - an exceptionally complex and challenging spell - which, in certain conditions and with significant caveats, can repeat a single day, allowing the opportunity for substantial training in the fundamentals of cultivation during that time.

As I said. Colossal bullshit.

***

Let's start with the conditions.

It turns out - in a *deux ex machina* kind of way - Merlin could cast a spell to make me exist in a perpetual Groundhog Day of training. So far, so good. However, for this spell not to cause the end of the universe, I needed to have no interactions that would alter anyone's settled destiny.

So, no saving Ealdgyð.

Apparently, it's absolutely fine for me to be fucking around in dark age history to sort out Merlin's personal project, but heaven forfend I help out a poor woman who got her family killed and her head blown off.

That's not quite how I put it, my dear.

It doesn't matter how he put it; it's what he means.

As I tried to explain . . .

Anyway, to avoid being remotely helpful to humanity during my training day, it turns out I have to find a solitary place in the woods and give up any thoughts of being Bill Murray, catching boys falling out of trees.

So, here I am. In a cave. Alone.

Awesome.

The second condition is that, as has been explained multiple times to me, while Merlin might be the one to actually cast the spell, all of the Qi being used for this little venture would have to come from me. And it would take all of what I had right now to make it work. So, I would be starting my 'day' of intensive cultivation training with zero Qi.

When the Big M first explained this to me, I was fine with it. After all, I was just over a day into this cultivation lark, so it hardly felt like much of a backward step.

It was when Merlin explained that the pathetic amount of Qi to which I had access at the moment was the result of it building up over thirty-seven years that I began to feel . . . concerned.

It's not as bad as it sounds, my dear. By developing a proper Qi-cycling routine, things will refresh pretty quickly. It will just put a hard ceiling on how much improvement you can achieve on each reset day. Because you'll be starting empty, you'll need to cycle for long enough to have the reserves back by the end of the evening to reset things all over again.

So, basically, it looked like I'd be spending most of my training 'day' getting enough energy together to restart the day again without making any tangible gains. Apparently, Qi cultivation is basically the model for late-stage, carceral capitalism.

And then there was the final condition.

"Seriously?"

Seriously.

"This seems like a lot of effort to make if you're saying the maximum amount of cultivation improvement I can achieve with this method is to end up with the foundations of . . . how did you put it?"

A slightly slow ten-year-old.

"Awesome. So, days upon days of isolation and deprivation, and all I can expect is to reach the level of a thick ginger kid preparing for his first day at Hogwarts."

Well, as most of the time will be spent cultivating rather than training, I can't help but think ten years of improvement is not too bad. To really develop as a cultivation of power, you will need time to move forward correctly. However, your options will be much broader if we can get the groundwork done this way.

As I say, colossal bullshit.

***

Are you ready, my dear?

I looked around the crappy little cave we'd scoped out in the middle of nowhere to train. "Sure. Looking forward to it. Rarely have I anticipated being so fulfilled by a day's work."

My dear, I know you are feeling frustrated, but let us remember that we are doing this for your own good. We cannot use this technique to turn you into the powerhouse you need to be to save your sister, but it can at least give you a starting point. Nonetheless, I appreciate it is going to be difficult.

'Dude, I have been on every diet known to mankind 'for my own good'. I'm the world expert in doing things to myself that make me miserable in the hope they'll eventually make me better. Although, you probably need to understand that I usually find myself tits deep in KFC a few hours in."

I have no idea how to respond to that. Here we go.

***

So, fun fact.

If you are sat in a dark cave, and your wizard mentor casts a complicated spell to reboot time, very little changes. You are still, basically, in a dark cave. Just a few hours earlier.

Well, not quite the same.

Because this spell needed every last drop of my Qi, I now felt like absolute shit.

I'd become very used to having my purple paint sloshing around my veins - *channels, my dear. If we're going to do this, let's at least try to get the terminology correct* - the absence of it was like having the world's worst hangover, but without the deep feeling of contentment and pride from knowing what you'd got up to in the club's toilets.

Right, here we go. You have twenty-four hours to generate enough Qi to be able to cast the spell again.

I settled in for the long haul.

***

I lost count of the number of times Merlin had to reset the day before I started to have any spare Qi left over to actually begin some training . . .

You really are ridiculously overdramatic, my dear. It's been two days. We're hardly talking about One Hundred Years of Solitude here.

Two days I spent sitting on my arse doing fuck-all. Do you have any idea how torturous that was?

You forget I have access to your memories, my dear. There have been many occasions across your life when you have spent days lying in bed, staring at the ceiling, doing nothing whatsoever. In many ways, I may suggest you have the perfect experiential skill set for what we are attempting.

Fuck you, Merlin.

***

We eventually got to the stage where I had generated enough Qi to restart things about an hour before the end of the day.

This did not, as I had hoped, lead to 'Morgan's Hour of Chill and Pampering'. Rather, it appeared to be an opportunity for Merlin to engage his drillmaster fantasies.

As someone who found any cardio more strenuous than hunting around the living room for the remote utterly impossible, this was not a joy.

It wasn't even anything as interesting as jumping around a swamp with my wizard mentor strapped to my back.

I spent that hour doing lots and lots of press-ups - *Five. You can manage five before you start crying* - followed by hundreds - *two* - of star jumps.

What is particularly impressive here, my dear, is that you are currently in the body of someone at the peak of human fitness and endurance. The very fact your mind is managing to convince your body you cannot do any more exercise demonstrates the iron will of which I was speaking.

I didn't get a chance to share my thoughts on this before the patronising judgemental wanker restarted the day again.

***

I lost track of time.

It's impossible not to, really, when every day is the same, and you spend most of it meditating anyway.

The only thing I could really use to judge my progress was the amount of time it took me to reach the level of Qi required to power the restart. On the one hand, I was pretty pleased to see the effectiveness of my cycling improve, but considering this meant the amount of time I spent Rocky-montaging increased, I guess I was ambivalent at best about it.

Actually, I did find cycling to be an increasingly enjoyable experience. The process would start from my palette - *your dantian* - where my paint - *your Qi* - would collect. I'd carefully ensure that all impurities were removed, filtering out lumps to achieve a smooth consistency so that the paint's purple colour was as vibrant and pure as possible.

With each breath, I'd then direct the paint with a brushstroke around my meridians - *meri . . . oh, you got that right. You do listen, after all* - and then rinse and repeat. I could tell, in a very, very, very small way, that each cycle made slight improvements.

As the days went by, it made sense to me that missing out on this experience - even if it wasn't making any real difference to how good a cultivator I was - would probably leave me the poorer.

Sorry, was that you saying this was actually a good idea?

Fuck you, Merlin.

CHAPTER 16 – IN WHICH I MAKE SENSE OF CULTIVATION THROUGH THE LENS OF MRS. ROWLING

After a while - and I honestly no longer have any idea how long 'a while' was - I found I needed to concentrate less and less on the actual mechanics of cycling. It was like I had built up some muscle memory around the whole thing, and the paint's ebb and flow became something almost instinctive. Like breathing. Or stealing mascara in supermarkets.

However, like a vulture circling for the precise moment of a deer's death, Merlin swooped in the second I sensed I might have had some spare mental capacity with a bit of lecturing . . .

I say 'a bit'.

If Satan was seeking to freshen up his circles of Hell - you know, to attract some new business - he could do a lot worse than lock someone in a cave for eternity and have Merlin explain, in punishing detail, the mechanics of cultivation. To contextualise, it was so bad that I looked forward to the moment it stopped, and I got to do some burpees.

Listening to him drone on and on about 'tiers' and 'arcane insight' and 'elemental harmony', I found myself reliving one of the less fulfilling of my short-term relationships.

A few years ago, I'd read something in Cosmopolitan - or one of those other terrible magazines designed to make women hate themselves - about one of the best ways to keep a man was to be fascinated by his interests. I'd recently fallen into bed with a reasonably presentable guy from work and thought - in lieu of anything better to do with my time - I'd give being 'fascinated' a whirl.

Basically, I was entirely up for some football-related banter. I was not specially prepared for the avalanche of Progression Fantasy that suddenly engulfed my life.

There were books. There was anime. There were graphic novels. There were figurines - Oh. My. Word. The figurines - but then there was the final breaking point. The convention.

I'm sure you've picked up that my vibe is to be open to most things. At least once. Usually twice for me to really get a feel for whether I was appalled by it or not. But the morning he presented me with the costume he wanted me to wear to that convention . . . well, that crossed about every line of morality I still had left.

And I've been known to rock a gold bikini.

Anyway, I mention all this because by the fiftieth day of Merlin outlining the various pathways by which Celestial Mastery could be achieved, I was in such a state of bad relationship PTSD I could barely breathe.

"Dude, you need to stop!"

What? Why?

"It's too much. I can't keep it all in my head. You're going on and on about all this stuff, and it makes no sense. All I need is the cliff-notes version of the rules of Cultivation play.

I don't know what you mean.

"Okay, think about it like this. My favourite Tolkien story is The Hobbit. Love me some Bilbo. I sense you'd be more at home with the full-on Lords of the Rings Trilogy - which is fine. It takes all sorts. However, what you are currently vomiting all over me is like listening to the Silmarillion read backwards. In Elvish. Without pictures."

You are asking me to dumb down cultivation theory?

"I'm asking you to shut the fuck up. However, in the clear absence of that being an option, I will accept you slowly and carefully explaining things to me with a limit of complexity or philosophy."

Well, that's no fun.

***

So, here we go. This is what I've gleaned.

Cultivators are all in different leagues.

Tiers, my dear.

Zip it. You had your chance. At the very bottom is where I am at. Merlin calls it the Initiation Tier, but I'm terming it **Neville** for ease. (Yes, I know he has an epic progression arc throughout the novels and comes out on top. That's the point I'm making, you pedantic mansplaining sealion.)

As a **Neville**, I'm pretty much useless. Basically, it sounds like it's a blooming miracle that I can sense Qi at all, let alone do anything with it. The point of this 'day' of training is to get me to the point where I can effectively cultivate, move my Qi around my body and enter a deep state of calm and mindfulness.

That will upgrade me to a **Ron**.

Elemental Alignment Tier, my dear.

As a **Ron**, I'll make the first step towards actually being any good at all this. I'll begin to pull in different flavours of Qi and use these energies with more complexity. Apparently, most cultivators with a decent mentor would become **Ron** around the eighth or ninth birthday. Considering I woke up last week in a pool of my own sick, an eviction notice taped to my front door, an empty bank balance and a worrying rash, I felt this was distinct progress.

Once I get a handle on one particular type of Qi - I'm making an early call for flinging fireballs - I could look to progress into becoming **Harry**

Arcane Fusion Tier . . .

Where, as well as probably having some nifty scars, I'd be able to put my Qi inside stuff. Oh, and live much longer.

Honestly, you really are making this sound much easier than it actually is.

After that, there's a few other tiers of various bullshit leading up to **Snape** - which is where everything went a bit wrong for Merlin - and then just a few more until you reach the very top of the tree with **Celestial Mastery**. Or, as I prefer to term it, **McGonagall**.

I am a touch disturbed that you have reduced my learned dissertation upon thousands upon thousands of years of complex thought to that summation, my dear. On the other hand, who am I to argue if that makes sense to you?

Damn straight.

***

Cycle. Lecture. Train. Reset.
Cycle. Lecture. Train. Reset.
Cycle. Lecture. Train. Reset.
Cycle . . .

***

I think that may well be our lot, my dear.
The day had barely reset when I realised I had fully replenished my Qi.
"What do you mean?"
We have exhausted all the improvements we can make in this fashion. You have developed a rudimentary understanding of cycling that would be akin to a promising cultivator just leaving childhood.
'So I'm **Ron**?"
*I am still not entirely sure what that means, but yes. If that makes you happy, you are now indisputably **Ron**.*
"How long did it take me?"
Merlin paused before answering. He did not like to tell lies, but he was unsure how well his apprentice would take the news that she had spent the equivalent of three years pushing a relatively small amount of Qi around her body and completing several million press-ups.
It is probably best to think not of the time taken but rather appreciate the journey we have been on. One of the . . . interesting side-effects of the spell I have been using is that you will, in pretty short order, lose the sense that you spent more than a day training. You will retain the progress and any insights you developed during this time, but your memory of the resets will vanish.

***

In his wildest dreams, Merlin had not thought reaching this stage would take more than a few months of resets. But the very fact Morgan had stuck with it must mean something. He couldn't help but think Sisyphus would have thrown in the towel long before if he'd been in her position.

But, it had served its purpose.

He had managed to move his newest apprentice into a place with a solid enough foundation to begin to press forward.

However, it would never be enough if she took this long to even reach **Ron** - no. Under no circumstances was he going along with that - to reach the Elemental Alignment Tier.

What he needed now was a way to dramatically speed her up on her cultivation journey.

Oh. Interesting. He actually had just the thing.

69

Now that you finally have a decent foundation, we need a reasonably rapid way to advance your skills, but one that neither infringes on your somewhat fragile morals nor places us in immediate danger.

"And that would be?"

We're going to go and slay Vortigern's Dragon.

CHAPTER 17 – IN WHICH THERE IS AN INEXPLICABLE MASH-UP OF MYTH AND INTERIOR DECORATING.

"A dragon?"

Yes.

"As in a giant fire-breathing lizard famously antagonistic to knights in armour?"

It sounds like you are familiar with the concept.

"I'm also familiar with the concept of trying not to be roasted to death. Do you really feel this sits slap-bang in the middle of the risk/reward continuum? Was there not, I don't know, a really strong pill I could take or something?"

Now that you are at the Elemental Alignment Tier –

"Ron."

No. Now you are at your current level, there are natural treasures I would like to get you to digest, but in order to be able to recover from swallowing them, we're going to need you to be an awful lot stronger. I'm reasonably sure the spiritual herbs I have back in my Tower would burn away your nasal cavity if you so much as sniffed them, let alone ate them.

Having dabbled, in my youth, with a powder that did its uppermost to compromise my nostril integrity, I was willing to take this one on trust. "Okay, so no natural treasures until I am a bit more buff. But still, a dragon!"

Ah, but you see, this is not just any dragon. It's Vortigern's Dragon.

***

Once upon a time, far, far away - by which I took Merlin to mean 'a few weeks back' and 'just over that hill' - there lived a king called Vortigern. He was your average mythical ruler, which is to say, he was an appalling despot who spent most of his time oppressing the peasants, polishing his crown, and being involved in the constant struggle to impregnate every passing wench.

However, one thing marked Vortigern out as being a little different from the other local warlords. You see, Vortigern had himself a bit of a situation. His castle, perched atop a hill, was constantly getting rocked by earthquakes. You might question the existence of hitherto undocumented localised tremors in the South West of England, but let's not pick at narrative threads at this stage.

Earthquakes. Lots of them.

And if there's one thing rulers hate more than having their morning tea served cold, it's an unstable castle. Oh, and women having a voice. And a transparent tax system. And democracy. And pitchfork-wielding crowds. But, certainly, an unstable castle was definitely in the top ten pet peeves.

71

So, after one too many disturbed nights of creaking wood and stone, and not in a good way, Vortigern decided to do what any reasonable person would do – consult his local wizard.

Enter a particular cultivator with a hat so pointy it could double as a weapon. Merlin scratched his chin, which even in his youth had been a lot more beard than chin, and muttered something about ley lines, magical disturbances, and inconvenient home improvement projects.

"But the castle keeps sinking into the ground!" exclaimed Vortigern.

"Ah, yes," said Merlin with a twinkle in his eye, "that's where the dragon comes in, you see."

Vortigern blinked. "Dragon?"

"Yes, yes, a proper one with scales and fire-breathing and all that. You will need a dragon to stabilise your castle, or so the old scrolls say."

And thus, Vortigern embarked on a quest to find a dragon. A real one. He posted notices around the kingdom, which mainly attracted suspiciously eager dragon enthusiasts and one enterprising young man who insisted his pet iguana was a rare 'dwarf' dragon.

Weeks turned into months, and still, no dragon graced Vortigern's castle with its fiery presence. The kingdom wondered if their ruler had gone completely off his rocker. And then, one day, just as Vortigern was about to give up and invest in some heavy-duty foundation magic, a distant roar echoed across the land.

There it was, in all its scaly glory – the dragon! Flames flickered in its nostrils, and its eyes glinted with a mix of curiosity and menace. Vortigern felt a combination of terror and a strange kind of awe.

The dragon, however, seemed more interested in the castle's architecture than in roasting anyone. It perched itself on a tower and started advising on curtain arrangements and optimal lighting for dungeons. It turned out that the dragon had a passion for interior decorating, which Vortigern found incredibly odd and somewhat endearing.

And so, instead of being the menacing force of destruction Vortigern had expected, the dragon became the kingdom's most sought-after interior designer. It transformed the castle into a place of wonder and magic, all while sharing handy tips on keeping your hoard of treasure organised.

And that, as Merlin explained it to me, is the story of Vortigern's dragon – a tale of unexpected friendships, unconventional solutions, and the realisation that sometimes a little bit of fire-breathing flair can turn a disaster into a castle fit for a ruler and a dragon with impeccable taste.

***

"You're taking the piss out of me, aren't you?
Maybe.
"This is because of the rapping, right?"
Amongst other things.
"There isn't really a 'Selling Sunset' Dragon, is there?"
Not as such.
"It's going to be a terrifying monster, isn't it?"
Most definitely.
"What really happened to Vortigern? The dragon ate him, right?"
I'm sure it did. Eventually.

***

As a newly minted **Ron**, there were a couple of more interesting things I could do with my Qi. Well, that Merlin could do with my Qi and I could watch. I was able to move us to Vortigern's castle. It wasn't quite the teleportation beam that Merlin used to move us to the village after the battle, but it was still quicker than hiking our way there.

Apparently, the trick was to see where you were, imagine where you wanted to be, and then pinch the two destinations together using your Qi. So, not a million miles away from fast travel in any number of MMPORG with which I had whiled away the hours.

Apparently, I found this approach more manageable than most apprentices of Merlin's experience because of how very visual the conception of my Qi was. Rather than needing to tear a hole through the fabric of space and time, I simply flicked from one picture to another. One moment we were walking along a dirt track, and the next...

We were stood in front of, what used to be, a castle on a hill.

I'm sure there was a day, probably not that long ago, that this castle was just standing here minding its own business, with its turrets pointing proudly at the sky like fingers trying to grab hold of passing clouds. It was probably the sort of castle that said, "I'm here to stay, and I've got the cobblestones to prove it."

But, you see, Fate – and I'm not wholly convinced here that a certain wizard did not do more than a bit of interfering - has a wicked sense of humour. Just when the castle was at its most smug and satisfied, a dragon suddenly appeared on its doorstep. Not just any dragon – oh no, this one was the kind of dragon that believed in making a statement. It had roared with the type of authority that makes knights rethink their career choices, and peasants question whether they really needed to venture out for that morning stroll.

Even now, so many years hence, I could tell that the dragon's approach had not been subtle. Flames had licked at the sky, swirling like a painter's brush strokes gone wild. And trust me when I say I know of what I speak. In the face of that inferno, the castle's walls had puddled to the ground like the proverbial chocolate teapot.

I closed my eyes on the ruin before me and was transported back to the moment of destruction.

With a casual flick of its tail, the dragon had taken care of the drawbridge, sending it tumbling into the moat with a splash that would have earned him high scores at the Dragon Olympics. At which stage, it would probably have eaten the judges, flambéd the crowd and taken a dump in the pool. Yes, in my mind, this dragon was the Donald Trump of losers.

"This is one burnt-out ruin."

The dragon was certainly thorough.

"And you are absolutely convinced that I have the chops to defeat something that has literally brought the house down?"

Let us say that I think we might have some advantages that Vortigen lacked.

"Which are?"

The knowledge gained from aeons of exploring the very limits of the universe. The experience of dealing with monsters from the darkest corners of hell. The power earned from —

"Hello, Merlin. Surprised you had the balls to show up around here."

I whirled to see a MAHUSIVE dragon land a few feet from us. It was red and scaly and — I must say, I think this is the crucial detail about the bloody thing - the size of an aircraft carrier. Flames curled from its mouth, and its eyes blazed with a hatred I had only encountered from a prospective mother-in-law who absolutely did not appreciate my tattoos. That being said, the fact it also appeared to speak with the voice of James Dean was pretty disconcerting.

But not quite as disconcerting as realising Merlin was no longer about.

It appeared I was just a girl, standing in front of Godzilla's big brother, praying for it not to eat her.

CHAPTER 18 – IN WHICH WE DISCOVER THE PROPERTIES OF A DRAGON'S FART

"I'm not going to eat you," said the dragon in the voice of the Rebel without a Cause.

I felt myself relax ever so slightly - as in I somehow managed to squeeze some oxygen into my lungs before I passed out. Everything else, though, remained tight as a drum, and I was utterly rooted in place beneath this behemoth.

"There's really not enough of you to bother, if I'm being completely honest. I could have summoned up the motivation for a morning snack if you'd ridden in on a horse - been a while since I had a good horse - but you look a bit bland and stringy on your own. I never could be doing with the ginger-flavoured ones, either."

You may be expecting a quip from me in reply here. But did I mention the fucking size of this monster? It's one thing to like a good bit of banter, but there's a time and a place. Like, as far away from my current position as possible.

I tried to follow the steps Merlin had shown me to fast-travel back to our starting position, but my Qi had seemingly dried up as a response to my panic. As survival mechanisms go, this felt as helpful as when deer freeze in the headlights of oncoming vehicles.

"That being said, I cannot stand the smell of Qi at the best of times, and you absolutely reek of Merlin. So, unless you have any amusing last words, I will move right along to the fireball thing. I'm listening."

Of all the times for words to fail me, this felt like a particularly poor one.

With that, this lizard the size of a small town took a deep breath, and smoke began curling out from its nose and out of the side of its mouth.

I closed my eyes to prepare to die.

Again.

At the very least, it seemed I should get credit for the increasingly exotic nature of my demises. There cannot be too many people throughout history that were hit by a lorry one day and then flame-grilled by a dragon less than forty-eight comparable hours later.

Or maybe there were. Perhaps, as with so many things in my life, other people were out there doing these amazing, weird things, and I was the one missing out. Maybe what I thought was the absolute cutting-edge of shuffling off this mortal coil was actually painfully vanilla. Like the first time you sprinkle salt on your chocolate muffin and rave to your housemates. Or... nope, I'm too scared to complete what was going to be an unnecessarily lewd comparative sentence there. Please use your own imagination.

Knock yourself out. Go really smutty.

But, and I was surprised about this as you, no fiery death occurred.

Realising I was still alive, I cracked open my eyes again to see the dragon observing me, almost thoughtfully, through its amber eyes.

"What are you doing?"

I cleared my throat and squeaked out an answer. "I was preparing to die?"

The dragon blinked. Once. Twice. And then the smoke vanished.

"For fuck's sake," and like the world's most enormous burst balloon, the dragon began to deflate, accompanied by the sound of epic flatulence and some Premier League complaining. "After all this time, he finally bothers to show up with another apprentice, and it turns out this one doesn't even have enough Qi to summon a proper shield. I mean, I have my standards. If I'm going to bother to drag myself out here and puff myself up to defend my lair, it better be worth it, is all I'm saying. And what do I have? Some little pissant fledgling with barely enough Qi to warm my tea. Fucking liberty, Merlin, that's what this is. A fucking liberty."

At the end of this monologue, the dragon had shrunk down to the size of a small pony. It was, therefore, somewhat disconcerting that it... pranced towards me precisely like one too.

"So, where is he? Where is that good-for-nothing-Qi-hoarding-beardy-lair-robbing-bastard?"

Now the scale of the thing was somewhat more manageable for my brain to handle, I seemed to have regained the power of speech.

"That's a slightly more difficult question to answer than you would think."

The dragon snorted at me, utterly incinerating the tree to my right. Like, full-on reduced it to ashes in a moment. Proper Nazi-frying Arc of the Covenant stuff.

"Try."

I had no idea where Merlin had gone, but as this particularly flamey shit show was his idea, I didn't feel any particular desire to protect his secrets. He could feel free to pop up and try to resolve the situation to his satisfaction whenever he wanted.

"I think it best if I start right at the beginning..."

***

In what used to be a village, a short ride from Morgan's current predicament, Pæga licked his lips.

He liked doing that. He thought his tongue whipping up and out around his mouth gave him a wolfish aspect.

Everyone else thought it made his face look like a pasty worm exploded out of the earth on regular occasions. It goes without saying that they would have agreed with Morgan's designation of him as Dick #1.

As far as he could tell, the invasion was working out pretty much as the High King had predicted. It had taken years of negotiations, and no small amount of gold, but he and a bunch of his fellow Warlords had been persuaded to stop fighting each other long enough to cross the Tamar and start laying waste to everything they found in Uther's kingdom.

Of course, he still flinched every time he saw a burst of Qi, expecting Merlin to appear and slaughter them at any moment, but so far, it had only been his own wizard, Melehan, who was bringing the magical doom.

"And we're still at the forefront of the advance?"

Melehan cycled his Qi to make it appear he held his eyes still whilst rolling them in massively expansive circles. He had no idea which god he had angered which had led to his attachment to Pæga's force, but he was making nightly sacrifices to all of the ones he could think of to make amends.

"Yes, my Lord. We are the tip of the High King's spear. My fellow wizards speak in awe as to your belligerence and bravery. They cheer you onwards whilst chastising their own cautious commanders."

Or, to be more accurate, they offered Melehan their sympathy and were extremely glad they were not in the section of the army that Merlin was going to vaporise first. Despite the High King's assurance they would not see him on the battlefield, all of the invading army's wizards had a fast-travel spell prepped to get them back home the second that dread presence appeared. No one thought, due to Pæga's apparent need to dip his cock in every comely native first, that Melehan would get a chance to cast his.

And yet...

There was far more Qi in this land than there ought to be. Legend said that Merlin's cycling needs had drained all the power from the surrounding area, and yet he had never been anywhere that felt so alive with Qi. And he had travelled overseas to some of the great sites of power: Uppåkra, Uppsala, even the incredible energy at Schnippenburg felt like thin gruel compared to the bounty here.

And hadn't he seen that Celt literally glowing with power in that first village they had come to? If there was so much Qi in the land that cultivators could just allow it to leak out of them in such a way, what did that say about those who actually had proper control?

But they hadn't come across any other cultivators.

And Merlin had not turned them into smoking corpses...

Melehan's nose wrinkled in distaste as he thought about the skirmishes thus far. He'd barely been needed to cast a spell, such had been the paucity of resistance. The High King had been right; these people had become complacent.

"Who is the nearest to us?" His 'master' was speaking again.

Melehan reached out to brush against the Qi-presences in the other invading forces. As he feared, they remained well in front of his fellows: the first response from Uther, or more likely Merlin, would smack them right on the nose.

"Warlord Heard is just reaching the last of the villages we sacked to the North. His wizard reports he is much angered to find it despoiled."

Pæga smiled and licked his lips again. "Excellent. So where next?" There was a pause. "Wizard, I asked where do we push to next?"

But Melehan was not answering. He had gone white as a goose, his tattoos showing in stark relief on his face.

Whilst questing out for the other cultivators in the army, he had touched on a power signature he recognised as the Celt from the village.

Was she following them?

That seemed a peculiar choice, having been given every opportunity to run the other way. But there was no accounting for stupid, he guessed. He pushed down on her presence, wondering if he could panic her to flee to safety, and was surprised to feel she appeared much more in control than she had been the night before. In fact, if he had not known the taste of her Qi from their previous meeting, he wondered if he would have noticed her at all.

Interesting. It was like she'd advanced an entire tier in a few hours.

Ignoring Pæga's question, he tried to get a fix on the Celt's exact whereabouts, but his senses were quickly engulfed by a presence he had never experienced before.

But, my word, he knew exactly what it was.

Pæga licked his lips and reached out to cuff the wizard out of his reverie. "I asked you a question!"

Malehan focused his eyes and, in fear, moistened his own lips. "My Lord, what do you know about dragons?"

CHAPTER 19 – IN WHICH WE LEARN HOW THE SAUSAGES ARE MADE

"And then he buggered off as soon as you appeared, and, well, here we are." If the dragon was remotely impressed with my tale, its face gave no indication. Although, I'm not sure what expertise I'm claiming in this area. For all I know, it was giving it the full "Oh.My.God!" with its eyes throughout my story, and I was just missing the subtleties of draconic micro-expressions.

"What a crock of shit." Or maybe not.

"Sorry?"

"You're telling me that, not only is Merlin dead, but that you are the only possible cultivator in all the realms he felt could help him 'save the world.' And that, knowing how weak you are, he thought the best way for you to advance was to bring you here?"

"Yes."

"Bollocks."

"Look, I don't know what else to tell you. Do you think I would be making this up?"

"Did Merlin tell you what happened to the last couple, I think it was five actually, of his apprentices he bought to me here?"

"He didn't mention it, no."

In much the manner that Merlin pulled me into his memories, the dragon suddenly did the same thing and showed me, in graphic detail, what it did to those poor souls. It was a horrific storybook collection I'm going to call 'Five Go to Dragon's Castle and Get Brutally Pounded by a Giant Lizard.'

"These were some of the most advanced practitioners of the age. Merlin had even forsaken his own cultivation to allow them access to enough Qi to advance, and he'd personally tutored them in different methods of facing me. And not one of them lasted more than a few minutes before going up in flames. You expect me to believe that he plucked you from the back end of nowhere on a super-secret mission of huge importance and then brought you here to face me without so much of a shield spell?"

The horse-sized dragon was getting quite up in my face now. It seemed super pissed off at the very idea that I was there to fight it. I had a friend, let's call her Michelle (for that is her name), who considered herself a stone-cold 10/10. She applied for all those terrible reality shows like 'Love Island' and 'Take Me Out' and generally thought an awful lot of herself. If anyone she deemed 'unworthy' even so much as glanced her way, she'd kick off in much the same way as the dragon was here: a real 'know your place and be pleased to breathe the same oxygen as me, Elephant man' energy about her.

I understood I was hardly Sorcerer Supreme material, but I couldn't help but feel a touch hurt by its visceral anger at the ideal I could even think about challenging it.

Also, I didn't particularly appreciate being made to feel a kinship with the host of Darrens and Deans that Michelle sent away with a flea in their mishappen ears.

Then something occurred to me. In all the visions of battles with the other apprentices - and the awful, awful slaughter that was at each of their conclusions - the dragon was in its colossal, town-sized form.

None of the others had faced this smaller version.

"I don't know what you think you're playing at coming here with such a crappy story, but I don't buy it for a second. Merlin's up to something, and as soon as I figure it out, there will be a wailing and gnashing of teeth the like of which the world has not witnessed in centuries." It butted its head aggressively against my chest once more. I was really getting quite fed up with this attitude. "If he thinks sending me a baby cultivator with barely a drop of Qi and not a single technique to their name for a snack is going to make up for all those efforts to try and steal my hoard, he has another thing coming. First, I'm going to -"

The dragon realised I had my arm raised. "What are you doing?"

"I just wanted to correct something you said."

"You what!?!" I had the impression not many people interrupted this dragon. It did not seem keen on the experience. Again, a bit like Michelle.

"You said something that's not quite right."

"You have a few seconds left to live. What are you blithering on about?"

"How you described me. It's not quite right."

"Do you think I care? You're nothing more than -"

"I understand. Take all the invective as read. I just wanted to make sure we are all on the same page."

The dragon opened its mouth and took in a huge breath. I could see right down its throat to where flames had started to creep upwards.

"You see, this **Ron** does have one pretty useful technique . . ."

In the air, I heard glass shatter and the opening bars of "I won't do what you tell me" boomed out across the sky.

My fists glowed bright purple as I opened a [Can of Whoopass] on a dragon.

***

Fun fact, the neck of a giraffe has the same number of bones in it as a human. Apparently, a dragon is much similar.

I mention this because, as my technique was completed and I crashed the dragon's head into the top of my shoulder, the force exerted appeared to be too much for the small number of bones that were supporting such a long neck.

What I'm saying is that [Can of Whoopass] tore the dragon's head from the rest of its body.

I'm not sure which of us was the more surprised - I mean, obviously, it was the now decapitated dragon - but I was pretty damn shocked by the outcome too.

I stood there, agog, for a few moments, holding the head like some sort of post-modern Hamlet. The torso slumped to the floor, pumping out waves of sludgy green blood as if the dragon's heart simply refused to believe what had just happened.

Considering the dragon had spoken with the voice of James Dean, it felt pretty ironic it ended up just being a disembodied head. Or, actually, that was not ironic at all, was it? Damn you, Alanis Morissette and your misleading of a generation as to the meaning of basic linguistic terms.

I love it when a plan comes together.

I didn't quite have it in me to answer Merlin immediately. There was so much adrenaline racing around my body that I needed to gulp in several large breaths before even beginning to think to formulate a response.

Oh, look at Mr I've-Turned-all-Your-Apprentices-into-Charcoal. Who's laughing now?

"Merlin -"

Didn't see that coming, did you? Nope. Thought you'd got one over on Merlin, didn't you? All that swanking about. All that bragging to the other spirit beasts. But I play the long game. Even dead, I turned out to be too crafty for you, right?

"Merlin -"

Two hundred years I've been bringing my apprentices here, and I finally got you. With the worst of the lot and without my physical body even being here. Head torn right off your shoulders by a non-entity of a cultivator. How humiliating for you.

I threw the head to the floor and put my hands on my hips. "Did you just use me as bait to settle an old score?"

There was a pause.

Not exactly. I think you'd describe what we did here as sandbagging. We lured the dragon into thinking you were a tragically weak specimen through - you know - you being wholly inadequate. Then, when its guard was down and it was back to normal size, you got to use your trump card and said goodnight, Mr Dragon. It was a great plan which you carried off flawlessly, my dear.

"But crucially, Big M, this was not a plan I had any idea about."

Well, no. The dragon needed to see your genuinely pathetic display when it first appeared. They're very good at reading emotions, and it was only because you were so guilelessly useless that it made itself vulnerable to you—a brilliant, brilliant plan, if I say so myself.

"And if it had simply blasted me the second it appeared?"

Cultivating is all about risk and reward, my dear. Faint heart never won fair lady. Necessity is the mother of taking chances.

"If the chance is me being eaten by a dragon, it's probably polite we talk about that first!"

For someone who was dead yesterday and seemed pretty happy to return to that state, you are moaning an awful lot about being in mortal danger.

That bought me up short. Merlin was quite right. When had I made the transition from not caring one way or another about being alive to feeling indignant at having my, second, life put in danger?

Merlin took advantage of the pause to press his advantage.

If you learn one lesson under my tutelage, my dear, it is that the ends always justify the means. Always. No one ever cares about how the sausages are made; they just want them on their plate first thing in the morning. We need you to get stronger. Quickly. We've spent considerable time shoring up your foundations, but now we need to see some real growth. There is no better way to do so than defeating and consuming a spirit beast: particularly one as old and as wily as this one. It's why I kept bringing my apprentices here. I hoped one would be able to take that next step. But none of them managed it, no matter how strong or how well I prepared them. But you? You took its head at the first time of asking.

I wanted to shout and stamp my foot. I wanted to rail against how unfair Merlin had been, how irresponsible. I wanted to slap his smug, satisfied face and scream and scream until he went deaf.

But it was not just him being a voice in my head that halted that desire. It was the glowing light that suddenly started leaking out from the chest of the dragon's body.

It was a colour I had never seen before. To try to draw comparisons with words seems somewhat redundant, but the best I can do is to say it was the colour of overwhelming strength. It pulsed and writhed in the air, seemingly looking for a new home.

Now, this is very important. You need to gather that Qi – can you remember how you did it with the wolf, my dear? Excellent. However, you need to do so exceptionally carefully. Breathe it in. But do so slowly. It is absolutely vital that you don't take in more than you can handle in one go or –

So, of course, I inhaled the whole lot in one snort.

CHAPTER 20 – IN WHICH HAVING FUCKED AROUND, I FIND OUT

It turns out that trying to cycle the Qi of an ancient spirit beast as a brand-new cultivator is a bit like attempting to fit an elephant through a mouse hole.

You will doubtless make note of the entirely safe-for-work simile that I used there, despite the obvious potential for a crass, sexual image and use that as a guide for how discombobulated the experience was leaving me.

You'd think that after all that time, alone, in a cave, waxing on and waxing off over and over again, I'd have learned to avoid such predicaments. Or maybe to listen, even slightly, to the voice of the undying expert warning me to go easy.

But, alas, here I am, feeling as if I was holding a hive of angry bees in my throat and trying to persuade them to settle down and be swallowed whilst delivering a presentation on appropriate insect behaviour.

The first indication I had probably made the latest in a long line of poor life choices was hearing Merlin say: Well, this will be interesting. I wonder if I can... Yes, I can. Incorporeal popcorn is the best. Salt AND sweet? Don't mind if I do.

I did not take this as a supportive comment.

The essence surge from Vortigern's Dragon hit me like a tidal wave of concentrated chaos, as if the universe had decided to play a particularly rowdy game of leapfrog with my internal energies. I felt my eyes bulge out of my head like a startled frog's, and my hair stood up on end as if it were auditioning for the part of a lightning conductor in a particularly eccentric theatrical production. Having all this lovely, pre-Raphaelite knee-length hair made this an especially visual spectacle.

I gritted my teeth, determined to weather the storm—or, in this case, the tsunami—of Qi.

However, whereas the wolf's essence had appeared in my studio as a small blob of red which was quickly absorbed into my broader palette, this was not working out like that.

The first issue was that this essence was a brand-new colour, and my poor purple Qi had no idea how it was supposed to absorb it. Every time my plucky little blob reached out to touch the dragon's Qi, it started shimmering and flashing through the full range of rainbow colours. Basically, my internal artist's studio was being lit up like the worst school disco you'd ever been to.

The second issue, and on reflection, I should probably have flagged this one first, was that there was an absolute fuckton of dragon Qi. Like, I'm stood knee-deep in my studio, nearly swimming through the stuff, and it was still pouring in.

Oh, dear. Look at that. It's almost like it would have been better to do this a little bit at a time. Who would have thought this would be the outcome? Oh, yes. That's right. Me.

The smugness in Merlin's voice was considerably amplified by, in my view, an unnecessarily loud crunching of popcorn.

"I think we can take the 'I told you so' as read now, Big M. Anything more constructive to say? Like any words of advice at all?"

Silence, save the sound of popcorn munching.

The pain. Did I mention the pain?

The bees were now unionised and conducting collective action against my insides. My muscles were protesting in a symphony of cramps, and, most alarmingly, my bones were creaking as if they were auditioning for a role in a horror novel.

Sweat poured down my face, and I'm sure that the noises I was making would have earned me a significant living on a few of the more exotic OnlyFans sites.

In my increasingly delirious state, I vaguely recalled the words in one of those anime series that said Qi, like a river, should flow smoothly and without obstruction. Well, let me tell you, what was going on inside me at the moment felt less like a serene river and more like a rampaging lava flow incinerating everything in its path.

Then it hit me. No obstructions.

If the point was to have nothing in the way of the flow, then white-hot lava would probably get the job done more effectively than my pretty purple paint.

I turned the page to the image of me as Vitruvian Man. As before, I could see all my veins lit up with that soft purple glow.

With a flick, I started directing the undiluted dragon's Qi straight into those channels.

This hurt. A lot.

Hang on a second, my dear. You need to assimilate that external Qi into your own essence before doing that. You risk -

But I wasn't listening. Merlin had his chance to be the wise sage over all this and had chosen to be a dick.

The dragon's Qi continued to pour into my studio; it was up to my waist now. If it carried on like this, I was in danger of, literally, drowning in it. My own blob of Qi had given up trying to assimilate it and gone to sit in the corner, continuing to flash and change colour as it sat there with, I imagine, a somewhat overwhelmed expression on its face.

I knew how it felt.

So I kept flicking that Qi like I had never flicked anything before. Again, please note the lack of smutty innuendo here as evidence of my level of distraction.

If cycling my own Qi pushed against blockages - hello, repaired liver function - then the dragon's lava Qi simply scoured my channels completely clean.

This hurt exactly as much as it sounds like.

But in the midst of this agony—this cacophony of pain and misplaced essence— I could see that the flood of Qi into my studio was beginning to lessen.

The more of the dragon's essence I was able to flick into my channels, the perkier I felt my own blob of Qi become - I sensed if I could get the amount in the studio down to something manageable, with the rest flowing around me, there was a chance some absorption could take place.

Of course, all this indescribable colour blazing around my veins was absolutely ruining me, but I could only worry about so many things at once.

With this newfound perspective, I tried to relax my clenched jaw, loosen my tense muscles, and keep washing the alien Qi out of my studio and into the rest of me.

The pain didn't vanish, but as I fell into something of a rhythm, it transformed into a pulsating symphony that, against all odds, started to make a twisted sense.

And so, there I stood, a baby cultivator caught amid an essence tempest, swaying and twisting like a leaf caught in a gale.

And if those tortured metaphors don't tell what a shitshow all this was, nothing would.

Just so you know, I am doing everything I can to hold you together. If it wasn't for all the tempering the boy had done to his, well, I guess your body, you'd be dead already, irrespective of anything I am doing.

"Can't talk. Burning alive. Internally."

Yes, that's pretty much the guaranteed outcome from forcing thousands of years of spirit beast Qi down in one go.

'Really? You should have said something."

I did!

I tuned Merlin out and looked back at my artist's studio. The flood of Qi seemed much more under control now. In fact, my blob of paint was being quite the little Qi mop that could, soaking up the remaining patches of dragon essence. I noticed that as it did so, the seizure-inducing colour flashing was lessening.

And, unless I was quite mistaken, it was becoming quite the hench paint blob.

The pain was still there, but it had become strangely exhilarating, like riding a roller coaster through a lightning storm.

Again, I want it on the record as to the incredibly complex and complicated work I am doing here to keep you alive. You don't need to be feeling you made a good choice here. This is literally the most stupid thing I have ever seen. And the prevailing worldview in this part of Britain is that trees can talk.

I wasn't going to give him the satisfaction, but I could dimly sense how hard Merlin was working to keep me alive. The undiluted dragon essence may have cleared out every single blockage that existed in my channels, and yet the thing was, it had almost entirely destroyed those channels too. To try to mitigate the damage, it appeared that Merlin was directing the flow to areas of my Vitruvian man that, up until now, had not had channels going to them.

This, by the way, is absolutely cheating. When I was alive, I would have ordered the execution of any apprentice that had tried this as a way to circumvent centuries of study and meditation to open up all these areas. I don't want you having any illusions that this speed of advancement is in any way normal.

"Mate, is this your way of dealing with me progressing at a greater pace than you managed? Didn't I crack the technique thing faster than you too?"

Everything I achieved was hard won by my own skill, ingenuity and effort. You're skipping out on all of the things that cultivating is supposed to teach you. And I am not sure that is going to turn out to be a good thing.

"On the other hand, and I may be misquoting you, so please stop me if I am, I think the ends justify the means, right? Right?"

He did not seem to have much to say about that.

CHAPTER 21 - IN WHICH MERLIN ADMITS HE WAS WRONG AND APOLOGISES SINCERELY

I don't think Merlin and I are talking.

Normally, this wouldn't bother me. I can hold a passive-aggressive silence with the best of them, so if he thinks I'm going to crack first, he has another thing coming.

What's that? You don't think I have the patience to stare down a legendary cultivator in a bottom-lip pouting contest?

You know me so little.

I have a 'friend' from Nursery I haven't spoken to in about twenty-five years: bitch took the last block of yellow Lego from the tub and, well, you don't do me like that.

She made somewhat of a power move a few years back by inviting me to her wedding. If you'd seen me ostentatiously blank a two-hundred-pound woman, in a puffy white dress, on the happiest day of her life, you need to believe I can cold-shoulder a wizard whose only presence on Earth is as a disembodied voice.

But, as I left my internal artist's studio and returned to the real world - one in which I found myself lying in the slimy, congealed blood of a recently decapitated dragon - it's hardly surprising I felt up for a chat.

"Big M, you there?"

Silence.

"Okay. I get you're pissed at me for not taking your advice. But you need to remember I have no idea how any of this works. You dropped me into a mortal combat deathmatch with a dragon, and I admit I was feeling a bit raw about it. However, I get that I shouldn't have gulped all that stuff down in one go, especially after you told me not to. But let's be fair, it doesn't seem to have worked out too bad, does it?"

Silence.

"I guess what I'm trying to say is that we both could have been our better selves over all this a little more, and we should probably put it behind us and get back to, you know, saving my sister. And the world."

That was a terrible apology.

"Excuse me, mate? Did you hear the word 'sorry' anywhere there? I'm not apologising to you; I'm saying things were done, and we can agree we both might have done them better. No harm, no foul. Look, think of it like I'm the loveable, impetuous one that the audience loves to hate, and you're the sanctimonious know-it-all who gets a spin-off series that is cancelled after three shows when the producers realise who had the real star power. We've got different skill sets. I'm telling you, we should totally team up and fight crime."

That's an extraordinary way of saying you made a colossal error, despite my advice, and that you are so grateful I swooped in to help. And that you are very, very sorry for being such a silly, silly girl.

"Dude, if you're hoping to out-petty me here, I can show you an official wedding photo with me giving such exquisite stink-eye to the bride that they had to stick one of those yellow smiley faces over me in post-production."

More silence.

I shifted around a little on the ground, feeling extremely high levels of ick at the resulting squelching noises. My back was thoroughly coated with the dragon's blood, making staying much longer in my current position feel very unattractive.

I'd only just gotten over the experience of being covered in wolf guts, and I feared the tunic I'd been gifted in the village was probably at the end of its serviceable life.

I pressed down with my forearms and elbows to start the process of standing up and, somewhat surprisingly, found myself catapulted several feet in the air.

Fortunately, to make sure this was even more ungainly, the back of my tunic was stuck to the ground by all the blood and was ripped clean away as I shot upwards.

The result of this, as I fell back to Earth with quite the thump, was that my arse was once again fully exposed to the elements.

"What. The. FUCK! Merlin, what was that!"

Fine. I am going to need to explain what has happened, so you don't injure yourself while getting used to the changes. However, I don't want you to take me engaging with you over this as any sign that I either accept your apology -

"I didn't apologise!"

Or that I believe I have done anything at all for which you are due an apology of your own. My position is that you are entirely to blame for everything -

"Mate, tell me what's going on with my body!"

You will recall that I have mentioned several times that the body you have possessed has gone through a significant process of physical tempering.

"So?"

Do you remotely understand what that means?

"You know what? I think it was unfair of me to describe you as a sanctimonious know-it-all. What on Earth made me think that was a fair thing to say?"

I am saying that the customs and practices under which your body was trained by its previous owner are nothing particularly advanced or unusual for the culture from which the boy was from. However, they are extremely impressive by modern standards. During our little day of training, we've further tightened up on what he had achieved there. You are thus what I believe is known in the trade as ... buff.

"Okay . . ."

However, whilst I was heroically keeping you alive after your latest foolhardy escapade, I seem to have pushed the physical potential envelope of your body a little.

I looked down at the divot my elbows had left in the dirt as they had propelled me into the sky. "In what way 'pushed the envelope', Big M?"

This seems like an apt moment for me to outline some further details around cultivation.

"It's not that long ago since your last infodump. Am I going to find this remotely interesting?"

I could put this another way, do you want to know what's happening with your body? Or should we just let you flounder about in what I am coming to recognise as being your signature style?

"Are there any other choices?"

You really are a child.

87

***

I will spare you the lecture Merlin gave me that seemed to last most of my adult life.

At one stage, I had to check time was still passing and he wasn't looping things again as I was sure there was no way there could be that much monologuing in just one short day.

We're talking Grade A Bond Villain oversharing here.

There were a whole heap of words I didn't understand and an awful lot of stuff I kind of did, but those sections sounded largely like Merlin was making it up as he went along.

But, to try to summarise with the highlights, it is apparently essential to have as a starting point that there's an awful lot of Qi in the British Isles.

Like, a lot.

Have you ever wondered why so many myths, legends and general wackiness have been generated on such a small island?

Well, now you know. It's not hallucinations caused by the toxic build-up of ingesting too much tea. It's Qi—lots of it.

The thing is, though, when he was alive, Merlin simply hoovered most of this energy up. The way he tells it, he needed to pull so much of it out of the land to keep up with his advancement that it left the rest of the island somewhat bone-dry.

The reasons there are no dinosaurs any more? Merlin sucked up all the Qi they needed to survive.

Atlantis? Merlin on a Qi bender.

Hang on. I never said anything like that...

So, the lesser folk - that's absolutely what he called the rest of us, by the way. Don't worry, I'm keeping score of all the many and various ways I'm not wholly sure the Big M is the good guy of this tale - by necessity, would focus on physical cultivation and body tempering in order to survive.

Essentially, in the absence of any Qi because of Merlin-the-magic-hog, a whole culture built around maximising physicality grew up. Thus, a fine young dark-age warrior like Wulfnoð would have spent most of his life pushing his body past its limitations in such a Qi-deprived environment.

Hence the henchness of our ancestors.

And, incidentally, nothing to do with all that paleo-diet bollocks your mate's dad would swear by as he paraded in front of you with his shirt off and in his ancient budgie-smugglers.

So, take one Qi-deprived but very well-drilled body and enter me and my fantastic idea to flood it with some high-quality dragon Qi. When that all became a touch intense, and Merlin needed to pull some epic cultivation shit to keep it from exploding under all the stress, that's where the magic happened.

To cut a long story short, the outcome of all that coming together was that I'm now the proud owner of a superhero bod capable of jumping small buildings in a single bound.

That is so far from what I have just explained to you that I assume you simply weren't listening to a word I said.

"That was the gist, no?"

No. Not even slightly.

"Come on. You as good as said it yourself. Dragon Qi equals gamma radiation, and my body is now permanently Hulked up, right? Next, we need to focus on flinging some force lightning around and sharpening up the old lightsaber action. After that, I'll be good to go to meet Arthur and save the world.

I think I preferred it when we weren't talking.

CHAPTER 22 – IN WHICH THE CAT LEAVES THE BAG

A midst the clamour of the skirmish, Arthur reigned in his horse and removed his dragon helm. His sweat-slick hair fell forward to cover his eyes, and he swept it back with his forearm.

His gaze fixed upon the shield wall that had formed, almost out of nowhere, ahead of what remained of his spearmen. Each member of the first line wore intricately wrought mail, suggesting he was in the presence of someone's elite bodyguard, but their shields were blank, with no symbols of their tribe. The sun's golden rays kissed the steel of their spears and swords, casting a heavenly glow upon their tightly packed ranks.

"Fuck this."

Arthur was thoroughly over being ambushed. It seemed he could not even travel a short distance to a neighbouring town now without one of his father's thegns trying to have him assassinated. Even then, he would respect them a lot more if they would, you know, own the attempt.

This whole 'anonymous strike team' thing was getting old.

"I feel I should once again mention there is a perfectly serviceable brothel in the castle." Bors drove his mailed fist through the face of a warrior that had strayed too close. With a flick of his wrist, he dislodged the teeth embedded into the metal.

"Been there. Done them."

"It just seems like we're pretty much asking for it at this stage. Anyone with a grudge can just park their húscarlas on any road leading to a big pair of tits, and sooner or later, we'll walk right into them."

"What can I say? New is always better."

There was a disgusted whinny, and Arthur's horse shook itself. He leaned forward and nuzzled against its neck. "Apart from you, obviously, Llamrei. There's no horse better."

"I'm no fertility witch, but maybe try doing that once in a while with the wife? A little Arthur would go a long way to cut back on the wear-and-tear on the spearmen."

Ignoring his friend, Arthur, unslung his own spear, Rhongomyniad, and held it high into the air.

"Gather up," he called out to the rest of his horsemen. With a smoothness born of years of practice, the figures around him quickly fell into a triangle formation with Arthur at the tip. "We all know the drill, quick charge, break the line, slaughter, slaughter, slaughter and back home to Tintagel for mead and muffins. Big stack of treasure for anyone who finds out who these guys serve."

There was an approving roar and the remaining spears fell back to reinforce the sides of the horsemen. They'd have to sprint outrageously to keep up with the flying wedge formation, but whatever made them happy, Arthur guessed.

"And charge!"

As the thunder of hooves began, the members of the shield wall started to rethink their career choices.

At no stage was the plan for them to hold against a bloody cavalry charge: they were simply here to block the escape by a broken force once the ambush had done its work and taken out the Prince.

They were a touch light on the details, but what had seemed like a reasonably straightforward hit-and-run job on a wastrel who dipped his wick in any passing puddle of wax seemed to have gone badly wrong.

They'd seen their commander lead a quick charge against the convoy's flank which, on a normal day, should have been that. But instead of causing panic and chaos, they'd been repelled with a ferocity that shocked them, and things had quickly descended to a rout as they saw their fellows cut to ribbons.

What was heading their way, very quickly, with the earth itself seeming to tremble, felt sub-optimal.

But it was probably a touch late for such regrets now. If you came for the Prince, you better not miss, and, for whatever reason, their gambit had failed.

The only thing all involved could be sure of was that if Arthur escaped to tell tales, Merlin would curse them to the twentieth generation. A resolve that came from certain and painful death strengthened their arms, and their shields snapped to overlap like scales. The rhythm of their breathing synchronized, a collective heartbeat that echoed the completeness of their purpose.

As they prepared themselves, the sound of thundering hooves grew deafening, the ground vibrating beneath Arthur's charge. However, the shield wall remained still, awaiting the moment of impact.

What else could they do?

The clash was seismic, the collision of forces creating a shockwave that reverberated through the ground. The charge met the shield wall with a force that shattered bone and crushed people under hooves.

For a moment, it seemed like the forward momentum would stall, but the flying wedge's true power emerged in the chaos that followed.

Arthur, at the tip of the thrust, broke through the line and created an opening in a fairly conclusive manner. His horse reared up, lashing out with its hooves, whilst he swung his spear in a wide arc. The defenders staggered as their cohesion began to shatter, and the rest of his forces surged into the gap he created.

Arthur dismounted, his feet hitting the uneven ground with a solid thud. The din of battle surrounded him - a symphony of clashing metal, cries of triumph, and anguished screams. This was one of the few times that he felt truly alive. The adrenaline surged through his veins as he engaged one of the spearmen at close quarters. His spear became an extension of his arm, striking out in calculated arcs.

Every movement was a dance of survival and conquest. The clash of weapons sent sparks flying, and the acrid smell of sweat and blood filled the air. Arthur's focus narrowed to the enemies before him - their eyes filled with desperation and defiance. He ignored Bors at his side, bellowing his strange battle cry, and drove forwards exploiting the openings in their defences his charge had caused.

He might have been unaware, but a small group of knights formed a protective circle around him that melded into a singular unit. Each relied on the other, their movements complementing and reinforcing one another. The rhythmic clash of weapons marked the ebb and flow of the battle as they pushed forward, and the enemy began to collapse under the pressure.

As the momentum of that initial charge began to fade, fatigue started to creep in. However, the flying wedge's initial breach had created a domino effect, and the enemy shield wall was almost wholly disintegrated.

It was over.

Or, at least, that was what should have happened.

Instead, Arthur found himself facing one warrior that seemed to be holding the last vestiges of the line together on his own. At his feet were several of Arthur's men. That in itself meant little to him, but he had an image to maintain.

He adjusted his grip on Rhongomyniad and flung it straight at that final opponent. In his experience, that should have been that and certainly, things would have worked out poorly for that warrior had he not raised his hand and pushed the onrushing spear to one side.

It was such a surprise that, for a moment, nothing else happened. Arthur's eyes met those of his opponent who, he was sure, seemed to wink at him.

"Wizard!"

The warning cry went up from those around Arthur. It may have been a generation since anyone had fielded magic against Uther's forces, but they had trained extensively to counteract such a foe. You did not share a castle with Merlin and have any complacency around the power of magic and its potentially devastating impact on a battlefield.

When facing a cultivator in the open field, Merlin recommended there were only two courses of action that would keep you alive. For reasons only Bors and Arthur we're aware, Option A - *Run like bastards and get a message to me to come and pull you out of the fire* - was not on the table.

Thus, it was time to give Option B a whirl. Merlin had codenamed this '*Operation It's-All-Fun-And-Games-Until-Someone-Loses-An-Eye.*'

In seconds, Arthur's men changed formation into two short lines: one kneeling in front of the other. "First row. Present. Loose. Reload." Bors quickly led his men through a drill none of them had ever thought they would use. "Second row. Present. Loose. Reload. First row..."

You are missing out if you've never seen knights in full chainmail speed load and shoot crossbows before. You would think it would be an absolute carriage wreck, but give people twenty-odd years of practice and some pretty clear motivation, and you'd be amazed what could be achieved.

The opposing wizard did a pretty decent job of deflecting most of the projectiles. The thing is, with crossbow bolts, 'most' didn't really cut it.

After the tenth volley, there was not an awful lot left to provide opposition.

Bors threw the recovered Rhongomyniad back to Arthur, who caught it one-handed. "That was intense."

Arthur nodded. "I don't suppose there's any chance the men will think that was a drill, is there?"

Bors looked around at a lot of confused people, all of whom were having some version of the conversation: "Holy shit! That was a wizard. How did they have a wizard? Do the bad guys have wizards now? Where was Merlin? Isn't he supposed to deal with anything like that?"

"I fear, my Lord, that the cat may be out of the bag."

CHAPTER 23 – IN WHICH I MAKE A NEW FRIEND

I think it is something of a record that I was having the "I think we should see other people" chat with Merlin barely seventy-two hours into our relationship. I had some wild weekends in my youth, but even within that dark context, this was a bit depressing for someone of my age and experience. Although, twenty-four of those hours were repeated over and over again . . .

So maybe I'm being a bit unfair on myself.

"Mate, I'm not going to lead you on here. The fact is, it's absolutely you and not me. I need to spend some time with actual people who a) aren't trying to kill me and b) don't get their heads blown off by evil wizards within minutes of me meeting them. Also, having a face to talk to in the corporeal world would be peachy."

As I keep trying to explain, you need to focus -

"Yes, yes, yes. I 'need' to focus on my internal journey and advance my cultivation to thwart the great evil casting a shadow across the land. Yada,, yada,, yada. Bit of emotional blackmail about my sister. Etc,, etc. I also 'need' someone else I can talk to about this stuff."

I don't wish to puncture any illusions you may have here about the plethora of Qi guides in Dark Age Cornwall, but there is no one else who understands this better than me. I am, quite literally, the greatest expert on cultivation in the known - or indeed the unknown - world.

"But you are also the guy that dropped me into single combat with a dragon that killed at least your last five apprentices. Let's say I'm having some trust issues."

And that battle with Vortigern's Dragon has advanced your cultivation beyond anything that could possibly have been imagined. In a few days, you've reached a level of power that should have taken, at the very least, decades of focused study. I do think a little credit where credit is due would not be beyond the pale.

"So now you want the credit for getting me to the cusp of **Harry**? You've been nothing but pissy with me from the second I absorbed that dragon's Qi. You can't have it both ways, mate. I'm either nailing this cultivation thing - in which case you can back the fuck off and give me a quick breather to get my head together, or I'm utterly useless, you are needing to do everything for me, and this whole plan is a waste of our time. You can't double-dip here. And either way, just for the sake of my own sanity I need to talk to someone who isn't you for a bit."

We don't have space for you to have some 'me time' here, my dear. I can see in your memories that this is a recurrent theme in your life. Things get hard, and you have a tendency to go missing to 'find yourself'. But I'm afraid the stakes here are a touch higher here than when you ran away from home because your father took his belt to you -"

'Fuck off!"

And then a strange thing happened.

93

I felt the Qi in my channels go white-hot, and then it was exploding outwards in a shower of purple stars. The brightness of the light blinded me, and it was several moments before I could see the ruins of the castle again.

Once I could, I realised two things had changed.

Firstly, I had burned a pretty impressive crop circle twenty feet around me.

Oh, and secondly, I couldn't feel a certain wizard anymore.

"Fuck me, I've exorcised Merlin."

***

It hadn't been the first time he'd left me alone since I found myself in this world. But it felt a bit different this time. Whereas before, when Merlin had gone a bit quiet, I still felt connected to him in some comforting way: like having the mobile number of a guy you were never going to do, but was helpful to have around when you needed to move furniture.

Now... well, it was like there had been a shell around me, and it had suddenly cracked and fallen away.

That, and the fact that the back half of my tunic had been unceremoniously ripped away when I flipped myself in the air, I was suddenly feeling pretty vulnerable.

I cycled some Qi into my fists, which made me feel a little less like a damsel in distress and had another look at my surroundings.

Castle ruin. Tick.

Decapitated dragon corpse. Tick.

Giant purple crop circle. Tick.

Yep, everything was pretty much as it was before I forcibly banished the only person who had an idea who I was or what I was supposed to be doing.

I'd basically killed Tom Nook.

I forced down a jolt of panic. This was what I had wanted, wasn't it? To be left alone for a bit? That was when I was at my best, after all. I had never needed anyone else in my life before, and I wasn't going to start now.

Although - a traitorous part of my head chimed in - there were worse places to start learning the value of friendship, found family and working together than when you were teleported to a time fifteen hundred years before you were born and when you were, for the second time in as many days, butt naked.

Well, no use weeping over the puddled lactose.

I summoned my inner Beyonce, pulled myself together, shed the tatters of my blood-stained tunic, and tried to pick a direction that looked like the sort of place a tailor who worked for free lived.

I'd taken two steps before my brain finally caught up with my ears. I did have another option before becoming the naked rambler...

What had the dragon said... "defend my hoard."

***

It turns out dragons don't tend to be too surreptitious about where they keep their stolen booty. I guess when you have the power to go all Kaiju on unexpected visitors, not that many thieves come calling.

At least not twice.

Vortigern's dragon had scooped out a massive spot to call home in the castle's centre. It had also used this hole in the ground into which to pile an extraordinary mishmash of the precious, the peculiar, the profound and the perplexing.

It was clear that, when not battling Merlin's apprentices, the dragon had existed in its horse-sized form, as everything about the lair was scaled for a reasonably sized dobbin. The path from the castle gatehouse to the dragon's lair was strewn with discarded oddments of all shapes and sizes. A signpost fashioned from a gnarled tree branch indicated, in scrawled, slightly singed letters, the way to "My Trove of Tidbits and Trinkets".

I took a moment to consider that sign.

It seemed a touch... unusual for a dragon to advertise its hoard in this way— particularly one whose response to visitors was fiery death. Maybe I wasn't the only one around here that needed people to talk to but was a bit spikey with it.

That metaphor felt a bit on the nose, so I continued down the path.

After a short while, I found myself standing before an entrance that reaffirmed my sense that the dragon may have been a little more needy than I had first thought. A worn-out doormat, with the embroidered image of a rather befuddled-looking Kraken, lay at the foot of the lair. The words "Speak Friend and Enter" were written on it in an ostentatiously flowery font.

"Yep," I thought to myself. "Needy as fuck."

I stepped carefully over the doormat and turned a corner into the cave proper. Hoard.

That was a word that had lingered into my own time. Of course, nowadays, it is used more to describe crazy cat ladies and their collection of random crap.

Looking around this dragon's space, though, I could see more than a few similarities.

It was as if the treasures of a thousand realms had collided, mixed up and then stacked themselves floor to ceiling in the most incongruous way possible.

I found myself humming a little ditty about gadgets, gizmos, whosits and whatsits but quickly stopped: the way things were going, I would probably trigger some sort of transformation spell and end up losing my legs but gaining an ability to sing and talk to crustaceans.

I kept walking further into the lair; the columns of crap in this hoard were just unbelievable.

Gold coins gleamed beside a pile of mismatched socks. Tarnished goblets rubbed shoulders with broken timepieces and forgotten trinkets. Stacks of precious gems lay jostled for space in one corner with half-finished jigsaw puzzles. A pile of dusty tomes teetered precariously on top of bags upon bags of tiaras.

The air was filled with the scent of old parchment and slightly charred teacakes. From looking at the covers of some of the books, this curious juxtaposition spoke of the dragon's dual interests—intellectual conversations and the occasional baking misadventure.

Stacks of ancient volumes on philosophy and history lay cheek by jowl with curious contraptions of gears and cogs that hinted at the dragon's forays into inventing, often with rather explosive results.

And then there were the artworks, each telling a tale in its own right. A portrait of a dapper ferret in a top hat hung beside a series of landscapes that seemed to shift with my gaze. Murals of fire-breathing chickens cavorted across the walls, commemorating an incident that had, presumably, become the stuff of legends.

However, there was one particular area of the trove that truly captured my interest. My gaze was drawn to a corner where suits of armour stood like sentinels, frozen in time and memory.

In my naked state, my eyes fell upon one particular set that looked exactly my size. It was bedecked with colourful ribbons and feathers that fluttered with a life of their own. It was as if this suit of armour had attended a masquerade rather than a battlefield, and something about it really appealed to me.

I reached out to touch it.

The second my finger made contact, I was wearing it: like I had equipped it from my inventory in every video game I had ever played.

I moved my arms forward and back experimentally. If it had any weight to it, I didn't feel it—big thumbs up to my new dragon-enhanced superbody.

I turned to admire my reflection in a stack of gold coins - everyone should do that once in their life. It felt AMAZING - and my covetous eye was drawn to a sword in an elaborate scabbard floating in a glass case.

I told Merlin that I felt I needed a different approach to things than simply throwing hands. I'd got lucky so far with my three fights, but I couldn't help but feel a sharp piece of metal in my hand might be advantageous. Don't get me wrong, I had no secret sword expertise - short of enacting every lightsaber fight I'd ever seen - but I was oddly attracted to this blade.

With barely a second thought, I smashed the glass with a Qi-infused gauntlet - did I mention how kick-arse I suddenly was? Real Xena: Warrior Princess stuff- and, with a flourish, drew the sword from its scabbard.

Fuck yeah. Freedom! Me and you, baby. We're going to tear the world a new one. Let's FUCK. SHIT. UP!

Well, I did want someone else to talk to...

CHAPTER 24 – IN WHICH FAR, FAR TOO MANY FUCKS ARE GIVEN

Hang on, who the fuck are you?

Some people might find the idea of a speaking sword odd.

Not me.

After looping the same day over and over again, energy-beam-throwing wizards, farting dragons, and Qi-infused WWE moves, this barely warranted a raised eyebrow. I mean, when the sword swivelled in my hand to point its edge towards my face in a way I instinctively knew meant it was looking at me, I might have had a slight moment.

But the speaking? Cool beans.

Where's Rhydderch?

"Who?"

Rhydderch.

"Nope. You can keep saying the same thing over and over again if you want, but that's not going to help me, I'm afraid."

Do you think you're funny?

"Yes. I'm afraid I do."

The sword twisted in my grip as if looking around the cave.

Oh, for fuck's sake! We're in a hoard, aren't we? The dragon got us, didn't it? I told him this would happen. I said, 'fighting fire with fire' is a cautionary tale, not a fucking assault strategy. But he wouldn't listen, would he? He always knew best. That's Rhydderch for you. Or was, I suppose.

"Sorry, what do you mean, 'fight fire with fire?'"

The sword burst into flames. I mean, I did ask.

I'm Dyrnwyn, the Sword of Rhydderch Hael. Fire is kind of my thing.

"Thanks for clarifying. Could you, you know, stop?"

The fire went out, but the sword kept swinging about in my grip, clearly looking around at the hoard.

Fucking dragons. No sense of organisational framework. Look at all this stuff. It's got a bloody Scroll of Resurrection mixed in with old copies of 'Teeth and Tails' over there. You will want to grab that, love. It twisted again to 'look' up at me. **Whatever the fuck you are. Who did you say you were again?**

"I'm Morgan Le Fay."

Like fuck you are. The things Morgan would do for hair and skin like yours would make your teeth fall out in shock. She's five foot nothing and built like an especially fat fucking barrel. And she knows who Rhydderch is. Try again.

"Okay. Look, it's going to be a long story. Can I put you down while we talk? Doing it like this is uncomfortable."

You can stick me up your arse if you want, love. My previous bearer is an ash heap, and you're wearing my scabbard. So, I'm your sword now. Whatever the fuck you are.

"Oh, goody."

***

I was starting to look back at my time with Merlin as a golden age of wit and sophistication. Drynwyn, although a lively conversationalist, was not quite what I was looking for when I told the wizard I wanted to see other people.

For a start, there was the swearing. I'm no shrinking violet, but I like to think I have somewhat of a varied vocabulary range.

The sword, not so much.

You're telling me you're a fucking cultivator? Fuck me. I thought Merlin fucked over those fuckers years back.

I shrugged. "I don't really know what I'm doing."

You ripped the fucking head off a dragon that cooked Rhydderch Hael. They don't name fucking swords after you because you're a lovely chap. He was a fucking legend. A stone-cold, fucking nightmare on two legs. He had stones you could grind walnuts with. There was a brief pause as the sword seemed to be considering. **Although, I'm not sure why he kept doing that, to be honest. Bit odd, now I think about it. And all that stuff with the baby oil...**

When it didn't speak again for a while, I started to look a bit more at the hoard. From the hints I'd picked up from Drynwyn so far, there was some good stuff mixed in with an awful lot of crap.

For example, the armour I was wearing didn't have a proper name or anything, but according to the sword I could use it to store my Qi. **It's just your standard cultivator armour. Force some of your stuff into it, which'll make it tougher. The better sets can hold fuckloads of your swirly stuff. Rhydderch never bothered with any of that, though. He was a loincloth and tassels kind of guy.**

I was starting to get an impression of my sword's previous owner.

My search of the hoard was proving fruitful. There were all sorts of rings, necklaces and pendants lying around in different bags that I figured had to have some useful properties. According to Drynwyn, I wanted to sort out any with the same colour stones as my Qi. **But don't put anything on until I have a look at it. There's some nasty shit in here, and the last thing I need is for you to get fucked up with a curse. That'd be just my luck. Freed from a dragon's hoard one moment to get saddled with an adventurer cursed to seek out ever increasingly complex sexual positions. Don't want to go through that again.**

"Again?"

I'd made quite a pile of amethyst-embedded jewellery before the sword snapped out of reconsidering its memories of what sounded to me like the kinkiest barbarian warrior since Red Sonja.

That's quite a nice haul, actually. Purple Qi? Unusual. But then, who knows what the fuck is going to be usual for you. You definitely want the one on the left. That's an entirely unique Mystic Gem. Irreplaceable. Unlimited power. No, my left. Left. Fuck's sake. That one. That ONE!

The sword shot up into the air and landed on the ring it had identified. Unfortunately, in doing so, it also sheared that ring in half.

Fuck's sake.

*

It took us most of the rest of the afternoon, but at the end of things, we were able to properly gear me up with all sorts of useful bits and pieces. The sword was the only true treasure, closely followed by my armour, but I was now wearing several seriously decent quality-of-life things that I was sure would be helpful down the road.

But by far the most helpful bit of advice was when Drynwyn wondered, ever so politely as I'm sure you can imagine, why I wasn't hoovering up all the gold coins.

"My armour doesn't have pockets" was apparently not an acceptable answer.

You're a fucking cultivator. Stick it all in your soul space.

"My what?"

If you were any wetter behind the ears, my previous bearer could have used you as a lubricant. Your soul space. You know, where you keep all your important shit.

It took a while, and some expletive-loaded explanations, for me to realise that I could 'add a page' to the book which housed my artist's studio and the Vitruvian-me.

Once you've done that, call it something like 'Fucking Loot' and just sweep the gold in there.

I'd like to say there was more to it as I was desperately clinging to the idea that the laws of Physics existed in some way in this world, but apparently not.

If I held a bag of money and... willed it onto the page, it vanished and reappeared there. It even helpfully added up for me how much I had. It was utter bollocks, to be honest, and shook me more than when I tore a wolf in half.

As you become stronger, you'll be able to hold more in that space, so don't be worried if you're quickly as tight as a nun's woozy. Just grab as much gold as possible - having a few coins on hand is always helpful.

I was up to my twentieth bag before Drynwyn cleared its throat and asked how much of my page was still empty.

"There's just one bag in the top left-hand corner filling up with each addition. There's nothing else showing in there."

Fucking hell. Change of plan. Swipe everything you can. Fill her up, as the bard said to the shaman.

The sun was just starting to go down when we'd finished looting everything my sword thought had any value whatsoever.

Apparently, I'd made out like a bandit.

Rhydderch had arrived to face the dragon with an entire support network of porters, wagons and merchants to pick over the aftermath once he'd done the slaying business.

He'd expected to be here for weeks whilst they sorted through it all. He'd even had the Exotic Dancer's Guild send him fifty of their best guys to keep him entertained. You're probably holding enough in your soul space to pay Uther himself to give you a lap dance.

We were making our way to the top of the path, just where it passed through the ruined castle gatehouse. I could understand Drynwyn just fine when he was in his scabbard, so I slung it around my shoulders with the sword hanging down my back in a way that made me feel all Henry Cavill.

99

Drynwyn was reminiscing happily about all the times he and Rhydderch had fucked over this or that warrior. I was starting to think we had a different interpretation of the meaning of that verb.

Then I stopped abruptly.

What the fuck?

I swore myself then, because, there in front of me, was a familiar-looking group of blue spearmen complete with two Dicks out front and... Yes. A wizard that could throw Qi with his hands.

"Fuckadoodledo," I whispered, stepping back into the castle's shadows.

CHAPTER 25 - IN WHICH WE TAKE AN ARGUABLY UNNECESSARY DIGRESSION TO A CHARACTER YOU DON'T CARE ABOUT

Melehan stared down at the decapitated body of the dragon for a few minutes without speaking.

It was hard to look at what had happened here and feel anything other than deep unease. He'd never seen the like before. Of course, his experience with dead dragons was reasonably limited, but at least in those he had seen there had been a consistency regarding how that state of being had been achieved. The motto of the Dragon Hunter's Guild was, after all, "Big balls, big axe, big loot."

But this dragon had not lost its head to any sort of cutting blade. Someone had, quite literally, ripped it from its shoulders. He did not know exactly how much strength that would have required, but he was willing to bet it lay somewhere between 'a lot' and 'a fuckload'.

He glanced at the man who had asked for his opinion on this particular blood-drenched scene. "I'm not sure what you want me to say, my Lord. But I'm happy to confirm that this is definitely a dead dragon."

"I know that, you cretin. I want to know what killed it."

"Having its head torn off would be my guess. I mean, it might have been poisoned, maybe even an especially acute toothache, but I'm willing to go out on a limb and say the 'no head' thing seems favourite right now."

Pæga licked his lips and cuffed Melehen around the head. "Do not forget your place, wizard."

Melehan took a breath and cycled away the Qi which had gathered in his hands. The High King had been clear as to the consequences for any practitioners that stepped out of line during this invasion. As much as he would enjoy kicking Pæga's arse every step of the way back over the river, it would not be worth the price.

Disrespect was temporary. Damnation was forever.

"I apologise, my Lord. I misunderstood the direction of your question. On reflection, I would suggest that this must have been the work of a cultivator of unusual capacity."

"Explain."

"Contrary to popular opinion, dragons are, naturally, this more modest of sizes. But, when threatened, they have the capability to increase their mass a hundredfold. Therefore, whoever was able to kill this dragon did not only force it to return to normal size - and that would take power beyond my comprehension - but then proceeded to decapitate it without using an edged weapon. Frankly, my Lord,

101

whoever did this pulled the dragon's head off. As these creatures are deadly even at this size, I am wholly baffled as to how they managed it."

Pæga's tongue whipped out and around his suddenly dry lips. "Do you suggest, therefore, the presence of Merlin?" He cast his eyes fearfully at the sky, expecting that particular boogeyman to appear instantly.

"Merlin would certainly have the required power, my Lord. It's just -"

Melehan paused and looked around the ruin. He could feel that Celt was somewhere nearby but could not get the sort of fix as to her location that he was used to achieving. He was as troubled by that as anything else he had seen this day.

"What?"

"I am not sure why he would bother, my Lord. This is Vortigern's Dragon. It's not one of the great Spirit Beasts of the realm, and it has been around these parts forever. If we believe the stories, and I always believe the stories where Merlin is concerned, he made a habit of feeding his apprentices to it. Not like for sport, but as a threshold test."

"He used a dragon for an aptitude test?"

"He's Merlin. He can do whatever he wants. And regularly did. Who's going to stop him?"

Pæga nodded. "But if he had the power to achieve this, why don't you think this was Merlin?"

The wizard knelt and touched the pooled blood of the dragon. There were pieces of some sort of material in it. He rubbed them between his fingers. Was this hemp? Like from a dress. "It just would not be worth his time. For someone as advanced as him, the Qi he'd gather here would be like a grain of sand on the beach. It would probably actually end up costing him essence by the time he was finished. Even with what might be found in the dragon's hoard -"

"There's a hoard?"

Melehan sighed and cursed his loose lips. Any hopes he had of getting his master to turn around and get back on mission were now thoroughly dashed. If there was one thing guaranteed to get Pæga's attention, it was unclaimed stacks of coins. Or claimed ones, to be honest. He was not too picky either way, from what Melehan was able to tell.

Not for the first time, the wizard found himself questioning some of his recent life choices.

Melehan had always been interested in cultivation and had been fortunate that his father had the resources to indulge his much-loved youngest son. Almost as soon as he could read, he'd had access to the very best technique scrolls and cultivation manuals that could be located. Moreover, no natural treasure would pass nearby without Melehan having the first claim on it.

Of course, even with all that, he was, at best, a minor talent, but his family had been proud of him, and he enjoyed being the source of that pride.

And then, six months ago, the levels of accessible Qi in the land unaccountably surged.

In the blink of an eye, Melehan went from spending days and nights diligently prodding desultory grains of sand around his channels to being buried up to his neck in the stuff. Thanks to his years of patiently building a solid foundation, he found he could make far better use of this bounty compared to all the other hedge wizards that were suddenly popping up everywhere.

He was now a talent that could, by no means, be considered minor any longer.

And then the High King came calling.

The rumour was that he - or at least those with his coin in their pockets - had conducted some sort of arcane ritual that had uncorked the bottleneck of Qi that had forever strangled the land. Melehan was not so sure about that, but he was certainly not going to question it if that was the story that terrifying man wanted out there. That sort of thinking got people nailed to walls.

A host of practitioners had responded to the High King's summons for all those whose powers had recently blossomed. The unspoken message had clearly been: "Come and say thank you". Melehan was happy to do so, although that happiness had waned somewhat when the nature of the 'thanks' required became clear: all those with sufficient talent were expected to join the long-anticipated invasion of what remained of Uther's Britain.

"What about Merlin?" they had all asked in the same tone the recently condemned asked after the executioner's axe.

"Myrddin Wyllt Emrys will not trouble you."

There was confidence, there was arrogance, and then there was using Merlin's full name like you were his father chastising him for farting at the banquet table.

Melehan did not know what to make of it, but he had seen enough of the High King to realise that - even should Merlin incinerate him where he stood the second he laid toe on Uther's land - it would still be a better option than denying an order from the man who insisted on being addressed by that long dead title, Brytenwalda: High King of Britain.

So, Melehan had gone to war.

The glory of the practice, which his father had often spoken of, had yet to be seen.. The one battle worthy of its name - the confrontation with the fyrd a few days back - had been over before it had begun. There were myriad ways to defeat a cultivator, but none involved standing still in a shield wall whilst fireballs were thrown at you.

The entire invasion was based on the premise that Uther's armies would not be able to adapt quickly enough to this tactic and, of course, that Merlin did not take the field.

As a man who had developed clear notions of honour in his life, he found much of what he had witnessed on the road thus far pretty distasteful. And the least said about the murder of the chieftain's wife, the better.

But, for all that, here he was: standing in a bright purple fairy circle, with the blood of a dragon on his fingertips and an unhinged paederast - Melehan did not let the ostentatious pillaging fool him - as a master.

"There is a hoard, my Lord. But, as I said, Vortigern's Dragon was a minor Spirit Beast. I doubt there will be anything to interest someone as powerful as you in there."

For a moment, he thought the flattery would work, but then the tongue licked out, and there was a gleam in Pæga's eyes. "By no means, wizard. There has been precious little loot thus far, and I have demands upon me. Minor Spirit Beast or not, there will certainly be treasures it will have acquired over its life. We will explore this hoard."

And at that moment, Melehan could finally lock down the presence of the Celt. Of course, as she was currently charging straight for them, bellowing an unusual war cry, it was not one of the more remarkable feats of magic he had ever achieved.

103

Pæga watched the approaching warrior with interest. "That Celt appears to be charging our entire army on her own."

"She does, my Lord."

"Is she shouting something?"

"I think so, but I know not what it means."

"Me either. I wonder who Frodo is?"

CHAPTER 26 - IN WHICH YEARS OF BUNKING OFF PE COME HOME TO ROOST

We need to charge them.

"There's at least a hundred of them. We're not going to charge them."

They'll run. I'm Drynwyn, the fucking sword of Rhydderch Hael. Bigger armies than this have fled, screaming at my fiery approach. Let's go, girlfriend.

I felt the sword prod me in the small of my back as if it was a particularly impatient OAP in the queue at the post office. One that had just spontaneously caught fire. And was screaming for the chance to bathe in the blood of its enemies. Otherwise known as a standard Tuesday morning on Dudley High Street.

"Well, now you're Drynwyn, the sword of Someone-Who's-Never-Held-a-Fucking-Sword-in-Her-Life. So you need to settle." I felt the flames behind me die back down.

I was worried about the wizard.

Who am I kidding? I was pretty damn concerned about the spearmen, the archers and the horsemen too. But I sensed the most pressing danger was the bearded guy in the flowing robes and the extremely pointy hat.

Drynwyn pushed me again in the back, and I staggered forward one step. **All you need to do is hold me in the right direction, and I will fuck them up for you.**

"Quit it! They're not going to let me get close enough for you to do anything. There's one path out of here, and it leads straight into the middle of them. I'll be a pincushion before taking more than a few steps: there's not going to be any hacking and slashing. I think I'm going to try to beam us out of here."

I dropped into my artist's studio and tried to flick the page back to the field of the giant purple cock. But nothing happened.

"Why's it not working?"

What are you trying to do?

"From what Merlin said, I should be able to fast-travel back to my last location. It worked when I tried it before: this is how he showed me how to do it."

But there's another cultivator out there.

"So?"

Are you a fucking moron? You can't fast-travel from within another cultivator's aura. That's like qi-travel 101. I'm a fucking sword, and even I know that. There's mould growing on that cheese over there that knows that, and it is shaking its mycelium in disbelief at your ignorance. You are a fucking dullard.

105

I pressed my fingers to the bridge of my nose. I was suddenly very aware of how much I'd been relying on Merlin to cheat code my way through things. "As I said, I don't really understand how any of this works. I've only been here a few days. So, no beaming out of fights with cultivators?"

No. But why would you want to flee? Rhydderch never ran away from a fight in his life. Even when naked, surprised in his bed-chamber and with me locked away in storage, he'd still take on six, sometimes seven foes in one go. Oh, the cries and moans from those he brought low.

"But Rhydderch's now dead, and you're my sword. So shut up while I think of a plan."

I poked my head out around the wall of the gatehouse to get more of a sense of where things were at. Dick #1 was taking an especial interest in the dragon's body. Dick #2 seemed more involved in setting up a perimeter around the castle. My extremely limited knowledge of military tactics had all been gleaned from the Total War series, but even I knew a competent pincer manoeuvre being prepared when I saw one. If I stepped out onto the path, I'd be exposed to attack from both sides.

For fuck's sake.

Why did I have to come up against competent bad guys? Like, this felt like a good plot moment for me to come up against the Arthurian equivalent of stormtroopers - cool-looking but ultimately useless cannon fodder that I could carve up with limited danger and learn something new about my spiritual journey - and instead, it looked like the deathtroopers had turned up and were going to tear me a new one the second they saw me.

I watched Dick #1 call the wizard over, and they both looked down at the dragon's body. I couldn't shake the feeling that, despite everything, the cultivator was the biggest of my problems.

If you're that worried about the wizard, throw me at him.

"Excuse me?"

The cultivator. Throw me at him. I'll fuck him up, and when he's dead, you can fast-travel away. Not that I'm on board with the 'flee-like-a-panty-wetting-child' plan, but I'm all about the solutions.

I looked at the wizard. He was several hundred feet away, up the hill and to my right. I'm not saying it was quite magic bullet, second gunmen on the grassy knoll territory, but it was certainly a testing shot.

"I can't throw you that far!"

What the fuck is the matter with you? You're a cultivator. You tore the head off a dragon. You are the motherfucking bearer of Drynwyn! I'm not going to allow you to crap all over my reputation by pissing around hiding in the shadows. Now, in the words of my late lamented bearer: "Get off your knees, strap this on, and brace yourself for something memorable." Throw me at the fucking pointy head!

Reader, I did.

***

"Well, that worked out pretty much as I expected."

As I watched Drynwyn arc through the air, I reflected - slightly too late - on the fact that just because my time training in the cave had massively increased my strength, it did not necessarily mean there had been a commensurate improvement in my physical skills.

Sure, I was now in possession of a cultivator's body who had spent considerable time buffing it up and tempering it with all sorts of natural goodness. And, sure, I had further enhanced that body with God knows how many days of time-looped training and the Qi of an ancient spirit beast.

But, despite all that, I still had the hand-eye coordination and innate athletic skill of Mr Tumble. In fact, I'm doing the Tumblester dirty there. That guy could juggle.

I'd given the 'it's not the size that counts, it's how you use it' chat to a plethora of insecure beaus in my time; and even, on rare occasions, might have meant it. And it turned out this homily was as true when throwing flaming swords at wizards as anything else.

Basically, what I'm saying is that I had thrown Drynwyn at the wizard with all the skill of Lenny gently stroking his fiftieth mouse of the day.

Good news: the sword flew through the air like a veritable Exocet missile. I was amazed there wasn't a sonic boom as it streaked from my hand like an arrow of flaming, inevitable death.

Bad news: my appalling aim propelled it at least half a mile to the left of the intended target.

Good news: the throw was *so bad* no one in the besieging army noticed I did anything at all.

Bad news: I'd just, quite literally, thrown away one of my few remaining advantages.

Fuuuuuuuuuuuuuuuuuuuuuuuuuuuuuuuuck

Drynwyn's voice gradually faded away in my mind as it vanished off and up beyond the horizon. There was a tiny part of me that had always wanted to be good at sports that grinned at that throw. The rest of me, the parts that were keen to avoid immediate death, pounded it into the dirt. Ah, just like being back at school.

While this was going on, the wizard and Dick #1 seemed to be having a very intense conversation, leading to Dick clocking the wizard. Then they both looked my way, and I realised my time was running out.

Apparently, I wasn't the only person that realised when you found a dead dragon, the next obvious thing was to come and look for its hoard.

I cast around for anything that might help me get out of this hole. My eyes fell on a bunch of other swords lying around on the ground. Drynwyn had insisted it would be disloyal to store any of them on my looter's page.

I picked one up, drew it, and waggled it experimentally. I sensed describing what I was doing as 'waggling' probably demonstrated my precise level of incompetence.

Things were looking bleak.

One thing of which I was sure was that I wasn't going to let myself be captured by the Dicks. They'd made clear the direction in which their appetites lay when it came to prisoners, and to be frank, I was a smoking hottie. They were not going to get the satisfaction. If I went with Drynwyn's plan and just charged, I reckoned either the archers or the wizard would take me out before I had to think about anything else.

However, for someone who'd recently sought to examine the bumper of a truck while it was still moving, I was oddly no longer all that excited to do the mortal coil shuffle off. I kept hearing Ealdgyð talking about different sorts of grief. It felt oddly disrespectful to her for me not to try and get back to my own timeline and fix things with Zizzie. Of course, slightly lower down on my fuck-giving scale, I also idly worried about where Merlin was and what he would do when his last potential apprentice died. It sounded like I was the absolute final option on the table when it came to saving the world.

It was quite a conundrum.

But ... fuck it. Not my circus. Not my monkeys. Even if I wanted them to be.

Brandishing the sword above my head, I stepped out from the shadows and charged the small force.

You live by the meme; you die by the meme.

"For Frodo!!!!" I bellowed.

CHAPTER 27 - IN WHICH, WITH REGRET, I INDULGE IN SOME CASUAL XENOPHOBIA

Two archers were watching the lone, red-headed warrior run towards them. She'd been charging for some time. The only thing that made sense about what she was doing was that they figured she'd misjudged the distance somewhat.

That could happen on a battlefield. You saw a big group ahead of you and instinctively thought it was much closer than it was. It was just a basic survival instinct. Both of them had known others in their war party do the same; they'd panic and let loose shots when the enemy was still several miles away.

The taller of the two bent, picked up some grass and tossed it into the air to check the wind. "What do you reckon? Right tit?"

Dæglaf glanced at his friend and then back at the running woman. Not only had she spectacularly misjudged the distance to them, but she'd delivered her battle cry far too early in the piece. All credit to her, she was trying her hardest to keep it going, but you don't pick a battle cry that ended in 'O'. That was just common sense. For the last ten seconds, the charging warrior had sounded like she was doing an impression of a rather camp ghost.

"From this distance, a tit? Even for you, that's too easy."

"What do you reckon then?" Ingwald had drawn an arrow and was in the process of notching it.

"She's got a mole above her right eye. You hit that, today's mead ration is yours."

"Fuck off. A mole? I can't even see it."

Dæglaf shrugged. "That's the bet. You hit that mole, and the mead's yours. Or we can just agree I'm the superior shot."

"Fine. The mole." Ingwald tracked the running warrior for a few seconds down the arrow shaft. Then, as was his custom, he took and held a breath for a few beats. He led her slightly, and as he breathed out, he took the shot.

The two watched the arrow streak towards the warrior and then ... impact.

After a few seconds, Dæglaf was the first to speak. "Well, that was unexpected."

***

I'd given up on my 'Frodo' battle cry.

Instead, as I plodded onwards towards the encircling army, I was going for the much less Tolkienesque - or, I guess, Jacksonesque - "Fucking. Enhanced. Eyesight. Making. Everything. Look. Very. Close."

If I had imagined a glorious arrow-filled Leonidas-inspired death, I sensed I was going to be disappointed. As far as I could tell, most of the army was just ignoring me; I was still a few minutes out, but that felt pretty disrespectful.

Although, saying that, there were a couple of archers that finally seemed to be taking an interest. I saw one of them pull an arrow from his quiver, and I changed course to run towards them. The second he released the arrow - after what I considered to be quite an elaborate set-up. I mean, come on, mate, it's a bow and arrow, not a religious experience - I realised something pretty important.

I absolutely didn't want to die.

Almost in instinct, I filled my hands with Qi and 'wax-on-wax-offed' the area in front of me, creating a shield of purple that, a second later, the arrow smashed into. I say 'smashed into', but the arrow was utterly obliterated just before it hit.

There was a beat, and then it would be fair to say I was suddenly very much more of interest to the rest of the army.

***

Melehan's eyebrows rose so quickly it was amazing they stayed attached to his forehead.

"What the fuck was that?" Pæga shrieked.

"It was just a standard shield spell. It's just ..."

"A shield spell? The arrow exploded!"

"Cultivators usually carefully calibrate the power they give to their shields to deflect projectiles away, rather than destroy them. To waste so much Qi on a single arrow. Well..."

"Will you fucking complete your sentences! It doesn't make you seem mysterious, wizard. It just makes you annoying."

Melehan, once more, cycled his Qi away from his hands. He was envisaging ripping out Pæga's tongue, and it would be best if he didn't have the strength to do it. "My apologies, my Lord. I was just a little startled. I was going to say that for a cultivator to waste so much Qi in such a careless manner, they must be a significant powerhouse."

"It's not Merlin in disguise, is it?" Pæga was peering into the distance where the cultivator was hidden behind the barrier she'd erected.

"I doubt it. But I will tell you one thing, I think we've found who killed the dragon. The reserves of power she must have to use so much like that..."

***

So, it was another good news, bad news situation.

I was alive—big tick. But I seemed to have used up all of my Qi- not ideal, just one arrow into the battle. A quick glance in my artist's studio showed that the cupboard was absolutely bare: there was barely a drop of purple paint to be found anywhere.

Then, I was dragged back to the real world as the sky darkened, and seemingly every arrow in the universe was launched towards me.

***

"Cease fire. Cease fire!" Beornulf, Pæga's second-in-command, arrived running. "What the fuck are you doing?"

Melehan had even less time for Beornulf than he did for Pæga. Whereas the force commander was a petty, vicious tyrant, there was nothing 'petty' about Beornulf. The only true 'veteran' in the force, the big man had reportedly fought successful engagements across the world. When in his cups, he would admit to having been somewhat of a 'naughty pirate' in his youth, which most considered to mean 'brutal slaver'. Nothing Melehan had seen in the man's behaviour would have argued against that.

"That's a fucking cultivator!"

"Yes. We'd noticed, Beornulf. Thank you", Pæga sneered. "We're dealing with the situation."

"You don't fire arrows at someone that strong. You fucking run! Or," he said, turning to Melehan, "you point your own cultivator their way, and *you charge with everything you've got!*"

Melehan felt his throat go dry. He knew he would have to try to deal with this threat, but ... well, the profligacy with which the Celt had used her Qi stunned him. If he'd poured that much into a simple shield spell, he'd have nothing left for the rest of the day.

The idea of, casually, throwing that much out there just to catch an arrow ... Well, he figured he'd be lucky to make it down the hill before she flayed the flesh from his bones.

"Don't be a dick, Beornulf. We need Melehan more than we need a dead enemy wizard. I'm not wasting him in our first proper enemy action. And I'm certainly not 'charging' in these circumstances. We will withdraw if we cannot destroy this threat by conventional means." Pæga turned to look at his wizard. "Unless you feel up to it, of course?"

Melehan tried to keep his voice level as relief flooded through him. "I regret to say I may well be overmatched one-on-one here, my Lord."

Beornulf went bright red. "He doesn't get to choose whether to engage an enemy cultivator! You know our orders. We exterminate any wizards we come across with extreme prejudice. Get your arse down there or, by the heavens, I will -"

It was unclear what Beornulf was planning to do as a bouncing, cartwheeling, flaming sword scythed straight through him on its way back towards the enemy cultivator.

Melehan and Pæga watched the two burning halves of the body fall to the floor and then raised their eyes to follow the sword as it flew to nestle in the hand of the Celt.

"Fuck. Me. Sound the retreat!" Pæga shouted, scrambling back on his horse. "Wizard, get the word out. We have been engaged by enemy practitioners and are retreating, with some losses, back to the muster point."

Melehan nodded dumbly, staring down at the two halves of Beornulf's body. He hadn't even seen her throw the sword ...

***

My purple shield slowly failed under the hail of arrows. By the time I heard someone shout 'cease-fire!' there was nothing more than a thin purple mist in front of me.

One more volley, and that would be that.

I looked back in my artist's studio to see if, by some miracle, my channels happened to be flowing with paint again, but no. Utterly dry.

I shook my head to try to clear an odd buzzing sound in my ear, something like a slightly disgruntled bee.

I wondered if that was a side-effect of complete Qi exhaustion? But then, the longer I listened, the more it sounded like ...

FUUUUUUUUUUUUUCCCCCCCKKKKKKKKKIIIINNNNNGGGGG HAAAAAAAAAAAAAVVVVVVVEEEE IIIIIIIIITTTTTTTTTTTTT

With a start, I peered through the rapidly discharging mist and saw a bouncing, spinning, flaming sword crashing across the ground back towards me.

It passed through the little group of Dick #1, Dick #2 and the wizard (I think it literally passed through Dick #2) before smacking, hilt first, into my outstretched hand.

Boomerang attack, baby. Fucking A.

I looked up to see the army that had me utterly and entirely at its mercy retreat faster than ... no, on reflection, that sort of bellicose xenophobia about another country's armed forces should be beneath me.

They can't help being cheese-eating surrender monkeys.

CHAPTER 28 - IN WHICH WE LEARN OF PAINTING RESTORATION AND LECHEROUS OLD MEN

"Yeah, you better run!" I shouted after the retreating army.

Or, at least, I whispered it forcefully. In my head. From behind a pillow. As the last of the rearguard vanished over the hill, I collapsed in a heap to the floor. Qi-exhaustion was only part of it; I was utterly rung out by the whole experience.

And, if I'm being honest, I wasn't entirely sure what had happened to change my fortunes.

Sure, the boomeranging re-appearance of Drynwyn had put the wind up them: one of your commanders being eviscerated by a flaming sword was the sort of thing that would put a dent in a good day. But that didn't seem enough to cause them to literally turn tail and flee.

If anything, I'd have expected that to have encouraged them to indulge in a little retributive slaughter. Running away seemed odd.

Drynwyn! Fuck, yeah! Coming along to save the motherfucking day. Drynwyn! Fuck, yeah!

If it was possible for a sword held within a scabbard to do a victory dance, Drynwyn was giving it its best shot. I was finding that, coupled with its newly written theme song, a touch gauche.

It seemed best I tried to distract it before more verses were composed.

"How did you find your way back to me? I figured the speed you were going, you'd be ending up in another country." Depending on where I was stood, that could have been anywhere from Scotland to Spain. Although, if my watching of Highlander had taught me anything, the accents encountered would have been the same.

You mean after you fucking yeeted me as far away from the target as possible like a complete fucking unstoppable moron?

"I'm not sure I'd choose to quite put it like that -"

Fucking come off it. I'm adding 'throwing' to the list as another thing you need to work on if you want me to hang around. And believe me, it's a fucking extensive list.

It felt like one thing when Merlin, the greatest wizard in the history of mankind, took time out from his busy day of trying to save the world to criticise me. But it hit a bit different when such scorn came from a piece of metal whose only previous owner was some sort of masochistic barbarian nymphomaniac.

"Do you think we could dial down the constructive criticism for a bit? It's been a long day, what with the dragon and the battle and all. Should we take it as read that I'm terrible and leave it there for a bit?

113

You really are a fucking pathetic specimen; did you know that? First, you plan to run away. Then you -

If I had a superpower, it was the ability to tune out lectures from aggrieved authority figures. And, I'm happy to tell you that when it came to reaming me out, Drynwyn was an absolute amateur compared to some true masters of the craft I'd come across in my time.

Give a little wave, Dad.

I left the sword, ranting about my inadequacies, and dropped back inside my artist's studio. I was disappointed to see that my channels were still empty of Qi - no fast travel for me in the near future - and that, on closer examination, they all looked pretty sore. I knew Merlin had said he'd needed to pull up trees to get them to hold together, but when they were filled with Qi, I hadn't been able to appreciate the extent of the damage.

Looking at the Vitruvian version of me, I could see that every single line around my body was red and inflamed.

On the plus side, there were no blockages remaining at all - the paths were all smoother than a Kardashian's forehead - which I sensed, don't ask me how, was going to be a massive long-term benefit. But it was obviously going to take quite some time for everything to heal up.

I'd basically had a triple-strength magic colonic irrigation and needed to stay away from curries for a bit.

That doesn't quite convey how peculiar this feeling was, mainly as I'd not even known what channels were, two days before. Weirdly, though, I found that if I concentrated on any particular channel, I could zoom in even closer until a section of it filled my vision.

What I could see from this perspective reminded me of the year I took painting restoration classes. I'd been looking to earn a few extra quid, and a posh acquaintance had come up trumps. She'd said her dad was looking for someone to cast their eye over some modern originals damaged by 'some awful colonials' in their spare house. That's how she'd put it, by the way. Their 'spare house'.

Not wanting to dive in without any knowledge - I saved that sort of behaviour for my love life - I'd signed up for a couple of free restoration classes to ensure I at least looked like I knew what I was doing.

When older paintings need work, it's typically because the canvas reacts to changes in the atmosphere, and it all gets pretty fragile. You definitely don't want an enthusiastic amateur just looking for a way to pay the rent playing around with things there. But, with modern paintings, which was what these were, damage and flaking is pretty much due to how the artwork surface was prepared. Often, heavy impasto paint layers crack and flake away from the canvas because the guy blasting out something every few days to sell to the tourists hasn't made an appropriate ground layer. So, pretty soon it all starts lifting away and breaking apart.

I was actually quite looking forward to giving it a go for a bit, but I never got around to doing any actual restoration. Turns out 'spare' houses weren't the only thing the man of the house was interested in keeping on the side. Without a word of a lie, he was old enough to have been my grandfather. Full disclosure - as I think we've been through some stuff together - he was kind of dishy in a distinguished way. But then he offered me money and - well, you know. As a perennial crosser of uncrossable lines, even I could see that was one it was going to be a journey to come back from.

I mention all this - not only because my enchanted sword has moved on to criticise **the way your fucking hair falls on top of my scabbard** - but because, when they were zoomed in upon, my Qi channels had the same sort of cracked and flaky appearance as those paintings.

I pressed my hand to the wall of the channel. It was hot to the touch, and some of the surface came away with the contact. Remembering my lessons, I tried to see if I could conjure up my palette and brush. It appeared to my right and was, of course, empty of purple Qi. However, I was pleased to see it held a clear solution that I felt would serve in what I wanted to achieve.

Dipping my brush in the solution, I carefully used it to reattach the bit of my channel that had flaked away into my hand.

As soon as my brush touched the channel, replacing the shed piece, I saw the cracks and fissures begin to melt away. This quickly spread until the whole section I had zoomed in upon was self-repairing, even though I had only worked on a tiny area of it.

I took this to mean that the repairs my channels needed were more metaphorical than literal. It was the *act* of restoration, rather than the repair itself, that was going to be necessary.

I remembered back to what Merlin had told me about cultivation. It was all about quality, not quantity.

I zoomed out and back in onto another small section and repeated the same process. I was pleased to see that, with every new attempt, I smoothed out the sore channels and prepared them to receive the flow of Qi once I was back to normal.

Whatever 'normal' was any longer.

I knew that time passed differently when I was within my artist's studio, but it felt like I worked away, restoring my channels, for hours.

It was, therefore, a little disappointing to reappear in the real world, drenched in sweat but with an entirely healthy Vitruvian man to show for my efforts, to hear Drynwyn still on his rant.

And that is without thinking about the shameful way that you -

"Drynwyn?"

What?

"If you do not wish to become my sword, I am perfectly happy to put you back in the hoard, bury you under the biggest pile of crap I can find, and leave you be. I don't need a sword. I don't want a sword. And I especially don't want a sword that's going to be a colossal throbbing dick to me.

Don't talk to me like that. Who do you think you are?

"I'm the bearer of Drynwyn. I doubt Rhydderch Hael took this shit from you, and I'm damned if I'm going to be different. I'm new to this, but I'm doing my best. You played your part in getting me out of what's just happened, and I'm grateful. Also - to be frank - I look badass wearing you. But, I'm on the fence as to whether the good outweighs the bad. Do you get me?"

I get you.

"So, you get to choose. You come with me, and you take it down a notch, or you can wait for the first looter that comes along once word of the death of the dragon gets out. Who knows, they may be more to your taste. What's your pleasure?"

The sword mumbled something.

115

"Sorry, I didn't hear that."

I'd like to stay with you.

"Okay. And was there an apology in there somewhere?"

Don't fucking push it.

Fair enough. He was a sword after my own heart, after all.

CHAPTER 29 - IN WHICH I EXPERIENCE A HAMBUSH

In lieu of, literally, any better idea, I set out in the opposite direction from the retreating army. I'd initially hoped that Drynwyn might have some sense of the surrounding countryside, but apart from having a vague idea there was a brothel **over yonder,** it was light on helpful details.

I've mentioned it before, but I want to stress how utterly desolate this part of the world is. The ruin of Vortigern's castle dominated the skyline, but there was nothing in any direction to indicate where there might be other humans. I guess, given a choice, you probably wouldn't seek to settle anywhere near a fire-breathing dragon. But even so. Bleak, bleak, bleak.

Ultimately, I fell into following something I was choosing to believe was a makeshift road. It curled from near the gatehouse up and around the hills and woods and disappeared into the distance. My thinking was that the castle must have had some sort of local trade route going on, as there were no apparent farms nearby to feed its population.

Speaking of which...

"I'm absolutely starving."

Drynwyn was sulking a bit, so I didn't get any immediate answer.

"I mean, absolutely famished. I don't think I've eaten anything since I've been here," I paused for a moment, "I don't think I've drunk anything either. That's not normal, is it?"

Cultivator.

"I told you to dial it back a bit; I didn't ask you to take a vow of silence. Until Merlin comes back," *he was definitely coming back, right?* "you are the closest thing I've got to a wise mentor. So, suck it up, buttercup, and get with doling out the exposition."

Cultivators don't need to eat and drink like ordinary people. Rhyddrech Hael once went a whole week sustained by nothing more than drinking ...

"Nope. Do not complete that sentence." I walked silently for a few minutes, trying to get that particular image out of my head. "So, why am I so hungry if I don't need to eat and drink that much?"

Your Qi usually sustains your body. All the things that food and drink did for you, your Qi now does. But, as you used it all up to hide like a plate of beets when Twrch Trwyth calls, you need regular sustenance again. Probably more than usual as you're pretty shit at this.

I thought about that for a while. "Twrch Trwyth is?"

Fucking huge wild boar.

"And it liked beets?"

Infamously.

117

"I could eat a wild boar right now."

Probably hundreds of them in those woods.

"Really? Do you reckon I could catch one?"

You? Fuck no.

"Could you catch one?"

Sure.

"Really?"

Yeah. First, I'd dig a pit and maybe stick some sharpened stakes down there. Then I'd lure one away from others, possibly weaken it by firing arrows into it. Eventually, I'd enrage it enough so it would charge me, and then I'd trick it into the trap. Then I'd wait until it died or maybe finish it off with some rocks.

"Seriously, you could do that?"

Of course not, you fucking moron. I'm a sword.

***

Turns out, without having access to any Qi, digging a pit is really, really hard work. And doing so while starving hungry was not hitting the spot at all.

"What do you think? Deep enough?" My whole body was drenched with sweat, and my long red hair was utterly matted with all sorts of woodland filth. I'd tried to tie it up and out of the way with some random twine I'd looted, but I couldn't shake the feeling that the resulting pigtails made me look like a waifu from nasty anime porn.

Sure. Absolutely deep enough.

I looked sceptically at what my efforts had produced. "You're sure? This is deep enough to catch a wild boar?"

A boar? Fuck no. I thought you were making somewhere to shit.

This wasn't going to work. And I was beyond hungry. In frustration, I threw the shield I had taken from my inventory to use as a makeshift shovel away into the trees.

This had a couple of unexpected and, ultimately, unwelcome effects. First and foremost, it caused an ungodly screeching noise to emerge from the woods. This did little for my fragile mental state, Secondly, and I probably should have led with this, to be honest, it caused the emergence of a giant, tusked and furious pig.

Well, this is going to be interesting ...

It was at this moment that I became the unwitting star of an impromptu play entitled: "The Scampering Idiot and the Charging Boar."

A hulking mass of bristly fur and sharp tusks burst forth from the foliage, charging straight at me with a fervour like I'd said something about its sister. Or thrown a shield at it when it was sleeping. One of the two. Probably both, to be honest.

At that moment, I did what any sensible person would do when confronted with a charging boar: I screamed like I was karaokeing the opening moments of 'Won't Get Fooled Again'.

My legs, seemingly possessed by the spirit of a particularly motivated hare, took me bounding backwards, at which stage I stepped into my pit, turned my ankle, slipped and fell.

As I collapsed to the ground, my mind raced even faster than my limbs, concocting elaborate plans involving feats of acrobatics that even the most daring circus performer would hesitate to attempt. But as I crumpled into a heap on the floor and the boar's snorts grew louder, and its thudding hooves seemed to echo through the very earth itself, I realised that my repertoire of spectacular gymnastic techniques was relatively sparse. Anything more complex than a gamboll was well beyond me, in truth.

In that unfortunate moment, with a triumphant snort and a last defiant charge, the wild boar crashed headlong into the pit on top of me.

In the ensuing chaos, there was a blur of flailing limbs, flying dandelion puffs, and a symphony of oinks and groans that would've done justice to a porcine opera.

And then, bizarrely, it was over as quickly as it had all begun. I lay there, panting and dishevelled, with the wild boar sprawled out between my legs in a most undignified manner that doubtless would continue to increase the popularity of my graphic novel in some parts of the world.

There I was, nose to snout, with a rather dead and somewhat shocked-looking boar. And I didn't think I'd done anything that could have possibly caused it.

I think you embarrassed it to death. Seriously, I think it felt so fucking bad for you, it just up and died out of empathetic shame.

I was struggling to get my breath. "You're not being especially helpful here. Seriously, what do you think killed it?"

Two theories. Well, three, if we're going to continue to entertain it being a particularly sympathetic hog. No? Okay, well, you may have broken its neck when you collided with it.

Looking at the size of the thing, this seemed unlikely. It was built mainly to charge long streaks of piss like me. "Or?"

Or the guy over there with the bow and arrow took it out.

I swung around to meet the somewhat startled gaze of the woodsman from every version of Snow White you've ever seen. Especially the ones on the internet you needed passwords to watch. And a locked room. And lotion. Seriously, the only reason he wasn't wearing a lumberjack shirt was that it would have distracted from his insanely overdeveloped muscles. And that would just have been a waste of good beefcake.

"Are you okay? I'd been stalking it when I saw it charge at you. I was so worried it would hurt you. I fired as fast as I could." The hottest man in all of the dark ages leaned down over me and reached out to take my hand. "Are you sure you are okay?"

I stared into the eyes of the most ridiculously attractive human I had ever seen, not just in the dark ages but in any part of the multiverse. It wasn't just the muscles - well, not wholly - but in a realm where I had only ever encountered hostility, lust and anger, the sheer compassion on his face utterly stole my heart.

I suddenly felt things would be okay for the first time in a very long time. It was always darkest before the dawn, and this gloriously buff man was very much my dawn. I smiled, rubbed my thumb against the back of his hand and then opened my mouth to answer.

You fucking want some?

Drynwyn flew, unbidden, from its scabbard at my back and neatly chopped off the woodsman's head. His angle was such, bending down over me to help me out of the shallow pit, that the blood utterly fountained down on top of me for a good few seconds before his heart realised there was now a lack of brainpower and it could stop pumping.

119

But not to worry, for his corpse immediately fell down on top of me, wedging tightly between me, Mr Pig and the blood-soaked ground. And to keep the hits coming, my erstwhile boar trap quickly filled up with the gore of the most desirable man in the world who'd just terminally lost a foot in height,

No matter how resilient, everyone has a tipping point.

It turns out mine was being starving hungry, having narrowly avoided being murdered by a boar and then seeing the most beautiful man in the world lose his head the second you fell in love with him.

I lay trapped, covered in mud, blood and viscera and sobbed.

CHAPTER 30 - IN WHICH ARTHUR'S PERFORMANCE ANXIETY IS LAID BARE

It had been a long and chastening few days for Arthur.

The shock of one of his father's thegns having their own, hidden cultivator - and then seeking to use it to kill him - had sent Uther's court into a spiral of paranoia.

With no knowledge as to whom had set the trap, Tintagel had been purged of all but those whose loyalty to the King was absolutely certain. It said nothing good for everyone's perception as to the severity of the situation that this turned out to be such a small list. Neither, it was fair to say, did expelling ninety per cent of the courtiers and retainers do too much for the administrative capabilities of the kingdom.

As if, what appeared to be, wholesale insurrection by a number of the ruling class was not enough, rumours of Saxon incursions up and down the border did little to quell rising tensions. Likewise, Arthur being unable to blow off steam in his usual way was making for a pretty untenable situation at court.

"My Lord, I do not understand why you do not consult Merlin."

"And I don't understand why my father hasn't cut your cock off and thrust it down your whining throat, Sir Pascent."

"Arthur," Uther rumbled warningly.

"Apologies, Sir Pascent. On reflection, I recognise that, due to the size of your member, it is unlikely to reach your throat. Maybe it would be better going up your nose? Although, even then, you have somewhat wide nostrils ..."

"My Lord, do I need to suffer this?"

"You do not, Sir Pascent. Arthur, you will be quiet, or you will leave."

"To be allowed to leave is all I ask, Father. We have tales of Saxon war parties moving, unopposed, across our northern border. Our people are dying. All I ask is to be able to respond."

Uther was not a religious man. In his youth, he had travelled extensively and come to realise that every tribe had their own version of the same, bloodthirsty paternal figures. It seemed to him that people the world over fashioned gods that gave them an excuse to do all sorts of horrible things to each other. The acts were appalling, but they were treated as 'just' because they were done in the name of a higher power. 'Sorry to have burned your village and murdered your children. Tartalus, eh? What's he like?'

Even so, for all his atheistic scorn, he found himself offering a little prayer to whoever may be listening to give him the strength this morning to deal with his son.

"Arthur," if Uther's teeth were more gritted, they'd splinter, "I say with all sincerity that there is nothing I, nor anyone else in the room, would like better than to unleash you upon our enemies."

"Then, why -"

"Have some sense, boy!" Uther roared, his patience snapping. "The Saxons are advancing in unheard-of numbers. You've seen the same reports as I, and you know they appear to have wizards numbering amongst their forces. We have questions as to the stoutness of our allies, and there are an unknown number of hostile cultivators across the realm. We are in the middle of an unprecedented crisis."

"All the more reason -"

"All the more reason for you to shut up and fuck your wife!"

There was an awkward silence as all eyes in the room did their level best not to glance the way of Princess Guinevere. For her part, she merely shrugged and poured herself another goblet of wine.

Uther pressed on. "You are my only heir. You have no legitimate children of your own. All the Saxons need to do, all the traitors in our own halls need do, is kill - or god forbid, capture - you and that will be that. No one doubts your efficacy on the battlefield, my son. But we need Leodegrance's ten thousand spears more than we need you in the saddle, and those spears are contingent on your wife's swollen belly. I, therefore, order, once again, that your sole contribution to this war effort is to take your wife to your bedchamber and lay siege upon her! Until then, and only then, will we discuss whether you get to leave Tintagel!"

All eyes turned to Arthur, who, red-faced, turned and stormed from the room.

"Thank you, my Lord. Now, if we could return to the question of Merlin -"

"Pascent?"

"Yes, my Lord."

"Shut the fuck up."

***

Arthur managed to hold on to his temper long enough to reach the stables. Once out of sight, he let forth a bellow and punched the wall once, twice, three times before collecting himself. It would be much easier to bear this frustration if anything his father said was wrong. But he'd pretty much hit the nail squarely on the head.

Leodegrance had promised ten thousand spears the moment it was confirmed Guinevere was pregnant. At the time, that had been seen as pretty much a foregone conclusion - the number of little Arthur bastards running around Britain was almost legendary. Rumour had it he just had to look at a serving girl in the right way, and nine months later, there'd be another modest drain on Uther's treasury.

But, no.

It was not that he did not find his wife attractive; gods knows, he had eyes. It was just ... he found the whole thing rather distasteful. It was as if he was being treated like a prize bull, and the whole world was waiting for him to breed. Every time he saddled up, as it were, to fulfil his part of the bargain, it was like he had an audience of the whole of Britain holding their breath and urging him on.

It wasn't just Leodegrance's spears that depended on his virility. It was, as his father kept making very clear, the future of the entire British race.

That seemed like quite a lot of pressure to rest on his actions in the bedchamber and, to speak the truth, he was having a touch of performance anxiety.

Give him a shield wall, bristling with ill-intent any day.

Bors appeared at his side. "My Lord? What would you have us do? The boys aren't wild about facing cultivators in the field, but neither do they want to sit here whilst the countryside burns. Many of them have families out there, and the news is pretty dire. If we leave it much longer, they're going to go out there themselves in ones and twos. Have to say, I don't blame them."

Arthur shook his head. "I know. It's slaughter out there. And it's not just the wizards - and gods know they're bad enough - but there's so many different points of conflict. If it continues like this, we will be flung back towards the sea before we draw our swords in earnest."

He reached into the saddle bag of Llamrei and unfurled his map tracking the disposition of the enemy forces. It showed the latest news they had of the Saxon advance. Without Merlin, it was, by its very nature, massively unreliable, but it was the best they had been able to cobble together. Not that it told them anything they did not already know; there were signs of an unchecked Saxon advance all over the border.

Although now he looked at it again, that was not entirely true.

"What do you think has happened there?"

"My Lord?"

"We know there's been a pretty much uniform advance from around twenty different war parties. An unusually coherent advance, to be sure, but that makes sense if they've got cultivators to keep communication channels open. And that's true everywhere we've gathered reports apart from there. It looks like the advance stalled at that one point, and the force retreated backwards."

"That's near Vortigern's castle, sir."

"Ah, the dragon. Do you think they've decided to go around it?"

"Doubt it, sir. That dragon's gnarly. You wouldn't want it at your back if you were looking to stretch your supply line across the countryside. It'd be feasting on the wagon train as soon as the soldiers were out of sight. It collects things, too. I wouldn't want to take the risk of it seeing a shield it liked the look of and wanting to gather up."

"Fair. So, why do you think they halted there?"

Bors shrugged. "Perhaps they engaged it and were defeated?"

"Maybe."

"You want me to go and have a look, don't you?"

"I do."

"You want me to go out there, in the middle of a wholescale invasion and see what a famously grumpy dragon has done to a Saxon army, potentially containing a cultivator?"

"That sounds like an absolutely wonderful plan. If you'd get right on that, that would be peachy."

"And I'm doing this rather than devising an elaborate ruse for you to sneak out, perhaps dressed as a washerwoman, and do it instead?"

"I'm going to have to play the 'once and future King; card again, I'm afraid."

"If I'm honest, I'm getting pretty fed up with that card, sir."

Arthur looked back at the throne room and grimaced. "So am I, Bors. So am I."

CHAPTER 31 - IN WHICH, ACCIDENTAL CANNIBALISM ASIDE, THINGS START TO LOOK UP

I'd lay in my pit of dead pig, headless love interest and various body fluids for quite some time.

That's a sentence they don't tell you at school you will ever write.

You're going to get up at some stage, aren't you?

I didn't say anything.

Look, I can see, in retrospect, that I may have overreacted slightly there.

I still didn't say anything.

In my defence, it was just good defensive instincts. He looked like he was going to attack you. I took care of business.

I said quite a lot to that.

"What part of the gorgeous man bending down to help me up - who had just killed the monster attacking me, let us not forget. A monster you'd singularly failed to attempt to deal with - looked like it needed you to 'take care of business?'

There was a gleam in his eye. I could see the signs.

"Well, there's no fucking gleam there anymore, is there? What is it with this place? I can't move for new acquaintances losing their heads within a few minutes of meeting me."

I wouldn't blame yourself entirely for that, if I was you.

"I don't blame myself! I blame the Dicks. I blame you. And most of all, I blame the fucking wizard who got me into all this and then fucked off when the going got tough!"

Didn't you banish him?

"And you can fuck off and all!"

The silence stretched out for some time after that.

In the end, it was the buzzing of the flies that stirred me from my torpor. There had always been something about that noise that massively unsettled me.

I'd been seven when my mum had walked out on us. She'd soon return, and this vanishing act would be a regular occurrence by the time I was in my teens, but they say you always remember your first time.

I'm not sure what finally pushed her too far. I assume he'd come home drunk once too often and, that night, had said something or done something out of line. Whatever it was, she'd had enough and packed an overnight bag.

And she'd just left.

That first time, she was gone for two weeks. Looking back on it now, I see this was just about the most irresponsible thing ever.

By the time she returned, complete with a suspiciously healthy tan and an appetite for tapas that lasted a month, the household was in utter shambles.

Dad worked, and he drank. That was his role in life, and everything else was down to be organised by the women. In the enforced absence of Mum, that meant me and Zizzie. Seven and five, respectively.

I mean, he wasn't so delusional he expected us to cook for him - we had a glorious fortnight of takeaways to sustain us - but he didn't have any interest in any of the things that, you know, responsible adults keep an eye on.

The bins built up. We ran out of clean dishes. Clothes were re-worn again and again. And the unused food in the fridge rotted.

So, by the time Mum bothered to return, it would be fair to say we had somewhat of a fly problem.

I give you that little bit of trauma porn because it's important for you to know why when the flies appeared around my deceased axe-husband, I utterly lost my shit.

Like, a complete Brittany-shaving-her-head, Mel-being-pulled-over-existential breakdown crisis.

Being wedged tight into the pit hardly helped me dial it down once the panic started.

I don't know how long I'd been freaking out before Drynwyn cleared what passed for its throat.

I can probably do something about the flies if you want?

I wasn't really in a place to answer, but after a few moments, I felt the warmth of its flames kick into life.

This had a number of exciting impacts.

Firstly, it turned out that Drynwyn's flames were napalm death for the surrounding insect community. This cheered me up no end. It's the little things.

Secondly, by flash-frying everything in the pit, I was suddenly not as stuck tight as I had previously been. Clambering out from the white-hot hole in the ground and stretching my legs a little further equalised my mood. All those self-help books weren't lying. Exercise really did help.

Thirdly, and this kicked in a little while later, once I had adequately got my shit together, it appeared that Drynwyn, as well as being a stunningly effective fly flamethrower, possessed some nifty butchery/cookery skills.

I guess what I'm saying is that, in pretty short order, I was happily munching on warm slices of crispy wild boar, and the least said about my epic meltdown, the better.

Things were starting to look up.

Hang on one moment.

"What?" I put down my handful of boar and looked around for danger.

No. I think it's okay.

"What!"

I thought, for a second, I might have mixed something up. But I'm sure it's alright.

"Mixed up what?"

It's not like I have all that many senses to rely on. The one looks just like the other.

I was starting to feel a bit less perky. "What are you talking about?"

You'd be able to tell the difference, right? I mean, you've eaten wild boar before, so you'd know, wouldn't you?

I looked down at the pit that was still glowing red-hot from Drynwyn's heat. I'd thought that the ash of bones which lay at its very bottom was all that remained of the woodsman.

"Are you hinting that there's a chance you may have muddled up pork loin for... longpig?"

No. Not at all. Not a chance. Well, not a big one. Probably not. There was a pause. I mean, fucking hell, if you're so picky, you cook next time.

Having heartily thrown up for several minutes, I went for a dip in the river.

***

Scrubbing myself clean of the filth that had attached itself to me in the last couple of days turned out to be just what I needed.

I'd found residue of that first wolf under my fingernails, and that was quite apart from what had covered me during that brief and disastrous first date. Sloughing that all off was a page that absolutely needed turning.

I'd left all my armour on the riverbank, and Drynwyn was scouring it clean with its flames. Fortunately, the dragon had hoarded various chests that contained serviceable underclothes, so I'd been able to add what remained of my tattered garments to the pyre. We'd had a brief disagreement about me being naked in front of it.

I'm a fucking sword. You all look the same to me. Squishy sacks that leak from various places when prodded. Rhyddrech Hael might have used me in ways for which I was not designed, but I'm thrilled not to repeat the experience.

I didn't think there was much to argue about after that.

The water did a great job of calming me down. Yes, things had been a touch intense for the last few days, but, on the plus side, I was alive and - for the first time in a long time - I was actually glad to be so. When that arrow had streaked towards me, I'd had the chance to have let it hit me and tap out from it all. Again.

That I'd instinctively thrown up the shield suggested I wasn't quite as nihilistic as had hitherto been the case.

Basically, there were worse things in life than to be a wizard.

Of course, one of those worse things would be it turning out I had cannibalised the remains of a potential soulmate. Still, I had some world-class 'bottling up your problems' skills and would be putting them into effect in the near, medium and far future.

I self-consciously left the water - **I'm still a fucking sword; you don't need to cover up the fatbags -** and found I could equip the clothes in my inventory just by thinking about it. That was good news, as it meant I was finally starting to regenerate some Qi. A glance in my artist's studio confirmed the cupboard was no longer completely barren: a thin trickle of purple was making its way around my pristinely clean channels. Even with this tiny bit on the move, I could see the whole system was working much more efficiently.

With a touch, I had my shiny suit of armour back on and, remembering what Drynwyn had said about it being cultivator armour, I encouraged the tiniest drip of paint to find its way to it during the cycle. Every little helps.

Are our panties now sufficiently unbunched?

I looked down at the sword and, for a moment, thought about dropping it in the river. Who knows, maybe that was what I was supposed to do? Perhaps, in a few years' time, someone was supposed to find it in the water and conjure up a whole mythology over the woman who had left it there. Then they'd maybe even give it to King Arthur at just the right moment to secure the kingdom ...

But no. Strange ladies lying in rivers distributing swords was no basis for a system of government.

Or something like that.

With a sense of regret that I might be making a colossal error, I swept Drynwyn up into its scabbard, took a deep breath and walked back to rejoin the makeshift road.

Merlin was bound to make it back from wherever I had banished him sooner or later, right? Right?

CHAPTER 32 - IN WHICH WE CATCH UP WITH OUR FRIENDLY NEIGHBOURHOOD ANCIENT WIZARD

In a realm of untime and unplace, where the boundaries of reality danced to a discordant tune, there floated a lone figure.

Regardless of your individual choice of reading matter, movie experience or breadth of imagination, you would doubtless recognise this figure as Merlin. Or Santa Claus. But most likely, Merlin.

He was unmistakably Merlin from the root of his long white beard to the tip of his pointy hat.

If he seemed more discombobulated than in more traditional depictions, that was probably due to the recent death of his corporeal body and the subsequent banishment of what remained of his spirit to this strange place.

I am getting too old for all this.

For someone who had just died from old age, this was a pretty solid description of his current situation.

The space that held him was a curious blend of the forgotten and the unachieved. Vague echoes of long-lost spells drifted through the air like the ghostly mutterings of a somnolent librarian. Half-formed dreams and unrealised aspirations floated past him, each a bubble of possibility, tantalisingly close yet now to be forever beyond his grasp.

He was in the place where reality came from. All realities. All the time. This was really not somewhere he should be.

It should have been impossible for a baby cultivator – a **Ron** as she insisted on calling her tier - to so much as direct him to sit down, much less banish him to this part of existence.

All very interesting. There is far more to Morgan than meets the eye. However, unless I can get back to her, there will not be much I can do to explore it further.

Merlin closed his eyes and sighed, feeling himself adrift in this unplace. He was not too proud to admit he'd made mistakes with Morgan. You'd have thought he'd have learned his lesson, what with dying and all.

If - no, when - he made it back, he needed a sign made: 'Sometimes you do not always know best.'

The gambit with the dragon had been foolish, the sort of 'all-in' move that should have been beneath him but to which he so often resorted. After all, how many apprentices had Vortigern's Dragon chomped down on over the years?

Ultimately, things had not worked out too poorly, and they could have been much worse. But what had been his plan in the event of history repeating itself? There were no potentials left, after all. He'd hazarded everything on being smarter than the dragon.

Reckless.

That it had worked did not make it less so. Sometimes - and it hurt him to admit it because it was one of his favourite sayings - the ends did not justify the means.

Even though he'd kept Morgan alive after she'd ingested far more Qi than she could possibly handle, he could see she'd been right to be angry with him.

He was just so focused on getting her ready for the challenges to come that he was not adequately giving her time to adjust.

He needed to remember that she too had died—and in far more traumatic circumstances than simply ageing out of existence.

It was hardly surprising, when forced into such a terrible situation, she had lost her temper. And then he had pressed buttons he should have been wise enough to know should remain untouched.

Daughters and their fathers.

No, he could not blame her for sending him here. He just wished he had a better handle as to where 'here' was.

And some plan for how he would get back would not hurt, either.

He moved his arms around experimentally and found, with not too much effort, he could swim through the nothingness.

With no real sense of up, down, left or right, that was, of course, of limited benefit. But he had always felt that acting was better than staying still, so he kicked his feet and started swimming forward.

He was in the place where the tapestries of reality intertwined with the threads of possibility. All very interesting, but how on earth Morgan had the strength to push him here, he could not conceive.

He drifted along for a few centuries (or minutes, who knew? Was time even a thing here?). The mists of the space swirled around him like spectral tendrils, whispering secrets and riddles alike. He recognised that spending too long in such a formless environment would doubtless send a lesser mortal mad.

Fortunately, he had already crossed that bridge, burned it to the ground and urinated on the ashes.

Reality would have to work much harder if it hoped to cause him any bother. In fact ...

I appear to have found myself at the nexus of all that is and might be, Merlin mused aloud. He assumed someone, something, was observing him to see what he would do. A less benign soul than I could do some severe damage here. A wise astral being would probably want me as far away from here as soon as possible.

The space swirled as if reacting to his words, and a doorway formed ahead of him.

Wise choice.

With a flourish, he extended his hand - he still had hands, right? - towards the door, his fingers suffused with an ethereal glow. The door, an archway really, its boundaries as fluid as a river's current, responded to Merlin's gesture and surged towards him.

It was not just a door, he knew. It was a gateway between the realms, a passage to domains where the fabric of reality could be reshaped. He assumed when she told him 'fuck off', Morgan had unknowingly ripped one of these doors open and pushed him through.

Within this realm of mists, the journey is not one of mere chronology but of growth. He rubbed his hand on the door frame. I am both here and everywhere at once. Imagine what I could have achieved had I found this place whilst alive.

As if in response to his words, the doorway opened, and he felt a tug from within it.

Do not worry; I will soon be on my way. I will not linger here any longer than necessary.

His form melded with the mists, and he stood for a second on the threshold between this space and the 'real' world from which he had been expelled.

Everything was telling him to step through, but he sensed there was more to this doorway than met the eye. With a significant effort, Merlin's awareness expanded, and he felt the currents of Qi surging all around him. It was as if the mists themselves were an intricate web of energy waiting to be harnessed and refined.

Merlin closed his eyes, his consciousness delving into the currents. It caused his spirit physical pain to be so close to all of this energy and to be unable to make use of it. Even disembodied as he was, whilst standing in this doorway, he felt connected to the very heart of creation, his presence resonating with the echoes of countless souls of existence.

I would have made my breakthrough if I had found this space while alive. If I'd even known it had existed, that might have been the last push I needed. He was unsure if that knowledge caused him sorrow. Sometimes it just is your time.

The mists responded to that thought, swirling with a renewed pull of intensity as if anxious to be rid of him. Each breath he took seemed to draw in the essence, infusing his very being. He was sure he felt his awareness expand, his senses heightened to perceive the energies that flowed through all things.

But no. Of course it didn't. He did not have channels of his own anymore. He no longer had Qi to cycle. He was a parasite on someone who knew no better. *But I am a parasite who still has a role to play.*

In this interstice between existence and ascension, Merlin sensed he could become a true conductor of cosmic energies should he abandon his final quest and leave Morgan to it. As if in response to that line of thought, the archway pulsed, its light intensifying until it was as blinding as a star at its zenith.

You want me to leave. I will not disagree.

With no further thought, Merlin stepped through the archway with purpose and poise.

He could do better. He would do better. He had a purpose. And he had Morgan.

The mists embraced him, their currents carrying him across realms uncharted and possibilities unfathomed.

CHAPTER 33 - IN WHICH WE LEARN OF THE PETTINESS OF SWORDS

I don't know, but I been told
Goblin pussy's mighty cold
Mmm good.
Feels good.
Real good
Taste good
Mighty good
Good for you
Good for me

I cannot express how fortunate Drynwyn was that we had long left the river behind. As someone whose natural environment was not the great outdoors, I had already been a little leery about hiking across Cornwall on the lookout for any sign of civilisation. Doing so to a succession of my sword's marching songs - **Rhydderch Hael said he found them soothing** - was not improving the experience.

I'd played along at first; the call-and-response structure reminded me of being in the Brownies. Wise Owl would gather us all up every few months and take us for a walk in the park. To keep us moving, she'd sing us songs like the ones of which the sword seemed to have an unending supply. Not, I should add, did she have us chanting about Goblin pussy. Although, if I believed the rumours, that was about the only sort she hadn't had an interest in.

Nevertheless, that was several hours ago, and whatever nostalgic charm the game had initially generated had long since palled.

If you'd thought my not joining in would put a stop to the whole thing, let me say, 'Bless you, my sweet Summer child'. All my chilly silence changed was that Drynwyn started doing an impression of my voice, providing the response.

This proved to be both as creepy as it was annoying.

I said a boom chicka boom (I said a boom chicka boom)
I said a boom chicka boom (I said a boom chicka boom)
I said a boom chicka rocka chicka rocka chicka boom (I said a boom chicka rocka chicka rocka chicka boom)
Uh-huh (uh-huh)
Oh yeah (oh yeah)
One more time (one more time)
Dragon style!

I couldn't take it any more. I stopped, drew it from its scabbard and held it before me.

131

What the fuck's going on?

"Mate, I can't take it anymore. You need to stop."

Stop what?

"Dragon style. Giant style. Elf style. Let's start with stopping any more fucking styles at all and then move our way down the list. You're being too much."

Too much what?

"Too much everything. It's fine just to be quiet sometimes. In fact, it's more than fine. I find it to be my overwhelming preference. I don't need a constant running commentary on everything we see. I don't need you singing songs to pick me up. I don't need inspiring stories from your history to help pass the time. I don't need any of that. I just need you to shut up while we walk."

Drynwyn didn't say anything. The people pleaser in me sensed that I had hurt his feelings. The bitch in me - who pretty much always had control of the conch - didn't give a fuck.

"Do you understand? I don't want to hear from you for the rest of the afternoon. Do you think you can manage that, or will I need to put you in storage?"

Drynwyn still didn't say anything.

Satisfied I had successfully gotten across my point of view, I resheathed him behind my back and turned back to continue my journey.

Or I would have if I hadn't walked straight into a swinging fist.

***

I have a song about noticing approaching danger if you'd like to hear it?

I was slowly regaining consciousness. Blobs of colour swam in and out of focus. I swear I could see little birds spinning around my head.

It goes something like this:

Oh, no. A man is creeping up behind you.

But you're too busy bawling me out to appeal to.

If you were less of a bitch I'd warn you.

But you are, so I'm not fucking going to.

I agree it needs some work, but I think it captures the essence of the message. I am not sure what the title will be at the moment, but I'm working with: "My new bearer got punched in the face, and it was fucking hilarious." I will keep drafting it, though, if it turns out you have any notes?

I experimentally clicked my jaw from left to right: whoever had sucker-punched me had certainly given it their all. Nothing seemed to be broken, and, running my tongue around my mouth, no teeth were missing.

That was about the extent of my good news.

As far as I could tell, I was lying on the floor of some sort of barn. I mean, I'm no expert, but there were bundles of hay everywhere and a smell I associated with farmyard animals. But being bound from head to foot with some reasonably substantial rope limited my room for casual exploration.

"Am I to take it that you let me get captured on purpose?"

I didn't like to interrupt. You were explaining how fucking important the quiet was to you. I felt it would have been rude. You were being pretty insistent about it.

"I think it's pretty clear I'd be okay with you speaking up to stop me being kidnapped."

You'd think. But I have a fucking vivid memory of coming to your aid just this morning and you giving me all sorts of shit over it. You know, you're something of a prick tease. Kill this guy! No, not that guy. I love that guy. How am I supposed to tell the difference?

"Let's agree that moving forward, it's a pretty solid rule that anyone who wants to tie me up is not someone I want getting close to me."

You sure? Rhyddrech kind of had that as a pre-requisite.

I opened my mouth to speak, stopped, and then shook my head. This was a conversation for another day. Maybe. I wasn't sure there was enough water in the world to get me clean after opening that particular Pandora's box. "Never mind. Let's chalk this one up to experience: a funny bump in the road on the journey of our developing relationship. Now, can you cut me free?"

I don't think I want to. You're mean.

"Excuse me?"

Do this. Do that. No, not like that. Like this. You're too loud. You're too sweary. Cut me free. Stop talking to me. Save me. But do it without bothering me. The more I think about it, I'm not sure we're equal partners in this relationship. I seem much more into 'us' than you are.

I wasn't sure how Drynwyn had transformed into my Art School boyfriend, James Sutherland, but he had the nasal whingey argument down-pat. Problem was, I was pretty sure showing the sword my tits wasn't going to shut him up.

I gritted my teeth and sought my soul for some droplets of faux-sincerity. "You're right. I've been taking advantage of you, and I'm sorry. I shouldn't be taking you for granted, and I need to listen more to the things that matter to you. If you could, please, just see your way clear to freeing me, I'll work on being more open."

You don't mean it. It's just that you need me now. As soon as you're free, you'll go back to being nasty again.

"Drynwyn, I can't promise to change who I am. But I will try to remember you have feelings and that I need to be kinder." Fucking hell. Life was so much easier when you could simply screw the frowning away.

Do you mean it?

Nope. I was out. I'd had enough. "Drynwyn, you cut me free right now, or I will tell whoever captured me that it was your fault they got the drop on me. I'll scream to anyone that will listen that Drynwyn, the sword of Rhydderch Hael, let its new bearer be captured because it was being a whiny, needy little bitch. How does that sound? What will all the other talking swords say if that got out?"

You wouldn't!

"Look at my face. Do you think I've been mean so far? You need to wait until you hear the stories I can spread. "Yes, couldn't even use him in a fight. He'd droop straight over whenever I swung him. Yes, that's right. Like a wet noodle. Totally useless. I'm sure that's how the dragon got the better of Rhyddrech. Drynwyn the Flaccid is what you'll be known as by the time I'm finished."

There was a tense silence.

Fucking hell.

"Yeah, sorry. I sensed I was going too far."

I mean, I was just playing around. Now, I don't know if I actually want to save you. You're horrible.

"Sorry. Can we talk about this more once I'm free?"

There was a flash of heat, and the rope holding me was incinerated instantly.

Not for nothing, but you don't question a sword's virility. That's like sacred shit.

"I understand. Sorry. I won't do it again." I rubbed my wrists like I'd seen every freed hostage do a million times on TV. I was, as I thought, in the stall of a barn. Looking around, there was space for five or six other animals in here, but nothing else seemed to be about. I was particularly pleased to see the other stalls were not similarly crammed with unconscious women.

"Did you get a good look at who hit me?"

Big guy. Probably a blacksmith. He has long brown hair and a thick, braided beard. It would seem to be a dangerous amount of flammable material in a forge, but there you go. Leather apron, fleece tunic. Thick hide boots. Oh, and one blue eye, one brown.

"You got all that from one look at him?"

No. Of course not. He's standing just there.

I turned round to meet the heterochromic eyes of the angry-looking, yet surprisingly silently-moving, man two feet behind me.

"For fuck's sake, Drynwyn."

CHAPTER 34 - IN WHICH YOU SHOULD LISTEN VERY CAREFULLY. I SHALL SAY THIS ONLY ONCE.

 "**D**rynwyn?"

What?

"Just checking, we're both on the same page if things need to go all Operation Stabby-stabby-hack-hack here?"

We're not calling it that.

"Let's give it a few minutes to see how things play out. But you know what to do if things go south. This guy has one strike already."

"To whom are you talking?" The voice of the big man was a deep baritone. Of course it was. What with his build and his clothing, he was the most blacksmithy blacksmith ever to smith the black.

"I think the more pressing question is who are you, and what's with all the attacking lone women in the woods and tying them up?"

I had prepared myself for any number of responses. This guy had laid me out with one punch, after all: even though I was totally unprepared, that felt like it was probably a significant thing to achieve against a cultivator. Particularly one that ripped the head off a dragon with her bare hands. So, I was cycling my Qi everywhere I thought it could be useful, and if he so much as looked at me funny, I was opening a [Can of Whoopass]. If that didn't decide things, I was sure Drynwyn was dying for an opportunity to re-establish its destructive credentials.

Thus, as far as these things go, I felt I had most of the bases covered. It all depended on how the big guy was going to play it.

I was, therefore, somewhat thrown when he sank to the floor, put his head in his hands and began sobbing.

"I know. I know. I don't know what came over me. I thought you were one of them, but when I realised you weren't, I didn't know what to do. Sǣþrȳð said to leave you here until you woke up."

That sounded like a whole new host of letters I wasn't going to seek to learn. "Dude, you'd tied me up."

"You're a wizard!" His voice was now less a baritone and more a castrato wail high enough to attract passing bats. "Everyone said you'd kill us as soon as you woke up. I thought if I tied you up, it would give me time to negotiate. Please, it was me that hurt you. None of the others. I am the one you should punish."

This wasn't going quite the way I thought it would. I let the Qi slip away from my hands and told Drywyn to keep a close eye but hold back on the flaming death for now.

"Let's all take a beat here. I'm not going to kill you." I paused; no need to give up the initiative. I quite liked being the sort of person big, bear-like men wept in front of. "Yet. But I need to understand more of what's going on here. What's your name?"

"Beocca."

"And you're a blacksmith, right?"

For some reason, that set the big man off sobbing again. "It's true what they say. Wizards know everything! You can read my mind!"

The man's clearly a simpleton. Maybe some sort of traumatic head injury. Be a kindness to kill him, really.

I felt the sword start to leave its scabbard.

"Stop it!" I bent down to kneel next to the wailing giant. "I am a wizard, but trust me, I don't know everything. And I'm not reading your mind. You just look like a blacksmith. And you're wearing a massive leather apron. And, yes, you have a series of small hammers in a belt around your waist."

He wiped his tears away with his massive, calloused hands. "Honest truth?"

"Honest truth, Beocca. Why don't we look to start again? Let's begin with who the 'they' are you thought I was, and then we can try to fill in some blanks from there."

Still think it'd be easier to kill him.

***

We'd relocated to the smithy, and Beocca had poured himself a glass of something lethal smelling to calm his nerves. He sent a small boy to 'bring everyone,' which was initially alarming until it turned out 'everyone' was five or six women of various sizes and ages.

One of them, Sǣþrȳð apparently, wrapped her hand around his the second she arrived, giving me some epic stinkeye. Honestly, she couldn't have marked her territory any clearer than if she'd pissed on him.

She was welcome to it, though. With the size of Beocca, we'd have needed to fashion up some elaborate pulley system to make it work. At least without endangering some bits of me I was pretty fond of. Mind you, as a blacksmith, he would probably be able to produce all sorts of exciting mechanisms that might make a dabble viable ...

I quickly shut down that line of thought. Rhyddrech Hael seemed to be rubbing off on me. Which I imagined he'd have enjoyed immensely.

Of course, even before the tale of woe was delivered, I'd already worked out what was happening. The complete lack of men and the generally tense atmosphere, plus Beocca's weighty mention of 'them,' made it all pretty clear what was going on.

"The fyrd passed through a week back. Most of the young men joined it; we don't see many raids this far from the border, so, as you can imagine, it was pretty popular."

"Beocca tried to talk them out of it, but boys will be boys." Sǣþrȳð chipped in.

"Not just the boys. Any man who could carry a spear tagged along," a sour-faced woman added. "My Harnult went with them happily enough."

There was a moment of silence as everyone thought about those who had been lost. Even while still holding out hope of seeing them again.

"We started seeing fires at the end of that first day. Columns of smoke in the sky from the direction of the other villages hereabouts. At first, we didn't pay them no mind. You get wildfires this time of year. But then, on the fourth day, with no sign of the men returning, we began to get nervous. A few of us rode out over yonder to see what was occurring."

I could see where this was going. "And?"

"We're surrounded by death, and worse, on all sides. Men, women, children. Even the animals. It's a slaughter. As far as I rode - and I went as far as I dared - I didn't see another living soul. Not until I heard you singing, in any event." Beocca didn't need to say much more. His eyes told the story of the horrors of his journey. I could almost forgive him clocking me first and asking questions later.

Almost.

"So, if you know what is coming, why are you still here?"

Sæþryð eyes flashed, and she raised her chin at that. "And where should we go, wizard? The fyrd has clearly been defeated, and our friends and neighbours lie dead for as far as we can ride. Who will protect us? Who will give us shelter? At least here we have roofs over our heads and walls we can defend." She obviously read the scepticism on my face. "What's to say we won't walk straight into whatever force is out there? We're as safe here as we would be on the road."

That sounded like giant, sweaty bollocks, and judging by Beocca's complete lack of poker face, there was another story here. These people were staying here for a reason that had nothing to do with worries about the road. But I couldn't blame them if they didn't want to confide in the wizard they thought was about to massacre them.

But what was I supposed to do now?

I'd been looking for people, and here people were. But I'd been hoping for, you know, a village with an inn, a spa, maybe a travelling circus. You know, just your basics. But the whole vibe here was a bit too French Resistance for my taste. And I fucking hated *Allo, Allo*.

I had no desire to watch anybody else whose name I knew die, but neither did I have any illusions that I would fare any better on my own against an entire army than I did last time.

I still had no idea what made them evacuate in their moment of triumph - General Tarkin would *not* have approved - but it seemed unlikely it would happen twice.

I looked around at all the grim faces. They were hiding something, but it was their lives, and they could do whatever they wanted. I just needed to decide if I was willing to risk having more arrows fired at my face for people I barely knew - one of whom had punched me in the face, and another kept looking at me like she'd like to.

On the balance of things, and with surprisingly little regret, I thought not.

Ignoring Drynwyn's cries of protestations, I stood and wished them all the luck in the world.

But then, who would have guessed, the decision was taken out of my hands. A small boy appeared at the door to the smithy, sweaty and with a face white with fear.

"Riders. Lots of them. Coming from the East. They're blocking the road."

Awesome.

137

CHAPTER 35 - IN WHICH I TAKE THE TIME TO INVEST IN MY VISUAL BRAND

"How many of you are there?"

Sæþrȳð was looking sick. "Half a dozen adults. Twice as many children. What do we do?"

"What's your strongest building?"

"Probably here," Beocca was wringing his hands like a Lady Macbeth tribute act. "Walls are pretty thick, but the doors won't stand up to a wizard."

"Let me worry about the wizard. Get everyone in here, then, and block up the doors and windows."

The group quickly left to gather up the rest of the village. I stepped outside to get the lay of the land. What I saw did not inspire me.

This is a shithole.

And it absolutely was. Apart from the smithy, the only other buildings worth the name were a few ramshackle huts. The whole place looked like one of those early episodes of Survivor where they're still in their pile-up-branches-and-call-it-a-shelter stage. This wasn't a village. It was collective homelessness.

Beocca had followed me out and caught the expression on my face. "I know. But we're in the middle of nowhere; the soil's too thin to farm properly, so we grow barely enough to feed ourselves, let alone keep any animals."

"But you have a forge. And you won't leave even with the certainty of impending death. What the fuck aren't you telling me?"

Beocca shook his head. "Not now."

I bet if I set his beard on fire, he'd tell you.

The blacksmith's eyes went out on stalks, and he looked around for who had spoken. I held my face still as if I hadn't heard anything. We could both play at the keeping secrets game.

"Okay. Well, if we're still alive at the end of the day, I look forward to hearing what's here that's worth dying for."

I wandered a little distance from Beocca and looked towards the direction from which I assumed the army would arrive. He chose not to accompany me, clearly thinking at least one of us was haunted.

I took up a position just to the side of the road and gave my best Luke-staring-at-twin-suns-at-the-start-of-episode-4 impression. Helpfully, the wind blew through my hair, streaming it behind me like a banner of flame, and - fuck it, in for a penny, in for a pound - I loosened my Qi control a little to let it bleed out my skin, giving my whole body a soft purple glow. To complete the image, I drew Drynwyn and held it down at my side. Sensing the mood, it helpfully burst into fire.

I am sure, to anyone who was watching, I looked absolutely EPIC.

Which was good because I had no idea what I was going to do.

Part of me, a giant pulsing massive section of my conscious thought, wanted to leg it as far away from the army as possible. But glancing back at the pathetic sight of this tiny, bedraggled community herding themselves into the smithy gave me pause.

These people were done if I ran. Who was I kidding? They were pretty much in the exact same situation if I hung around. But - and I am as surprised about this as everyone here - it didn't seem like I was the sort of person who could walk away and that desertion not seriously fuck me up.

"Drynwyn, I could use some words of advice here."

The burning sensation will go away if you ignore it.

"What?"

Sorry, force of habit. What sort of wisdom are you looking for?

"Is there any sort of tactical masterplan you could suggest that might get us all out of this alive?"

You're facing an unknown number of attackers - but the context suggests it will be a decent-sized war party. Spears. Archers. Probably, on past experience, a wizard. You have no allies upon whom to rely. Your combat experience to date is a wolf, a dragon and a boar. Oh, and you hid behind a shield whilst an army took potshots at you. You've gathered up all the non-combatants into the only moderately defensible building. And they won't leave.

I waited for the advice. "And?"

There's no 'and'. You're fucked. Those people are fucked. Probably literally. The best-case scenario is it happens after you're dead.

"Seriously, no sunlit uplands at all here?"

Not unless you can bluff them that you're much more capable than we know you are. But they're not going to fall for that twice, are they?

And with those words, Operation Lucy-Removes-the-Ball-At-The-Last-Minute-Once-Again was born.

***

They'd left this hamlet until now simply because it hadn't been worth the effort to exterminate.

The fyrd had walked straight into them four days back: it had been a short and bloody confrontation, putting them ahead of schedule compared to the other war parties. So, they had been in no rush to mop up the surrounding countryside. Certainly, there had been better prizes to be plucked than this sorry excuse for a village.

But, they'd received word that the other invasion parties were finally ready to push deeper into Uther's territory. So, for completeness, they'd come calling.

Ealhhere took a pull from his wineskin as he watched the vanguard move slowly forward. They'd not come across much resistance at all, but there was no need to get sloppy.

He'd heard from his wizard that Pæga had taken some casualties and had needed to retreat back to the border, but his group hadn't seen anything like that. As far as he could tell, anyone who could run had done so, and those who had been left behind were simply placidly waiting to become collateral damage.

139

One of his men appeared at the side of his horse. "Our scouts report that the population have barricaded themselves in the forge."

Ealhhere's brows rows. Maybe this might be worth his time after all. "Must be a huge forge!"

"More a tiny population, I'm afraid."

"Fuck's sake." Ealhhere took another mouthful of wine and looked over to his wizard, Tata.

He didn't like him, but he didn't like anyone. He would admit the slim, dark-haired man had done his work soundly enough so far. The fireballs were hot, the healing was adequate, and the moaning was kept to a minimum. He'd heard tale that the High King had been pretty brutal in his manner of conscripting cultivators for this invasion. So, he'd expected no end of whining from the one assigned to his force. But the man had kept mainly to himself and done his business. You couldn't ask for much more that.

"If they're all in one building, Tata, can you just burn it down? Save us the hassle?"

Tata slowly shook his head. "If it wasn't a forge, sir, sure. But I'm not sure fire will have much impact there."

"Fuck's sake." Ealhhere repeated. "So be it." He signalled the attention of one of his men; he hadn't bothered to learn the names, but this one had seemed particularly enthusiastic about this sort of work. "You know what to do here. I doubt there's anything worth looting, but bring anything you find so we can have a look."

"And the women, sir?"

Ealhhere shuddered. The last few villages hadn't yielded anything with more teeth than eyes. "Place like this? I wouldn't risk it with someone else's. You're welcome to them."

The soldier grinned and directed a small group of spearmen to push forward to surround the forge. His chosen few had nearly made it to the door when Tata's eyes suddenly widened, and he started to shout a word of warning.

It was to no avail.

As if from nowhere, there was suddenly a knight in armour, holding a flaming sword, scything their way through some very surprised spearmen. There was something odd about how they held the sword; it was a technique none of them had seen before. It almost looked like they were clinging on to the hilt rather than directing its path. All very curious.

The noise the sword was making, likewise, was bizarre. It was something like a buzzing hum whilst also making a 'schwum' noise with each swing.

In a blink, four spearmen were down, and the knight was stood alone before them.

She, he could see it was a woman now, replaced the sword in its scabbard behind her back with a smooth movement. As it snapped into place, the buzzing hum stopped with a sound like the soft crackle of cooling metal.

The woman looked at him, red hair streaming behind her and spoke. "You can torture these people and burn their villages to the ground. But do you see that?" She pointed to one of the smouldering corpses of his spearmen. "Fire is catching... And if they burn... you will burn with them!"

The knight took a step forward, gesturing towards the forge. "Those people in there will not go quietly into the night! They will not vanish without a fight! They're going to live on! They're going to survive!"

She opened her arms wide, then, and it was as if her accent seemed to become more ... Celtic. "I am Morgan Le Fay! And I see a whole army of Saxons in front of me. You've come to fight as free men... and as free men, you will die. What will you do with that freedom? Will you fight? Aye, fight, and you will die. Run, and you'll live... that I promise you. And dying in your beds, many years from now, would you be willing to trade ALL the days, from this day to that, for one chance, just one chance, to come back here and tell your enemies that they may take your lives, but they'll never take... YOUR FREEDOM!"

Ealhhere frowned then looked, bemused, round at his men. "I don't ... I don't think that made sense. It sounded like you stuck together three speeches you'd learned by heart. But they didn't really link together. And the last bit? That sounds like you're encouraging us to attack rather than to leave you alone. Did anyone else think that?"

There were several nods.

Told you that wasn't going to fucking work. I mean, I told you your bit wouldn't work. My bit went like a fucking dream. Even making those stupid noises you wanted.

"And I told you, if I'm going to have a flaming sword, it's damn well going to sound right. We'll work on getting the flames to go green. Right. No worries. That was always going to be a bit of stretch. Okay, let's move on to Plan B."

Which one was that?

And the world went up in flames.

141

CHAPTER 36 - IN WHICH I'M FAIRLY SURE I COMMIT A WAR CRIME

Fun fact.
When Beocca had mentioned 'wildfires' earlier, I had thought he had meant the woodlands going up in flames. But the more I'd thought about it, especially after seeing the landscape around the village, the more that didn't make sense.

Quite apart from the soggy weather – if you're British, I don't need to explain, and if you're not, it's hard to put into appropriate words the draining grey, dreariness of living on this island – there simply wasn't anything around that looked especially flammable.

A few hurried minutes of conversation with the blacksmith clarified what he meant, and thus, Plan B was born.

It turned out, the people in the village were used to seeing columns of smoke in the sky because, in the surrounding area, there were little pockets of gas under the ground that regularly, and with minimal prompting, went boom.

Apparently, throwing around Drnwyn's flames provided just the sort of encouragement the area on the outskirts of the village needed to become excitable.

I'm not sure how comfortable I am with this.

I watched the last of the running, screaming figures in front of me and couldn't help but agree.

Killing people one-on-one, I don't have a problem with.

"I'd noticed."

But at least they have a chance. I mean, not much of one because I'm fucking awesome. But it's still theoretically a possibility. Those guys ...

We watched silently as the last of those caught up in the explosion smoked and died.

Merlin used to do things like this. In the bad old days.

I nodded. "He showed me a vision of him taking out three whole armies. It was pretty grim."

Rhyddrech was terrified of him, you know? Merlin. Said people were never meant to have such power. Wouldn't have anything to do with him.

The smoke was clearing now, and the full extent of the devastation was revealed. Of the bulk of the army, there was pretty much nothing left. A crater about the size of a football pitch stood in its place, tastefully decorated by various odd and sods of human remains. Those that had been at the edge of conflagration had fared a little better. In that, rather than be summarily exploded into pieces, they had been afforded the opportunity to be flash-fried.

I wasn't convinced many of them were genuinely grateful for that.

"These were bad guys, Drynwyn. The things Beocca said they'd done to the people in the other villages ..."

Some of them, for sure. Maybe even most. But we've just wiped out a bunch of people whose only actual crime was being conscripted into an army. I don't know. Not sure I'm feeling too heroic right now.

"There will be a battle here in five, six hundred years. It'll be over religion: most of them are, really, when it comes down to it. A city will be asked to hand over all the people living there who are the wrong religion. They'll, being decent humans, flatly refuse. One of the commanders, a delightful wet-wipe called Arnauld Amalric, will order the army to "kill them all. God will recognise his own.' I don't know what made me think of that."

I stared at the space in which the army had stood. I wasn't feeling too heroic, either. Mind you, I don't think I ever had done so before, so there wasn't that much comparative data available. I was pretty familiar with shame, though, so my current mood was like putting on a comfy old jacket.

Which god?

"Sorry?"

Which god will recognise his own? That sounds like some seriously vengeful Odin shit.

"Ah. You might not have Him in these parts yet. He'll be pretty big in this part of the world."

God of War, I guess?

"Funnily enough, peace and love."

Fucking hell.

"I know, right?"

***

The people inside the smithy took the extermination of the soldiers coming to rape and murder them pretty well. I mean, from their point of view, one moment, the fat lady was giving the final chorus some serious welly, and now she was back at home shouting at her agent for the lack of a gig. They were wholly on board with the smoking wreckage now on their doorstep if it was a choice between them or the army.

I was finding the party atmosphere a bit harder to stomach. Sæþrӯð even smiled at me, which freaked me out even more. It didn't help that they seemed determined to ascribe the victory to my control of unearthly powers rather than introductory chemistry.

"It is true what they say about Wizards. You are truly all-powerful."

"I appreciate the props, but honestly, you could have done it yourself. All you needed to do was fashion a strong enough ignition mechanism, and the whole thing would have gone up spectacularly without me." Beocca stared back at me like a dog that had been shown a card trick. The awkward silence drew out before he grinned and clapped me on the back, knocking the wind out of me. "And humble too! Truly, you are one of the great Mages of the realm!"

I stopped trying to argue after that. If I wasn't careful, they'd decide I was a nice person, and there was only so much I could face keep pulling the wool over the eyes of these good people.

143

I say 'good' people as if they weren't all currently scrabbling through the crater, extricating anything lootable they could get their grubby little hands on. There was something of an unhealthy disregard for the sanctity of dead bodies being displayed. But, as the one who had made the mountain of corpses, perhaps I shouldn't be throwing stones through the massive glass windows of my hypocrisy.

Sæþrȳð brought me a glass of something that screamed moonshine, and I gulped it down gratefully—anything to get the taste of death out of my mouth.

"You don't like what you did."

I looked at her appraisingly. "What, no 'all hail the mighty spellcaster?' I'm horrified."

"We were going to die, and now we're not. None of us care how you achieved that. We're just extremely grateful. Follow me." She held out her hand for me to take and gave me a look I thought I had copyrighted after five vodka cokes.

I felt myself blush, and I hesitated. "Look, not that I'm not flattered, but there's no need …"

The stare I received in return suggested my gaydar remained wholly and irredeemably broken. "You wanted to know why we wouldn't leave. I'm going to show you."

Somewhat chagrined, I followed her back to the smithy.

"My family have lived in these parts for generations, and this forge has been here for all that time."

"Okay …"

Sæþrȳð bent to pull a chest filled with metal offcuts away from the wall. Behind it was a hole that led down some stone steps deep into the ground. With some difficulty, she squeezed herself through the gap and indicated for me to follow. Call me a bluff old traditionalist, but I was not excited to pursue a strange woman into a mysterious cave: I'd seen the film Descent at an impressionable age.

"I'm fine with a verbal explanation. This doesn't need to be a whole show and tell performance."

"For a wizard, you are very skittish. Is not exploring the unknown supposed to be your thing?"

"I'm more from the 'what you don't know can't hurt you' school of thought."

Sæþrȳð had vanished down the hole, and the peer pressure was fairly insistent for me to follow. And whether it was cigs, booze or jumping down foreboding pits in the ground, I was a sucker for it.

The steps went down quite some way, and torches recessed in the wall lit as I walked towards them and flicked off once they were behind me. I could be wrong, but my carefully honed senses suggested some magical shenanigans may be taking place here.

Watching my step, I dipped into my artist's studio to ensure everything was topped up if needed. My Qi was cycling happily around, the benefit of my Dragon-cleansed channels being obvious now as the purple paint positively sluiced around. A pretty decent squirt was going into my armour now, too, which I'd have to experiment with later.

I was dragged back into the real world by walking into the back of Sæþrȳð.

She glared at me and then pulled me to her side.

"Here. You can see now, wizard. This is why we couldn't leave."

For a moment, I didn't see anything; it was just a long tunnel that vanished into the blackness beyond the torches. But then my eyes adjusted, and I realised the walls were alive with tiny, brown-green creatures.

Each was no bigger than my hand, and they were mining the tunnel. Like full-on hi-ho shit. Most had little pickaxes in their hands, while others were running about with wheelbarrows, transporting the debris away.

If they noticed us, they didn't react. But then, there were thousands of them, and they probably could take us if they needed to. We've all seen Gulliver's Travels.

"Do you know who these are, wizard?" Sæþrȳð's expression was hard to read.

I went to shake my head, then stopped. I actually did. A memory from twenty years past sprung, fully formed, from my brain. "Knockers. They're fucking Knockers, aren't they?"

145

CHAPTER 37 - IN WHICH BORS DEMONSTRATES HE IS NO SIXTH-CENTURY MISS MARPLE

Bors had no idea what to make of it all.

He'd been on more battlefields than he cared to remember and had, in his own words, *seen some shit*. But he couldn't make head nor tail of the scene around Vortigern's castle.

There was a dead dragon.

He felt it was wise to start with the things everyone would be able to get on board with. He'd not seen so many of them to be blase about it, but neither was it a wholly remarkable sight. Some people dedicated their whole, by their very nature, shortened lives to taking down these giant lizards. Like that lunatic, Rhyddrech Hael. Now there was someone who lived by the maxim if you can't eat it or fuck it, you'd better kill it.

Thus, in his time, he'd seen his fair share of dragon bodies. So he was pretty surprised at how tiny the corpse lying at his feet was ...

He'd last seen Vortigern's dragon some years back. As was his practice, Merlin had thrown one of his apprentices at it to see what would happen, and Bors had been charged with overseeing the clean-up detail. It was not one of the more prized duties, but - provided you made it clear you were no threat - it would usually pass without too much unpleasantness.

This last time, the dragon had decided to be a twat and had hovered over the top of them the whole time they were ash collecting. Being under that massive shadow - particularly when it started to muse aloud on how each of them would taste - had not been one of the more restful experiences of his life.

Looking at the shrivelled, headless body of all that now remained, Bors was unsure how he felt. The dragon had been a fucking terrifying presence in this part of the world, but, well, it had been pretty magnificent in its stomach-churning way. To see it like this was ... sad.

But, more than that, he couldn't understand why it was in its 'normal' size. The whole area stank of Qi, so it had definitely been a cultivator that had taken it down. Likewise, there was no chance anyone strong enough to rip the head from its shoulders had just 'snuck up' on a dragon this old and wily and caught it unawares.

So, what? Had an unknown wizard of unusual strength and capacity somehow inhibited its battle state? If so, someone with the skill to forcibly shrink down a dragon was precisely the sort of magic the kingdom needed right now.

And he guessed that was the story. A serious cultivator of unknown origin had taken down the dragon. Tick. File that one as solved. That made some sense, and whilst there remained some pretty troubling questions about 'who?' and 'on whose side were they?', they were problems for later on. Bors was very much a punch-the-problem-in-front-of-you-in-the-face-and-then-think-about-next-steps,' kind of guy.

Moving forward, then, Bors tried to make sense of what had happened next.

A decent-sized war party had shown up and taken up a competent attack position around the ruined castle. The horse manure he found was considerably fresher than the dragon's body - sadly, he'd needed to taste to check - so he figured these guys had rocked up a little while after the unknown cultivator beheaded the dragon.

That felt like the first bit of good news for a while. He'd been worried that it would turn out the Saxons had bought some serious dragon-slaying talent with them. That these two events seemed separate was a positive.

Bors made his way down towards the gatehouse, almost missing the two halves of a Saxon commander that had been left lying on the ground. As far as he could see, this appeared to be the only casualty, other than the dragon.

This body was sliced neatly down the middle, but there was no blood whatsoever.

He settled on his haunches and ran his hands down the inside of both the halves. He had a glamorous life, sometimes.

Utterly cauterised.

So, a flaming sword. And wielded by someone strong enough to bisect a fairly substantial enemy combatant. That vibed with his image of a powerful cultivator suppressing down the aura of a dragon and then pulling its head off like a popping a ripe plum.

But why were there no other casualties? Everything he saw pointed towards something approaching Merlin-levels of power. And he wasn't known for restraint when encountering enemy armies.

There should be bodies everywhere. Not just one neatly halved soldier.

What the fuck was going on here?

His confusion wasn't improved by the fuckton of arrows scattered halfway between this body and the gatehouse. The Saxons had opened up on someone coming out from behind the gatehouse. That much was clear, but as he drew closer to the site of that confrontation, not much else was.

Bors picked up a shattered arrow. It, and hundreds of its fellows, had hit something solid and turned to matchsticks. Again, the whole area stunk of Qi, so was it some sort of shield spell? He hadn't seen one of those in years.

"A ridiculous waste of Qi," Merlin had said when asked to use them over Uther's army. "Nothing burns through energy as quickly as protective spells. It's more efficient for me to kill the people shooting the arrows than waste Qi protecting your men. Both of those resources are replaceable, and one is much less hassle to get more of than the other."

Merlin could be a dick at times.

He followed the signposted path into the dragon's hoard and finally felt the pieces start to fall into place a bit more. The cave had been almost entirely cleared out. Rumour had it that Vortigern's dragon had been one of the more obsessive collectors of artefacts in this part of the world. That all was left were some crappy swords helped make more sense of what had happened.

The speed needed for this type of operation would have called for a team of wizards working together to cram everything possible into their soul spaces. Thinking back to what he had seen further up the hill, it seemed clear there was really only one story here that made sense.

He needed to get back to Arthur as soon as possible.

***

"A cadre of expert, treasure-hunting cultivators are sweeping through the land, exterminating dragons, Saxon war parties and stealing valuable treasures."

"Yes, my Lord."

"They suppressed the dragon's aura and pulled its head off. Then, they looted the hoard, at which stage the war party showed up. They weathered enemy fire using an insanely overpowered shield spell, chopped one single combatant in two, at which point the Saxons pissed themselves and went running back to the border."

"Yes, my Lord."

"And then, a short distance away, they stopped, for no apparent reason, to conduct some sort of unholy ritual using a boar and a local woodsman. The result of which is that they consumed both bodies and carried on their merry way towards Isca Dumnoniorum."

"That's what I found, my Lord."

"Well, that sounds like the sort of shitshow we would want Merlin to deal with, doesn't it?"

"It does, my Lord."

"And it is in no way suspicious or coincidental that such a team of cannibalistic super-wizards appear just at the moment we have no clear way to defend ourselves against them."

"It does seem rather sus, my Lord."

Arthur rubbed a hand across his face. The stories of Saxon incursions across the border were increasingly alarming. There was seemingly wholescale extermination of any Britons for the length and breadth of the border villages.

Only around Vortigern's castle was there any sign of the invasion being repelled, and it turned out whoever had managed that was a whole headache all on their own.

"Latest reports are that the Saxons are marching to Isca Dumnoniorum themselves, right?"

Bors nodded. "As far as we can make sense of things. It's what I would do if I were them."

"Okay. Two choices. We cross our fingers and hope that we have Saxon Invasion Force against Unknown Treasure Hunters Round 2 outside its walls. Maybe we get lucky, and they wipe each other out before we need to get involved. How are we feeling about that?"

"I think I'd like to think we could come up with more of a plan than 'let's see what happens,' to be honest, my Lord."

"Second choice, then, is that we gather up everyone that we think will follow us and hightail it out there to see what we can bring to proceedings."

"I do like a good hightailing."

"Agreed. So, if you could run and tell the King that's what we will be doing, that would be lovely."

"You mean the King who has expressively forbidden you to leave the castle?"

"That's the one. You might want to wait until I'm a few hours out so that he can't stop me. He will probably lose his shit over it, so best of luck."

"And you didn't want to do it in person, yourself, because?"

"Once and future king, card, dear boy."

"Fuck's sake."

CHAPTER 38 - IN WHICH YOU NEED TO UNDERSTAND THE BRITISH FIND THE WORD 'KNOCKERS' SO HILARIOUS, THIS CHAPTER IS BASICALLY 'CADDYSHACK'

On seeing the Knockers, my mind flew back to that dreary Cornish summer when Mum and Dad dragged Zizzie and me to visit a mine.

It had been a shocker of a holiday. The weather was vile - *plus ca change*. And *the plus* did never *change* - and I was hating everything about the enforced closeness of the family experience. To be fair, looking back, I recognised I was having equally as dreadful a time as my parents. But show me a teenager with empathy for others, and I'll call you a liar.

Nevertheless, there was something about exploring a hole in the ground that did precious little for any of us. And I could only think it was the inevitability of literal hand-to-hand combat between me and Zizzie that incentivised them to drag us out of the tent and into the rain.

When we'd pulled up to the entrance, the sight of rusted machinery and towering rock walls emerging from the drizzle did very little to lift my spirits as to the fun and japery that was about to commence.

"This is going to fucking suck."

My Mum managed that impressive parental feat of reaching back and slapping my legs from the car's front seat. "Don't swear in front of your sister. And it's not fucking going to suck."

We stepped out of the car, and I was immediately struck by the smell of earth and minerals that hung in the air, a caustic mix of dampness and something metallic. It was the kind of smell that absolutely inspired a teenage girl that this would be her kind of place.

With much sighing and eye-rolling, I'd been coaxed to join a small group of foreign tourists, and our guide, an older man with a greying beard and a voice that oozed, 'I hate each and every one of you with a passion and would gladly skin your still screaming body if I thought I'd get away with it', began his spiel.

He rattled off a host of historical facts and figures about the mine, its role in Cornwall's industrial past, and the sheer scale of the tunnels beneath our feet. My eyes glazed over as I did my best to tune him out and focused on the many ways I would make Mum and Dad suffer for this, wishing I were anywhere else.

After all the warnings about wandering off, floods and the unseen perils present in big holes in the ground, the group descended, following the guide's flashlight beam. Old Man Mine's patter was giving off big 'step out of line once, and I will

149

leave you down here' energy. To be honest, I remember being borderline as to whether, in my current mood, this was a dealbreaker.

But as we continued our descent, the temperature dropped noticeably. My t-shirt-clad arms prickled with goosebumps, and I wrapped them around myself, suddenly wishing I'd worn something warmer. The only light source was the guide's flashlight, which cast eerie shadows on the rocky walls.

I remember being genuinely unnerved by the experience.

Every step I took felt heavy, like I was trudging through solid air that resisted my intrusion. I couldn't even check the time on my watch to see how long we'd been down there, as it had long since given up on life in this lightless place.

Eventually, the walking downwards ended, and we reached a cavernous chamber where the guide explained the mining process in painstaking, somewhat punishing, detail.

Then, just when I thought I couldn't stand it anymore, he began recounting a local legend that took my mind off the darkness. As he spoke, his voice finally lost its bitter edge and took on an enthusiastic yet somewhat hushed tone.

"Now, we come to everyone's favourite bit of the tour. All you fine folks with a hankerin' for a tale of misery and toil, this is what you have been waiting for." Honestly, this was how he sounded: I imagined he practised at home. "I will tell you now of the heartless Knockers, and, should one of them take offence and pull me into the walls, you take this torch and run straight back the way we came, you hear me?"

He paused as we tried to take in what he'd just said. Then, he took a half-eaten Cornish pasty out of his pocket and brushed the lint off it. "But I always come prepared and hope my offering will be enough to keep them sweet on me. I've been doing this tour for thirty years, and I ain't never angered them yet. But there's always a first - and a last - time."

With great ceremony, he laid the pasty on a rock, adding a little thimble next to it into which he poured something from his hip flask. Satisfied that the creepiest little picnic in the world was now appropriately prepared, he turned to look back at us.

"Close your eyes, ladies and gentlemen, and listen to the echo of the distant moans of the earth. Hear the sounds she makes and the secrets she holds. Now, picture miners, gaunt and grim, walking by your side, with pickaxes in hand, trudging along these cursed passages, chasing after a mere glimmer of tin. It's a hard life—an unforgiving one. One mistake and the earth could fall on you. One wrong turn, and you would be lost forever. And just when you thought their luck couldn't get any worse, enter the Knockers!"

On that word, the volume of his voice raised and boomed around the chamber.

"These mischievous creatures, oh, they have a particular fondness for driving miners to the brink of madness. They'd scuttle about, their eerie laughter echoing through the tunnels, causing noises that would make a man question his own sanity. They'd imitate the sound of hammers striking metal, making the miners believe they were close to striking it rich. But alas, 'twas nothing but their wicked games!"

Here, he flicked off his torch, causing more than a few of us to scream in the blackness. Say what you like for crazy tour guides; they certainly have a sense of theatre.

"Knockers have a knack for extinguishing lantern flames and causing mine carts to derail. Can you imagine? A miner, his eyes heavy from exhaustion, his hands blackened from the toil, pushing a cart full of tin, only to have it career off course thanks to these malevolent imps."

I knew, intellectually, that the guide hadn't moved, but it was as if his breath was on the back of my neck.

"Hear my words, and hear them well. Beware the fae, ladies and gentlemen. For they wish you harm."

He went quiet for just long enough, then, for us to fear we were being left down there. I felt the sort of panic I'd never experienced before rise in my chest, and I'd grasped at my sister's hand, squeezing it tight. But then the torch switched back on, and his tone had shifted.

"But the Knockers aren't all devilry and doom. Sometimes, if a miner was kind enough to leave out a little treat – a corner of pasty or a sip of ale – they might earn the favour of these tricksters. Some say the Knockers guided miners to hidden veins of precious metals, though more often than not, it was just another cruel joke. Ah, my offering had been accepted. We'll make it back to the surface this day, ladies and gentlemen."

Our eyes turned to the rock, and it was true: the pasty was gone, and the thimble was empty.

"So there you have it: the Knockers, pint-sized tormentors of the Cornish mines. If you've got an itch to experience the thrill of being driven to the edge of your wits while chasing after meagre riches in the earth's bowels, well, you've missed your chance by a century or so. But fear not, for the echoes of their laughter still linger in these haunted tunnels."

As the guide spoke, I caught snippets of conversations among the other tourists. Some seemed genuinely intrigued by the legend, while others scoffed and dismissed it as mere folklore. I, on the other hand, was watching, right at the corner of the light, a small green and brown figure munching on a Cornish pasty.

It saw me looking and saluted back. I mean, I think now it was giving me the finger, but at the time, it felt like a moment of kinship entirely removed from my typical experience.

We'd exited shortly after, without me even nagging to go to the gift shop. I think Mum and Dad were quietly triumphant about the excursion's effect. I never told them about what I saw.

And I hadn't thought about it since.

***

Fucking Knockers. You need to get me out of here.

Due to his uncharacteristic silence during the journey underground, I'd almost forgotten Drynwyn was on my back. "What's the matter?"

Knockers can put out fire. I'm a flaming sword. Do your fucking sums and, whilst you're doing so, get me the fuck out of here.

"Calm down. They haven't even noticed we're here. Anyway, they're basically subterranean Smurfs. I'm fairly sure you could take them."

What's that? The sound of someone tempting fate in a faintly reckless fashion? Yep, you'd think I would have learned from a lifetime of my words coming back to smack me in the face. But, no. There I am, my mouth writing cheques my body is going to have to cash.

151

From my side, I heard Sǣþrȳð' take a sharp intake of breath, and I noticed that all the sounds of mining had stopped.

With a sense of crushing inevitability, I realised that thousands of pairs of luminous eyes were now staring my way.

CHAPTER 39 - IN WHICH WE WHACK SOME SMURFS

In the dim recesses of time, my school had needed me to undertake 'work experience' for a couple of weeks. As far as I could tell, the whole thing existed because our teachers were at the end of their tether and were looking to outsource the crowd control for a bit. True to form, I'd left it to the last minute to organise anything and ended up working in the local Nursery. I mention this because the way those Knockers are looking at me is faintly reminiscent of the cold, dead-eye regard of thirty toddlers sizing up the fresh meat.

In response to their sudden interest in us, Sæþrȳð started fumbling in the pouch at her waist, producing a pie of some sort. She broke it in two and then held it out to the little creatures. It seemed to me that unless she had some serious loaves-and-fishes shenanigans planned, this was unlikely to be sufficient.

One of the closer Knockers scampered forward towards Sæþrȳð. It grabbed one of the halves out of her hand and was instantly tackled to the floor by two or three others. In seconds, a swarm of these things were fighting over what was left of the crust.

I couldn't help but feel like I was stood helplessly by, watching Brody chumming the waters. We were going to need a bigger pie.

"Is that a good idea? It seems to be winding them up."

"You have to make an offering to the Knockers. Everyone knows that." Sæþrȳð seemed oddly unconcerned about the voracious way the rest of those in the cave were looking at the remaining half a pastry in her hand.

The words of that tour guide so many years ago (or was it so many years in the future? Time travel was tricky) echoed in my head: "Beware the fae, ladies and gentlemen. For they wish you harm."

Right now, I could well believe it. My hands filled up with Qi, and because you can never have access to enough instant death, I tried to draw Drynwyn.

Nope. Not going to happen. Not against Knockers.

"Quit it. Now is not the time for you to get murder-shy." But try as I might, it steadfastly refused to leave its scabbard. "Fuck's sake, Drynwyn, strap on a pair and get ready to whack some Smurfs."

But it remained silent. In a burst of cultivator-chivalry, I tried to push Sæþrȳð behind me, but she slapped my arm away. "Stop it. I'm telling you, there's nothing to be worried about. But they'll start getting cranky if you don't stop shouting and leaking Qi everywhere. I didn't bring you down here to fight them. They're friendly!"

And the Knockers immediately demonstrated their peaceful friendliness towards me by swarming forwards, a horde of tiny figures moving as one, their sharp teeth and malicious intent pretty damn obvious.

153

My fights so far had tended to be against things much bigger than me, so I was momentarily stumped as to how to approach it. The malevolent little things took advantage of my confusion, and, in no time, my legs were covered in nipping, biting imps slowly climbing their way up my body.

I swept downwards with both hands and managed to dislodge several of them, but the others grabbed a hold and clambered onto my shoulders.

Within seconds, I had Knockers crawling through my hair and nibbling on my ears.

There's a scene in The Mummy where a host of scarab beetles munch down on some treasure hunters. There's skittering, and chirruping, and chomping, and screaming. The whole thing had given me nightmares for weeks. If I even saw so much a ladybird, I ended up in a gibbering heap of PTSD.

Thus, I was so glad to have the opportunity to relieve that horror in real life. Like, absolutely cock-a-hoop about this state of affairs.

In my growing panic, I dropped into my artist's studio. My Qi was flowing around freely, including into my armour to top up its reservoirs of power, which dipped down each time one of these hell-sprites bit me.

I was aware of Sæþrȳð shouting near me, but the tone sounded more like she was pissed off rather than experiencing the agony of having the flesh stripped from her bones.

I needed to get these things off me. At the best of times, I was leery about being touched - apart from in very specific circumstances - so the feeling of thousands of little hands, feet and mouths all over me was proving to be a very specific ick.

Seemingly, in response to my growing horror, a single drop of my Qi solidified into a hard ball. Having this form inside me was a peculiar feeling- almost strange enough to block out the nips and bites now starting to cover my face. As soon as I focused on the ball, it began whizzing around my channels.

Think 'marble run' designed by Escher if you need a visual.

With each circuit the sphere completed, it was like the ball appeared to absorb more and more of my purple paint. As it grew, from frenzied ricochets around my channels, its movements became smoother and far more controlled.

Soon, its movement actually started to calm me down some. I was even able to fade out the teeth and claws digging into my flesh. Eventually, even the thought of being covered by them wasn't causing me quite so much terror.

Then, just when it seemed like the sphere couldn't grow any bigger and still move, at least not without splitting the channels, it screeched to a halt just behind my belly button and, with no further ado, exploded.

The words [Personal Space Invader technique created] floated across my vision. The effect was fairly dramatic.

A wave of purple Qi rolled out from an origin point in my stomach and threw all my attackers away and off my body; they crashed into the tunnel's walls to fall limply to the ground.

The wave also hit the wall, but - much to my surprise - rebounded back towards me, hitting the Knockers for a second time and flinging them against the opposite wall before returning to the spot above my belly button.

I waited to see if that ball of Qi would do anything else, but, no, it seemed quite happy to sit there with my paint continuing to move around it. It was spinning like an ornamental water feature.

After all the frenzied noise of the Knockers attack on me, I very much welcomed the silence that descended. It didn't last.

What the fuck was that?

"I don't know. I think I created another Qi technique."

You think? Fuck me. Isn't the whole point with you cultivators that you, you know, 'cultivate' shit? Shouldn't you know?

Sǣþrȳð was suddenly at my side. She was also not pleased. This was not my day for making new friends and influencing people.

"What was that? You could have hurt them!"

"I could have hurt them? Did you not see what was going on? They were trying to eat me!"

"Eat you? They were just being friendly. That's how Knockers say 'hello'. And now you've gone and upset them."

"Sǣþrȳð! They were attacking me."

"They're three apples high. You've just massacred an entire Saxon war party. I think you were probably going to be okay. They're very affectionate creatures when you get to know them."

The Knockers were pulling themselves upright now and casting somewhat reproachful glances my way.

"Let me get this straight. The reason why the village wouldn't evacuate when the Saxons were closing in was because you wanted to protect these fucking chaos goblins?"

"Don't be stupid. Knockers don't need the likes of us protecting them. They've mined these tunnels since the beginning of time and will keep doing so long after we've all gone." I thought back to the one I'd seen during my mine tour. She had a point. "They don't care if it's us or the Saxons living above ground."

The Knockers were watching us carefully now: I wasn't feeling bathed in the warm glow of their positive regard.

"So, why wouldn't you leave?"

Sǣþrȳð sighed in frustration. "Are you blind? Look at what they're doing."

I looked over the head of the glowering little imps at the walls they had been excavating. I saw seams of what I took to be tin running through the rock. The Knockers had been smashing it out of the walls into their little wheelbarrows. On the floor, discarded as rubbish, was something else. Little lumps of shining stone.

I felt a surge of Wulfnoð's memories for the first time in a while. And these memories said: 'gimmie!'

"Are those ...?"

"Finally, you get it. There's not many things in the world anyone here would risk facing a Saxon war party for. Those? Those are right up there."

What are you talking about? I felt the hilt of the sword tug to the left as if Drynwyn was trying to look over my shoulder. **Fuck me! Those are uncut mana stones. There's hundreds of the fuckers.**

And there were.

While cutting out their tin, the Knockers seemed to be uncovering and discarding hundreds upon hundreds of mana stones.

This, if the clamour from Drynwyn and the positive drooling from Wulfnoð's memories was anything to go by, felt like kind of a big deal.

CHAPTER 40 - IN WHICH THE PROPERTIES OF MANA STONES ARE REVEALED

After we got back above ground, thankfully avoiding any further molestation from 'affectionate' Knockers, Sǣþrȳð sat me down in the shack that doubled as her family home and took me through the history of the village.

It turned out one of her ancestors had literally stumbled into the tunnel entrance while hunting. After picking themselves up and dusting themselves down, they, in the wholly reckless manner of humans everywhere, decided to go for a stroll down the foreboding hole in the ground into which they had fallen.

After a few hours of pointless wandering, they were very lost and very hungry. Finding an appropriately inviting rock, they sat themselves down and unpacked some food. When they were subsequently set upon by a host of small, chittering creatures, they showed quite the sang froid in realising that it was their pie, rather than their lives, the monsters were after.

And, in that first moment of lunchbox sharing, humans and Knockers established a bond that ran right through until this very day.

"At least," snarked Sǣþrȳð, "until some unstoppable moron threw them around their cave when they were just excited to say hello."

I felt our recollections of the meeting below ground somewhat varied.

Going back to her story, she explained how, very quickly, her intrepid ancestors had realised that, in the process of their mining - an activity they carried out with an obsession only usually seen in unmarried women of a certain age and their collection of cats - the Knockers were creating giant waste heaps of incredibly valuable mana stones.

So, several bake sales later, the people of the village were in a position to establish a way of gaining regular access to one of the rarer materials in the world. They built a forge on top of the tunnel entrance, magnanimously offered to keep the tunnel clear of all those pesky shiny stones, and Robert was your mother's brother.

Scroll forward several generations, and all of the families in the village were sitting on a veritable mountain of precious materials, which helped make a bit more sense as to why they weren't so keen to take to the hills when the Saxons arrived.

"But, and I mean this with love, if mana stones are as valuable as you say .."

They are.

"They absolutely are," Sǣþrȳð added.

Wulfnoð's memories nodded enthusiastically.

"Okay. So, they're valuable. Got it. Then why are you living in a place that would make Victorian slumlords wince? Shouldn't you be Beverly Hillbillying it up in downtown St Ives?"

I felt Drynwyn turn in its scabbard to face Sǣþrȳð. **I'm sorry. I had the chance to let this fuckwit die, and I didn't take it. I blame myself.**

If she was somewhat startled to be directly addressed by a magical sword, Sǣþrȳð didn't show it. "You can't sell mana stones. Well, you can try, but it rarely works out well. Things got quite desperate a while back, and my grandfather took one to the city to try to sell. He was robbed and killed before he could so much as introduce himself."

"So, if you can't safety sell them, what makes them valuable?"

For fuck's sake. You're embarrassing me in front of the pretty lady.

"Do you truly not know?" Sǣþrȳð was looking at me in that faintly horrified way we all have when we need to explain to elderly relatives why they probably shouldn't use that word about their Asian neighbours.

"Explain it to me like an idiot."

I wonder how on earth she will make that stunning, imaginative leap.

***

So, I'm going to paraphrase here.

Mostly because I didn't really understand much of what was said, but I was damned if I was going to give Drynwyn an opportunity to take the piss anymore by asking questions. But also because I feel we know each other quite well at this stage, and you don't info dump on friends.

Here goes: mana stones are the Mega Mushrooms of cultivation.

There, how hard was that?

Okay, so it's a bit more complicated ...

First up, these things are great in rings and necklaces. Like a battery, you can fill them full of your Qi and draw down on them when needed. Drynwyn had smashed one like this in the dragon's hoard. Having experienced the sinking sensation of going cold Qi-turkey, I could see the benefit of having a bunch of quick recharge packs hanging around. Especially if they're refillable.

Secondly, if I used one of these when cycling my Qi, it turned out it would make the whole thing much more efficient. I didn't think I had been doing it long enough to understand the undoubted benefits here. From what Merlin had said, I knew that – if you ignored the cave training to reach **Ron** - I had been moving through things an awful lot quicker than other cultivators. So I could see if I'd been doing it for years, and progress was slow, I'd be grasping at anything that sped things up a little.

Thirdly, and I guessed this was the one that would have the most significant impact on me right now, cultivators could completely absorb these things, and it would give a permanent boost to Qi levels. I'd already felt the colossal impact on my available paint from inhaling the dragon's essence, so I could see the attraction of something like this. Mainly as it wouldn't involve battling with terrifying spirit beasts.

Looking at my inventory, I could see that I had looted a whole host of scrolls from the dragon's hoard that seemed to describe the techniques for absorbing mana stones. These would be worth my time looking through, apparently.

Or, you know, not. You doing a fucking bang-up job figuring it all out on your own. Who needs the distilled wisdom of ages, eh?

Finally, and this is why Sǣþrȳð's family had been so keen to settle on top of the mine, and why people would literally kill to get their hands on them, they could also be used by 'normal' people to improve their various attributes passively.

157

When in close proximity to a mana stone, such as if you happened to be hiding hundreds of them under your ramshackle floorboards, people who were not cultivators would experience heightened senses and awareness. This would aid them in their daily lives and endeavours, even improving their health and longevity if they spent long enough around them. They didn't gain any of the abilities that came with cultivation, but it was, basically, like having access to some superhuman fertiliser.

I told you I wasn't listening that carefully.

"Beocca's almost doubled in size since he came to live with me."

I waggled my eyebrows. "In both the places you can see and the ones you can't, right?"

"Are you sure you're a cultivator? You're nothing like I'd imagined one would be."

"In a good way?"

Sæþrȳð's expression suggested she did not mean in a good way.

"We will, of course, want to reward you for protecting us from the Saxons. Each family will donate from their private store of stones. You can either absorb them, or Beocca will happily set them in whatever form suits you."

Kill them all and take the lot.

"You realise you are speaking aloud, right?"

So? What's she fucking going to do about it? Trust me, if there's anywhere close to the amount of mana stones around here that she's implying, it will be worth it. I tell you what, if you're feeling squeamish, I'll do it for you.

Drynwyn started to slide out of its scabbard, and I pushed it firmly back. "No. That's not how this is going to go." I turned to Sæþrȳð, whose eyes were wide. "Ignore it."

"Ignore the talking, magical sword that's expressed a desire to kill us all? Sure. No problem. I have no follow-up questions or comments whatsoever."

***

After Drynwyn tried to slip out of its scabbard for the third or fourth time, I'd been forced to stick it in my inventory. This wasn't an ideal situation, as I could still hear it ranting, but at least I wasn't constantly on edge that there'd be genocide committed if I wasn't constantly on watch.

At the same time, I'd taken out any scrolls that were obviously about mana stones from my soul space and started working my way through them.

I very quickly encountered a problem which I'm going to describe as 'being thick as mince.' These were all written for someone who understood what cultivating was about and I . . . well, I had renamed my tier progression in honour of a series of books where I remained baffled a character called Luna Lovegood had not, at any stage, tried to blow a member of the faculty.

Essentially, I'm not sure I was the target audience for this.

In order to absorb a mana stone, you needed to use a whole bunch of techniques that the scroll's authors obviously expected the reader to understand. For someone like me, who'd cheat-coded their progress thus far, I was clearly missing lots of essential pieces of information. Like when someone at level 80 boosted you through a dungeon and, when you returned to do it yourself, you realised your level 10 Holy Smite wasn't quite the wrecking ball you'd thought it was.

Still, I hadn't made it this far successfully through life by recognising my limitations and failing to dive, unheedingly, straight into things.

Weren't you dead when Merlin found you?

So, I'd piled up my gifted mana stones - I couldn't help but feel the villagers had been slightly more generous than they needed to be after word of my sword's Thanos-like impulses got out - and prepared myself to absorb them.

As far as I could tell, I should be able to draw the coalesced Qi out of them in much the same way as I did with the wolf and the dragon. There were a bunch of health warnings around taking on too much at once, but, hey, I swallowed the Qi of a dragon. How much more could there be in one little stone?

I put my vision into 'Magic Eye' mode and inhaled deeply, seeking to draw in the Qi from the stones. Immediately, I felt a connection being made between my artist's studio and all of the shiny rocks in front of me. I extended my hands, and a luminous aura enveloped the stone on the top of the pile, creating a bridge between us from which the energies to flow.

So far, so good.

Then, using what the scrolls called the Qi Infusion Method - which I assumed meant 'suck the fucker in' - I tried to guide the influx of energies into my body. The first of the mana stones hummed in response, the heat of its power quite unlike anything I had experienced before.

As the first tendrils of its energy trickled into my channels, I realised I'd fucked up.

Like, replying-to-your-mate-highlighting-at-length-what-a-colossal-wanker-your-boss-is-and-ccing-in-the-whole-company, 'fucked up'. If you'd also critiqued his technique in the sack and ccd in his wife. And his kid's primary school teacher. With some home-made video.

That sort of 'fucked up.'

The mana within just one of these stones was boundless; its purity and intensity overwhelmed my senses to the extent that, despite knowing what a disaster I was courting, I couldn't make rational choices anymore.

I clenched my teeth so hard I felt them crack and sweat poured from me. My body quivered under the sudden onslaught of power I couldn't control, and my channels felt like they were once again being stretched and torn beyond their limits.

I thought it would be difficult to find you again, my dear. After all, you could have travelled anywhere since my, well, since my banishment. Imagine my delight, and no little consternation, therefore when I returned to see a giant throbbing column of Qi towering into the sky, no little distance from where I'd last seen you.

Pieces of shattered teeth were shook from my mouth as I tried to speak. The shaking became so profound I felt bones splinter, shards of white piercing out from skin.

Who could that be so recklessly channelling powers far in advance of their levels and capabilities, I thought to myself? Why, what are the chances it might be my apprentice who was last seen absorbing a dragon's Qi?

"Can't - talk - being - ripped - apart."

Yes, I imagine you are. Would you like me to help?

I couldn't answer. I wasn't sure there was much 'me' left to speak.

Because I helped before, and you were quite the bitch about it ...

I felt each and every one of my atoms start to split.

159

Fine. You can have this one on me, and then we can have a little talk about respect, cultivation and agreeing to fulfil our destiny.

Looking forward to it, Big M.

And I lost consciousness.

CHAPTER 41 - IN WHICH WE DIGRESS TO THE SIEGE OF ISCA DUMNONIORUM

"They stink, don't they?"

Anlaf looked at his brother and frowned. "They what?"

"The Saxons. They stink." Aldwine leant over the top of the stone walls and spat towards the gathering enemy.

"Can't say I've ever noticed. I mean, if you're looking for things to hate on them for, I'd probably go with all the raping and the pillaging. Bit weird to bring their smell into it, isn't it?"

"I said what I said, and I means what I means."

It wasn't the first time Anlaf had cause to curse his mother's last words: 'take care of your brother.' It wasn't always easy looking out for a half-wit.

The morning mist outside Isca Dumnoniorum clung to the ground like a shroud, obscuring much of the impending carnage that lurked beyond. It had been the worst kept secret in the land that the Saxon invasion would pass beneath what remained of these Roman walls. Anlaf and Aldwine were just two of the spearmen who had been funnelled into bolstering the settlement's defences.

But, thought Anlaf, there were worse places to be in the world than behind stone walls.

Like being the ones preparing to attack it.

The Saxons stood in grim silence on the plain before the town. Their war parties had started to arrive a few days earlier, and now, with them all apparently here, and arranged in one massive group, they made for a pretty intimidating sight.

It had been generations since anyone had seen the Saxons gather in anything like these numbers. Putting this many bodies in the field with Merlin around was a fool's errand. And the defenders, raised on stories of his power, were looking forward to seeing the legendary wizard in action.

Of course, they'd heard that the Saxons had their own practitioners in the lines arranged before them, but hey, they had Merlin. You didn't worry about fighting a guy packing a butter knife when you had a broadsword, a mace, eight crossbows and twelve rabid cave bears.

Such was the upbeat mood amongst the defenders, that bets were running on what he would turn them into when he arrived: 'puddles of white-hot goo' was currently the odds-on favourite. But 'turtles' was running a close second. No one could quite explain why.

With no apparent reason behind it, across the whole army, there were many versions of the following conversation taking place: "It's not like he has a history of reptile-based transformations, is it? Why would anyone bet on that? It sounds like someone might be in the know; maybe one of Arthur's boys has had a chat and is trying to pull a fast one. So, I stuck everything I own on it." Either way, there was a lot of money on the line when he finally showed up.

Anlaf watched the Saxons' preparations with a critical eye.

'Fair play to them,' he thought, 'they were fronting up as if this wasn't a foregone conclusion.'

He turned back to his brother, who had returned to mining for gold with a finger embedded up his nose. "You remember the plan?"

Aldwine paused his prospecting and consumed what he had found with relish. "Sure. I stick anyone who tries to climb over this bit of wall with my spear."

"And?"

"And I don't fall down, or the stinking Saxons will kill me."

"Again with the stinking?"

"I saids what I said."

Anlaf shrugged and went back to watching the Saxon preparations. He figured when they got enough of a head of steam up, they would charge and try to climb the section a little way down from their bit. The stone was pretty patchy down there, and anyone determined enough, and with a long enough ladder, would have a good chance of finding a way up it.

The section the brothers were defending would make a pretty uninspiring focal point for an attack, but it offered a good view of the assault for the moment Merlin showed up and unleashed hell. Or created an impromptu aquarium. One of the two.

Having sensibly spread his bets across all options, all in all, Anlaf felt today would be a good day.

He noticed movement and nudged his brother to draw Aldwine's attention. "Oh, here we go. They're going to try the walls."

One of the Saxon war parties had split away from the others and were obviously getting themselves psyched up for a charge. Their chieftain, a massive bearded figure, raised his sword high and shouted something fairly uncomplimentary about Arthur's parentage.

Aldwine shuffled uncomfortably. "No need for that. Don't need to bring the Queen Igraine into it. Bit classless that."

"Seriously?"

"What? I always liked Queen Igraine. She gave me a biscuit once."

"What are you talking about? You've never met her."

"I did, too! The Queen came to my naming day party, and Prince Arthur was there too and she gave me a biscuit and told me I was the bestest boy in the whole world. And then they flew away on a unicorn."

Anlaf closed his eyes momentarily and undertook his customary five count before answering. "You're absolutely right. I forgot about that that. Lovely woman, Queen Igraine."

That seemed to satisfy Aldwine, and he went back to gazing absently at the Saxon horde.

In response to the Chieftain's declaration, the war party shouted back, and, with a roar that echoed through the mist, they surged forward as a single entity, a living avalanche.

Anlaf could see the defenders perched atop the fragmented wall, watching as the enemy advanced. He could see their fingers tighten around spears and bows and knew that unease was sweeping through their ranks.

Given a choice, you always wanted the high ground, but no one liked to stand there and wait for the enemy to come into range.

At just the right moment, the first volley of arrows took flight, a lethal cloud that darkened the sky. At least, that's how Anlaf assumed the chronicles would record it. To his eye, it was fired a touch early - nerves, he thought - and was a more gentle sprinkling of pain than anything especially lethal. You didn't dump your load too early in the piece, and, anyway, arrows were expensive. This wouldn't be the only charge of the day, and you didn't want an empty quiver when things really hotted up.

Nevertheless, the sound of wood striking wood was like a concussive drumbeat. Saxon warriors stumbled, their screams swallowed by the shouts and jeers from those above them. But the gaps in their ranks were swiftly filled by those who pressed forward, driven by a hunger for revenge.

"Right, now we'll see how much they fancy it. What do you reckon, any of them reach the top?" The brothers watched as ladders were propped against the least well-maintained wall sections.

Aldwine considered. "Nah, not this time. Looks a bit half-hearted to me."

To be fair, the clash near the top of the ladders was pretty brutal, a maelstrom of clashing steel, splintered wood, and anguished cries. Shields met shields, and the impact of men being thrown from the top of the wall was like a thunderclap reverberating through the bones of those below.

Spears rose and fell, driven by the primal instinct to survive and conquer. Blood mingled with the dust beneath boots, and flowed down the walls in long streaks.

"Yeah," Anlaf nodded, "all a bit tentative, ain't it? You can't fanny about like that. Get to the top and fuck shit up."

Aldwine gasped and covered his ears. "You said a naughty word. I'm telling."

His brother sighed and restarted a five count.

Amidst the chaos, heroes amongst the Saxons emerged, their voices like beacons in the storm. Commands were shouted, strategies attempting to be carved from the chaos. But it wasn't to be. The defenders fought with a clinical resolve, determined to hold the top of the wall and protect their homes from the encroaching tide of violence.

"Oh, hang on. He's looking a bit lively." Aldwine was pointing excitedly at the Saxon chieftain who, in the midst of the fray, had reached the top of a ladder and was carving a path of destruction amongst the British spears. He was a force of nature. With each swing of his blade, he carved through spearmen, his path marked by fallen bodies.

Anlaf nodded approvingly. "Yeah, got to hand it to him, he's not fucking about." He ignored his brother's gasp of horror. "Mind you, unless he gets some back up soon he's going to be - ah, that's a shame. You hate to see it."

Three defenders had isolated the chieftain and he fell from the wall, their spears thrust through him.

"Think that will be it for a bit?"

Anlaf nodded in agreement. "Yeah, they'll need to rethink that attack formation a bit. You don't want to leave the ones who can handle themselves exposed like that. Rookie error. Although -"

Both brothers glanced at each other as a single figure walked towards their part of the wall. He was wearing robes and a pointy hat.

163

"What's this stinker doing?"

Anlaf shrugged. "No idea. But it looks like there's a bunch of them doing the same thing."

Across each length of the wall for as far as Anlaf could see, one of these oddly dresses figures was now standing. A few archers made half-hearted efforts to shoot towards them, but the range was too far.

They started to, for want of a better word, 'wriggle' their fingers towards the defences.

Anlaf suddenly had a terrible feeling. "Aldwine, mate, we just need to step back a bit."

"What? Why? I want to watch!"

"I just think we might -"

And then the fireballs struck.

CHAPTER 42 - IN WHICH WE APPROACH ALDERAAN. I MEAN ... NO, YOU GET IT, RIGHT?

And she will be waking up right about ... now. As much as I wanted to keep my eyes closed so that I didn't have to deal with Merlin being insufferably correct, I did not quite have that amount of churl in me. He had just stopped me from ripping myself apart through reckless pig-headedness. Again. He was owed a win.

Oh, thank the gods, you're awake. It's fucking Merlin! Merlin is right here. You need to get up and run!

I don't know if you've ever experienced having competing intrusive voices in your head - if so, welcome to our support group! Please collect your SSRIs at the door. I recommend the Paroxetine - but it's not ideal to experience arguing disembodied voices as you wake up with a concussion.

How are you feeling, my dear?

It's Merlin! Didn't you fucking hear me! What are you waiting for? Leg it!

"I'm struggling a bit, to tell the truth, Big M. Drynywyn, can you take a breath and stop screaming? My head feels like it's about to break in half as it is. All this noise is a lot to process."

Ah, so it is Drynwyn. I thought I could taste the residue of that degenerate sword somewhere. It was in the hoard, I presume? A significant find! Well done. I imagine Rhyddrech was somewhat surprised to finally come up against something that hitting with a sword or impaling it... in another fashion couldn't solve?

Keep his name out of your mouth, you fucking lunatic. I saw what you did to those people at the river Glein. They were retreating, and you -

I think that's quite enough from it for now.

And there was silence. And She saw that it was good.

"How did you do that? If I'd known it had an off-switch, things might have been an awful lot smoother." I felt a brief, entirely slutty, pang thinking of the beautiful, now headless, woodcutter. But then, without the sword's particular brand of unhinged aggression, I probably would not have made it out of the hoard at all. "Well, maybe not, actually."

Not so much an 'off-switch; more a temporary mute button. I can let you hear it again if you want? There was a brief pause. *Although, we might be better letting it burn off a bit of steam first. It has quite the mouth on it and seems to be fairly unhappy with you. I remember a time when enchanted swords were more respectful. Speaking of which ...*

I imagined the Pinteresque pause was left there for my grovelled apology. Ah, poor Merlin. You know me so little.

I lay in silence for a few minutes, enjoying the peace and quiet.

Do you have anything you want to say to me, my dear?

"Sure. I'm glad you've seen the error of your ways, are ready to apologise and have chosen to come back. So, what did you learn from your time-out?"

My time-out?!?

"Yes. We go on the naughty step when we forget to use our kind words, don't we, mate? Classic behaviour management technique."

You banished me to the place that exists between realities! It was certainly not the naughty step. Do you have any idea how dangerous that could have been?

"Not really. The whole acting-without-any-real-knowledge-about-consequences thing is kind of my vibe right now. So, did you properly think about what you did? Are you going to do better moving forward?"

This conversation is not proceeding in the direction I was anticipating.

"You've missed this, haven't you?"

Like you would not believe.

***

So, it turns out the whole 'absorbing mana stones' thing is something for MUCH later in my cultivation journey. With my literal hours of cultivation experience, I shouldn't even have been able to make a connection with them, much less start to pull in their Qi.

What can I say? I've always been an earlier bloomer.

This was a touch disappointing. However, the massive pile of precious rocks I now held in my soul space would not be going to waste.

Firstly, as Beocca was adept at quickly knocking out rings, bracelets, earrings and necklaces, I was soon positively jingling with mana stone drip. Under Merlin's careful guidance, I adjusted the flow of my Qi so that it cycled through all the new jewellery, and these backup batteries started filling up in no time.

There's something to be said for subtlety and moderation in all things, my dear. Even at the height of my power, I might only wear one mana stone ring. Do you think you need to be this ostentatious?

I fanned my face in the manner of a Southern belle. "Why, Mr Merlin. A lady never goes anywhere without her pretty things."

Sæþrýð couldn't decide if she was horrified or, I thought, a touch jealous. "You do realise you will be attacked as soon as anyone sees you? People lose their minds when they encounter mana stones."

Initially, I had asked Beocca if he would fashion me a gauntlet so that I could have the stones inset into the knuckles. Merlin vetoed that with a haste I felt was unseemly.

But, quite aside from the battery power of my new shinies, Merlin was clear that just holding these things in such a high number in my inventory would have significant benefits.

We're going to need every advantage we can get moving forward. I don't mind sharing that you are exceeding my expectations for someone with such a poor grounding in the art.

"You can stop with the flattery, mate. This **Ron** ain't sleeping with you."

Quite. But with the progress you have made thus far -

"Did I tell you I created a new battle technique? All on my own?"

You have mentioned that, yes. Once or twice. As I was saying -

"Had you created two brand new techniques when you'd only been cultivating a few days? I can't remember what you said before."

Yes. You are quite the powerhouse. All hail, Morgan, our new lady and master. May her rule be benevolent and the fact she has no idea what she is doing not result in either her untimely demise or the implosion of the universe.

"It sounds like someone might have picked up a portion of sass in the world between realities."

Indeed. As I was saying, the passive improvements these stones will make to your senses and the quality of your cycling will be immeasurable. I do not mind sharing that, with enough work, I would expect you to reach the Arcane Fusion Tier –

"Harry."

There was a pause and I SWEAR I felt something within him die.

*Yes. **Harry**. With the passive power of these stones that tier may well be reasonably achievable in our time frame. I cannot tell you how important that would be in being able to draw on enough power to maintain the timeline.*

It didn't go unnoticed that every time the Big M wanted to get me back on track, Zizzie's name appeared in his mouth. I wasn't wild about that. "Guys, look, I've got it. Stones be good. I'll wear all this stuff now to fill it up and then stick it in storage. The earrings Beocca made are subtle enough to have in all the time, and the rest I'll just equip when I need it. Or when any of them needs filling up. That sound okay?"

That ... that actually sounds sensible. Are you sure you are feeling quite yourself?

***

Despite Sæþrȳð's protestations that the stones were gifts, I'd forced on her several bags of my looted gold. The village was a shithole even before I blew a giant crater in the ground. Following the death of most of their men with the fyrd, there would need to be some changes if the people left here were going to flourish. Mana stones were all well and good, but proper housing and a regular supply of food were what was going to be needed moving forward.

Ignoring Merlin's palpable frustration, I'd offered to hang around, help them with the clear-up, and start the rebuild. But, much to my chagrin, I'd pretty much been shooed out of town. Apparently, cultivators who are audibly conversing with Merlin, in possession of genocidal swords, and who have single-handedly wiped out Saxon war bands are not the ideal house guests.

Before we left, Merlin showed me how to set the village as one of my fast travel destinations on the appropriate page of my artist's studio, and I promised to pop in now and again to make sure things were going okay.

Sæþrȳð and Beocca had exchanged a look at that. "Sure. We'll warn the Knockers. No rush, though, right? You must have important things to be doing."

I'd heard warmer 'see you again soons' in my time, but I'd take it.

With a muted Drynwyn strapped to my back - *hmmm, he still seems quite angry. Maybe another day or two for him to simmer down?* - my mana stone earrings rapidly filling with Qi and with Merlin critiquing everything from my stride length, to my breathing rate, to the way I scanned the landscape, I made my merry way inland.

We'd been travelling for a few hours (or eighteen ways-in-which-I-was-not-being-a-proper-cultivator, which seemed to be an equally regular way to mark the time in Merlin's world) when the steady deluge of criticism - *valuable advice, my dear* - suddenly stopped.

167

"You okay, mate? You've not bitched about the way I'm swinging my arms for a good few minutes."

Something terrible has happened.

I opened my mouth to quip, but the tone of his voice shook me. "How do you mean?"

I'm not sure. But, even in my current reduced state, I can feel significant uses of Qi nearby. It's how I was able to find you after my ... no, I will not be calling it a 'time-out'.

"You mean there's a cultivator nearby?"

No. I mean, there are many cultivators nearby, and they've just completed a massive casting. Even now, I am still feeling the aftershock.

"I'm getting a real 'millions of voices suddenly cried out in terror and were suddenly silenced' vibe here, Obi-Wan."

That Merlin did not immediately answer was not reassuring. "Okay, Big M, I hear you. Big Qi boom nearby. Which way should we be heading - towards it or in the other direction?"

As much as I am loathe to put you, untested, in proximity to so much power, I need to understand what has occurred. We must reach Isca Dumnoniorum as soon as possible.

CHAPTER 43 - IN WHICH ARTHUR DECIDES TO KILL SOME FUCKING SAXONS

"All I'm saying is that there're two ways of looking at the situation, and you are picking the single most negative interpretation."

As they were riding in single file, Bors had been monologuing to the back of Arthur's head for some time. "Could we have reached Isca Dumnoniorum faster if you hadn't wanted to spend an evening with the blonde with the long legs? For sure. No argument there. You're bang to rights on that one. We were delayed at least half a day by the time we'd rescued you and paid off her father."

They'd reached the end of the easily passable parts of the trail, and Arthur pulled on Llamrei's reigns to bring her to a halt. Bors took the opportunity to kick his horse forward so that he sat alongside the prince. One glance at his face showed that his mood had not improved.

"But this is where I think you need to look at things differently. Think about it. If it weren't for your nighttime dalliance, we'd have been behind Isca's walls when the attack happened."

"Do you think that helps, Bors?"

"It should do, yes, my Lord. Because - and take it as read that I'm speaking with all due respect, yada yada yada - in your current wallowing pit of self-recrimination, you seem to be forgetting that those walls simply aren't there anymore. Like, at all. Like, they've been blasted out of this realm of existence."

Arthur turned and met Bors' eyes. "What's your point?"

"You seem to think us being there might have made some sort of difference. What I'm telling you is that your cock is the only reason we're all still alive." Arthur didn't answer, so Bors pressed on. "They blew the place out of existence, my Lord. None of us have seen anything like it. Not since Merlin last took to the field. If we'd rocked up on schedule, we'd have been just two hundred more corpses amongst the ash."

"But at least we'd have fallen with my people!" Arthur fired back with a snarl.

"For fuck's sake, my Lord! You need to snap out of it and stop moping around. At the time, were any of us happy with the delay? Of course not. We were riding to save Isca from the Saxons! None of us signed up to sit and play dice outside a haybarn whilst you plucked some farmer's daughter. But we all saw what was left of the town, and not one of us doubts we're only alive because we were late. If you're saying you're keen to spend time wishing you'd have died alongside them rather than plotting how to hit the bastards back then, with all due respect, can you fucking give up command and let someone with a working set of balls take over?"

169

Bors and Arthur momentarily looked at each other before turning to regard the diminutive knight who had spoken.

"Balin. That was ... unusually blunt for you." Arthur's voice was tight.

"I know, my Lord, and I'm sorry to speak out of turn. But we've been picking our way through Saxon sentries for a while now like a maiden at her first orgy, and I think I speak for most of the boys when I say, by your leave, I'd quite like to off a few of the fuckers with extreme prejudice. You know? To relieve some tension."

Arthur turned away from the smallest of his men – four feet tall If he was an inch - and looked out into the distance. He could still see the smoke climbing from what was left of the settlement he had sworn on his honour to protect.

Isca Dumnoniorum. Gone.

How many of his and Uther's schemes had been built around having that fortress as a bulwark unto which to retreat? Nearly every plan they'd devised had the Saxons razing the borderlands as much as they liked, but then their rising tide would crash against Isca's solid walls and fade away to nothing.

That had been British military doctrine for generations.

Well, that strategy was going to need a rework.

He still struggled to comprehend the scale of the devastation inflicted by the Saxon wizards. Every section of the stone walls had been destroyed, taking the majority of the town within with them when they . . . melted. If there had been any survivors after whatever spell had been cast, none remained by the time Arthur's warband had ridden through the smoking ruins.

He knew - of course he did - how lucky they were to have been delayed. Had they made the expected progress, Uther's kingdom would now be without both its heir and its two hundred, most storied warriors. With that single fiery blow, the war would have been over in a stroke.

Of course. It may still be if he didn't find a way to slow the pace of the Saxon invasion.

"Sir, if I may -" Bors began.

"It's fine. He hasn't said anything the rest of you aren't thinking. Sir Balin, you are absolutely right." Arthur raised his voice so that everyone around him could make out his words. "He's right, and I apologise to all of you. This isn't the time to dwell on personal failings. I'm being self-indulgent, and this isn't time for that. It isn't even the time to honour our fallen people, as much as I might wish it were. No. It is not yet time for that. And do you know why? Because it is time for something else. What is it time for, boys?"

Balin and Bors exchanged a glance. "Is it time to kill some fucking Saxons, sir?"

Arthur drew his sword. "It is absolutely time to kill some fucking Saxons."

***

It was child's play for Arthur's war band to begin isolating Saxons around the fringes of their advance. I mean, obviously it wasn't. Any child playing a jolly game of vicious guerrilla warfare needs to spend more time playing football in the garden with an appropriate adult. Instead, let us say it was a straightforward thing to achieve.

Nevertheless, however we might choose to describe it, over the next few days, there were quite a lot of fucking Saxons killed as they meandered their way inland.

In many ways, the Saxons had become victims of their own success in having such big numbers of soldiers. There were so many different war parties all mixed together that Arthur's men were able to slip in and out of sentries with ease -

particularly once they'd looted a number of cooling corpses and availed themselves of some pretty snazzy disguises.

This wouldn't have been too disastrous - in the grand scheme of things, it was only a few hundred very capable warriors picking off people at the edges of a massive, advancing column - had the leadership of the Saxons been able to agree on any sort of coordinated response.

However, just as having lots of little war parties, all with their own commander, had been a tactical masterstroke in causing efficient chaos along and across the British border, it was now an administrative nightmare since all of these commanders had come together after the fall of Isca.

When everyone is in charge, no one is.

And when no one is in charge, no one can agree on how best to stop the constant predations on their numbers. Indeed, such was the level of distrust, back-biting and paranoia that had settled over the leadership of the army that four days after the destruction of Isca, the invasion had simply ground to a halt near the port of Topsham.

"Team meeting. Now." Arthur whispered as he walked past each of his men's fires in the growing gloom. Bors waited several beats, yawned, and excused himself from his new Saxon friends. "I'll be right back, lads. Need to water the daisies."

No eyes followed him to the edge of the camp - why would they? - and in moments, he and all the others who had made similar excuses were lost to the dark.

It was just a short walk into the woods until the small group of soldiers directing Operation Stab-as-many-of-the-fuckers-as-you-can-in-the-dark had reconvened.

Arthur had learned the art of codenames from Merlin.

"Any trouble?" Balin had risen in status since his motivational talk to Arthur a few days earlier.

"Nah. As best as I can tell, they've got so many spears, the higher-ups just aren't arsed about looking into all those going missing. The men on the ground are getting pretty pissed about it, though. Morale is low. But it's all just 'acceptable losses' at the moment. They're pretending its desertions, not that anyone believes it."

"So, we keep killing them. Maybe crucify a few of them. Hard to spin that as anything other than a pretty determined form of desertion. Eventually, they'll need to do something about us. They've stopped advancing, after all. That's got to mean something." Balin's words got approving nods from the other knights.

"No. The halt is not to do with us. They're just figuring out a pecking order. Once King Shit of Turd Town floats to the top, they'll be off and marching again. And it'll be different. With someone calling the shots, they'll tighten the whole thing up, and we'll start losing people." Arthur's tone cut through and stilled the others. "We've probably got one more day and night of working like this, and then we'll have to cut and run to Uther."

Bors and Arthur had discussed how this meeting would go, and it was time for him to do his part. "So how do make best use of the time we have left, my Lord?"

"Glad you asked, Sir Bors. We're going to catch ourselves a wizard."

CHAPTER 44 - IN WHICH WE SUSPECT A SNEAKY EFFORT TO ACCELERATE TO 88MPH

I'd known, intellectually, that the sight that would greet us at Isca Dumnoniorum was unlikely to be a good one. Merlin had gone all quiet the closer we'd come to our destination, and that hardly suggested he was expecting positive news.

So, with the Big M in an unusually contemplative mood, and with Drynwyn continuing to stew in its muted state, it was really the first time I'd had proper headspace to myself since I'd been portalled here.

I took the opportunity to drop in and out of my artist's studio as we walked, trying to smooth out some of the adjustments to my cycling technique that Merlin had 'suggested' before he went and got all maudlin on me.

As much as it hurt me to say, it seemed like he might have had a few points. Yes, things were working for me, but I was doing it all in a pretty cackhanded way. No one would disagree that my Qi was smoothly cycling around my body, but without all the cheating I'd done with the dragon essence, Merlin rewiring my channels on the fly, and now a shedload of mana stones, it was obvious that my technique was shambles.

My channels - post dragon - were Brazillian smooth, meaning there was simply no resistance for my paint as it flowed around. However, had there been even a touch of friction - and Merlin had indicated, even for experienced cultivators, it was customary for there to remain significant blockages for decades - the path of my Qi would have been, at best, sluggish.

I'd never, after that first time, really had to struggle to push my energy around me-as-Vitruvian-man, so I hadn't developed any good habits. The time spent training in the cave had made me a more effective cultivator than most other humans, but that was just the first step on a fucking mahusive journey.

Even with all the lucky breaks I'd received, I still wasn't at a level where a giant man with a wild beard would show up at my door and whisk me away on his motorbike. That was pretty humbling.

Full disclosure, something very similar to that happened on my twentieth birthday. And I suppose it did lead to warts of a different type.

My state of being objectively quite shit in the grand scheme of things reminded me of when I absolutely nailed my first attempt at a still life in Mrs Morrison's Art GCSE class. She was so bowled over that a) anyone had actually stopped flicking paint at each other long enough to draw something and b) that my effort wasn't utterly rancid, that she'd given me a pass all year.

I still can't draw bananas for toffee.

There was a reason why people spent decades practising to get this cultivation lark just right, and just because I'd bumbled my way through it so far was no reason to ignore all the useful - if somewhat archly delivered - advice as to how I could improve.

I cannot tell you what a triumphal moment of self-growth admitting that is for me. I kind of felt it should have been rewarded with some sort of celebratory *ding* from whatever passed for a System in this version of the multiverse.

That my only acknowledgement was a gull shitting on my head kind of felt a little on the nose ...

Checking Merlin wasn't paying too much attention, I did a quick [Personal Space Invader] to force the sticky whiteness out of my hair (and that's not the first time I've ever thought that sentence, I'm afraid).

Newly birdshit free, I continued wombling on my way, fundamentally aware that my life was the equivalent of blasting around Arthurian England in a snazzy, souped-up Ferrari with the engine of a Reliant Robin under the bonnet.

If my disastrous effort in following the instructions of the looted scrolls had taught me anything, it was that there were significant gaps in my education. I didn't know what I didn't know. This made me really vulnerable to the kind of misjudgements that were pretty much my calling card. Kind of like trying to watch The Last Jedi without having seen any of the others and thus being denied the opportunity to build up decades' worth of resentment and unrealistic expectations.

Thus, pressing cleaning ritual moments aside, I took advantage of the unusual silence to work on my breathing and get my mind into the right state to reflect on what I was doing.

So, I was in a decent frame of mind when, several hours later, we crested a hill and looked down on Hell.

It won't surprise you to know that I'm a big John Martin fan. His paintings fully embody all those themes of doom and despair, which - shock horror - had been very much my thing once upon a time. If you've never seen his work, there's one particular one, *Pandemonium*, which he based on the bit in 'Paradise Lost' when Satan is talking to the devils outside the demonic palace they'd just constructed. As you can imagine, it's pretty heavy on the fire and brimstone and just *bodes*.

Looking down at the remains of Isca Dumnoniorum, I couldn't help but feel Martin had slackened off a little in his depiction of sparse, gothic horror.

"What could have done this?"

Me.

Merlin did not need a face for me to read his expression.

I walked down the hill, getting as close to the smoking ruin as the heat would allow. That I needed to replace substantial energy in my Qi armour to get even this close should tell you all you need to know. I guess if you looked hard enough, you could still make out the lines where the stone walls used to be. But you'd have needed to be really committed to the effort. And comfortable no longer having eyebrows.

What I'm saying is that what was left of the settlement looked like a blancmange to which someone had taken a blowtorch.

That's it. That's the simile.

I don't have much else to say about it all.

It was stark as fuck.

"You've done things like this?"

173

I have. Many times.

"Does that mean the Saxons have someone as strong as you?"

No. This was the work of thirty or forty cultivators working in concert. They formed a ring outside the town and combined their Qi in a ritual I don't think I recognise. And even then, I can feel ... someone adding significant power from the outside. This cost those present almost all of their accumulated reserves and then some. I can feel that many of them did not survive the casting.

"So why do it - if it's cost them so much?"

They are making a point, my dear. When you are waggling your dick in the air, you don't worry about some of the hairs you pull out. I'm sorry. That was a horrible metaphor.

I looked at the wasteland of ash. "All of this was just to make a point?"

Yes. It's a surprisingly effective tactic. If I was Uther, I'd be seriously considering whether to summer in Frankia this year.

"Do you think anyone made it out alive?"

I honestly don't see how.

I had to agree. Isca was a fiery tomb.

We stood looking at the smouldering rock for some time. It didn't feel there was much else to talk about.

Then, with a strange tone in his voice, Merlin suddenly became chatty. *This is going to be an odd question, but in your own time period, did you ever visit Isca Dumnoniorum?*

I pulled a face. "Mate, I don't think what's left of this place is going to be standing next week, let alone in fifteen hundred years' time ..."

Exactly. I'm testing out a theory I dislike very much, indeed.

I rolled my eyes and was about to answer in the negative, but then a memory stirred.

I could see myself, first as a teenager and then as a young adult ten years later, walking the stone walls of Exeter. I remember being told that they had existed since the Roman times. For such a little shit, I had been quite taken by the sense of timelessness that demonstrated. Certainly, enough to bring a boyfriend back in tow years later.

But even as I remembered it, the memory sparked, flared and became entirely indistinct. It was still there if I thought hard enough about it, but more like it was a dream I was half-remembering. Certainly, it wasn't as firm a memory as it was before.

"I think so. But ... it's weird. It's like it didn't really happen. If I concentrate too much on it, it fades out."

Shit. It is as I feared.

"What?"

This shouldn't have happened.

I didn't have to ask him what 'this' was.

There shouldn't be any Saxon wizards, and there shouldn't be enough Qi available for them to cast this spell. Isca Dumnoniorum should still be stood in your own time. Someone is changing history.

"So what changed?"

I died.

"Help me out, Big M. How does you dying lead to the Great Fire of Exeter?"

At my tier level . . .

He paused to give me the chance to add "at **Snape**" but in a heroic act of self-development, I restrained myself (seriously, System. Where is my *ding?*).

At my tier level, every time I breathed, I pulled in as much Qi as the British Isles could easily maintain. As a general rule, I tried not to drink so deeply as to destroy all the magical flora or fauna, but the drain was still significant enough that no other cultivators could thrive. I paused my own progress a few times over the years to try and train apprentices but, well, they were all essentially useless, and I became bored.

"So you fed them to Vortigern's dragon."

So I fed them to Vortigern's dragon. Merlin agreed.

"But with you dead, the Qi is available, and, what, the Saxons have grabbed it?"

Yes, but that's not the most pressing question.

"Which is?"

I'm not convinced Arthur knows I am dead yet. So how have the Saxons managed to steal a march with their cultivating?

"Good point, well made."

Of course, I'm Merlin. But now, here's the big question, and it's based on some big assumptions, but we shall accept each of them for now. Let's assume whoever is training the Saxons knew the exact moment I died. Thus, therefore, let's assume they had something to do with it. And let's not even get into what achieving such a thing would need. If we take all that to be accurate, I think we can assume it's not just the future of the walls of Isca Dumnoniorum they are looking change.

Merlin was silent for a few seconds; I didn't like to interrupt him. *Describe your sister to me, my dear.*

I opened my mouth . . . and nothing came out. I could see her, but I also couldn't. There was an absolute place she had in the universe, and there was also an aura around her sucking her away.

And the worse thing was, I couldn't even feel panic about it. Because what was a panicking about? That someone who had never existed, did not exist?

Fuck.

"Merlin, mate?"

Yes, my dear?

"We need to find who is doing this and end them."

For once, my dear, we are in complete agreement.

175

CHAPTER 45 - IN WHICH, IN RESPECT FOR THE FALLEN, THERE IS ONLY ONE DICK JOKE.

Melehan's hands were shaking.

He stared at them in the flickering light of the campfire. They did not even feel like his anymore. They had been doing this, without pause, for days now. Ever since ...

No more of that. He stood, smoothing down his robes and tucking his hands under his armpits, pressing them tight to stop the movement.

None of those around the fire marked his hurried departure from their company. The warriors milling around the camp opened a wide gap to let him through as he walked away, as if none were willing to be too close to him.

As if shame were somehow contagious.

It didn't help, but he knew it was just not him who was being shunned in this manner. It was the same for any of the wizards that had survived the ritual at Isca.

Or what used to be Isca.

As he walked, Melehan was once again struck by how hard he was taking that summary rejection by the others in the army. He had never been an especially gregarious soul, but during the invasion, he had come to enjoy the camaraderie of the warriors around their campfires. He had been surprised at how much he welcomed their company and their easy acceptance of him as one of their own.

Now, more than ever, he needed that normality, and it was being withheld from him.

Ever since the conflagration at Isca, the rest of the army treated the wizards with something akin to horror. Nobody who had witnessed the aftermath or heard the shrieks and pleas of those within were comfortable sharing a meal with the architects of that infernal blaze.

And that included those who had cast it.

They'd all intellectually understood the plan. Of course they had. Had they not practised their role in the casting day after day on the march through the countryside? The ritual needed each of them to complete, and hold, the High King's spell in precisely the right way. It was an intricate casting - far ahead of what any of them could summon on their own - and needed extensive focus.

But there was a big difference between the theory and seeing all their rehearsals in full production.

What had been an interesting Qi exercise for the last few weeks had become appallingly real for each and every one of them.

The shaking of Melehan's hands became so intense he held them out in front of him - would they ever return to normal? - before clasping them tightly to his chest to try to bring them under control.

He could still hear them. The people inside the walls. The moment when they had recognised that no help was on the way, that there was no escape, had been the worst of his life.

The shouts and screams had become wails, and he knew it had broken him. As soon as he heard that animalistic noise, his Qi had lurched wildly out of his control. His cycling had abruptly halted, snapping him out of his connection with the other cultivators. As that happened, the eyes of the cultivator beside him widened, recognising her need to channel the excess energy that Melehan was no longer holding. It had proved too much for her - did he even know her name? - and she had exploded, like an overripe pear falling to the ground.

The pop and hiss of overloading cultivators - someone had told him five or six had perished around him at that moment - was just another awful part of the soundscape that now haunted him.

Melehan was unsure how he felt about the deaths of those wizards. He was completely out of available guilt at this stage.

The true irony, of course, was that Pæga's war band had barely made it back in time to join up with the rest of the army at all. After their ignominious retreat in the face of that powerful enemy cultivator, they had returned to the border to regroup. It was only Melehan passing on the scorn of the other embedded cultivators for the sole section of the invasion to be repelled that had spurred the commander to turn around and attempt to catch up - taking a longer way around to avoid any chance of crossing paths with that wizard.

And, of course, by the time Pæga was swapping stories with his fellow war chiefs, what had occurred had been massively embellished.

Was it not amazing, Melehan thought, that we had been able to defeat a dragon, vanquish ten enemy cultivators and execute a brilliant tactical retreat with the loss of only one warrior?

Certainly, since being back, Pæga had been swaggering around the camp with all the unearned bravado of the untested school bully. One of Melehan's few remaining pleasures was to look forward to the moment that the bluff was called.

It was irritating, therefore, that the loss of Ealhhere's war band, near the vicinity of where Pæga had reported significant enemy action, had added credence to the tall tale being spread. As none of Pæga's forces were eager to recount they had fled in the face of a solitary cultivator, soon everyone was convinced a puissant British fightback was underway.

And that cast the events of Isca in an even more worrying light.

That demonstration of overwhelming power could work both ways, after all. If, as intended, it quelled the Britons into immediate surrender, then it may be that the horror he had helped deliver saved further bloodshed.

However, Pæga's exaggerated experience and the loss of all of Ealhhere's men was giving the leaders of the invasion pause. The word 'Merlin' was being muttered around every campfire Melehan had stopped at over the march inland.

There was a significant fear that, rather than supplying a stunning knockout blow, was there not the chance that the Saxon wizards had prodded the biggest, angriest bear in the woods?

Melehan flashed back to that gathering months back. "Do not fear Merlin," the High King had said. "His days have long since passed." It had been thrilling to hear

177

such a thing said at the time, but now, having committed a great crime against the people of Britain, the whole army feared they had been unwise to discredit him so blithely.

"Are you okay?" Ula, one of the cultivators he had known from before the invasion, was at his side.

"I don't know," he smiled thinly to her, "How would I tell?"

"You're still shaking, I see?" Melehan tucked his hands back under his armpits. "I'd probably swap maladies with you, to be honest. It's the dreams for me. No matter how much I drink, I can't seem to get a dreamless night."

Melehan looked at his friend, concern in his eyes. "They're still that bad?"

Ula nodded. "I think we did a terrible thing."

They walked onward in an uncomfortable silence. Soon, they reached the edge of the encampment and put their backs against the trees that loomed above.

The invasion had stalled.

They were within a day's march of the sea where, in theory, half their numbers would embark on the waiting crafts to speed down the coast towards Tintagel, and the other half would continue with the trail of destruction inland.

But there was no clear decision on which war bands would do which. The loss of Ealhhere had upset the balance amongst the Saxon commanders, and uneasy alliances were now becoming open warfare.

"How long are we going to be stuck here, do you think?"

Ula shrugged, "Who knows? From what I hear, there's going to need to be a few heads banging together, removing and stuck on pikes to get us moving."

They both stared at the hundreds of campfires blinking away. Ula seemed less able to cope with the silence than Malehan. "Have you heard the latest rumours? The soldiers think someone's picking them off."

"They're still talking to you? No one's so much as met my eyes since Isca."

"I have tits."

Melehan waited, unsure if there was more to be said. Apparently, there wasn't.

"It'll just be desertions, no?"

"That's what I said. But they're convinced there's a war band out there, waylaying people in the dark."

Melehan didn't care.

He was shocked to realise it - these were people's lives, after all - but he simply did not have it in him. What did it matter to him if warriors were killed now or in a week's time? The only thing that was certain about this march was that the flow of blood and the stink of death would follow them until the end.

Ula was still talking. " - do something about it."

"Sorry? I missed that."

She rolled her eyes at him, and he could see the dark circles that marred her otherwise pretty face. No, Ula had certainly not been sleeping of late. "I was saying it might be wise for some of us cultivators to try to do something about it. They're looking at us as if we're feral beasts. We'd generate some goodwill if we could ferret out anyone preying on the men."

There was a soft whisper of quickly moving feet, and then both of them were dragged backwards into the woods. Their heads were quickly hooded, their hands expertly bound, and knives pressed at their throats.

"For future reference, the time to put in place a plan to deal with dark forces grabbing people in the dark is, ideally, just before, you know, the dark forces grab you in the dark. All becomess a bit moot afterwards."

The two captured cultivators were lifted off the ground and carried further into the woods. "I know the Prince wanted one wizard; do you think he'll be happy with two?"

"One of them's got tits. I imagine he'll be a cockahoop."

CHAPTER 46 - IN WHICH, NO MATTER WHAT MERLIN MIGHT SAY, I ABSOLUTELY BECOME CAPTAIN PLANET

No, no, no!

Training was going well.

I know of babes in arms still draining their mother's dug every morning and night that could achieve this.

Merlin was really pleased with the progress I was making.

How can you not follow the most basic of instructions? Have you received a recent blow to the head?

To be honest, everything was proceeding so smoothly that we'd talked about taking a few days off from travelling towards Tintagel and just chilling out on the beach.

If you cannot better control the passage of your Qi through your channels, how can you possibly think that you can command it when it leaves?

I was looking forward to kicking off the armour, throwing caution to the wind and going skinny-dipping. My new body lent itself well to such displays of wanton abandon, and - having never had the gall to try it in my previous life - I feared I was missing out on the full 'hot girl' experience.

Are you listening to a word I am saying?

"To be honest, Big M, I tuned you out a few miles back. I'm all for cranking up the training regime since we realised the Saxons are going all Quantum Leap, but nowhere in my contract did I sign up for Qi boot camp delivered by Gunnery Sergeant Hartman."

You need to ...

"Let me stop you there. I don't 'need' to do anything at all, and if you can't chill your jets, you're taking another trip to Camp Naughty-Step."

I waited and was pleasantly surprised by the silence that followed.

For the last day or so, we'd followed the rather unsubtle tracks left behind by the giant, town-destroying army sweeping inland.

Merlin has ummed and ahhed about us blasting ahead and trying to slip past them, but, in the end, we agreed it seemed sensible to shadow them for as long as we safely could. The chances of being spotted and brought down by a bunch of cultivators who knew far more about what they were doing than I did were too high.

As I'd walked, we'd been trying to double up with some serious 1:1 cultivator training. However, and who would have thought it, it turned out I might not be a natural student.

"Okay. Now we've remembered that I'm a human being with hopes, dreams and feelings of my own, shall we try that again?"

I'm sorry, my dear, but I cannot understand why you find these basic techniques challenging. Some feats you have achieved suggest you are a prodigious talent, but sometimes, it feels as if you're barely sentient.

"Hopes, dreams and feelings, Big M. Hopes, dreams and feelings."

It shouldn't be possible for a disembodied voice to take a deep breath, but Merlin gave it a good old-fashioned try. *Okay. Let's try this again.*

"Can I sit? I feel like I should sit?"

If it will help you concentrate, please feel free to stand on your head.

I spotted a suitably inviting-looking tree stump and perched myself upon it. *And the reason for the crossed legs and the humming?*

"Just centring myself, mate. I am one with the Qi, and the Qi is with me."

Quite. Now, as I have explained, linking your Qi to an element, in this case, water, will be a crucial part of mastering your abilities as a cultivator. You have gained a significant amount of control through treating Qi as a medium with which you are intimately familiar - and that was very sensible.

"You see, you can be nice to me when you try."

Indeed. However, your Qi is the very essence of your being. It is your life force. Whilst there are advantages to how you have organised your ... ah, your artist's studio, seeking to link it to an element will give you far more control, power, and insight.

"You mean it will help me stop shooting my full load whenever I cast anything?"

If that is how you would like to phrase it, then yes.

"So, linking my Qi to an element is the spiritual equivalent of a cold shower?"

There was a pause, and when he next spoke, the scholarly tone to Merlin's voice, which he always adopted when seeking to 'teach' me something, was gone. In its place was, I don't know, something rawer. More intimate.

I know what you are doing, my dear. And I appreciate it; I truly do. This irreverent mask you wear is wonderfully diverting. We have seen an appalling sight and fear for further horrors in the future. The weight that we - well, you - need to carry to avert disaster feels crippling. Would you like to talk about Zizzie and your fears for her before we carry on?

I thought for a moment. 'If it's all the same to you, Big M, I think I'll just keep up the steady stream of verbal bollocks. It's been pretty much my coping mechanism forever. Go with what you know, you get me?"

Of course. I just thought it was worth saying.

There was a beat while we both rearranged our mental armours. We had been shaken by what we had seen at Isca and in our consideration of potential consequences. In order to continue to function, I'd locked my worries down as tight as I could. Fortunately, I had decades of experience on which to rely here.

Now, where was I? Water, my dear. Water is the essence of life itself. It's the ebb and flow of existence, the very thing that sustains us all. I linked my Qi to water at the very beginning of my journey of cultivation. Through it, I gained a deep understanding of balance, adaptability, and resilience. When your Qi is linked with water, you learn to go with the flow, adapt to challenges, and become as flexible as the reeds by the riverbank. For example, imagine harnessing the tranquil strength of a calm river or the unstoppable force of a raging torrent. Picture yourself as fluid as the water, adapting to any situation that comes your way. That's what linking your Qi to water can do for you.

I thought about what the wizard was telling me. It seemed sensible but simply didn't resonate. "I don't know, mate. I get that water is your thing, but it's never been mine. I just don't look at it in the same way that you do."

There was a pause whilst Merlin restrained another burst of frustration. *Alright. I disagree, and it would make things much easier if we had a shared elemental sense, but let's give this another go. This time, we're setting our sights on the air element. I've got a feeling, with all the hot air you speak, that this might be more appropriate.*

I felt the atmosphere around me ... I think 'harden' would be the word? It was as if Merlin had pooled all the available nearby oxygen into a bubble and cut me off from the wider world.

Now, close your eyes and take a deep breath. Let's go through this step by step and see if we have more luck linking your Qi to air. Clear your mind. You're sat in a serene, open field. The small space around you is still, and the only thing that exists is the air you breathe.

I followed his instructions, and rather than the damp and uncomfortable sense I had when trying the same thing with water, I actually found myself relaxing.

Inhale slowly. Fill your lungs as much as you can. As you do so, think of your breath as more than just air; it's the essence of the element with which we are aiming to connect. Imagine you're drawing the very spirit of the wind into your body.

Strange to say, but that actually made sense to me. It was how I had brought the wolf and dragon Qi into my body, after all.

Now, with your eyes closed, start to feel the air around you. Picture it like a cloak, flowing gently around your body, resting against and caressing your skin. That soft contact fills your senses with its presence. Concentrate on your intent, my dear. Think about what you aim to achieve through this—this connection with the element. Focus on the qualities of air—its freedom, adaptability, and its ever-changing nature. Let that intention become a burning beacon in your mind.

The word 'freedom' resonated with me. If water represented calm acceptance and stillness - a state of being that absolutely did not suit me - then the unrestrained nature of air certainly called to me. With a start, I realised I could feel bubbles begin to form within my Qi as if the paint was fizzing in some way.

As you breathe deeply and slowly, envision your Qi merging with the air, like a drop of paint being added to a portrait. Feel the boundaries between yourself and the surrounding air blur and fade away. And with each breath, let the connection grow stronger. Imagine yourself becoming as free and limitless as the wind itself.

The bubbles in my Qi multiplied exponentially and became smaller. Soon, it was like the paint itself was composed of millions upon millions of tiny pockets of air.

Remember, my dear, this isn't a race, and it's not about getting there in a hurry. I can feel you stepping closer in your understanding. But it's a process, much like a blacksmith crafting a fine sword, requiring patience and dedication. You won't see a dramatic change right away, and that's perfectly normal. Keep practising, keep focusing, and you'll see your connection to the air element strengthening.

Even just from this short period of meditation, I could tell that my Qi was ... lighter? It wasn't a massive change, but the flow around my channels felt noticeably more directable.

I sat in a contemplative silence for a good few minutes, just enjoying the experience of breathing in and out. Then, a thought occurred to me.

"Merlin, your element is water, right?"

That is correct, my dear.

"And mine is on its way to being air?"

More than on the way. I can feel the strength of your developing connection already.

I pulled Drynwyn from my inventory. "And the sword's element is fire, I presume?"

If you were interested, its reply suggests you undertake some creative and anatomically impossible sexual practices.

"Okay. Let's leave the mute on for a bit longer." The hilt of the sword glowed white-hot in response. "The mana stones from the Knockers ..."

Yes?

"Do they have any sort of elemental affinity?" I touched the earrings Beocca had fashioned for me.

Of course. Mana stones are the embodiment of ..." There was a pause. "That is absolutely fascinating, my dear. Do you understand what this might mean?

"Well, I'm hoping it means that I'm a hero that's gonna take pollution down to zero. With elemental powers magnified, I'm going to fight on the planet's side. And, as a side note, I'm gonna put asunder bad guys who like to loot and plunder. Is that what you're thinking too?"

No.

CHAPTER 47 - IN WHICH, FOR SHITS AND GIGGLES, WE SPEND SOME TIME IN THE MIND OF A FLAMING SWORD

D rynwyn was not, naturally, given to introspection.
Few swords are.
In a pretty short space of time, though, it'd had a couple of enforced periods of solitude, and it hadn't overly enjoyed the experience.

The first was in the dragon's hoard following Rhydderch Hael's untimely flash frying. Although it had no fundamental concept of marking the passage of time, it recognised that the distances between stabbing people had become significant.

After raging against the unfairness of it all for an unknown amount of time, Drynwyn had settled in for some lengthy seething. This had led to some uncomfortable reflections about the nature of its time with Rhydderch, which it had squished down nice and tight and was never going to think about again.

I am my bearer's sword. There's nothing like me, and I am theirs.

Then, out of the blue, she'd freed it.

It understood there were a couple of different 'types' of person. But Rhydderch Hael didn't seem to care about that, so it hadn't either. Its new bearer was one of those whose soft bits stayed soft, rather than hardened up, but that made no mind.

My bearer is my best friend. They are my life. They must master me as I must master death.

Of course, it recognised that they hadn't established the smoothest of bonds thus far, and, to be fair, it had probably been due a period of enforced silence.

However, the return of Merlin had completely freaked it out. From its experience, there was only room for one disembodied voice in a bearer's mind, and it worried it would be pushed out.

My bearer, without me, is useless. Without my bearer, I am useless. I must swing true. I must cut deeper than my enemy, who is trying to kill my bearer. I must kill him before he kills my bearer. I will.

It didn't know what happened to a sword that was never drawn. It had never needed to have that sort of existential thought before. Rhyddrech wasn't the type to keep any of his weapons sheathed for a moment longer than necessary.

But, if Morgan never drew it again, what did it become? What would happen if it turned out it was trapped in the silence of this inventory for the rest of time? Could it even call itself a sword anymore?

Interficiam ergo sum. It was all it knew how to do.

My bearer and myself know that what counts in life is not the cuts we make, the heat of our fire, or the smoke we make. We know that it is the killings that count. We will kill.

It knew that its new bearer was pretty inexperienced in such things. After so long with Rhyddrech, there were things in battle that had become second nature. You both knew what the other one was thinking without needing to spend too long thinking about it.

Looking back at its time with Morgan, it could see that it was still following old patterns of behaviour. That wasn't good enough. It needed to do more to try to adapt to her and how she wanted to go about things. It couldn't rely on instincts that weren't appropriate anymore. One headless woodcutter demonstrated that.

My bearer is human, even as I am immortal, but they are my life. Thus, I will learn her as a sister. I will learn her weaknesses, her strengths, her parts, her accessories, her eyes and her heart. I will ever guard her against the ravages of weather and damage as I will ever guard my grip, my pommel, my blade and my tang against damage. I will keep my bearer clean and ready. We will become part of each other. We will.

It remembered the creed it had sworn so many years before when it was first removed from the blacksmith's fire and handed to Rhyddrech.

It didn't know where the words that it spoke came from, but it recognised they said something about its intrinsic 'swordness'. It was these words that connected it to its bearer, and until now, it had not truly tried to apply them to Morgan.

Before the forge, I swear this creed. My bearer and myself are the defenders of the world. We are the masters of our enemy. We are the saviours of Britain.

As it thought these uncomfortable thoughts, it dimly recognised that it had been taken from its state of stasis in Morgan's inventory and had returned to its favourite place on her back. Its voice was still being muted by that bastard Merlin, but - all in all - being out and about significantly improved its situation.

She won't let you keep me silent forever, you know.

Indeed, not. But it is not my intention to remove your voice in perpetuity.

So why've you still got the muzzle on me?

Have you spoken your creed yet?

Drynwyn bit back from releasing a stream of invective. It had never come across anyone who was not a sword who had spoken of this before. **How do you know about that?**

I'm Merlin. I know everything. Have you?

You're an evil bastard, that's what you are. Don't think I'm going to stay quiet about the things you've done the moment I can tell her.

We can both agree that, of her many flaws, Morgan does not number self-delusion amongst them. She knows exactly who I am and the things that I have done. At the moment, she needs my knowledge to gain in power, and I am happy to provide it. Are you going to help me?

If the sword could have spat, it would have done. **Help you! If I could find your wizened neck, I'd slit it in a second.**

And, should I have the hands to do it, I'd melt you down to slag and have you remade into a particularly decorative fruit bowl that I'd gift to an elderly female relative. You'd be engraved with all manner of flowers and a variety of frolicking woodland creatures. Anyone who looked at you would describe you as 'positively charming'.

You evil bastard!

But neither of us is wholly free to do what we would most dearly wish right now, are we?

Fuck you.

Hear me, Drynwyn, Sword of Rhyddrech Hael. Yours is a tale that, should we somehow maintain the current timeline, holds a place of reverence among the great swords of legend. You may not be Excalibur -

She's such a snooty bitch. Never could understand the attraction.

Quite, but you too are a named blade, and that will still mean something in a millennium if we can avoid the cataclysm to come.

Do you think I care about that? About how people I will never meet think about me? There was a pause. What sort of things did they say?

Drynwyn wouldn't swear to it, but he was sure he could hear a smile enter Merlin's voice. *According to legend, when drawn from your scabbard, you would blaze with flames, striking fear into the hearts of enemies.*

Too fucking right.

However, your legend also carries a cautionary tale. It is told that anyone unworthy who attempts to draw Drynwyn from its scabbard will suffer a terrible fate, as the sword's flames turn upon the would-be thief, burning them to ashes.

Happened more than once, I tell you. I've charcoaled enough sneaky fuckers in my time to open my grill station.

And so, in the grand tapestry of British legends, Drynwyn of Rhyddrech Hael shines as a symbol of the power of virtue and the consequences of greed and ambition. Throughout history, you remain an enduring emblem of chivalric power. And unless we can somehow work together to support Morgan, that future will be wiped out. No one will ever have heard of you. And I think that would be a shame.

There was a tense moment whilst the sword chewed over Merlin's words. Then, with a dip of its pommel, it accepted the wizard's words.

You get one chance. Fuck me over one time, and we're done.

Those are sound words to live by, dear Drynwyn. And they do you credit. Now, about the creed

...

The sword swiftly intoned its sacred words, reaching the final line, which it bellowed out in a crescendo.

So be it, until victory is Britain's and there is no enemy, but peace!

WELCOME TO THE DARK AGES

CHAPTER 48 - IN WHICH WE LEARN ABOUT ELEMENTAL CULTIVATION AND ITS DEEP DEBT TO DISNEY SONGS

Welcome back.

You'll be pleased to know you managed to miss the first three hours of Merlin's lecture on the theory of the five elements.

I mean, it's been a true joy. We've laughed. We've cried. We've explored the limits of human endurance.

To catch you up, the CliffsNotes version is that everything Mr. Barnes taught me about the elements in Year 7 Chemistry was wrong.

Apparently, it isn't all about Earth, Fire, Air and Water (and Heart. This is a hill I will die on). What I should be thinking about is Earth, Fire, Water, Wood and Metal. Who knew?

Anyway, I am glad you've made it back for the home-stretch. Strap yourself in, drink your body weight in coffee and prepare to get your learning on ...

You know, a less secure person would be hurt by your lengthy expositions into the empty space. But no, not me. No. I shall press onwards regardless. As explained, my dear, the five elements each represent a unique aspect of nature. When we consider them, in turn, we can see that they are in a constant cycle of generation and control. In their relationship and in their interactions, they form a harmonious and dynamic system.

"So, what I'm hearing is that, due to our world being in peril. Gaia, the spirit of the Earth, could no longer stand the terrible destruction plaguing our planet and sent five ..."

If you make any further references to that particular 90s cartoon, I am going to go on strike.

I took the hint. There's the joy of solid callback humour, and then there's pushing an all-powerful wizard slightly too far. I sensed I was creeping pretty close to that particular line.

To take an example. Wood represents growth, expansion, and vitality. It is particularly associated with the liver - which, with all the damage you had done to that organ, is why I do not think you have any particular affinity for it - and the Spring. Should you develop the capacity to cultivate it, Wood Qi will teach you the importance of flexibility and adaptability.

"Those are not traits I think anyone who knows me would suggest I possess in abundance."

No. Nevertheless, just as a tree bends with the wind but remains rooted, it would be good for you to learn to adapt to life's challenges whilst also staying true to your own ... quirky personality.

The Big M had a point. When I was alive, I was very much a shatter-into-a-thousand-spikey-shards person rather than a bend-and-go-with-the-flow type. Saying that, I did feel I was rolling with the isekei thing reasonably well, so maybe I wasn't so distanced from the power of Wood as Merlin was making out.

I thought back to my first experience of cycling my Qi and remembered the repairs that were undertaken to my liver. Was it a coincidence that my ability to "adapt to life's challenges" had improved once the damage of years of vodka-based assaults was reversed? It was something to consider once Merlin wasn't droning on …

And, of course, on the other hand, Fire symbolises passion, transformation, and warmth. It most closely links to your heart and to the Summer. Fire Qi, as embodied by your possession of Drynwyn, reminds us all to cultivate our inner passions and desires, using their energy to fuel our spiritual journey.

"Kind of like our id?"

There was a pause whilst I sensed a gathering of what remained of internal resources. *My dear, no one takes psychology seriously. Id, ego and Superego? It's bunkum. Freud made it all up.*

"But flaming swords, Qi and dragons are a big, realistic thumbs up?"

I don't understand your point.

I let it go.

As I was saying, the cultivation of Fire Qi also reminds us of the importance of balance in all things, as an uncontrolled fire can lead to destruction. Drynwyn is an excellent focus for you to consider when you seek to cultivate Fire Qi. There is a need to restrain aggression lest it leave your control. Together, the two of you could achieve amazing things. You could also literally cause the world to burn.

"So, what you are saying is that with great power comes great responsibility."

That is indeed what I am saying. I will note right now, though, that if you try to call me Uncle Ben even just once, I repeat my threat to undertake significant industrial action. Shall I move on?

"Absolutely."

Moving right along. On the other hand, Earth represents stability, nourishment, and the importance of being grounded. It is connected to the spleen …

"That what?"

The spleen.

"Five hundred quid on the table and a gun to my head, I could not tell you where to find my … what did you call it?"

Your spleen.

"You're making it up."

A spot to the left of my stomach suddenly glowed red-hot and then quickly healed.

Sorry, that was beneath me.

"Did you, in a fit of pique, just throw a tiny fireball at my spleen to show me where it was?"

I have apologised.

"Your approach to teaching is," I thought back to the vision Vortigern's Dragon gave me of him eating each of Merlin's previous apprentices, "entirely consistent. The spleen. I now know I have one. Thanks for the clarification."

Indeed. Now, Earth Qi is not linked to a season as such but is instead connected to the transitional periods between them. Fundamentally, and this is why I wish to stress it to you, it emphasises the importance of a strong foundation, both in our physical and spiritual lives.

"Hence me in the cave?"

Hence you in the cave. To help develop that, I have sought to support you in making a connection to the air element - as you can tell, an entirely minor player in Qi cultivation - to help fill the considerable foundational weakness you have. Whilst the mana stones you wear at your ears and that you keep in your inventory are going some way in supporting you to establish a strong foundation, we will need you to establish a much closer relationship with the Earth.

"Well, I didn't know I had a spleen five minutes ago, so the only way is up, right?"

Quite. Just as the Earth supports all living things, you must cultivate stability and balance within yourself.

I did feel the Wood Qi and the Earth Qi were being a touch judgy of me. They both seemed to embody aspects of my personality that were ... less developed. I knew one of the central premises of cultivation was personal growth, but I couldn't help but feel I'd be getting less shade thrown my way by a more classic System apocalypse.

Next, Metal embodies clarity, purity, and refinement. It is associated with the lungs and, in particular, Autumn. Connecting to Metal Qi teaches us the value of letting go of impurities, whether physical or emotional, to reveal our true essence.

So, I felt a bit of a musical mash-up singalong was appropriate at this stage. Although, it is safe to say that, while the storm raged on, in the light of day, Merlin did not care that the cold never bothered me anyway.

He was also highly anti-building a snowman.

Are you quite finished?

"Sorry, mate. I will be the good girl I always have been."

Please stop it. Crucially, and it is important to stress your clear affinity for this element, like Metal being forged and refined, Metal Qi shows us that we too can become stronger through adversity.

It did feel like Metal and Fire were much more my vibe than Earth and Wood. "Is it normal for cultivators to have an affinity with one element more than the others?"

It is, but to combat what is to come, we need you to have the ability to draw on all potential sources of power. It would be helpful if you could think of the elements as aspects of you rather than things you can do and things you cannot.

I wasn't sure that explanation quite worked for me, but I needed to think about this myself some more. If there was one thing I was learning about cultivating, it was a horse-to-water process. Merlin was giving me the info, but I needed to do something with it myself for it to be of any use.

Finally, we come to Water, the element with which I have the most connection. It symbolises wisdom, adaptability, and the power of flow. It corresponds to the kidneys and Winter.

"Bit on the nose, isn't it mate? Water Qi is wisdom and Winter? So it's basically a metaphor for a clever old man. You're sure you're not projecting a little in the descriptions?"

Merlin appeared to have decided to ignore me. When we cycle Water Qi it teaches us the importance of introspection and the ability to adapt to changing circumstances. Lord knows I've needed that. Water is the source of life, and in our cultivation, it represents the depth of our potential.

I sensed Merlin was reaching a crescendo of explanation. His voice became animated.

Now, why are these elements so crucial to Qi cultivators, you may wonder? The answer lies in their interconnectedness and the way they mirror the energies within ourselves and the universe. By understanding and harmonising with these elements, Qi cultivators can achieve balance, health, and spiritual enlightenment.

"Kind of like Planeteers?"

Silence was my only reply.

189

CHAPTER 49 - IN WHICH ARTHUR GOES A BIT COLONEL KURTZ.

Melehan did not know how long they were carried into the woods. In the darkness of the hood, it was impossible to keep track of time in any meaningful way.

This was not helped by, as they moved, the fact that the Britons were not especially kind in their treatment of the captured wizards. Heads crashed into trunks and branches. There were multiple sudden drops as though falling, and then explosive surges upwards as their limp bodies were thrown from one carrier to another carrier.

It was a terrifying, exhausting experience, but, he supposed, the Saxon wizards had done precious little to deserve anything better from their captors.

As they travelled, he kept trying to take an opportunity to reach for his Qi, but the disorientation of the journey was simply too great. He was sure there were calm, centred cultivators that might still have been able to cycle effectively in such circumstances, but he doubted any were still with the invading army. The events of Isca had done more than exhaust their stores of essence, it had shattered the foundation of their spirits.

Just when he feared he could not exist within the churning darkness any longer, they came to a sudden halt.

As abruptly as the black had descended, the hood was whipped off, and he found himself blinking into the eyes of an austere, bearded stranger.

"You've bought two of them, I see. I could have sworn I asked for one," the figure said, his voice oddly flat.

A huge man appeared from behind them to push the wizards to their knees. With a gesture, he indicated for figures to slink from the trees and to come forward with their knives. "You get a sense of anything tricky, you stab first and ask questions later, you hear?" He turned to face the bearded man. "Apologies, my Lord. We sort of figured two was better than one. You know, it's always good to have a spare. I can remedy that for you if you'd rather just keep the one with the legs?"

He placed a hand around Melehan's neck and lifted him to the sky. Ula shrieked and tried to stand but was forced back to her knees.

Even as his face darkened and his vision blurred, Melehan kept eye contact with the bearded man. He wanted this Briton to know he understood why this was necessary. That he was sorry. That he accepted this as a just punishment for what they had done. That, more than anything else, he was ready to die.

After a few moments, he felt blood vessels pop, and the final darkness began to descend. In welcome, he opened his mind for the coming peace.

"Wait. Let him go."

Air returned to his lungs in an explosive gush as he hit the ground. Almost unwillingly, he sucked a breath inwards, aware of a figure standing over him.

"What is your name, wizard?"

Holding his damaged throat, he tried to speak, but couldn't force out an intelligible answer. Ula answered for him. "Melehan. His name is Melehan. He's a good man."

"A good man?" The bearded man's face held an unreadable expression. "Then he'll be in rare company hereabouts. Are you a good man, Sir Bors?"

"Well, yesterday I strangled a Saxon with his own intestines whilst he cried out for his mother. I forced his own shit into his mouth as he died."

"So, would that be a 'no'?"

"Probably not, no. I mean, not classically 'good', anyway. I'm sure, in some cultures, I'd be looked on as quite the entertainer."

The man scratched his beard. "So, that's where Bors is at. Me? Well, I've been spending the last few weeks orchestrating the kidnap, murder and torture of around three hundred Saxons. I've quite enjoyed it, too. So, with regret, I don't think anyone will be stroking me with the 'good boy' stick any time soon either."

He swept his arms around the clearing. "Bors and I are well out. But you never know, we might have some takers. Is anyone around here still calling themselves a 'good man'?"

There were uneasy glances around the thicket. The brutal execution of enemy combatants was not traditionally an opportunity for some light call-and-response banter. Most of them felt it was a touch crass, to tell the truth.

Thus, silence was his only reply.

The bearded man knelt in front of Melehan, who was still struggling to catch his breath. "It appears, if your glamourous assistant is correct, that you might be the only good man for quite some distance. Well done you. How did you manage it? Is there a cream to draw out all of the impurities? Maybe a mantra you say to yourself to stop the filth of this world from sticking to you. Although, and forgive me if I'm speaking out of turn here, but I kind of think burning a settlement of men, women and children to the ground might just disqualify you from the running, too."

He cuffed Melehan around the ears, sending him back sprawling to the floor.

"What do you reckon? Maybe, just maybe, that might give the judges of 'Good Saxon Men' a moment's pause?" He pulled Melehan upright and held their foreheads together, their eyes almost touching. "What gives you the right, boy, to look at me like that? Where do you get the balls to look at me whilst you die, and .... and you were fucking forgiving me for killing you, weren't you? For fuck's sake. You still fucking are." He struck Melehan, sending him flying back against strong arms that held him.

"You don't get to say 'sorry' and just die and take your penance. I don't want your apologies, and I fucking don't want you to make it up to me. What do I want, boys?"

"Dead fucking Saxons, sir?"

"And when do I want them?"

There was a pause. "To be fair, sir, I was just killing him," Bors noted reproachfully. "Had him going purple and everything. You interrupted me to deliver that somewhat disconcerting speech that's done very little for the boys' morale. Make up your mind." He drew his sword and held it above the wizard. "You sure, this time? It's kind of a no-take-backs thing."

All eyes were on Prince Arthur, who continued to stare at Melehan.

191

He knew what was the responsible thing to do. He had captured two enemy wizards - doubtless a treasure trove of useful information - and he should gather them up and return to Uther for questioning at all speed. He'd get a nice pat on the head, probably gifted another castle or two, and maybe be hailed as the hero who, once again, saved the day for the people of Britain.

But for that, he needed to return home.

Needed to leave all of this wildness and go back to a world that measured his worth by the product, or lack of it, of his cock.

He wasn't sure he could face it.

It was all so different when he was in the field. Here, when eyes looked at him, it was for orders. For reassurance. For praise. That felt a world away from the snide judgements and political manoeuvrings of court.

The retreat from Isca had been, in many ways, devastating for his war band, but it had undoubtedly honed these warriors into a lethal edge. The fact they'd just managed to capture two enemy cultivators without alarm or casualties was evidence of that. It was the places of mud and blood where he found his true worth. Try as he might, he simply could not conjure any interest in taking these wizards and striking for home, a hot bath and more questions about how often he had his wife's legs in the air.

Part of him, a significant part, wanted Bors to sweep the head off this wizard and then do the same to the one with the legs. (although that could potentially wait a few hours as she had a certain something about her, and it had been a dry few weeks. If she was willing, of course.)

Then, they could steal and kill a few more. And a few more after that.

But no.

He knew which way that path lay. He'd been right when he'd said that there was a day, at best, left of this style of hit-and-run warfare. Soon, the invading army would realise it was being preyed upon - especially now wizards were vanishing - and it would raise itself from its internal arguments and seek to kill them all.

A force that could blast a town out of existence would not trouble itself in seeking a proportional response to their presence.

He looked at Bors, and then the others that had fought with him these last few weeks. They'd been formidable before Isca. They were a holy terror now. If Britain was to survive, Uther needed all of these fighters back home, not stalking the enemy in the woods. His heart sinking at the realisation, he decided to do the right thing. He looked down at the wizards and opened his mouth to order them to be trussed up and stowed on the horses.

Ula had been tracking the careful consideration in Arthur's eyes and, on seeing it sharpen to a decision, jumped to the wrong conclusion. She saw that cold regard rest on them and panicked: visions of rape and murder flooded her mind and broke her free from her paralysis.

Before the man holding her could open her throat, she cycled bright green Qi into her hands and used the intensity of her fear to push herself free. Bodies crashed against trees, and blades sliced up her arms but failed to make a fatal wound.

Bors, seeing the girl wrench herself free, swore and chopped down towards her with his blade. She caught the descending sword with one hand, firing beams of energy to scatter the rest of the warriors. In an instant, she twisted the blade free from Bors' grasp, bending the metal in half in the struggle for dominance before twisting and sending him to his knees with a punch, two, then three to his forehead.

With a cry, she raised the mangled sword into the air to prepare to drive it downwards into his skull when she was distracted by Melehan staring at her.

Sitting there, he looked so pathetic. He was making no effort to join her frenzied escape, slowly shaking his head at her. She dropped the sword and reached out for him, shouting for him, but he smiled sadly in response. "I don't have it in me, I'm afraid."

And she suddenly knew what he meant. Knew that she was not fighting out of a desire to live but rather from ingrained habit. But Isca has scoured that primal instinct from her soul, leaving ... nothing.

The two wizards smiled at each other one last time, and then Arthur's great spear, Rhongomyniad, pierced her from the back and through her breastbone, driving her to the ground, blood and Qi leaking into the soil.

There was a moment of silence before Bors rumbled "Told you it was good we got two of them. Well, what are you waiting for? Some fucker help me up, and let's get going back to Tintagel."

Arthur stared down at the body of the young wizard. "Yes," he said without emotion. "Let's go home."

CHAPTER 50 - IN WHICH TEAM MORGAN PREPARES ITS NEXT STEPS

"That's an awful lot of Saxons."

Although the plan had been to travel in the shadow of the invasion for as long as possible, that only really worked if they were, you know, actually moving. For whatever reason, the invasions progress through Cornwall appeared to have completely stalled. As the sun went down on the third day after the conflagration at Isca, I found myself perched on a hill looking down on a veritable ants' nest of blue-painted spearmen.

Now, I'd never been any good at estimating numbers. Not the way you'd see in a movie where a scout would take one glance at an approaching force and go: "thirteen thousand, two hundred and eight men. Six women, one with a limp. They've had beans for lunch."

Nevertheless, to my inexpert eye, their numbers looked to be anything between Merry-Hill-on-the-Saturday-morning-before-Christmas and Villa-Park-for-a-midweek-European-game.

Basically, there were loads.

Throw me the fuck down there, I've got this.

I wasn't sure I was absolutely delighted that Drynwyn was back on speaking terms with Team Morgan. Merlin said they'd had a chat, and he had helped it to have a 'come to Jesus' moment. Apparently, I'd be having much less trouble with it moving forward.

I can't say I'd noticed much difference.

"I think we'll keep that in reserve as Plan B, if you don't mind, mate. But you stay poised and ready in case we need to do something genocidally suicidal. You are absolutely our go-to guy there. Any thoughts, Big M?"

We are witnessing the plight of every invasion since the beginning of time, my dear. Everyone always thinks it is how the battles turn out that decides the direction of wars. More often than not, though, it is just good old-fashioned logistics.

"They've run out of loo roll, you think?"

Something like that. They have achieved their primary goal and now have all sorts of hierarchical niceties to arrange. Human nature is what it is, and there needs to be a pecking order established. They will certainly not be in any shape to get moving in the near future until all of that is resolved. A little blood will need to flow to lubricate the wheels.

"So, what do we do?"

I know we discussed following them, but this is too good an opportunity to miss. We should probably take the opportunity to slip past them.

"What about their wizards? You were worried they'd be able to sense me if we tried to get past them before?"

I know. But something seems to have happened to them. I can sense them, and there are some of significant power there – far in advance of your current capabilities - but they are all ... subdued.

The fluency of their cycles appear to be disturbed. They are not even efficiently gathering Qi as before. I wonder if the reverberations as to what they committed at Isca have been substantial.

"When you say shit like 'I can sense them', what actually do you mean? Is that something I should be trying to do?"

There was a pause. "Sorry, is anything wrong?"

Quite the opposite, my dear. That was a perfectly valid question, and I'm just calibrating my mental processes to accept the possibility you occasionally demonstrate such insight.

"I sense you're still not over me ruining your big finish to that elemental speech, are you?"

I don't know what you mean.

If we've all quite finished holding each other's dicks and singing kumbaya, can we get on with the attack?

Once again, I was left with the impression that Drynwyn had seen some shit with his last owner that he had yet to fully process. "We're not going to attack right now, Drynwyn. We're going to plan for a super-secret spy mission where we have to be very, very quiet."

The sword sighed its derision. **We seem to be doing far too many super-secret silent spy missions in the last few days. They don't seem quite right. Rhyddrech Hael never did super-secret spy missions.**

Which may be the reason he is no longer with us, of course.

He's dead because he decided to take on a fucking dragon without back-up. Don't patronise me.

That was not my intention, Drynywyn, I apologise.

I never thought I'd feel a touch left out listening to my talking sword and my ghost mentor merrily bonding. It's certainly a vibe.

"Sorry to interrupt, Big M, but you were about to share some doubtlessly crucial cultivator knowledge? How are you sensing all those wizards?"

It's not that difficult, my dear. If you think that each of us is constantly cycling our Qi, that process creates ripples that echo out through existence. Nothing hugely noticeable, of course - it's not like any of us are foolish enough as to allow a visual manifestation of our power to leak outwards.

"No," I thought back to my meeting with the head-removing Saxon cultivator, "that would be ridiculous, wouldn't it?"

Indeed. Well, I will describe it in a way that makes sense to me, and you will need to substitute your own metaphor for looking at cultivation. So, if you think of your Qi as a still pond, all other cultivators are causing ripples on its surface. With sufficient effort, I can locate those ripples and, with practice, can sense things about what caused them.

I mentally substituted a 'white canvas' for Merlin's water imagery and immediately noticed little paint dots popping up upon it. I thought that was it, but then I found if I concentrated on them, I was able to get a fairly decent sense of the wizard they corresponded to.

Nothing too invasive. I mean, I didn't get full-on character sheets or anything actually useful like that, but it was enough that I felt I could tell them apart from each other.

Panic suddenly struck me. "Can anyone do this?" I was alarmed at the idea of the internal radar of several hundred wizards suddenly pinging away and zeroing in on the enemy cultivator who thought they were hidden atop a hill.

In theory, yes. But they would need someone who has mastered the technique to show them how to do it. I do not think these wizards have had that lesson. Indeed, from the sense of the auras, they do not seem to have undertaken a traditional apprenticeship at all.

I quickly mapped the sense I had of my wizard-radar against what I could see of the Saxon army beneath me. From what I could tell, the cultivators all seemed to be grouped to the very edge of the force, which, as a tactic, felt pretty odd.

They're scared of them.

"How do you mean?"

Drynywn was silent for a moment, and I didn't think it would answer. **It's hard to explain. For those who are non-cultivators, it is difficult to spend time around those who have the power to change the world. Think of it from their point of view. They have spent their whole lives training and practising to be good at war. For many of them, they have risen high on the strength of their arm and their skill with a blade. There is significant honour in our culture of being known to be the pinnacle of your craft. Then, one day, you stand the shield wall against a cultivator, and it makes everything you are, or will ever be, redundant. It shakes the very core of a man. It makes friendships between the two difficult. It made Rhyddrech Hael very lonely indeed.**

That was the longest speech I'd ever heard from the sword that didn't have a 'fuck' in it. I awkwardly reached behind me and touched its hilt in what I thought was a comforting manner.

Did you just fucking pat me?

Or maybe not.

I was trying to formulate a response when I noticed that two dots on the far left of my canvas, ones that were already well away from the rest of the small cultivator grouping, started to move away from the Saxon camp quickly. I looked up to try to see what that movement looked like in the real world, and it seemed like two of them must be running into the woods just below us.

"Deserters, do you think?"

I doubt it. There would be no friendly welcome for Saxon cultivators in the villages around here. And they're too far from the border to think they can safely slip back on their own. Even then, though, I think the fear of the locals would pale into insignificance compared to what would happen should they be captured by their fellows. Saxons take cowardice personally.

"Well, something is making them run."

I watched the paint dots move on my canvas for a moment, trying to figure out what these wizards were up to. Then, they abruptly stopped, and a few seconds later, one of the dots vanished.

"I'm going to take a punt that doesn't mean anything good?"

Well, not for that individual cultivator, but, on the other hand, that might be some of the best news we've had for quite some while.

"What? Why?"

Because someone out there has found the wherewithal to kidnap a pair of Saxon wizards and the giant swinging balls to go ahead and fucking end one. That makes them very much my sort of people.

Worryingly, I found myself agreeing.

CHAPTER 51 - IN WHICH 'YO MAMMA' JOKES LOSE SOMETHING IN TRANSLATION.

The decapitated head bounced once and rolled to settle in the corner of the tent.

Nothing ever quite gets the attention of a room as effectively as a summary execution. All arguing ceased as eyes quickly turned to the giant figure brandishing a battleaxe.

"I have had a belly full of your bickering. I have listened - by Þunor have I listened! - to your petty squabbles, but my patience is now at an end. The sun has risen and fallen thrice since our army came to a halt, and none in this coven of complaining women seem ready to call an advance."

The headless corpse, which had managed to stay upright during that little speech, fell forward and splattered messily on the ground.

"Did anyone see who that was?" one chieftain asked another in the hushed silence

"No idea. Better hope it was no one important. Things are tense enough around here as it is."

"Fuck," another said, peering at the head that had come to rest near his foot. "That's Oeric. That mad bastard just offed Oeric!"

There was a quiet collective groan. Oeric the Smooth had spent the last few days ingratiating himself with just enough of the other war parties as to be the only thing close to a 'compromise' leadership candidate the Saxons possessed. No one liked the patronising snake, but everyone disliked him just the right amount to grudgingly follow his lead.

In the land of the febrile psychopaths, the half-bloodthirsty madman could be king.

After all, everyone within the pavilion knew and understood the High King's plan. That wasn't the issue. They were to split their forces and squeeze Uther's army in a pincer movement. Half the war bands would march to Topsham, lay waste to the port, and take to the sea on the vessels their wizards told them were already waiting offshore. The other half were to press inland towards Tintagel, enthusiastically undertaking the various and bloody pastimes favoured by invaders everywhere.

It may be thought a sensible invasion plan would already have decided who was going where, but mindful of the potential for casualties, it had been deemed prudent to await the achievement of the first objective - the destruction of Isca Dumnoniorum - before taking a view. That the only loss of substance was the one man everyone agreed was a shoo-in to lead their combined forces - Ealhhere - was proving somewhat of a stumbling block to collective unity.

Over the last few days, therefore, into that vacuum had oozed Oeric, and this night, the Saxons were finally within touching distance of starting the next stage of the invasion.

But then Hengist had - not for the first time, it must be said - shat the bed.

"So I say," bellowed the huge man, "that we march for the sea tomorrow. And if Merlin wants to make an issue of it, I say we spit in his eye and welcome it. No more cowering in our tents when there is fighting to be had. You are either with me or against me."

If Hengist had expected a cry of acclamation, he was to be disappointed. Too many of his fellow war chiefs had just seen carefully balanced schemes go up in flames. Or, they supposed, down in a puddle of rapidly cooling blood.

"And if we are against you?" One of the younger chieftains pushed forward. "You have had your time, old man. If any here wished to follow you, they already would have joined your camp. I hear, rather, your men flee to the hearths of greater men."

Older, more experienced heads started to pull back from the area around the speaker. Everyone knew how you handled Hengist. You agreed with him, promised to see him in the morning, and then just let him charge off alone after whatever goal had interested his berzerker rage. He never held your non-appearance against you. It was simple, really.

What you didn't do, crucially, was get him all riled up.

"Eberhard, I'm surprised you pulled your mother's tit out of your mouth long enough to speak in this company of men.'

"Did you not hear, Hengist? I left my mother's tit behind long ago. It's your mother's breast on which I've been sucking of late."

There was a pause. Eberhard was from the north, where it appeared there was a far richer culture of 'yo mamma' jokes than was to be found amongst more traditional Saxons.

"Hengist's mother is older than my sword. Did he just say he was fucking her?"

"I think so."

"That's pretty weird, ain't it?"

"He's northern. Maybe they go for the older woman there?"

"There's 'older', and then there's ... I think I'm going to be sick."

"Does she even still have her teeth?"

"Maybe that's the attraction?"

Hengist blinked back at the younger chieftain as if unsure how to respond. The circle of men backing away from Eberhard grew even more expansive. "Did you just say you are in a sexual relationship with my mother?"

The younger man sensed something had gone wrong in this confrontation. "Well, no. Of course not. It was an insult."

"It would be an insult to be in a sexual relationship with my mother?" The red spots on Hengist's face were now glowing like a forge.

"Well, no, obviously not. I was just saying ..."

Two figures slipped away and out of the tent just as things became interesting.

The first, a tall, thin man with long dark hair, kicked out in frustration at a passing camp dog. It instinctively snarled and snapped back, but then, seeing who had struck it, it cowered and slunk out of range. "That'll add another day to our wait. By the time tempers cool, we'll have five more war bands without leaders and no closer to pressing forward. I swear, nothing has gone right since Isca. It's like the gods have turned their backs on us."

Pæga licked his lips nervously and said nothing. He was scared of this man, Cedric of the West Saxons. All right-thinking folk were.

Since his ignoble retreat after his run-in with that cultivator, Pæga had known he'd need to shelter under another's reputation for a time. There had been some mutterings that others deserved their chance to lead his war band. He'd purged those with such views in his own spears ruthlessly enough, but there were others in the wider host from whom he needed protection. As his sister had married a cousin of Cedric's, he'd made his introduction the moment he'd caught up with the main Saxon force.

As soon as he spoke to the man, though, he knew he'd made a mistake. There was something about Cedric that exuded menace. He spoke of people as things, as obstacles to be removed, as tools to be used. Nothing ever seemed to bring him joy, and there was a flatness to his eyes that disconcerted all who met him.

Pæga had thought he would be gaining a measure of protection by demonstrating his links to such a feared chieftain, but by the time he'd realised he was trading one form of weakness for another, it was too late.

"The High King does not seem unhappy with our pause. My wizard tells me ..." Pæga began.

Cedric's eyes flashed. "Do not speak to me of wizards. I'll hear none of them."

Pæga's head dipped in instant supplication. Stupid. He knew not to speak of cultivators in this man's presence. The remains of the wizard assigned to Cedric's war band still hung from a tree at the edge of the camp. The chieftain had taken exception to what had been done at Isca. That poor woman had not had an easy death.

In many ways, the savagery of what had been done that night had greatly enhanced Cedric's reputation in the army. No one was comfortable with how the siege of Isca had been resolved, and much anger was felt towards the wizards who had perpetrated it.

"My apologies. I merely meant to say that from what we know, there is no urgency on behalf of the High King for us to begin the second half of the invasion. We know he is content for us to wait for a time. There is no remaining force between our lands and here. Uther has not left Tintagel, nothing has been seen of Prince Arthur, and there is no word of ... their most powerful ally. Our victory is thus inevitable - it is merely the moment the end begins that is to be decided."

Pæga shivvered under Cedric's cold regard. "So speaks the leader of the only war band to have been defeated in the field. A wise man may question from where you get that confidence. Are there not ten powerful cultivators somewhere at our backs?"

"Well, yes. But nothing we will not be able to handle now we are all together. My sole wizard was not enough in the face of such power. Bringing any of my men out of the battle was an achievement. If only Ealhhere had managed the same."

There was a silence as Cedric stared at Pæga. Then, after what felt like an age, the tall man smiled. Somehow, Pæga thought, the smile was more terrible than the silence.

"I like you, Pæga. Clever enough to be useful, but not clever enough to be dangerous. Yes, I like you."

And with that, Cedric turned and returned to the command tent, leaving a disconcerted Pæga alone.

He licked his lips thoughtfully. That hardly sounded like a ringing endorsement from a long-term ally. With a sigh and nimbly stepping aside to avoid a young chieftain missing an arm that ran screaming from the tent, he followed behind Cedric.

CHAPTER 52 - IN WHICH TOLKIEN WOULD TURN IN HIS GRAVE

We had a plan.

It was a good plan. It had clear goals, allocated resources and even some sensible redundancy measures built in.

I thought it was a good plan. Merlin thought it was a good plan. Drynwyn couldn't give a fuck but agreed, when pressed, it was a good plan.

We were going to carefully skirt the edge of the camp, lose ourselves in the trees, follow the paint blob trail left by the cultivators and seek to meet up with whoever had just offed a wizard. 'The enemy of my enemy is my friend', and all that.

As you can see, a solid plan. No obvious weaknesses. No notes.

It was, therefore, mildly disappointing that less than a hundred feet into executing said plan, we ran straight into a Saxon patrol none of us had noticed coming from the opposite direction.

For fuck's sake.

I don't know who was more surprised: us or the five blue-painted Jason Momoa lookalikes we'd just stumbled into.

On instinct, I activated [Personal Space Invader]. This had the advantage of blasting the Saxons far away from me, which was a big tick. But, on the downside, it landed them smack bang in the middle of the campfire of a larger group of Saxons who, once they'd overcome their confusion at the sky raining spearman upon them, identified me as the cause of their woe.

I may have suggested dealing with that initial confrontation a little more stealthily.

"You think?" I swept Drywyn from its scabbard and held it towards the group gathering itself before me. It looked like at least two of the initial five were out for the count, but their loss was more than made up for by the ten others whose supper time I had rudely interrupted.

"Anyone have any ideas?"

I quite liked Plan A, to be honest. You know, the one when we made sure we crept past all the guards without alerting them to our presence? That was a good plan. I could get on board with that plan.

"There's a certain amount of shutting stable doors after the horses have been turned into lasagne I'm not appreciating right now, Big M."

The only good news I could see was that the group of fifteen or so Saxons now spreading out around me hadn't alerted anyone else as to the appearance of an unescorted, redheaded woman carrying lots of lootable items at the edge of their camp.

I imagine everything I represented could only be shared out so far ...

Well, that was a cheery thought.

I tapped into my mana stone earrings and withdrew enough Qi to top up my reserves that had dipped alarmingly low after firing off [Personal Space Invader]. My armour was already at capacity, so I pulled as much energy into my offhand as it could hold. I'd still not mastered the art of firing bolts of Qi like that first cultivator I'd met a million years ago - or was it last week? - but I was keen to keep trying.

This is not a complete disaster, my dear.

"I mean, I'm fairly broadminded about such things, but even so, I think what these guys have in mind for me is going to be pretty detrimental to my general well-being."

Quite. What I mean is that they've clearly decided to deal with you themselves. I can sense no attempt to alert anyone else in the army. You should take this as an opportunity to improve yourself.

"There's got to be at least fifteen of them. How exactly do you see this playing out?"

Fifteen Saxon spears are nothing compared to you, my dear. Just think of the things you have already achieved. You slew a dragon. You faced down not one, but two armies - slaughtering the second to a man. You have bargained with Knockers, and as much as it hurts me to mention, you banished the spirit of Merlin to the netherworld.

"When you put it like that, I am pretty bitching, aren't I?" I was being steadily backed towards the treeline where, I was sure, a few strong, warm arms would be eager to wrap me up into an eventual terminal embrace.

"The thing is, Big M ..."

What is the thing, my dear?

"I really don't think I did any of those things on purpose."

Ah, yes. There is that.

And the Saxons attacked.

***

Hrolf would have first dip.

That was the way things were, and no one begrudged him that privilege. After all, he would ever be the first to charge a shield wall, so it only stood to reason he got a go on the women first.

He stepped forward a few paces, leaving the ring of his fellows behind, and threw a meaty fist at the stranger's head. Not too hard, of course. It wouldn't do to mess her up too much. She had a pretty face; no need to lose that right off the bat. That was the point of going first, after all. So she'd still look like a person,

However, rather than accept the blow and collapse to the floor - a scene he'd played out countless times before - the woman suddenly jerked her head to one side, and his punch met thin air.

That was unexpected.

So unexpected, in fact, that the lack of resistance to the blow caused him to stumble forward uncontrollably before coming to an abrupt halt. A fierce pain bloomed in the centre of his chest, and looking down, he saw she'd driven her sword straight through it.

With a twist, she pulled the blade free, pushed him away and turned to meet the forward surge of Ceol and Aidan. As his friends charged past his falling body, Hrolf had just enough time to ...

***

The two brothers did everything together, so it was little surprise they were next to each other, close on Hrolf's heels. It didn't seem fair they had to take a turn after him - he rarely left anything recognisable behind after he'd finished.

So caught up were they in the injustice of it all, that they barely noticed their leader's punch fail to connect, nor his subsequent demise. Ceol, therefore, ran straight onto a crossways slash to the throat that quickly emptied much of his blood into the air in a fountain.

Aidan watched his brother's death in horror before realising the woman had tossed her sword to him. It was such a strange thing to do that he reached out and caught it without thinking.

Fucking rookie move.

***

Inguc wasn't quite sure what was going on.

Nevertheless, he knew it was bad.

The evening had been pretty uneventful up to a few moments ago. He'd been on patrol when, out of nowhere, a ginger bird had crashed into him and then - and he wasn't sure about this bit - apparently made him fly twenty feet in the air to crash into Hrolf's campfire.

He'd come round and dusted himself off just in time to see Hrolf walk into a blade - no great loss, the man was a throbbing dick - Ceol get his throat cut, and then Aidan combust into a pillar of flame.

That was all bad enough, but then - somehow - that smoking corpse turned round and started to chop through anyone within easy reach.

Which, unfortunately, included Inguc.

***

All things considered, I was quite happy with the early exchanges here.

I mean, there were still ten of them left - nope, nine. Drynwyn was enjoying himself - but this felt like a pretty good start.

Leave the sword to its fun for now. Let us see if you can harness the power of Wood Qi in your defence.

Odd as it seemed in the middle of a battle, it did feel like I could afford to take a breath. No one at the other campfires seemed bothered by what was occurring - a quick glance around suggested such skirmishes appeared to be almost commonplace.

Drynwyn had welded himself to the crispy body of the Saxon who'd caught him and was engaging three or four of the others at one time. The charge towards me had all but stopped - violent death tends to put a dent in even the most ardent of would-be rapists' ardour - and those that were left were either trying to work out how to fight a flaming zombie or watching others fail to work out how to fight a flame zombie.

"Okay. So Wood Qi. I can do that. Lots of trees around. Lots of grass. I can call on that. Yep. So what do you want me to do? Can I make one of the trees go Groot on their ass?"

Well, no. Not really, I was hoping you would ...

203

New technique created: [We want our Ent-Wives back]

***

It took less than a minute before the last of the Saxons was dragged, screaming, into the woods by - and I'm afraid to say it - desperately horny Oak trees.

"I make that three new Qi techniques I've created in a week. That's got to be some sort of record, right?"

Actually, my dear, I think you will find you have simply renamed - in a somewhat anachronistic way, of course - one of my own early efforts to manipulate Wood Qi. A very primitive technique, I should note. I imagine there are Druids in Bavaria who might find it difficult to master such a skill, but certainly, it is no great achievement for cultivators of quality.

"I have any number of follow-up questions as to why you felt the need to create an army of trees that want a shag. Where would you like me to start?"

There was a lengthy pause during which I could hear several Saxons come to recognise why it was so important that sometimes 'no' means 'no'. Should any of them make it out of the woods alive, I felt sure they'd have a more enlightened attitude to the position of women in society.

Oh, and splinters. Lots and lots of splinters.

By which, of course, I mean, 'well done, Morgan'. Never has the world seen such a prodigious, intuitive use of Wood Qi.

"Damn right, Big M. Now, back to the plan?"

Back to the plan.

"Drynwyn?"

Fuck the plan.

"Awesome."

CHAPTER 53 - IN WHICH THINGS VEER DANGEROUSLY CLOSE TO A MOMENT OF HONEST SINCERITY

To avoid other possible ... entanglements, we ventured deep into the woods before slowly dog-legging towards where we'd thought a wizard had been slain. Once bitten, twice shy, and all that, so we were looking to make much more cautious progress.

To my delight, I found that I could make a paint drop 'breadcrumb' trail appear in my vision, leading to my desired destination. Basically, I was Qiing up my own Sat Nav. Merlin had been unimpressed when I'd gushed with excitement - apparently, the skill would have manifested at the same time as I'd gained the ability to fast travel - but I wasn't letting him kill my buzz.

As we followed the purple blobs through the trees, I played around with pulling in the abundant Wood Qi around me and cycling it around my artist's studio. As when I created the technique of the thirsty trees, accessing this mouldy-smelling essence seemed ridiculously easy. So much so, I'd asked Merlin about it.

After the usual patronising back and forth over 'what a good question' that was and how 'impressed' he was I'd thought it up on my own, he settled in to explain.

Think about it like ... I'm sorry, my dear, I'm trying to find an appropriate frame of reference. Did you ever lift weights?

"Absolutely."

Really.

"All the time. You couldn't get me out of the gym. Morning, noon and night, there I was. Pumping all the iron. I was the henchest girl on the checkout. Won awards and everything.

That's fascinating! I would never have expected ... you are having fun at my expense, are you not?

"Maybe a smidgen."

But you are familiar with the concept?

"Man lift heavy thing. Man's muscles grow. Man takes tablets to help make muscles grow faster. Muscles grow, dick shrink. I have a handle on the core premise."

Well, when you first start becoming ... I believe the colloquial term is 'swole'?

I cringed so hard, I nearly fell to the ground. "Mate, we need a list of words you absolutely are not allowed to say. And 'swole' is going to sit right at the top of it."

So be it. The point, my dear, is that your initial improvement can be quite impressive. You've transitioned from being an entirely sedentary potato to something more active. The muscles respond, and the, erm, the 'gains' are very visible.

"I am following your analogy thus far."

Well, cultivating is not dissimilar. In a very short period of time, you have moved from never having heard of Qi, to possessing pristine channels and a capacity to use energy that would be the envy of anyone in the world - well, apart from me, of course. Now, crucially, you have come by those 'gains' through entirely non-traditional means.

"The dragon Qi?"

That, and finding Drynwyn, the mana stones and the various tricks I had to pull to stop your very being vapourising.

"I could be wrong, but it sounds like you're suggesting I might not be wholly responsible for my own rapid self-improvement."

Quite. Well, the point I am making is that, because of all those incidents, things are currently coming too easily to you. You can draw in Wood Qi so easily because that, in and of itself, is not a significant achievement for an advanced cultivator. You have, quite by accident, reached a stage of development where it is utterly facile for you to do that.

"I was **Neville** and now I'm nearly **Harry**. All hail me. I'm not hearing much downside here? "

For now, there is not. You are performing feats that would usually correspond to a lifetime of practice, reflection and effort. However -

"No, don't spoil it. There's no need for 'however'. Let's leave it that I am awesome, I'll be awesome forever, and nothing more needs to be said about my intrinsic awesomeness. I am the Marysuest Mary Sue that ever Marysued"

And it's been suggested I'm immature.

Drynwyn is quite right, my dear. It is important you understand the full implications of your current predicament. You have short-circuited the process of cultivation. We did our best to catch you up with our cave training. But that has only taken you so far. I am delighted that things have progressed so quickly. I feel much more confident we will succeed in our goal than ever before. Nevertheless, I must make you aware that a wall is approaching - I have no idea how rapidly - and you will not be able to progress beyond it without learning how to cultivate traditionally.

"Okay. That doesn't sound too bad?"

It is a little more complex than I am making it sound. Apologies. Okay. Think of having the body of ... can you name someone with an enviably masculine physique for the point of this metaphor?

"Sure. Bill Gates. Massive guns. Obsessed with Broscience. Utterly peeled."

Thank you for those new and colourful words. Okay. So, imagine you are Bill Gates. At the peak of human physical perfection. However, you have no idea how you achieved that state. You have an impending Mr. Universe competition in a month, and not the first insight as to how you should prepare for it.

"I can see how Bill Gates would feel alarm in that situation."

I am not sure you are wholly following me, but the point is this. When you hit that wall, you cannot progress further. Unless you put in the time to build - and crucially, understand how you build - the appropriate foundations, every moment you spend without advancing at that wall, you will slip back a little bit further. Eventually, you will ...

"Win a massive prize, and everyone will applaud?"

No, my dear. You will suffer the same fate as me. It is, after all, the destiny of cultivators everywhere. We are to constantly progress. And if we don't, we will surely die.

***

The atmosphere of our jaunt in the woods darkened somewhat after the Big M spelt out my impending doom. There was something about seeing the approaching cliff-edge you were hurtling towards that ruined a good walk.

Although, to be fair, it's not like he was giving me a terminal diagnosis. He was just making clear that, at some unknown point in our uncertain future, my free cultivation ride was going to come to an end.

But that was okay. If I knuckled down now, paid attention and stopped fucking about, there was no reason why - especially with Merlin as my guide - that I couldn't lay down all the groundwork I needed to cultivate properly. Basically, if I put in a shift now, when the going got tough, I could get going.

The problem was, I wasn't sure I had it in me.

It had always been the same. Whether at school, university, Art College or a succession of unfulfilling jobs, everyone believed I "could try harder."

They were probably right, but, and this is what I found so hard to explain to anyone, I just didn't have it in me to do better.

All things considered, I've been pretty upbeat during my time in the Dark Ages. Yes, I've had my moments, but - and I am aware of how pathetic this sounds - this has probably been one of the most consistently enjoyable periods of my life.

It takes me a moment to process that.

But then, as sure as eggs is eggs, if there is one thing I know for absolute certain about being me, it is that there is never an 'up' without it crashing back 'down' straight afterwards.

Even now, walking through some lovely, dark and deep woods, with a wizard chattering away and a mythical sword for a companion, I can feel my mood starting to darken.

Rhyddrech used to feel like you.

The interjection was so unexpected I almost thought I'd hallucinated it.

"Sorry?"

Everyone thinks he was this happy-go-lucky guy. The life and soul of every fucking mead-hall. 'Hael' basically means 'bloke you want a drink with', you know? But that wasn't him. Not really.

"I would never have guessed."

No one would. But it was all an act. A mask he'd put on when out on business. "Have to live up to the legend", he would say. But when there was no one about, his Qi tasted like yours does now.

"You can taste my Qi?"

Not normally. But when you feel really fucking strong emotions, I sometimes get a flavour of how you are feeling. Mostly, of course, you've been squirting out non-stop blind terror -

"Nice."

Calling it like I see it. But now? Now you taste just like he did. Especially last thing at night when the fire burned low, and he would stare at nothing.

"And how is that?"

You taste sad, my dear.

There's all sorts of different types of therapy. Trust me, I've tried most of them. But until you've had a dead wizard and a talking sword feel concern for your mental health, you've genuinely never lived.

I know what I should have said then. I had, literally, a captive audience and a long hike ahead in which to explore some of my issues. I had one of the wisest souls to ever live to bounce thoughts off and a sword who'd seen in 3D what happened to you when you bottled everything up too tight. I'd probably never get such a good chance again to talk 'me' through properly.

Or I could mask it all with an inappropriate joke.

"That's what yo momma said."

Why change a habit of a lifetime?

CHAPTER 54 - IN WHICH I AM ENTIRELY HAPPY TO BE TREATED AS A SEX OBJECT

It's difficult to know the etiquette when seeking to introduce yourself to a mythical warlord. Particularly, when you have the voice of someone who knows them really well in your head, whispering pointers. And especially when his men have just caught you sneaking up on him.

***

We'd arrived at the spot where we'd assumed a cultivator had been killed a few hours earlier, and, as anticipated, we found one very dead wizard. This was not a nice place to be. The whole area was drenched with a smell of sour Qi, little improved by the horde of flies feeding on the bloated corpse with the giant chest wound.

As the extent of my forensic knowledge was limited to an entirely normal, and not at all unhealthily sexual, obsession with Benedict Cumberbatch's Sherlock, I was somewhat at the mercy of Merlin and Drynwyn's expertise in the matter.

She's dead.

Well, that cleared it all up nicely. Glad to have all that expertise on hand.

I wasn't wild that she'd just been left lying here like that. Speaking as someone who'd created their fair share of dead Saxons in the last few hours, I knew it was a touch hypocritical to worry about a dead body. But there seemed something wantonly cruel about killing this woman - girl, really - and then leaving her where she fell.

It was the work of seconds to open the earth and inter the body. I'd have liked to have added a cairn, but without a name, I left it be.

A few words from Poe came to mind, and with no one to take the piss out of me for being mawkish, I spoke them softly over her grave in the gathering dark.

I stand amid the roar
Of a surf-tormented shore,
And I hold within my hand
Grains of the golden sand —
How few! yet how they creep
Through my fingers to the deep,
While I weep — while I weep!

We need to get you laid.

I didn't have a lot to say to that. I hoped I wouldn't ever get to the stage where death did not bother me. I worried I might.

Fortunately, the tracks left behind by the men as they cut away from the scene were easy enough to follow, and, in no time, I was peering at a pretty grim group of armed men who were setting up camp for the night.

Well done, my dear, you've hit the jackpot. Do you know who these are?

"I'm kind of hoping they're a collection of men that have worked 'killing female cultivators' out of their system."

Indeed. But these are not just any collection of men -

"Are they M&S men?"

I fear I lack the context for what I'm sure was a witty rejoinder there, my dear. Please, imagine I laughed heartily.

"Tough crowd. So, you recognise these guys?"

Indeed, I do. These are Arthur's Marghekyon.

"Yay! I love a Marghekyon. And Arthur's Marghekyon? They're by far my favourite of all the Marghekyons."

Sometimes, I fucking hate being your sword.

"As if you know what a Marghekyon is!"

Of course I fucking do. Anyone who is anyone wants an 'in' to Arthur's Marghekyon. Rhyddrech tried to join once, but after a night of carousing and the three Virgin Knights becoming the two Virgin Knights and the one Sexually Awakened Horndog, they turned him down.

The camp was being set up with startling efficiency, the tents being established around a large circular tree stump in the middle of the clearing.

A Marghekyon is, I'm sorry, I'm trying to find a modern-day equivalent, I think 'crew' is probably not too far from the truth.

'So, this is Arthur's 'crew'? All heavily armoured, storied warriors, I presume? And they are currently laying out their evening meal on a big tree stump?"

Yes.

"One may almost say they are treating that large round object as a table, right?"

Are you okay, my dear?

"Oh, come on. Are you telling me you're not seeing this? Arthur. Group of warriors. Big circular dining surface?"

A shadow fell over me, and strong hands pulled me to my feet, whilst spinning me around.

"I don't know who you are speaking to, Celt, but I have a friend who will be very interested in making the acquaintance of all that red hair."

A hood was dropped over my head.

***

Arthur was studying a map of the countryside that he feared was, at best, startlingly inaccurate. Cartography was quite a skill, and it did not appear Uther had managed to recruit the peak of the profession. Where they were currently stood, for example, was apparently the middle of the sea.

He rolled up the scroll and was replacing it in Llameri's saddlebags, when Bors emerged through the trees carrying a bound figure.

"Really, Sir Bors. Whilst I appreciate your commitment to bringing back every waif and stray you come across, there must be a limit." He indicated the haggard figure of Melehan sitting, slumped, to his right. "I thought we decided that one Saxon wizard was enough?"

"Ah, but this is no Saxon, my Lord." He removed the hood with a flourish, and a cascade of red hair fell down to frame a heart-shaped face.

At that sight, Arthur let out an audible gasp. Bors elbowed the warrior at his side. "I told you, didn't I? Knew there was a way to get him out of his funk."

***

I'm not going to lie, it's quite nice having a figure from legend sigh when they look at you for the first time. I mean, I know this body isn't strictly speaking 'me', but I bet porn stars with fake boobs don't angst over whether people are lusting over the real 'them'.

So, yeah, I could totally get used to being a thirst trap for a mythical king.

You know I can hear you, right?

What do you want me to say, Big M? A girl's got to eat.

I feel I should be clear that our aim here is to provide support to Arthur as he rises to become king. Not ...

Jump him?

Yes. I think that would be an excellent first order of business. You are to do everything you can not to ... erm ... 'jump' the Once and Future King.

"I don't know, Merlin. He looks like a man who could do with a good jumping."

My eyes were adjusting to the camp now, and I took in the men that made up Arthur's Marghekyon. As unfamiliar as I was with military structure, even I could tell there were two different sorts of soldiers here. On the one hand, there were the basic warriors. Don't get me wrong, they were still fucking terrifying men that could bench press me with one hand, but they were all, I don't know, pretty nondescript. Some carried bows, some swords and shields and others spears, but all of them were wearing metaphorical red shirts. I didn't think there was going to be much point learning their names: they had big NPC energy, if you know what I mean.

On the other hand, there was a small group - probably not quite twenty - that were absolutely the business. If you had asked me to paint an Arthurian version of the Dirty Dozen, I - well, I would have told you to 'fuck off' and find someone else to fulfil your cosplay fantasy - but if you, by luck, caught me on a good day, these guys were exactly what I'd have doodled for you.

The guy who had grabbed me from the woods, for example, was a massive, strategically shaved gorilla that was carrying more weapons than seemed practical without having eight arms. And he wasn't the most intimidating of them. I'd not seen so much leather armour, giant biceps and waist-length beards since an ill-fated career as a waitress for 'Bear Night' at The Nightingale.

And amongst them all was Arthur.

He was tall, though not built on anything like the same scale as some of his Marghekyon. He wore his dark beard closely cropped, which made his severe features appear even less friendly. I'd always had somewhat of a thing for Roger Delgado's Master, and if you lopped twenty years off him in 'Terror of the Autons', you'd have the face of the Prince of the Britons.

I wasn't quite swooning, but if he wanted to buy me a vodka and coke, I would probably make a show of myself.

I still can hear you, my dear.

211

"What do they call you, Celt?" I even liked his voice. I could show that voice a good time.

Before I could answer, Bors dragged Drynwyn from the scabbard on my back and threw it to Arthur. I barely had time to register the impending firestorm this was likely to cause when the Prince plucked the blade from the air.

Showtime.

CHAPTER 55 - IN WHICH CEDRIC BEGINS TO SNARL.

A giant pillar of fire stretching leagues into the sky was the sort of thing even the least observant of sentries tended to notice.

The intensity of the blaze lit up the sky, transforming the still of night into the brightness of midday. It was as if a monumental finger had suddenly thrust itself upwards, pointing towards where the sun should reside and deciding to show it how to do the whole 'daylight' thing.

It was several seconds before there was any sound to accompany the blaze, but when it did come, it was a deep rumble as if of a thousand thunderheads. Anyone who had somehow missed the light show certainly had their attention grabbed by a noise that left all ears ringing and more than a few bleeding.

There were screams of terror at what felt like the world was ending, but within moments of the explosion, the first Saxon war bands were already gathering to set out and investigate its cause.

Whatever had happened was well beyond the scope of their patrols, and this put everyone on edge: no one wants to advance into enemy territory with powerful forces on your flank. The rumours of groups of enemy cultivators - or even worse, of Merlin - still haunted the dreams of this army. Thus, the sight of a massive tower of burning Qi was, at best, deeply unsettling to morale. Memories of Isca were still fresh amongst the warriors. No one wanted to be on the receiving end of some payback.

Saxons are very much all for the sowing, not so much about the reaping.

Amongst the foremost of those responding was Cedric, who could be found pulling on his wolf-fur cloak and striding to the edge of the camp, issuing orders as he moved. "There's someone gathering power out there, and I can smell cultivation. If there's a wizard fucking about behind us, I want to be eating their liver before daybreak. Fifty gold coins to whoever brings it to me."

Groups of his warriors howled in response to his words and loped through the trees towards the column of smoke that still lingered in the air. Although not one of the largest factions in the Saxon host, the numbers of West Saxons were significant. The other chieftains watched, somewhat in envy, at the speed and efficiency with which Cedric's pack deployed itself. There was a sleekness, a ferocity, a passion to the way these warriors moved, which spoke well to their proficiency in battle. There had been rumours about the path of destruction these men had delivered during the invasion. None of the Saxons could have been considered merciful, but the tales of atrocities committed by those who flew Cedric's standard were chilling even to them.

However, watching them now, none missed the quality of their gear nor the number of thick iron torcs they wore at their arms. Those under Cedric's command were given respect rarely afforded mere spearmen. They were, in appearance and action, among the elite of the Saxon forces.

A few of the other chieftains, sensing a shift in momentum in their perennial battle for supremacy, tried to organise their own warriors into a similar display. But none could miss how the man was being looked at by his fellows - this was a leader who could get things done and rewarded those that pleased him. Should this hunt return with a defeated British cultivator, there would be little remaining debate as to who was the foremost Saxon chieftain.

Cedric noted all this and was well pleased.

Amongst so many other contenders, he had despaired at ever getting an opportunity to showcase his claim. The camp was drenched in the blood of those who had tried to rise to the top without the backing to make it stick, and he was a wily enough wolf not to leap at his prey too early. You let the others wear it down first, and, when exhaustion began to tell, you picked the perfect moment to strike.

However, he had begun to fear he had tarried too long. There was no sign of anyone else coming over to his side and, amongst so many others, how could he differentiate himself sufficiently? Yet, now, the perfect chance to gain attention had come along. If all went well - and why would it not? - he would ensure that the blood would flow in thankful sacrifice for his good fortune.

Nodding to himself in satisfaction, he was about to join his spearmen in their hunt when he saw a familiar face hanging back at the edge of the watching crowd. At first, he paid him no mind, but - on second thoughts - there was an advantage to be made here. Now would be the time to fully tie this worm to him. If he leant him a little of this glory, he would be his forever more. He strode towards Pæga, grasped his arm and pulled the man into his wake. "I want your men with me, friend."

"Of course," Pæga felt the eyes of all the other chieftains fall on him, and he puffed out his chest at their regard. Of all of them, Cedric had selected him to join him in this quest; he could feel his standing rise almost as quickly as that column of fire itself. Then, the reason for this helter-skelter pursuit rammed home, and he found himself licking his lips nervously. "But, I am afraid, my wizard has gone missing. I'm not sure how much use my men can be if there's a cultivator out there." His heart skipped a beat at the thought of, once again, confronting terrible powers no human should wield.

Cedric grinned in response, but the smile did not reach his eyes. "There's nothing a wizard can do that the rest of us cannot overcome." He gestured towards where the remains of his own cultivator still fluttered in the breeze, crows seeking out any last scraps of meat. "If we cut them, do they not bleed? If we bleed them, do they not scream? And when they are done screaming, do they not die? Cultivators are nothing more than tricksters. For all their boasting, their lives leak out the same as the rest of us."

A vision of a spinning sword dissecting his second-in-command was, suddenly, at the forefront of Pæga's mind. It wasn't what they could do to the wizard that especially concerned him. He was sure Cedric was capable of inflicting all manner of horrendous things on an enemy wizard. It was what might come back the other way that concerned him most.

But his warriors, seeing their chieftain honoured by the terrifying West Saxon, were already striding forward, seeking to match the enthusiasm of Cedric's wolf-fur-clad forces. He didn't think he would be able to call them back, even if wanted to. Within a few heartbeats, and with more than a little regret, he joined them, following Cedric's lead, howling out his anxiety to the night air.

The cloud of smoke was dissipating slightly, but the focus of their charge was clear. Should they make good time, they would be reaching the site of the explosion before sunrise. And then they would see what their chieftain did to cultivators that displeased him.

The remaining Saxons watched them leave, then set about preparing for what was to come. Should Cedric return triumphant, the advance would begin immediately. If not, someone else would need to take their shot. Either way, the invasion would recommence imminently.

CHAPTER 56 - IN WHICH I BECOME THE DARK AGE EQUIVALENT OF SAVLON

I've had to endure more than my fair share of awkward moments.

There was vomiting down the front of my teacher's dress when I was seven. That was an early highlight.

Then, there was that time I went to a party wearing what I thought was a very flattering maxi dress. Turned out to be maternity wear, as Felicity Hurndall took great delight in telling everyone for the next two years of my life.

Probably near the top of the list would be that, a few years later, I sent nudes to my best friend's husband. To be fair, he asked. Often. But, no, that wasn't viewed as an acceptable excuse back then either.

What I'm saying is that I'm not unused to people looking at me with 'what the fuck?' written all over their faces.

What was a new experience, though, was being responsible for chargrilling a significant part of British culture.

I'm making it sound worse than it is.

Marginally.

***

As soon as Arthur caught Drynwyn, the sword did its thing.

Fucking A. Prince or Pauper, you handle me, you better be able to handle me.

"Merlin, can we have Drynwyn on mute for a bit, please? I'm catching the folks up, and I think we could all do without him adding his particular brand of colour commentary while I do."

Your wish is my command.

So, the giant silverback threw Drynwyn to Arthur, and the dopey fucker went and caught it. The sword went up in flames, at which stage, things became complicated.

As you would expect, Merlin had loaded his favourite future monarch with all manner of life-saving goodies. I'm sure they all had names and titles, but to spare me trying to pronounce words that will make me sound like I'm gargling granite, I'm going to refer to them all as 'plot armour'.

This is all very disrespectful to many priceless artefacts that your hooligan sword has just turned into ash. Llen Arthyr yng Nghernyw, on its own, was one of the wonders of the Dark Age.

"Yes, fare thee well, sweet cloak: we will never see your like again. In mourning, I'll pour one out for Llen the Voweless every bonfire night."

As I was saying ... When Drynwyn went boom, the various pieces of plot armour did their best to keep the timeline intact. They absorbed a fair amount of the fire, and when they became overwhelmed, they diverted quite a lot of the blaze straight upwards.

The keywords being 'a fair amount' and 'quite a lot', of course.

Yes, I'm getting there, aren't I? So, what I'm saying is that the Once and Future King is still very much alive. No worries on that score.

He's just a touch crispier than he formally was.

And you are all caught up.

∗∗∗

After the sonic boom that comes with a myriad of magical items going up in flames faded, all that could be heard in the clearing were Arthur's screams.

For a moment, none of us moved.

Then, as I squirted some Qi around to rebuild my shattered eardrums, I dashed forward to wrench Drynwyn from Arthur's grasp. I took most of the skin on his hand and forearm with me as I did so, which was nice.

If you need a more vivid description for this moment, think of popping a giant blister that smelt of KFC.

You're welcome.

I can feel his life force rapidly fading, my dear.

"That will be the full thickness burns across his whole body, Big M. Need a plan and fast."

I was aware of another figure kneeling next to me, and I scrabbled to get the sword back in its scabbard. I glanced over and met the eyes of the cultivator that beheaded Ealdgyð back in the village. Then his hands were on Arthur's chest, and he was ... doing something.

As I watched, the raw horror of the burns calmed slightly, and Arthur's screams reduced to sad little whimpers. A fusion of the scent of lavender, peppermint and juniper flooded my senses.

*Interesting. Whoever this is has an impressive facility for Wood Qi. He's soothing the wounds with the fundamental essences of nearby herbs. Ah, now that is clever. He even anaesthetising him with something from those thyme bushes, too. This is a **Harry**, my dear, if you are wondering.*

"Is it working?"

Define 'working', my dear. Merlin's voice was suddenly bitter. His ministrations will mean that Arthur dies in a few moments rather than right now.

The giant man who had thrown the sword was reaching out to pull the Saxon cultivator away. I glared at him.

"You touch him, and Arthur instantly dies. He's the only thing keeping him in one piece right now."

"He's a fucking Saxon." The man's teeth were bared.

"If you can't be helpful, fuck off." I activated [Personal Space Invader] and blew the man away into the trees. I was idly aware that I must have levelled that up as he was the only one sent hurtling.

"Merlin, come on, there's got to be something you can do to help. You've seen me through tighter spots than this."

I am linked to you. And you are a cultivator. There is not anything that connects me that way to Arthur.

217

I dropped inside my artist's studio and tried to direct my Qi to flow from me into the remains of the Wicker Man. But there was no pathway for my paint to flow. I was me, and Arthur was him. I growled in frustration and tried to get a read on what the other cultivator was doing.

I could feel him applying a thin coating of his Qi to Arthur's skin and that Qi was holding the properties of the soothing herbs. The thing is, even with my level of knowledge, I could tell this man's Qi was pretty thin gruel. For someone who had once seemed like an all-powerful, force-lightning-throwing Sith Lord, he was basically doling out nicely scented dishwater.

"Can we make what he is doing more effective?"

Merlin took a moment. *Perhaps. He would need to allow us to help.*

The Saxon cultivator's eyes were closed as he maintained the balm around Arthur. I tapped him lightly on his arm. "Dude, can you hear me?"

He nodded, his face a mask of concentration. "I dig what you're doing, but it's not going to be enough."

A frown creased his forehead. "I'm sorry. This is all I have left. And I'm afraid I'm nearly out."

Well, that wasn't great news. "No worries, mate. I am chockful of Qi goodness, you just need to tap me in."

"Tap you in?" It might have been my imagination, but the herby smell was getting distinctly fainter, and Arthur's cries were increasing.

"Sorry, WWE reference. Guess you guys aren't ready for that yet, but your kids are gonna love it. I don't know what you are doing, but if you let me, I think I can boost you."

"Do whatever you need to."

It was easier said than done. When I switched on my Magic Eyes, I could see his Qi, but it steadfastly refused to mix with mine. Wherever my purple energy touched the green light covering Arthur, it was pushed away.

Not like that. You're trying to dominate his casting. You need to merge with what he is doing. It's not like absorbing the Qi of a fallen foe. He won't be able to submit to that whilst alive, even if he is willing. You need to combine it with his spell.

You may have guessed, but I'm not good at performing under pressure. Bohemian Rhapsody, on the other hand ...

I needed to look at things in a different way. There was a rhythm, a pulse, to the Saxon's cycling. There was no point trying to do anything on his 'on' beat, but I could support what he was doing on the' off'.

Easy come. Easy go. Little high. Little low.

We fell into a rhythm, him pushing out the healing essence and me boosting it and strengthening the quality of what he was sending. I didn't need to know what he was doing to make it thicker. Soon, the smell of the herbs was almost overwhelming.

I know I seem to be saying this all too often, my dear, but you never cease to astonish me.

I don't know how long we maintained this give and take, but eventually, Merlin suggested I force a manastone into Arthur's curled fist and tie what we were doing to its Earth Qi. If that sounds complicated, it absolutely was. The fourth or fifth time I lost grip of the different Qi strands, I was happy to let the Big M take charge.

The relief I felt when the manastone maintained the spell around Arthur was huge. I collapsed against the Saxon, both of us exhausted and drenched with sweat.

We weren't quite post-coital, but, you know, that was about the most satisfying workout I'd had for quite a number of years.

"How is he?" The giant man I'd thrown around like a ragdoll seemed a bit more respectful now.

"He's alive. I don't know there's much more to say than that."

He looked like he was about to say more when the howling of wolves interrupted him. But no, that didn't sound like actual wolves. The man's face creased into a frown. "Fuck it. That's the Saxons. They've found us."

He started to bellow orders to the men who had been silently crowded around us before turning back to glare at me.

"You got anything left, Celt?"

And that was the question, wasn't it?

CHAPTER 57 - IN WHICH BORS AND CEDRIC SWAP POEMS AND ENTER A DICK MEASURING COMPETITION.

In a culture where tales of incredible feats of arms and scarcely believable deeds of courage are the currency of existence, it is, indeed, the innumerable stories of Arthur's Marghekyon that stand out.

Throughout his childhood, the young Prince's capacity to seek out all the most exciting forms of trouble attracted a score of like-minded friends to his side. Bors, Owain, Balin, dark-skinned Palemedes and Arthur's younger cousins, Gawayne and Cador, were the first to see the potential in following the lead of the boy with whom no one could ever stay angry. But, as he grew, others of a similar mindset quickly joined what everyone for leagues around called "Arthur's unruly pack."

By his sixteenth birthday, the bonds between these boys were forged stronger than iron, and as those friends rose to star in their own stories, they brought their followers into the Prince's orbit.

Thus, at its height, Arthur's Marghekyon numbered close to three hundred warriors, and if he did not quite know the names of everyone who rode with him to battle, no one thought any less of him for that. He was, after all, Prince Arthur, and where he led, his pack would follow.

"Are you writing a book, Big M? Because I kind of think there's other things to focus on right now."

I'm just providing you with some crucial context, my dear. You have, thus far, had limited experience of professional warfare. Wulfnoð's memories of the fyrd - primarily farmers and hunters, remember - and your own highly fortunate interactions with roaming Saxon warbands may lead you to underestimate that of which these men are capable. The elite warriors of Britain surround you. And they have a wounded prince to defend.

As far as I could tell, 'the elite warriors of Britain' were currently running around in a panic, shouting at each other, but my military experience was somewhat limited, as Merlin had noted. Maybe this was how it was done in the pro leagues.

The big man - Bors, I was to understand - raised his eyebrows at me, and I realised I hadn't answered him. "Sorry, Merlin was filling me in on what an elite fighting force you are."

"Merlin? But he's dead!"

As soon as he said those words, he snapped his mouth shut, and his eyes grew round. Interesting, I thought, so it's not quite the taboo secret the Big M figured it might be. There are at least some people who know he's passed on.

"Dead but not quite gone, I'm afraid. He's got somewhat of a Patrick Swayze 'unfinished business' situation. But no potter's wheel-related shenanigans. Not yet, anyway."

"I do not know what any words you've just said mean." Bors grabbed the shoulder of a man running past him and span him around. "Not that way, you fucking idiot. Form up against that line of trees. There! No, over there!" He propelled the man in the other direction with a bootkick.

"Basically, he's dead, but he's still talking to me. He says 'hello'."

Our eyes met momentarily, and I could see Bors trying to figure out how much of his available brain space he was willing to put into understanding me. It was a look with which I was intimately familiar.

As was the outcome.

He shook his head as if to clear his vision and returned to his original question. "What can we expect from you here?"

"Good looks, charm and witty banter."

I sensed from his blank look this was not an acceptable response. "I have no available Qi left if that is what you are asking." My artist's studio, my armour and my mana stone batteries were utterly exhausted. Keeping this particular English Patient alive had cleaned me out.

"Depending on how long the fight lasts, I might get enough back to be useful down the line. Maybe."

***

Bors cursed and immediately re-evaluated his planning.

He'd hoped the Celt would add some firepower to the left flank, but it just wasn't his day for being lucky. Studiously ignoring the melted thing that was all that remained of his best friend, he continued to seek to pull his small force into battle order.

On the plus side, he thought, the Saxons must be underestimating what they were coming up against. You didn't announce your impending strike by howling like lunatics unless you thought your opponent had poor discipline and poorer morale.

Sure, a descending horde of howling Saxon spearmen would be enough to rout a fyrd, but all they'd achieved so far was give Arthur's men time to form up.

That point was made, quite literally, when the first of the Saxons burst from the trees, to each be impaled by a flurry of arrows and javelins.

"Who fucking told you to throw!" Bors bellowed, striding forward to leave the cultivators to tend to Arthur. "The first person I see without a drawn bow or a shield ready for contact will be running home to his mummy with my spear so far up his arse he can use it to pick his nose."

***

I thought I could grow to like this man. If we survived what was coming.

The pincushioned, blue-painted Saxons each had worn a wolfskin around their shoulders. With the howling, that suggested we were up against a war leader who had a firm grasp of branding and a decent marketing strategy. I asked Merlin about it.

I rather fear we may have drawn the attention of Cedric of the West Saxons. I know of few others that favour such theatrics.

The Saxon cultivator, Melehan, quickly filled me into a lot of colourful backstory as to why it would be a spiffy idea, as both a woman and a cultivator, for me not to fall into this Cedric's hands.

The howling of the pseudo-wolves had stopped, leaving just the sound of Bors issuing orders in a somewhat eerie silence.

221

The Britons had formed a large hollow square, four or five people deep, around their unconscious Prince. Several terrifying-looking men were with us in the middle of the square. I thought of them as 'troubleshooters' or, more accurately, 'trouble-slaughterers-with-giant-axes' who would move to where they were needed.

Looking around at the determined faces of the warriors, I had an inkling as to what Merlin had meant earlier. These men did this sort of thing for a living. "I'm feeling pretty confident right now, Big M. Should I be?"

Perhaps. They can hold this position until doomsday against a single warband. Maybe even should two or three come against them. But Bors knows the rest of the Saxon army is just a small march away. They won't bother stirring for two hundred Britains, but -

"If they know Arthur is here, all bets are off?"

Indeed.

As if listening to our conversation, a voice spat incomprehensible syllables at us from the woods. Bors replied in the same language, and a few of his men grinned.

"Why can't I understand what they're saying? I've heard Saxon before."

Whoever is out there is speaking in a somewhat unusual dialect. I presume Cedric is addressing us in Kentish because -

"He's a cunt?"

I was going to say he's from Kent, but we can agree with your general sentiment. One moment, I should be able to help you translate what is going on.

In no time, the back and forth between the two commanders became comprehensible. "And what do you know, we came across a bunch of Saxons in a place no one expected you to be. Things were said, javelins were thrown, and here we are."

"And you want us to believe that you are a - sorry, what did you call yourselves?"

"A scroll club. We like gathering together in the woods, having drinks, and discussing the latest kennings. What was the one you shared the other day, Gawayne, heaven something?"

"Heofon-candel." A surprisingly high voice came from the press of warriors. "Means the sun. A heaven candle."

"See? We're always doing things like this. Just marching out into the wilderness and composing poetry and the like. A scroll club."

"And you would like us to believe your ... scroll club of two hundred warriors has found itself loitering on the edge of our entire army."

"I couldn't give a toss what you believe." I definitely liked Bor's 'fuck around and find out' energy. "Way I see it, we're going to get moving soon, and you can either try and stop us, and we'll kill you, or you can fuck off back to your mummy and daddy in the army and tell them the big boy is being mean to you and you need them to step in."

There was a tense pause. I'm not sure the sniggering in the British ranks did much to lower temperatures.

"I am fond of kennings myself, Briton. I have, for example, heard my war band described, by friends and foes alike, in the old tongue as the 'hrynsævar hræva hund'. Can you translate it?"

Bors voice was tight. "The hounds of the roaring sea of corpses."

And with that, the Saxons attacked.

***

I didn't really have the best view of the opening exchanges, huddled as I was in the middle of the formation and shielded from projectiles from above by several guards.

It would be hard to miss the noise, though. The Saxons hit us from all sides, and the square noticeably shuddered with the intensity of the crash of metal on wood.

This merged with the howling of the attackers, the shouting of orders, and the screams of the fallen to provide quite the unsettling soundscape.

Through it all, Arthur remained unconscious, his blistered body contorted in a boxing pose. As far as I could tell, the mana stone I had wedged between his grasp was still working fine; Merlin had said it should continue to self-sustain through its connection to me and from ambient Qi.

I was trying to encourage some paint to cycle, when I realised Bors was next to me again. "Don't you have a battle to command?"

"Nah. Shields have locked together, so it's all pushing and shoving for a bit now. They'll get tired before us and fall back to have a think about what to do next. They don't seem to have a wizard, so we'll do this the old-fashioned way." He grimaced. "Until, that is, Cedric decides to swallow his pride and send a message back to the rest of the army for help."

"What will we do then?"

A panicked shout from the far edge of the square grabbed Bors' attention for a second, but one of the 'troubleshooters' pushed their way forward into and through the press and, a few rises and falls of his giant axe later, he was making his way back to the middle.

"Fucking sneaky blue-skinned twat felt like making a name for himself." He answered Bor's questioning glance.

"And did he?"

"Dunno. Does anyone write songs about people who piss themselves when they get their arm cut off?"

"Probably not."

"Well then. Was hardly worth the effort."

The big man turned back to me and rubbed a hand over his face. "In this formation, we can effect a decent fighting withdrawal if we need to. It won't be pretty, but neither am I, and it never did me any harm. Cedric will have a choice to either let us go, or double down. We're good, but not that good. If the whole army comes calling, you're going to have to do us all a favour."

"What?"

"You're going to need to pull some wizardy-shit and get Arthur out of here."

CHAPTER 58 - IN WHICH SHIT GETS REAL

Sitting idly chatting in the middle of a pitched battle felt somewhat odd, but no one else seemed to think anything of it.

"Are you sure there's nothing we should be doing to help?" I asked for, seemingly, the fiftieth time as one of the troubleshooters strode out to hack at an especially troublesome Saxon.

"I'd take a fireball or two if you had one to spare?" Bors looked at me, hopefully.

I shook my head. Although there was a decent amount of paint now cycling around my artist's studio, my channels were painfully raw. New-Jimmy-Choos-two-sizes-two-small-and-an-eight-hours-bar-shift raw. Merlin kept muttering gloomily about 'ruptures', 'Qi exhaustion' and 'catastrophic decompression' every time he sensed me so much as glance towards my essence.

"Not really, then. It's what people don't realise about battles. Most of it is fucking boring. Until it suddenly very much isn't. More often than not, a shield wall press is just a brutal, monotonous grind until one side calls it a day. There's two different war bands hitting us - the fuckers who think they're wolves are giving us a bit of trouble on the left-hand side, but the other lot, fighting under a stag skull sigil, aren't much cop. Hearts aren't in it."

Melehan flinched at that. Bors and I gave him a chance to expand, but he went back to staring blankly into the distance. Since helping with the semi-healing of Arthur, he was giving off some serious Lieutenant-Dan-after-the-legs-were-gone vibes.

He looked a bit like Gary Sinise, too.

Bors, sensing there was nothing more to be added by the Saxon, resumed. "It's not all heroic one-on-one duels like you hear about in sagas. The boys are all packed together so tightly that they can barely move, and all most of them can see is the backside of him in front. There's not much for me to do right now, to tell the truth. There's no grand strategy to it. It's just a game of push and shove. As long as our lads keep their footing and don't get knocked to the ground, the Saxons are not getting through. But we're not going anywhere quickly, either."

The troubleshooter returned to the middle, the left-hand side of his face painted with blood. He accepted a waterskin from one of the others and sluiced it over his head. "They've pulled back a touch on the right, Sir Bors. Probably not gone far, but if we're going to move, now would be a good time."

Bors nodded, stood and brushed himself down. "Fair enough. This is where we earn our mead, gentlemen," he nodded at me, "and lady."

His voice suddenly ratcheted up in volume, so it boomed around the clearing. "Right, that's enough standing around weighing our balls and calling it foreplay. We've got places to go, people to kill. On my mark, we're going to withdraw, slowly, along the path the Prince was taking us. Any fucker wants to stand in our way and contest our progress is to be shown the error of their ways. With extreme prejudice. Are we clear?"

A roar answered him. Four of the troubleshooters came forward with a makeshift stretcher on which they carefully laid the body of Arthur. He hadn't been able to tolerate anything touching his skin, not even a light blanket, so the extent of his burns was fully displayed.

I very much like Sir Bors' confidence, my dear, but this is a profoundly delicate military manoeuvre. Once moving, it will not take much for the coherence of our square to be imperilled. And should that happen, you must be prepared to immediately fast-travel Arthur to a place of safety.

"I thought my channels were fucked by all the healing?"

If the shield wall fails, I think we can consider the rupturing of your channels to be the lesser of two very bad evils, my dear. Bors is quite correct when he says the survival of Arthur is to be our only consideration.

I looked at what, charitably, could be described as a cured block of corned beef that smelt vaguely of lavender. "I'm not being funny, Big M, but is there much point? I doubt there's enough Bio-Oil in the world at this stage."

There was an uncomfortable silence. When Merlin spoke, there was a heaviness to his voice. *My dear, in my long life, I was granted but a few pure glimpses into the future. Moments of genuine prophecy, if you will. The strongest of these was of the court of King Arthur and the age of peace that he brought to the world. I will not relinquish my faith in that future until we have exhausted all possibilities. Whilst the Once and Future King lives, I will hold on to the hope we can, somehow, bring that dream to pass.*

"There's being alive, Merlin, and then there's," I looked at Arthur's form again and suppressed a shudder, "whatever that is."

Should I be what I once was, I am sure I would have been able to heal him. Our key aim must be to enable you to find a similar solution.

I was about to carefully, and in great detail, explain why expecting someone who'd been cultivating for about a week to be able to match the achievements of fucking MERLIN was batshit crazy when the square in which I was standing started, very slowly, to walk to the right.

***

Pæga licked his lips and nodded with reluctant appreciation. "The balls it takes to try this. I doubt my men could execute it in the best of circumstances, let alone whilst under sustained attack."

Cedric spat in response and glared at Pæga's tone. "They're fools. What are they hoping? To walk all the way back to Tintagel with us hammering them every step of the way?"

Pæga thought that was precisely what the British commander had planned. It did not seem especially prudent to mention it.

"One slip, and we'll have them." Cedric gestured for his skirmishers to press in again. If they were weary of the struggle, Pæga did not see it on the faces of the warriors wearing wolf-skins. They howled and charged the line of shields again. His own spearmen held back, far less keen to tangle further with this determined and well-organised foe.

There had, considering the ferocity of exchanges, been relatively few losses on either side. The men in the square had, thus far, been happy to hold the line and allow the Saxons to exhaust themselves and withdraw when wounds were taken. Every indication Pæga could see was that, should the Saxons choose to fully disengage, the British would be happy to simply vanish into the woods.

After another assault was bloodily beaten back by the retreating square, he suggested as much.

"Are you such a fool? They must be here for a reason. Every fyrd we have encountered, every single one, has been crushed without thought. Yet here and now we encounter these formidable men. Why is Uther happy for such as these to flit around at the edges of our army? More so, we have seen nothing of wizardry - so what caused that pillar of flame that drew us to them? No. There is more to this, and I would know what before I let them leave."

"So let us alert the other war chiefs. Let us see if these men can still stand against double, triple our numbers and then -"

In surprise, Pæga rocked backwards at the force of Cedric's slap, slipped and fell into the mud.

Later, looking back on the incident, it would be that the West Saxon did not even give him the respect of a punch that would burn his soul the most. That and the faces of scorn turned his way by Cedric's men as he lay sprawled on the ground. More than a few of his own men turned their eyes away in shame.

Cedric stood over him, bellowing out his rage. "We do not turn tail and beg for help from allies! We do not show our stomachs to those we will rule and plea for their support. They must know we are strong and that it is their luck to be allowed to join us in the hunt! And we do not let prey slip away simply because it lowers horns and resists. We. Are. Saxons. Do you not know what that means?"

Pæga lowered his eyes, submitting to the other man's wrath. This was the Cedric of which he had heard so much. The one everyone, even the boldest in the invasion, feared. Suddenly, he was dragged upright by one wolf-fur-clad arm. "I shall not have you cowering at my feet. Take your men and break that shield wall. Do not come back until you have done so. I will, personally, skin anyone who takes a backward step. At the end of this day, those of the stag that still live will be shouting in victory or screaming in pain beneath my knife. Thus do I vow." Paega was thrown into the arms of his men, who backed away, unsure whether they felt anger, fear or shame for the dismissal of the war chief and the threats that spurred them on.

Cedric watched them go and, when they were out of earshot, spoke softly to his own spearmen. "Let the British spend themselves on the cowardly stags. The moment you see an opening, strike. I want their chieftain's heart."

There was no howl in response, the warriors merely slipped into the wake of Pæga's men, who, mindful of Cedric's threats, were all, each and every one of them, charging the front of the British line.

**

"Fuck me, something's crawled up their arse. Front line, brace!"

The square had moved maybe five hundred yards, leaving a trail of broken weapons, crushed foliage and the odd dead Saxon in its wake. It was painstaking going, as each warrior needed to move in complete synchronisation with the man at his shoulder to avoid disaster. I'd tried line dancing once, and if I'd thought Cotton-

Eyed Joe was tricky in a church hall whilst wearing cowboy boots, I now had a new appreciation for the complexity of the whole 'moving in unison' thing.

But it was going okay.

From what I could tell, Bors had no interest in his men killing Saxons, so keeping the small force compact and taking one step at a time was relatively easy. The edges of the square were where there was the most likelihood of the whole thing collapsing in on itself, and it was there that men who I most probably knew stories about were positioned. No Lancelot, as far as I could tell, though. Probably back at Camelot pumping Guinevere.

And then, for no obvious reason I could see, the Saxons went all Leroy Jenkins. Whereas there'd been something of a rhythmical ballet of charge, clash, and withdrawal going on, it was suddenly like someone flicked a switch, and wildebeests were coming down the mountain to crush Simba's dad.

The first inkling I had that some serious shit was going down was all the troubleshooters gathered up their things and ran to the front of the formation. Arthur's stretcher was on the floor, and Melehan and I looked at each other with our best 'I've got a bad feeling about this' expressions.

The noise of the collision was deafening.

I thought I had gotten used to the sound of battle, but this was up another level. Over the screeching of metal on metal, I could just about hear Bors shouting orders, but there was more than a little of the last few minutes of '300' about his tone.

Get ready, my dear. The pressure is too great, and the line is bending. One of the warbands seems to be undertaking an utterly suicidal charge.

I drew Drynwyn, who had been uncharacteristically quiet since turning the King of all England into a flaming sambuca.

"Can they hold?"

Not against men who don't care if they live or die. Rhyddrech Hael always said you never fucked with a Berserker. There was a pause. **Or was it never fuck a Berserker? One of the two.**

"Are my channels healed enough to fast-travel out?"

Merlin's silence was the least welcome, most awkward pause I'd heard since telling my ex I was pregnant.

What do you want to do?

Funnily enough, Warren had said much the same thing.

And, with a splintering shudder, the British line broke.

CHAPTER 59 - IN WHICH A BUNCH OF MYTHS AND LEGENDS LOSE THEIR HERO

B alin was the first to fall.

Bors had worried about placing the smaller man near the square's edge, but it'd been the same since they were children: you couldn't convince him his size was ever a disadvantage.

For the most part, he was right. If you had big enough balls and a belligerent enough attitude, what was a foot or so in height?

But when push, literally, comes to shove, you need consistency in a shield wall. You want a uniform line of wooden shields presented as one to repel the charge. What you don't want is a visible gap between them into which, say, a particularly motivated Saxon can suicidally leap through.

That attacker was dead, stabbed through by the men standing behind each of Balin's shoulders, before he could do any damage. But, as his corpse landed on top of the short knight, he toppled him to the floor.

His shield mate, Hrunn, stepped forward to provide cover, but the pressure of the rush of Saxons made this as futile as swimming upstream in a flood, and he lost his own footing, slipping and being crushed underfoot as the charge went up and over the two of them.

Slowly, and then very quickly indeed, a breach opened.

Bors watched the disaster play out as if in slow motion as the frontmost corner of the formation started to collapse in on itself. The men of Arthur's Marghekyon were hard, disciplined warriors - veterans all - but even they could not perform the impossible.

Saxons began pouring into the growing breach, and no amount of skill or bravery could force them back. Geraint was run through. Lamorak was stunned by a shield bash and beheaded by a swinging axe. Bedivere was cut off from support and, for a time, was an island of death for any Saxon who dared to try to close. But a flurry of arrows was his undoing, his shield long since crushed to splinters.

All around him, childhood friends were trying and failing to be bulwarks against an irresistible tide of destruction. Bors had always known it would end like this. You were only ever one miscalculation away from death in a shield wall, and he'd had more than his share of luck over the years. There was no bitterness here.

He'd just thought he'd have Arthur at his side when the worst happened.

"Fuck it," and with that, he shoved his shield forward with all his might. The Saxon opposite staggered backwards as Bors' spear drove straight through his chest. Instead of pulling back and resetting, which he had been doing for what felt like hours, the giant Briton braced his legs and charged forward, also impaling the man who stood behind his first opponent.

Eliwlod and Palamedes were positioned at his shoulders, and, seeing this anger-fuelled gambit, they copied it. Of course, lacking Bors' immense size and strength, they had less success at creating Saxon kebabs, but, nevertheless, the three charges combined made a spiked wedge, with the big man at the tip, tearing into the attacking force. Those around them, feeling a sudden release of pressure, flowed behind them.

In moments, two distinct battles opened up.

The square formation was no more, dissolving into two halves. On the one side, the cohesion of the British line had wholly collapsed, and the Saxons were running riot. Wolf-clad warriors surged past what remained of the war band whose frenzied assault had broken the line. They offered no quarter to the diminishing number of defenders who died where they stood.

However, just a short distance away, a vicious counter-thrust delivered slaughter in the opposite direction. Following Bors' lead, the British abandoned any thought of defence and were rapidly overrunning the surprised and exhausted Saxons.

And smack in the middle of these two disparate battles going in opposite directions, in a rapidly clearing area of space, was a time-travelling Celt, a Saxon cultivator and what remained of the Prince of the Britons.

***

"Give me the worst-case scenario."

Your channels explode, triggering a series of knock-on effects that rip a black hole in reality. All known and unknown life in the universe will cease immediately.

"Fuck! Seriously?"

Yes. Of course, the odds of that happening are, there was a brief pause, *vanishingly slight. I'm not sure I even have words for the numbers. It would be twice as likely, for example, for the sun to grow a face and begin serenading us with Joe Dolce's mighty hit, 'Shaddap your face.'*

"Unusual reference considering the circumstances, but I'm here for it. But if it is so unlikely, why mention it!?!"

You asked for the worst-case scenario of you trying to fast-travel in your current state of Qi exhaustion.

"Yes, in a cost-benefit way. Not in a Steven-King-fever-dream-of-the-most-unlikley-thing-possible kind of way."

My arm suddenly jerked to the left as Drywyn took it upon itself to defend against a charging Saxon. With two quick slashes, it opened the belly of the spearman, who collapsed screaming to the floor, clutching his intestines.

"Dude! What the fuck was that?"

What?

"Why did you do that? What's wrong with killing him normally?"

Fuck's sake. Don't disembowel them. Don't burst into flames when people catch you. What the fuck is it I am allowed to do? How about, just once in a fucking while, we try: 'thank you, Drynwyn. You are literally the only fucking thing standing between us all and immediate death, you fucking legend.'

"Look, it's not that I'm not grateful. Big thank you for the save. It's just," I looked down at the still whimpering man at my feet, "I mean, he's not even dead yet."

Drynwyn jerked downwards, splitting the spearman's head in half.

Problem solved.

I screwed up my eyes for a moment. What with the chaos of battle, Merlin being needlessly literal, and Drynwyn ... being Drynwyn, I was finding concentrating on saving our arses rather tricky. My empathy for Premier League football referees was rapidly increasing.

"Drynwyn, I need to give you to Melehan for a few minutes while I think about what to do. Do not burn him."

Sweetcheeks, I burn the unrighteous. Always have, constantly fucking will.

"Well, you better find him righteous when he grabs hold of you, do you hear me? Someone needs to have you so you can fight, and I need to work on getting us out of here. And if you ever call me that again, we're resurrecting the "flaccid noodle" nickname."

I passed the sword to Melehan, who, unsurprisingly, was less than delighted with this development. As he did not spontaneously combust, I presume he was either one of those good Saxons everyone talks about or Drynwyn finally read the room.

"Big M, what's the most likely, hear my words, downside of me just beaming us out of here?"

Thank you for being so precise. You see, it costs nothing to consider your frame of reference properly.

"Sure, let's debate semantics. I'm sure those three angry-looking Saxons coming this way will wait."

Melehan was bodily dragged towards them as Drywyn closed to engage.

The most likely downside would be the rupturing of your channels mid-transfer, and you - and everyone travelling with you - becoming lost in the space between realms.

"And that would be bad, I'm guessing?"

Well, yes. But on the plus side, not for very long.

The three Saxons were already cooling corpses, and Melehan was covered in blood and looking like he was going to be sick.

"Okay. And how likely is that?"

Let's just say, in your current state of Qi exhaustion, if it didn't happen, I'd be pleasantly surprised.

"Awesome. Do you have any other ideas at all?"

Nothing comes to mind.

I looked around at the battlefield. In front of me, things weren't looking too bad. Bors was a fucking nightmare and had, by sheer cussed violence, salvaged a good half of the Marghekyon into some sort of order. It looked to me as if they just kept pressing forward, they would be free and clear.

Behind me, though, was carnage. A few Britons still stood, mostly fighting back to back, but they just hadn't realised they were dead yet. We probably had a minute at most before the mop-up operation was finished, and those Saxons charged towards Bors' island of resistance, wiping us out as collateral damage.

There was, of course, an even worse outcome. Bors could notice our plight and drag men who had just fought their way to freedom back into the meat grinder and certain death. He'd asked me to get Arthur out of here if the line broke. I didn't want the cost of me, once again, falling short of expectations to be the death of over a hundred men. Even for me, that was an exceptionally high failure rate.

"Merlin, is there anything short of fast travel I can try that might be less dangerous?"

Not unless you happen to know how to open and maintain a portal, my dear.

"Funny you should say that."

I looked up and met Melehan's eyes.

Lieutenant Dan seemed to have found his way onto a shrimp boat and was fucking loving it.

CHAPTER 60 - IN WHICH WE GET A ROGUE ONE MOMENT. REMEMBER NOT CARING ABOUT MELEHAN? SHAME ON YOU

Bors screamed in triumph as the pulverised Saxon folded beneath the hammering of his fists. He'd lost his spear early on in the charge and had eventually resorted to driving punches into - and through - enemy shields.

He stared around , wild-eyed in rage, locating his next victim, but in front of him were only trees. It took a few moments to register, but then, exhausted, he dropped to one knee, gulping in lungfuls of air. Somehow, they'd, literally, battered their way clean through all the Saxons on this side of the battle.

Not bad from a standing start in a shattered shield wall, even if he did say so himself. There'd probably be a song in it somewhere.

He felt rational thinking start to come a little easier as the bloodlust began to fade: the tell-tale red sheen of his vision returning to normal.

As he sucked in a particularly deep breath, he felt his leather jerkin burst at the seams, ripping clean in half. The surprise instinctively made him bunch his bloody hands into fists, which flexed his forearms. This caused his copper bracers to ping off.

"Fuck."

"You okay, sir?" A waterskin was pressed into his hands.

"Nothing to worry about. I must have levelled up somewhere back there. Fucking grown again."

"And I'm sure Mrs Bors will be happy to hear it, sir. Heard she already walks like a cavalry veteran."

"Fuck off."

He poured the water over his head and shook himself like a dog to fling pinked liquid away. Ignoring his increasingly naked state, his boots ripped in two as he stood up, Bors turned to take in the state of play around him.

It was both better and worse than he had feared.

By his quick reckoning, a little under a hundred men were recovering on the ground around him. What had started as a glorious final charge into the jaws of certain death seemed to have actually rallied a decent number of men to safety.

"Never seen anything like it." Bors looked down at the speaker, a wounded spearman lying on his back, staring at the sky. "We kept thinking you were doomed. That one of the fuckers would remember they had a spear in their hand and gut you like a fish. But they just panicked as you ran into them. They folded like tents in a gale. It was all we could do to keep up as you butchered through them."

He winked at the man and moved on. If he was pleased with the numbers he'd pulled out of the chaos of the routed line, he was devastated to see so few of his childhood friends with them. He'd felt Palamedes be torn from his side quite early on, and he'd seen Eliwlod take a sword to the gut right at the end. It'd been that last wanker he'd beaten to a pulp who had done it.

But other than Gawayne and Peredur, he couldn't see any other of the original members of the Marghekyon. His head swam as he thought what that meant for the country. In one piddly little action, in the back end of nowhere, the Saxons had pretty much removed the heart - or at the very least the balls - of the British forces. It was a devastating blow, and he did not even think they knew they'd achieved it.

Then, his brain finally caught up with the hollow feeling that had been in his stomach since he returned to his senses from his battle fury. That wasn't the most important thing, though, was it? Had that Celt wizard got Arthur out when it all went to shit?

He swung round to look at the way they had come on their charge.

As far as his eyes could see, the forest floor was littered with dead and dying bodies. It looked like his assault had completely decimated the Saxons fighting under the banner of the stag. But he could just make out the fur-clad ones mopping up what remained of that half of his army down at the edge of the clearing.

And just in front of them, so close he couldn't believe the Saxons hadn't seen them yet, was a small group of figures Bors really wished he hadn't noticed.

"Form up!"

To their credit, what remained of his men pulled themselves into something approaching order. But it was a sorry sight. If they weren't unarmed, they were carrying injuries. It was some sort of miracle they'd made it out, and now they were going to spit that luck back in the gods' faces.

He didn't think there was one of them, including him, that would survive going back down that hill against those wolfy fuckers. He didn't know if he had the right to ask them to do it.

But he was going to. Because he'd asked a Celt for a favour, and she'd let him down.

"We seem to have left some of those fuckers unmolested, boys. Don't know about you, but that doesn't sit too well with me. I figure we go back down there and reintroduce ourselves. What do we all think?"

If there wasn't exactly a roar of approval, not one of them actively protested.

Fuck, he loved these guys. They'd done the impossible. They'd had their line broken, been utterly mauled, and still had the wherewithal to bite it off and shove it right back down the Saxon's throats. And now they were going to try to do it all over again.

And he had no doubt they'd be cut to pieces.

"On my mark, follow me down there, boys. Let's see if I can kill enough of them to earn another nice surprise for Mrs Bors."

An admirable sentiment, Sir Bors. If I could have a few moments of your time, though, we're about to try something.

***

Melehan closed his eyes, pressing his fists tightly together.

233

Behind him, much to my surprise, a hazy scene resolved in the air. It was pretty insubstantial, but I could make out rolling fields, little groups of sheep and even the odd cow dropping its guts on the grass.

I had no idea to where the Saxon cultivator had opened a portal, but there was no waiting horde of blood-thirsty spearmen waiting for me that I could see, so I was all for giving it a whirl.

"Give me a hand with Arthur," I bent down to pick up one end of the stretcher, but he didn't move. "Melehan?"

He has to channel the portal to keep it open.

"So?"

So he needs to stay on this side of it.

"Don't be stupid. If he does that, the Saxons will kill him."

He knows, Morgan. He doesn't want to be alive anymore.

I didn't know what to say to that. Not too long ago, I'd been stood, with my eyes closed, on the edge of a motorway, feeling pretty much the same way as Melehan did now. And, after I'd stepped off, I'd been gathered up and given another chance. After all I'd been through since then, how was I supposed to just let him do this?

Sir Bors is pulling the surviving Britons out and making for Tintagel. I took a slight liberty with your Qi and left him an exceptionally brief message. He says 'thank you'.

I thought about my interactions with Arthur's giant friend. "I doubt those were his precise words."

In the interests of continuing to build trust between us, my dear, I'll admit he said if you fucked this up, he'd rip your arm off and use it to sodomise you to death with the wet end. But, in his heart, I know he meant 'thank you'.

"Melehan, are you sure? We can still try fast travelling?"

The Saxon opened his eyes, and I was struck, for the first time since I'd met him, that he looked genuinely at peace. "My thanks, but I helped commit a terrible sin at Isca. I wasn't tricked. I wasn't fooled. I knew what we would do and practised as hard as anyone else to make it a reality. It was an awful thing we did there. I'd hoped that helping save your Prince would make amends somehow, but no. Some crimes just cannot be forgiven." He looked at his hands. "But they're not shaking any more. Not now I have made up my mind."

"Melehan, they'll kill you!" There were tears in my eyes.

"And I think that would not be before time. If it helps, we met over the body of an old woman I'd just murdered. And that action did not give me a moment's pause."

Morgan, I don't want to have to hurry you up here, but there are no Britons left alive on this side of the battlefield. Quite a group of Saxons are coming this way, and they look like they mean business. I can maybe dilate time for a few more seconds, but you must get Arthur through that portal.

Melehan had closed his eyes, and the expression on his face was almost beatific. I was now full-on ugly crying, snot streaming from every orifice.

I bent and gathered Arthur up in my arms. The burned man screamed at the movement. I put it out of my mind.

"Any idea where you're sending me?"

They're here, my dear. You need to run!

"All I can tell you is that it's somewhere on this tiny island of yours. I don't have the power to cross the seas. Beyond that, I am afraid I do not know. But the very best of luck to you."

I couldn't even look at him as I ran past and through the portal. What more was there to say?

***

Melehan felt her cross the threshold and immediately pulled his fists apart, collapsing the connection.

There were a few moments of peace, and then, opening his eyes, he was looking into the face of a man he vaguely recognised from the invading army. A West Saxon, he thought.

"Who did you just help flee, wizard?"

Melehan did not say anything.

The West Saxon smiled. "Excellent. I do so like it when they have spirit." He nodded to one of his men. "Bring him with us. Let us see whether I can find a way to make him more loquacious."

Melehan did not care. He closed his eyes and let his mind wander to an open field with a bubbling brook.

CHAPTER 61 - IN WHICH WE LEARN OF THE NECESSITY OF FUCKING GUINEVERE

Uther's face was stony whilst Bors, breathing heavily from running to the throne room to make his report, outlined his tale.

When the giant man finished, an awful silence stretched out.

Finally, after what seemed like aeons, the King spoke, staring resolutely into the middle distance. "Do you believe my son still lives?"

Bors shrugged. "My Lord, that I don't know. Merlin told me to pull the men back and get here as soon as possible. His view was that his apprentice had the matter in hand."

"How can you be sure it was Merlin that spoke to you? I am sure that the wizards who levelled Isca," the King paused at that fact, still unable to process the news. There had been rumours, but to hear of the fate of that great settlement from someone who had been there was something else. It staggered belief. And then the fall of Arthur? Calamity visited upon them after calamity. "I am sure that anyone with access to that sort of power would not find it hard to, for example, project their voice."

Bors nodded. "Yes, my Lord. I did think something very much the same. However, the voice that spoke to me had ... knowledge of me to which I am comfortable only Merlin would have access."

Uther felt his lip curl into a snarl. He knew he should not be directing his anger at this man. Gods know, if even half of the story he had told was accurate, Bors had performed acts of colossal bravery and stunning military cunning in guiding the shattered remains of the Marghekyon back home. But angry he was. The big man would take it and understand. "Heartened as I am that you are 'comfortable' with that assessment, I need a little more than your fucking comfort to convince me this realm still has a prince! It may have eased your conscience at leaving my son to die to not question a voice in your head that let you run away with your tale between your legs, but I'd like some damned evidence!"

Bors did not flinch. "Merlin thought you would say something like that, my Lord. He gave me a message to pass on, which he felt would quell your anxieties." He cleared his throat and then paused. "I should note, my Lord, that there is wording here I would hesitate to use in your presence in other circumstances. Should I not be wholly reconciled to the certainty that this comes from Merlin ..."

Uther flapped a hand to stem his words. "I have a vivid memory of you pulling me back to my feet in a shield wall and telling me if I ever dropped a fucking bollock like that again, you'd reach down my throat, tear off my dick through my gaping arse and use it to blind both my eyes. I think we're past the 'all due respect to the crown' stage of our relationship. Give me the fucking message, Sir Bors."

"Merlin asked me to remind you that only two of you know what went down behind the woodshed that summer, and if you persist in being such an enormous cock, that number will dramatically increase."

Uther felt the heat rise in his face. "Did he say anything else?"

"Yes, my Lord. Erm. Baa Baa."

The level of awkwardness in the silence that enveloped the throne room was substantial. Eventually, Uther cleared his throat. "I am happy to agree with your assessment that it was the shade of Merlin who spoke to you."

"Yes, my Lord."

Uther stood and came down from his throne. The room was empty save Bors, the King and Queen Igraine, who had not yet spoken a word. Resolutely avoiding eye contact, he strode past the younger man to stand at the window that looked out on the approach to Tintagel.

He visualised this view filled with a Saxon assault and felt a stirring of fear. If what Bors said was accurate, the number of invaders was more than enough to bring an end to the British presence on the island. And that was without whatever those damned wizards could do.

And he had no Merlin. And now, maybe, no Arthur.

He turned abruptly. "You say my son was badly injured. How badly?"

Bors did not see a benefit in mincing words. "Had not the Celt intervened, he would be dead."

"Assuming Merlin's plan worked, and they got him out, is he going to be able to play a part in the war to come?"

Bors opened his mouth to speak, paused, then began again. "My Lord, I have seen Merlin perform acts of such wonder and mystery that I hesitate to think there is anything in the world that is not possible. Should we have him with us today, I do not doubt we would see Prince Arthur on the field again. But in his absence ..."

"Were his wounds so dire?"

Bors nodded slowly. The aftermath of the fire that had consumed Arthur haunted his dreams all the way back to the castle. He suspected they would for the rest of his life.

"I thank you for coming directly with your report. Whilst your news is dire, you have, once again, performed us a great service. We will be forever in your debt."

Bors knew a dismissal when he heard one and gratefully gathered himself up to leave. He had jumped off his horse and ran directly from the courtyard. Even to a campaigner used to difficult conditions, he desperately looked forward to scraping off the thick coating of blood, dirt and sweat that clung to him. He knew his wife liked him to return from war "windswept and interesting", was how she put it. But there were limits.

Igraine and Uther watched him leave. "If it is possible, that man has grown even bigger."

Uther turned to his wife in surprise. They hadn't exchanged so much of a word in months.

"Oh, stop your gawking. If we don't talk following the death of our only child, what help for us is there?"

"You misheard, my Lady. Arthur still lives."

"Don't be an arse, Uther. You saw the expression on the big lad's face as well as I did when you asked about his wounds. If our son still breathes, then it is not for long."

The heaviness of that conclusion settled on Uther like an anvil. How had this all come to pass? The loss of Merlin had been a body blow. Then, no sooner had he begun to recover, but rumours came his way of the fiery destruction of Isca Dumnoniorum. As if that was not enough, tales of a giant Saxon host gathering to strike south came with them.

And now this. His son was dead. Or as good as.

He felt tears sting the corners of his eyes, and then Igraine slapped him.

"No."

He reeled back in astonishment. "Igraine!"

"Stop it. You stop that right now. You do not get to wallow in self-pity at the moment your people need you. Did you not hear what he said? There is an invasion force arriving at his heels. I am no military strategist, but I imagine there are all sorts of preparations to make."

"But Arthur?"

"Is dead. Washing the floor with your tears will not change that."

He stared at this woman. She had probably just said as many words to him in a few minutes as they had shared throughout the last ten years.

"I did not know you held him in such low esteem."

This second slap made his ears ring.

"If you think my heart is not breaking, then you are an even bigger fool than I've taken you for. But we do not have the luxury right now of falling apart. The kingdom needs you to show leadership. It needs to rally behind you to war. And, whilst the people mourn their prince, they must know there is a succession plan."

Uther's eyebrows hit the top of his head. "Igraine, I fear your days for bearing children are -"

The third slap was a doozy. Blood swelled in his mouth. A tiny, forgotten part of his mind flared to life, remembering that there had once been something about the spirit of this woman he had found highly enticing.

"Not me, you half-wit. Guinevere. We announce she is pregnant, call in Leodegrance's promised spears, prepare for a siege and make clear the Pendragon line is secure."

"But she isn't pregnant! How long do you think it will be before we find ourselves with a Saxon army on our doorstep and thousands of armed, pissed-off Kernish joining them in the assault."

"So we make sure she is pregnant."

Uther threw his hands up in despair. "A fantastic idea. Why didn't I think of that? If only her husband wasn't fatally injured and whisked away in the keeping of some mysterious Celt."

Igraine shook her head. "Oh, Uther. You really are adorably dense. Listen to me very carefully. Wash your face, put on your crown, go directly to Guinevere's room and fuck her each way until Sunday until it magically turns out that the fallen, heroic prince left a lovely and much hoped-for surprise behind."

Uther's face was white, and his eyes were wide, as his wife took her leave of him.

CHAPTER 62 - IN WHICH WE LEARN ABOUT FOOD AND WINE PAIRINGS

"And did those feet in ancient time
Walk upon England's mountains green:
And was the something something odd
On England's pleasant pastures seen!

And did da da da da da dee
Do da da da da do da do dee?
And was Jerusalem builded here,
Among these dark Satanic Mills?

Bring me my Bow of some sort of gold:
Bring me my Arrows of rhymes with fire:
Bring me my Spear: bold bold bold bold
Bring me my Chariot of fire!

I will not cease from doo da Fight,
Nor shall my Sword sleep in my hand:
Till we have built Jerusalem,
In England's green and pleasant Land."

There was an awkward silence in which there was no applause.
I wonder if the impact of that stirring melody is lessened somewhat by you not knowing all the words?

That and she can't fucking sing.

Well, that, too. But I cannot help feeling the overall thrust would be more inspiring with fewer ad libs.

And, for the love of all the gods, picking a fucking key. Any fucking key.

To be sure. Also, in our current circumstances, I think it would be prudent of me to advise against promoting the concept of 'England' whilst we're at war with the Saxons. Somewhat mixed messages there.

Mixed fucking everything, if you ask me.

And contemporary audiences will be rather confused by mentions of 'Jerusalem' and 'Satan', at least for the next few hundred years.

"If everyone is quite finished being critical dicks?"

We'd been sat in the grass on top of a hill for a few hours. Arthur's screams whenever I touched him were pretty inhibitive to my desire to carry him much further. After a few, harrowing, tries, I'd simply settled him down a few hundred

239

metres from where we'd come through Melehan's portal. Once on the ground, he'd calmed down and then passed out.

Looking at the state of him, that seemed like the kindest thing.

After that, I whiled away some time trying not to think about what had just happened in the battle.

We appeared to be in the middle of nowhere. The lushness of the grass, the rolling hills and the sheer volume of sheep made me think we might be somewhere in Wales - but considering my geographical knowledge was about two thousand years out of date, I was taking that with a bucketload of salt.

Merlin still had me on a strict 'no Qi' regime, so it wasn't even like I could spend the time working on my cycling.

I am not sure how we got on to the topic of national anthems - you try making small talk with a dead wizard and a psychotic sword, with a crispy legend whimpering in the background, and see in what direction the conversation takes you - but I was happy to pronounce forth on my firmly held opinion that 'Jerusalem' was a more stirring song for the country than 'God Save the King.'

The critical reception was not kind.

"All I'm saying is that if Camelot is looking to adopt a national anthem, it would do worse than go for something like Jerusalem."

You say your people sing the national anthem to show respect to the country? Sounds to me like your rulers need to round some fuckers up and get heads on sticks sharpish. Given a choice of summary execution or enforced dirge singing, I know which one I reckon would engender the most fucking respect.

I didn't have much to say to that. Fortunately, Arthur chose that moment to become lucid.

Slowly but surely, the manastone I'd lodged in his hands seemed to be calming down the worst of the burns. The scent of soothing herbs that emanated from him brought tears to my eyes, reminding me as it did of the Saxon wizard who'd given his life so we could escape.

I appeared to have entered the sniffing-his-old-sweatshirts-and-weeping stage of a relationship I'd never actually been in.

Don't get me wrong, the Prince of the Britons was an absolute sight. All his hair had been burned away, leaving his head looking like nothing more than a misshapen thumb. However, the raw lividity of the burns had faded to something that looked survivable.

His eyes opened, and he made a noise that sounded like, 'Where am I?' However, with no lips, it was pretty hard to tell. He might have been asking me for the most appropriate wine to accompany roast lamb at dinner. I mean, that seems pretty unlikely, but I didn't want to rule it out.

Once he'd finished gurgling up at me, I leaned into where his ears used to be. "You're safe. We left the battle behind, but now we're stuck in the middle of nowhere. We're going to wait until I have enough Qi to try fast-travelling back to Cornwall." His pain-filled eyes regarded me blankly. "Or, if I'm understanding you correctly, personally, I'd go for a Cabernet Sauvignon."

I do not think he can hear you, my dear. In the process of healing him, you moved his conscious mind behind some rather thick mental shields of imagination. If I know Arthur, his spirit is probably engaged in a rather licentious orgy right now.

So what's with all the fucking screaming?

Residual reaction. There is probably just enough of 'him' there to undertake spontaneous responses. But I can promise you, he is not suffering anywhere near as much as it looks like.

I wasn't sure I believed what Merlin was selling here. I didn't have the faintest idea how to hide someone behind mental shields - okay, even as I said that, I know that's basically my entire life, but I don't know how to do it to someone else, you know? Melehan as a **Harry** maybe had the knowledge, but he was focusing more on pulling in as much Earth Qi as he could without sparing time to fiddle around with Arthur's mental state.

I dropped down into my artist's studio.

My dear ...

"Cool your jets, Big M. I'm just looking around."

Things were still pretty ropey in here but were undoubtedly much better than they'd been. My Qi was moving relatively smoothly around Vitruvian-me, and there didn't seem to be too many inflamed areas left. I wasn't going to risk doing anything until Merlin gave me the all-clear, though: absorbing a mana stone taught me everything I needed to know there.

The hard core at my centre that appeared when I developed [Personal Space Invader] was still acting like a spinning water feature within my channels, but I sensed it was slowly starting to fill with Qi. It was less than a quarter full right now, but I imagined something either awesome or catastrophic would happen when it was full.

Probably both.

Interestingly, I could see a thick line of Qi leading from that spinning core to the mana stone Arthur was holding so tightly. That made sense. Merlin had said that I was, through the mana stone, maintaining Melehan's spell, but now I wondered if it was doing something more.

"Mate, you say I'm keeping Arthur's mind locked away in his Playboy Manor happy place?"

I do not recall using those words, but from context, I tentatively agree.

"Is the mental orgy being hosted in the stone?"

Indeed.

"And is the only place that mind can go is back to the body from where it came?"

Well, not strictly speaking. You are the exception that proves the rule, after all. Where are you going with this?

"Arthur's body is like, totally fucked, right?"

I am not sure I would put it that way, my dear.

Absolutely screwed. Fucked up beyond all saving. Borked forwards and backwards with a sharp stick.

"Thanks for that. So, what is to stop us from finding him another body, a healthy one, and putting his mind in that?"

Other than professional pride at not stealing the plot of a terrible Wonder Woman sequel?

"You didn't get a Playboy reference, but you're all into throwing shade at Patty Jenkins?"

I take my DC adaptations seriously. I understand what you are asking, my dear, but that sort of mental transplantation is psychically traumatic. You were only able to cope with it due to your own mental strength and considerable potential as a cultivator. Arthur, sadly, does not have access to either of those reserves of power. The most likely outcome would result in the complete shattering of his mind.

241

"Okay, let's not do that then. How about, I don't know, shapeshifting his body so it was healthy? Like you did with me?"

There was a pause.

That is not an absolutely terrible idea. However, I was only able to do that with you because of our Qi connection. I would not be able to achieve the same effect with someone else.

"Can't you guide me through it?"

Perhaps. But I fear reshaping Arthur's body when it is so damaged would cause a level of pain he would have no capacity to survive.

"But you said he's in his happy place. Fucking imaginary bunnygirls."

There was another pause.

In all honesty, I lack confidence you would be able to maintain the integrity of those mental shields whilst also reworking his physical form.

"But it's possible."

All things are possible for a cultivator. But I cannot condone us placing Arthur in such a situation. Even if it all went perfectly, the pain he would suffer would be beyond excruciating. We could repair his body but end up breaking his mind. I do not feel we can take such a risk.

The body at our feet gurgled emphatically.

"That was either 'stop fucking around and fix me', or he was clarifying he fancied the Côte du Rhône."

More frustrated gurgling.

"Pardon me. A good Rioja Crianza."

My dear, you need to understand if this goes wrong, it will be the end of the story of King Arthur. I think we both know what that could mean.

I looked down. "Dude, unless we do something radical, the only Sword and the Stone this realm is going to be seeing is when I flip out and bury Drynwyn in concrete."

Hang on. What the fuck did I do?

The eyes of Arthur stared up at me, unblinking. I knew what I would want to happen if I was in his situation.

"Big M, we're doing this. I know what it means. Zizzie depends on there being an Arthur on the throne. And I'm going to make that happen. As soon as I have enough Qi in the tank, we're going all Mystique on Arthur's arse."

Martian Manhunter would have been a better callback gag.

"Fucking critic."

CHAPTER 63 - IN WHICH I NAIL BEING A NURSE. AND ARTHUR NAILS SOME IMAGINARY NURSES

The moment that I came off my Qi cooldown, we made a start.
Merlin had talked me through our outline plan: skin first, bones, and finally, the brain.

But I cannot stress enough how challenging this will be, my dear. At the very least, the amount of essence this will take will pitch you right back into full-blown Qi exhaustion. There's a reason why cultivators try to avoid this state and twice in a few days? There could be consequences for that. And that is before we consider the immense strain this will put on Arthur's sanity. Should your command of the mental shields you have placed around him slip, even for a moment, that could well be that.

I wondered if I should have been more transparent with the Big M that I had absolutely no idea how I was maintaining said 'mental shields' around Arthur. But hey, it's not like we had any other plans.

I had an ancient wizard to guide me, a stack of fully charged mana stones, and a can-do attitude. I doubt I had ever been more prepared for an endeavour in my life.

I took a deep breath, and with the calm precision of a teenage boy removing his first bra, I reached out for all the Earth Qi I could lay my hands on.

"Point of order, Big M. If you are going to wince, tut or gasp throughout this, you might be better off putting yourself on mute."

My apologies, my dear. It's just when there is a task requiring such profound delicacy before us it is rather disconcerting, right at the start, to watch you flail about like a newborn octopus. We are going to be reshaping the most fragile thing you will ever have touched. So, more china doll and less bull in the shop, I feel. But, yes, I will attempt to keep my counsel. Regardless of the provocation.

The plan's first stage was to try to supercharge Arthur's own healing process. Melehan had, essentially, coated the prince's body with a thin layer of Earth Qi, which I was maintaining via the connection I had to that mana stone clutched in Arthur's hand. From what I could understand, the healing properties the Saxon had imbued there kept Arthur's burns in constant flux. They were not getting worse, but neither were they getting any better.

Before we could look to achieve anything else at all, those burns needed to start improving.

Burns are much more difficult to heal than any other type of wound. The body's inclination is to toughen up the injured skin. Typically, with a minor burn, that would not be too problematic. We could heal it and encourage some minor scar tissue to develop. However, the extent of the damage to Arthur is so profound that the level of scar tissue which would result from any standard approach to healing would be devastating. He would be, effectively, encased in a suit of boiled leather that would be agony every time he moved.

243

"I'm going to vote for us trying to avoid that."

Arthur gurgled a somewhat emphatic agreement.

Indeed. So, we will need to ensure a more gentle process of regeneration. This, of course, is much trickier.

Fortunately, we had plenty of time before my channels were in a good enough state to try anything for the ancient wizard to talk me through the theory. When we'd exhausted all possible options – okay, let's be honest, we'd exhausted Merlin's patience for talking me through all the possible options – we made a start.

As he wasn't a cultivator, Arthur did not have channels as such, so when I shoehorned a fuckton of Earth Qi into him, he immediately began to shimmer with a golden light. Honestly, it was all a touch Rachel Summers channelling the Phoenix Force for me.

With a deftness of touch that would make a watchmaker weep with envy – that's a very nasty cough you seem to have developed there, Merlin – I tried to hold the Qi inside Arthur while coaxing his skin to remember what it was like before an insane sword turned him into charcoal.

Bit by bit, layer by layer, Arthur's skin started to mend itself, the twisted red slowly giving way to a healthier pink, as if he'd spent a day sunbathing on the beach rather than being the unwitting main course in a barbecue.

Hours passed, and just when the moon was high enough to give the whole scene a dramatic touch, Arthur had something approaching a normal body. As the skin healed, though, Merlin urged me to delve deeper into our Qi arsenal.

A skin makeover is just the first start, my dear. We will need to oversee a complete rebirth of sorts, minus the inconvenience of being born all over again.

As per Merlin's instructions, I closed my eyes, directing my Qi to Arthur's bones, urging them to remember their original blueprints. I poured purple paint into the marrow, telling them stories of strength and resilience.

This feels like a good moment to mention I was known as the 'Bone Whisperer' by some of the mean girls in the office. I think they had a different meaning in mind.

At the same time, I was stretching out his muscles, willing them to reknit themselves into a network of power and agility.

My Qi flowed through Arthur's body like a river in full spate – *I told you seeing it all as water would make the process much easier* - carrying with it the essence of renewal and growth. His bones, once brittle and fractured, now began to knit together with an audible pop. If you need a 4D experience, imagine a creche of baby elephants rolling on the world's supply of bubble wrap. His muscles, previously a sorry tangle of sinew and pain, regained their form and strength, rippling with newfound vitality as if they had never known Drynwyn's judgment.

So far, so good, my dear. I am noticing spikes of pain from Arthur, but nothing thus far to suggest a shattering of his mind. Now, mending skin and bones is one thing, but tinkering with the human brain is akin to trying to unravel the mysteries of quantum sock folding—it requires finesse, patience, and a healthy dose of sheer audacity.

"If you could see me now, Dad. Magical brain surgery on mythological heroes. Who would have thought it?"

Sending my Qi into Arthur's mind was a bit like threading a needle in the dark, with the fate of the entire tapestry hanging in the balance. I could feel Merlin hovering at my shoulder like an especially nervous safety net, ready to catch any stray sparks or misfired synapses that might threaten Arthur's fragile consciousness.

My Qi responded to my call, weaving its way through his brain like a gentle breeze through a labyrinth of ancient trees. My little-purple-paint-that-could sought out the damaged pathways, the frayed connections, and the scarred memories, nudging them softly, coaxing them back into their rightful places. It was a dance of restoration, a delicate ballet where every move had to be precise, and every gesture deliberate. It would have helped if I didn't keep getting snippets of what he was visualising at the moment. It took a lot to make me blush, but I felt that should the kinging thing not work out, Arthur probably had a career adding some extra chapters in the Kama Sutra ahead of him.

Careful, now. You need to pull out gently.

I think it is a testament to how exhausted the experience was leaving me that I attempted to make none of the obvious jokes here.

I collapsed to the ground with the worst headache in the world, and I could feel that I had emptied out the last of the stored energy in the mana stones. "Did it work?"

Good news and bad news.

"Give me the good news first."

You are not going to have to worry about people inundating you with requests for makeovers.

I groaned and tried to sit up, but it was like my body was wholly out of my control. "And the bad news?"

"I'm going to need you to grow me some hair back, Celt."

I vomited over what looked like the largest naked molerat in existence and blacked out.

CHAPTER 64 - IN WHICH EVERYONE'S FAVOURITE WARM, LOVING QUEEN OFFERS MORE ADVICE

"I can do this all fucking day," Bors yelled into the face of the Saxon he had lifted a foot in the air by his throat. Terrified eyes stared back, and he casually tossed him off the narrow bridge that led to Tintagel's gatehouse. There was a short scream, then a loud splash and Bors turned to face the mass of Saxons pressing to line up to charge towards him.

"I mean, it's not like you weren't warned. Tintagel. Din Tagell. "The fort with the constricted entrance. Did you think you could slip in as easily as I did with your mother last night? Now, let me tell you *that* was an open entrance. A thoroughly well-trodden path, if you know what I mean? Could even make out some footprints."

"Why does everyone keep going on about fucking my mother!" A giant Saxon, easily the size of Bors, pushed through the crowd and dashed across the bridge in great strides. Of all the ways to attempt this perilous crossing, in a blind fury, running and swinging a huge battleaxe was pretty sub-optimal.

Bors watched him come and stepped nimbly inside the arc of the swinging axe, landing a ferocious headbutt right on the sweet spot.

The Saxon's eyes rolled back in his head, and Bors heaved the big man into the sea. "And that's still not as wet as I made your mother!"

Seeing another contingent of Saxon archers form up, he returned to the rest of the small force holding the bridge and accepted his shield from Peredur.

"Having fun?"

Bors snorted, slotting his shield into its place with the others above their heads. The pitter-patter of arrows striking leather and wood was oddly soothing, considering the context. "They're either being led by idiots, or this is just a distraction."

"With the numbers they've got, I'm not sure it matters either way."

Bors didn't disagree. There were more than he could count already on their side of the bridge, and more seemed to be arriving every day.

And that was without wondering what the wizards were up to.

There was no non-magical way to attack the castle but through Bors and the twenty men he had with him. However, the Saxons had the men to keep up an almost constant press on the beleaguered defenders whilst their cultivators plotted away.

The big Briton had been true to his boast and had been throwing Saxons to their death 'all day'. But they only had to get lucky once. It looked like his luck would need to hold several thousand times.

"My turn."

As the archers had fallen back, Peredur slipped forward, all grace where Bors was all strength. As he ran, his leather-clad hand tightened around the hilt of his thin sword, his shield braced in front of him.

The rhythmic thud of his footsteps was overshadowed by the thunder of arriving Saxons. They hadn't yet devised a better strategy than 'fucking charge', so their iron-clad boots clanked angrily against the ancient stone of the bridge.

Peredur met the rush calmly, his blade flicking out and back like a lizard's tongue. One was down in a moment, pierced through, and their collapse fouled the footing for the one following behind. That warrior tried to jump the body, but Peredur's sinewy frame moved with a practised fluidity, and he shield bashed him over the edge of the bridge and into the water below.

"This is getting fucking embarrassing," yelled Bors. "What's the plan? To fill the ocean with bodies and walk over that?"

"Stop. Giving. Them. Ideas." Peredur was a blur of parrying, sidestepping, counterattacking motion. The clash of iron rang out like a haunting melody in the mist-laden silence.

But such fighting was hard work. His breath grew ragged, his muscles protested under the unceasing exertion and, like Bors before him, he realised that his position was becoming untenable. Glancing over his shoulder at the dwindling stretch of the narrow bridge behind him, Peredur knew he had to pull back.

Summoning the last reserves of his strength, he slowly began to retreat, drawing the growing tide of Saxons with him. Step by measured step, he gave ground, each withdrawal a calculated manoeuvre to ensure the safety of those relying on him for protection.

Then, without them noticing, the Saxons had come too far to retreat safely. They were well over halfway across the bridge when those still on the mainland shouted a warning.

Suddenly, Peredur retreated in a run and dived to the side and there, facing them, had been positioned a massive, mobile crossbow.

"Ballista to the face, bitches!"

***

Igraine raised her eyebrows as Uther entered the throne room.

"Well?"

Uther shook his head. "Nothing to report. We're holding the bridge with few challenges. Their losses would be catastrophic if they didn't have more spears than Bors has cuss words. I'd worried there was something more to their battle plan, but for now, I think this is it. They're going to keep charging the bridge until they get through. What's really pissing me off, though, is if they keep at it long enough, it will probably work."

"I wasn't asking about that, as you well know."

Uther ran a hand through his hair. "It's complicated."

His wife's eyes were cold. "It really, really is not. Of the many things about Kingship, which I would agree are desperately complex, the mystic art of this particular battlefield should not be beyond you."

"I'm not raping my son's wife."

There was no sound save the faint noise of battle wafting through the windows. The splash of Saxons hitting the ocean had become little more than background noise throughout the day.

247

"Can we win without Leodegrance's ten thousand spears?"

Uther shook his head.

"Is there a way to fool that damned fertility witch that's supposed to send the confirmation?"

Again, Uther shook his head.

"She's not been near the Princess since before Arthur took to the field, but we're surely running out of time. If they cross paths and she senses there's no little prince growing, this plan will be at an end. Do you have any better ideas?"

Silence.

"So why are you stood here like a fucking spare cock at an orgy!"

That almost brought a smile to the King's face. "You've been spending too much time around Bors."

"And you, my love, have clearly not. Do you think for one moment that if you ordered him to impregnate Guinevere, he'd mope around angsting about it? He hasn't got eight kids because of his winning smile. That is a man who knows what goes where, when and how far."

"And what do I say when Arthur comes home? How do I look him in the eye after doing what you propose?"

Igraine felt her resolve waver and took a deep breath to steady her nerves. "Uther, I have done many things over the years to ease your burden. I would not be so cruel as to speak of them now, as I know you have a good heart, and I would not have it break. I merely mention it to stress that if I could do this for you, I would. If the only thing holding you back is what Arthur will say, then I say to you he is dead. We both know he is dead, and should that fact be wider known, this castle would already have fallen."

Uther opened his mouth to argue, then closed it.

"You know I was not an enthusiastic participant in Arthur's conception; that did not seem to bother you half as much."

"That's different."

"It really is not, Uther. What do you need to make you do your duty to your people?"

He was spared answering by the sound of running feet and then booming knocks against the door. "Enter!"

An armed man fell to his knees. "Your majesty, Sir Bors requests your presence at the bridge."

"Why?"

The messenger's eyes flicked to Igraine. She smiled. "Assume I will not be offended by Sir Bors' earthy vernacular."

"He says, 'you won't believe what these sneaky fuckers are trying. Get your bony arse down here and tell me what to do.'"

***

"I have never seen anything like that before in my life."

"In all honesty, my Lord, I was hoping for something a little more inspiring than 'fuck knows'. Did you want another go?"

The two men were staring at a giant structure of wood that was slowly growing on the Saxon side of the bridge.

"What do you want from me, Sir Bors? They're building a massive magical bridge that, I presume, will let their full force cross straight over our battlements in one go. How was that?"

"Do you have any orders?"

"What would it take to stop it?"

Bors shrugged his massive shoulders. "Once it's ready, nothing. We can't let them finish building it. I need to get over there with a few of the boys and kill all their fucking wizards."

"How many boys do you think it will take?"

"I could probably do it with ten thousand prime Cornouaillen spearmen. But you know, time is ticking."

Uther glared at him. "You need to hang around with my wife less, people will talk."

"Let them. It's not like I'd be doing something useful, like fucking my son's wife."

"Sir Bors, I need that bridge destroyed."

"My Lord, I need the men to do it," there was a pause. "Do you want me to do it? I've done worse."

Uther let the pause stretch out as he considered it. But no. It was the first, and only rule, of Kingship. You never asked for something to be done you wouldn't do yourself. Even this.

"I'm told Leodegrance has a portal ready to send the troops the second he has confirmation. Get what you need ready to go."

CHAPTER 65 - IN WHICH THE EUPHEMISMS FOR ARTHUR'S PENIS ARE MANY AND VARIED

The whole 'passing out from Qi exhaustion' thing is starting to get old.

There was a time, not so long ago, that waking up with a pounding head, a sense of deep spiritual emptiness, and a strange man looking down on me would just be a standard Sunday morning in paradise.

But that was then, and this is ... well, an awful long time before then, and I haven't seen sight nor sound of a Cosmopolitan in far too long.

I'm not saying I'm looking back on the excesses of my hedonistic youth with nostalgia, but there's plenty to be said for blackouts due to titanic alcohol intake rather than from messing with the nature of reality.

I'm glad you are back with us, my dear.

"Pleased to be here, Big M. Is there a reason a walking advert for Veet is looming over me?"

Chemo-Arthur (*Morgan, that's beneath you. You are not to call him that again*) was not looking at me in a way that suggested the eternal gratitude of a Prince of the Britons was about to be lavished upon me. Although, without eyebrows, it was pretty hard to read micro-expressions.

"Celt, am I to understand you are responsible for my healing?"

He still had that deep, smooth voice that had been so attractive before his unfortunate flaming. However, now I looked at him post-healing, I realised he had a face that absolutely needed the beard. It wasn't a weak chin, per se, but you could tell he was royalty, if you know what I mean. Likewise, there are men who feel a shaved downstairs makes their John Thomas look more imposing. Arthur's equipment was currently doing an impression of the last chicken in the shop following a salmonella outbreak.

To be clear, I obviously wasn't catching Arthur at his absolute best right now, but any squelchy notions that had survived learning how he'd smell if I cooked him were now utterly drying up.

Ignoring his question, I sat up and took in the scene around us.

We were still in the middle of a nondescript pastoral wonderland. The brook bubbled, the sun shone, and the wildlife continued to periodically fertilise the fields. In fact, the only thing remotely different from how it was when I lost consciousness was the bald, stark bollock-naked man glowering at me.

"Arthur Pendragon, I presume?" I held out my hand, channelling my best Henry Stanley.

The Once and Future King frowned and declined the handshake. Probably because he was covering his little prince with both hands rather than any fundamental rudeness on his part. But the day was young. It might have been both.

Be fair. He is feeling extremely vulnerable and self-conscious.

I could understand that. One moment, he had been crossing death's threshold; the next, he was standing in a field, with his junk exposed to the elements and as hairless as the minge of a pornstar with alopecia.

We've all been there.

"But, despite that understandable discombobulation, I'm sure he's feeling ever so grateful to the wizard who has just saved his life, right?"

"Who are you talking to, Celt?"

"In some cultures, taking such a tone with your saviour might be considered rude."

"And are we in any of those cultures right now?"

"Apparently not. Big M, I think I preferred him when he was screaming and gurgling."

You are not really allowing him a decent go, my dear. If you could give him a chance, you will find him quite impressive.

"I don't know ... I've seen quite a lot of him, and none of it was especially impressive. Mind you, it is quite cold."

Oh, burn.

It would be fair to say that if Arthur was not especially enamoured at my company, he was even less delighted at hearing Drynwyn speak up.

"Who said that?"

It is pretty challenging to take up a threatening defensive stance while naked. It's why most major martial arts have pyjamas as an absolute minimum.

I couldn't be dealing with this right now, so I dropped into my artist's studio for a look around. All in all, things didn't seem too bad in here. Certainly, having become somewhat of a connoisseur of the shambles left behind after Qi overuse, there wasn't much unusual to write home about here.

My channels looked sore, but they'd been worse. Likewise, I might not be drowning in excess Qi, but the well had certainly been drier.

I refreshed all the little threads I had established to fill up my armour, my earrings and the now-empty pile of mana stones in my inventory.

Interestingly, the thin line extending to the one I had given Arthur was still pulsing away. Knowing what his mind had been up to in there, I wasn't really sure I ever wanted it back. I wouldn't be shining a blacklight at it in a hurry, at any rate.

I must say, my dear, your Qi levels are returning to an acceptable standard at quite an impressive rate. It would not be uncommon, for example, for a novice to need days, maybe even weeks, to recover following similar experiences.

"That's me. Always bouncing back like a champ."

Quite. If I may, you have used that expression before. Why do you consider that 'champs' need to bounce back? Surely, a 'champ' - a 'champion' - is, by their very nature, rarely required to overcome adversity?

"I'm interested, does this feel like the moment for this conversation?"

Perhaps you are right. In the same vein, though, and far be it from me to lecture you on etiquette, but you are currently in the presence of the Prince of the Britons. Considering our overarching mission, it may be prudent for you to seek to ... make a better impression than you currently are.

"I'm not fucking him, Big M."

Thank you for clarifying that. May I suggest that there are other forms of social interaction available? For example, I imagine offering a naked man some clothing would go quite some way to laying the foundations for a sound relationship.

"As long as that's the only laying you have in mind ..."

I had all sorts of outfits in my inventory following the looting of Vortigern's Dragon. I left my studio and fired Arthur a set that appeared to be called 'New Starter Armour'. To be fair, his general mood did take a slight upturn once he had it on.

"I apologise for my brusqueness, Celt. I found the experience of suffering through your healing quite trying."

I thought back to what I had witnessed him up to behind his mental shields. 'Trying' was somewhat of a reach. I pointed at the mana stone he was still clutching in his hand.

"Can I get that back, please? It's probably worth more than your kingdom."

Arthur looked down with surprise. "This?"

"That."

He shrugged and tossed it to me. On reflection, the verb choice there is unnecessarily suggestive.

I caught it, making a mental note to bleach that hand, and quickly stowed it away, linking it back to my core. It seemed to have retained the healing properties that the Saxon wizard had imbued to it. Just holding it for a few seconds eased my headache, and my general mood improved. That was interesting. I played with a couple of labels for it before renaming it 'Malehan's Rock of Continous Curing'.

<Unique Artefact created>

Hmmm.

"Was that a 'goodness me, Morgan, you've once again achieved something far beyond your years and experience. Well done!"

Yes.

"You could sound more enthusiastic."

I am sure I could.

"Fine, be like that."

I have nothing against you achieving astonishing things, my dear.

"So what's with the attitude?"

*The creation of unique artefacts is something that should be so far beyond your abilities I do not have the words to adequately explain it. This is not you pushing the **Ron** envelope. This is an entirely different stationery set, and I am not wholly clear as to the possible repercussions for the world that you have achieved it. We will need to speak further on this.*

I snorted and looked over to the now-dressed prince.

What was it with the men in the realm and their inability to show proper appreciation for a strong, independent woman who kept getting astonishingly lucky?

"Fine, Big M. I'll pretend you're not feeling threatened by my awesomeness. Arthur, shall we start again? My name is Morgan, not 'Celt'. If you're interested in properly saying 'thank you' for the colossal effort I made to fix you up, I'm open to it."

The bald prince dropped to one knee and took my hand. "Mistress Morgan. I thank you for your service."

That was more like it. If I squinted, I could almost pretend the sun wasn't shining off his oddly shaped dome.

CHAPTER 66 - IN WHICH, TO ACHIEVE A PROPER ETHNIC BALANCE, SOME SCOTS ARE SLAUGHTERED.

'Melehan's Rock of Continous Curing' worked wonders on my sore channels. Even with it safely stored in my inventory, I could feel the stone's cooling breath wash over me in slow waves. The tingly experience is exactly how the tea tree and eucalyptus body wash I like to use as a pick-me-up makes me feel. Only inside. On a soul level.

I'm not explaining this well.

It felt pretty damn good, is what I'm saying.

Under its influence, my Qi exhaustion was quickly a thing of the past, Merlin pronounced himself happy I wouldn't destroy the universe if I started cultivating again, and I was all 'fast travel' ready.

As it turned out, though, this was another thing that made Merlin sulk.

I am not sulking, my dear. I am just saying that there is no way you should have Tintagel as one of your fast travel destinations. You've never been there. This is not how these things are supposed to work.

"Mate, I'm not disagreeing with you. But, look," I indicated the page of my artist's studio that held my 'fast travel' options, "Tintagel."

*The design of the fast travel system explicitly precludes cultivators from popping up in places they have never been. Can you imagine the chaos this invasion would have wrought if Saxon wizards could manifest themselves anywhere they wished? But it is more than that. Even **had** you been to Tintagel to plausibly have it as an option, I have, for obvious reasons, set up significant safeguards against anyone fast travelling to within many miles of the place!*

"I kind of think you're yelling at the wrong person here, Big M. I don't know, is there not a Big Cultivator Manager in the sky you can complain to? Just so you know, you're giving off big Mystical Karen energy, right now."

I know it is not your fault, my dear, but we cannot overlook that you appear to be at the epicentre of the basic rules of magic breaking down. If you are not creating Qi techniques far beyond your expertise, you are crafting unique artefacts or finding ways to circumvent the fundamentals of cultivation. Such things should not be possible.

"You just said all that like it was a bad thing."

*It is a hugely bad thing. Do you not see? Everything in this realm exists in a careful balance. The great powers wax and wane, and as one rises, another falls. Reciprocity in all things. But beyond all that, there are levels. There are thresholds. There are **rules**. And none of them seem to apply to you.*

"Okay, so I'm Up Up Down Down Left Right B A Start. What's the problem?"

Gods help me, I actually get that reference. This is about far more than you being a 'cheat code', my dear. It is part of a wider breakdown in the fabric of the way things should be. I should not be dead, Isca should still be standing, and Arthur should not have been nearly torched out of existence.

"I don't wish to interrupt what appears to be a very tense conversation between you and your imaginary friend, but someone is coming. Several someone's, actually."

I looked to where Johnny Sins (*My dear, no. That's as bad as Chemo-Arthur*) was pointing and sure enough, a small group of horsemen were galloping towards us.

For clarity, I mean men on horses. Not, you know, centaurs. Although that would have been cool. I have some questions about the anatomical distribution there, if you know what I mean.

Far be it for me to comment, but I think you need to stop using that mana stone. It seems to be making you more ... lascivious than usual.

"Fair point. Any ideas on the newcomers?"

None at all. There is a chance they could be friendly?

"Mate, the whole 'cheat code' thing aside, if we didn't have bad luck, we'd have no luck at all." I unslung Drynwyn from its scabbard, and it burst into flames. Arthur, to his credit, barely soiled himself.

From my inventory, I threw him a change of trousers, a sword, and a giant circular shield with a cross on it.

The shield was interesting, actually. Whereas most of the stuff I'd looted from Vortigern's Dragon stacked in my soul space, the shield was one of the things that took up a slot on its own. As it had its own name, Wynebgwrthucher, I'd kind of assumed it would be something I could speak to. Like I did with Drynynwyn.

Considering how that relationship was going, I did not know if I was pleased or disappointed when it didn't chat back.

As soon as Arthur caught the shield, however, there was a noise like the cracking of a giant stone table, and the cross at the shield's centre resolved itself into the face of a very pissed-off old woman.

Oh, great.

"What?" I was suddenly acutely aware that the last time Arthur had caught something of mine, it hadn't worked out too well.

No, it's nothing like that. Wynebgwrthucher's not dangerous. At least physically.

Oh, wonderful. All alone facing a charging enemy on horseback. I'm going to get smacked in the face again, aren't I? Great.

Who the fuck is that? Wynebgwrthucher? Where did you come from?

Some moist bint just threw me to this hunk of baldness. Drynwyn, is it? Well, isn't this the day that just keeps on giving? Never met an afternoon adding you to it wouldn't ruin.

Do not get me wrong, it is a very fine shield indeed. It is just not very good for morale.

Don't let me put you off here, baldy, but unless you hold me a touch higher, you'll be wearing that arrow as a necklace." There followed a sharp clang. **"Great. It's my first time out of that cave in years, and I'm already catching quarrels. Wonderful. No, don't you worry. Just leave it sticking out of me. I'm sure it'll just go away on its own. Oh, here come some more. Fantastic.**

The men on horseback had pulled up a little way in the distance and were, yep, shooting arrows at us. That struck me as unnecessarily hostile At least try to get to know me first. Each shot embedded itself on Arthur's shield, which kept up a running commentary on the various flaws of his defensive technique.

If we got out of this alive, I couldn't help but feel the shield might be good for the Prince of the Britons. I did not sense he was overburdened with voices not raised in his acclamation.

"Okay, Big M. Moment of truth. Tintagel or not?"

It is, without question, the perfect destination. That is what is making me suspicious. At every turn, we seem to be able to call upon the ideal solution to our problems. It is as if there is a guiding hand in all this.

Our attackers seemed to quickly tire of playing catch with Wynebgwrthucher. Two had dismounted and had drawn insanely oversized swords. With a war cry that sounded like a rock troll clearing its throat, they began rushing up the hill towards us. The others remained on their horses and followed behind at a cautious distance.

Ah, claymores. It's been a long time since I've seen one of them wielded on a battlefield. I guess that answers where the Saxon sent us. Caledonia is so lovely at this time of the year.

I watched as Arthur moved to intercept the faster of the ones on foot.

What the fuck are we waiting for? Don't show me up in front of that fucking mood killer.

The sword fairly dragged me forward to stand at Arthur's side. Even though I was not sure having Drynwyn's fire so close to him was all that helpful to his concentration, I am going to admit the man could fight.

Full disclosure, outside of memorising each and every version of a lightsabre duel, I have no real frame of reference for such things.

But, goodness, Dark Age Saitama knew how to handle his sword, if you know what I mean.

Sigh.

He'd dispatched the first attacker in moments, removing first his right arm and then, pretty definitively, his head. As he did so, he'd blocked the second's downward swing with the shield, pivoted and ran him through.

I take it back. Now I think about it, I recognise that guy is fucking righteous. See if he wants a new sword.

The remaining horsemen were preparing to fire more arrows and, yep, there were more quickly coming to join them. I hadn't felt this unwelcome in Scotland since finding myself wearing a Union Jack dress (damn you, Ginger Spice) in Century 2000.

"So, Tintagel, then?"

There was a pause, during which Arthur caught another flurry of bolts on Wynebgwrthucher. Much to the shield's vocal displeasure.

As long as we are open to the fact this could be all an extremely elaborate trap. Tintagel.

Warp speed. Mr Sulu, take us home.

CHAPTER 67 - IN WHICH, AS I AM SURE YOU WILL AGREE, MY ALEC GUINNESS IMPRESSION IS UNCANNY

For what felt like the hundredth time, Bors ran through how he thought this would play out.

The Saxons were gearing up to make another doomed attempt to cross the thin strip of stone that connected Tintagel to the mainland. Why they were bothering when their wizards were halfway through constructing a fucking giant bridge for their whole army to swarm over at once was anyone's guess.

Maybe they were bored?

Anyhow. The plan. The Saxons would attack, he'd kill a bunch of them, gloat about it, and the blue-skinned bastards would retreat with their tails between their legs. But this time, the Britons would be doing something a bit different.

Rather than disengage and fall back, Bors - and every other suicidal lunatic who'd signed up for a chance at immortality – would charge after them.

The hope was that this was such a colossally stupid thing to do that the Saxons wouldn't see it coming. Thus, their confusion at the manifestly ridiculous tactic would buy the plucky attackers just enough time to reach the bridge construction site, slaughter all the wizards – who he was sure would charitably not seek to defend themselves – and retreat back over to the British lines in time for tea and crumpets.

"To be fair, I've heard worse plans," added Gawayne.

"Really?"

The fair-haired Knight took a moment. "Actually, probably not."

"Then you've a short memory. I'm old enough to remember your efforts at bedding Lady Kendra. I rate our chances here far better than you ever had at riding her." Bors easily dodged the good-natured attempt to behead him in response and, in doing so, bumped into a tall figure in full plate that had arrived to join them.

"How's it looking?" Apparently, King Uther Pendragon had come down to see them off. Although, the way he was dressed …

"Your Highness, tell me you're wearing all that gear because the Princess Guinevere has an armour fetish."

The King tugged at a gauntlet self-consciously. "I'll have you know it all still fits like a glove. Forty years old, some of this is."

Using the laughter of the men as cover, Bors pulled him to one side. "I'm assuming you're in all your martial finery because the deed is done, Guinevere is growing fat as we speak, and there's a horde of battle-mad spearman portalling our way? You just want to make a striking impression when they arrive. Right? Right?"

Uther stared back in response.

"So, no reinforcements?"

"No."

"Did you even …"

"No."

"Couldn't make it stand to attention or ..."

"You know the line between King and subject you are never, ever supposed to cross?"

"I'm rapidly approaching it?"

"Look behind you." There was a pause, and then, because he knew he owed an explanation to a man who was about to die because of his decision, he added, "I couldn't do it. I explained to her what was going on, why we needed her with child, and all that. And she just looked at me with such ..."

"Lust at your kingly forcefulness?"

"Disappointment. But, and this was what made it worse, not too much of it. As if me fucking her would just be the next in a very long line of let-downs. Like it was hardly worth getting worked up about anymore. I think she even sighed."

"I can imagine that killed the moment."

"Just a little. So, here I am."

"I can't help but feel the vibe is moving from 'impossibly brave attack to relieve pressure on the castle" to 'courageous final stand with us all being killed.' Would I be reading that right?"

"I haven't given up, Sir Bors. I'm just not going to let you have all the glory when this insane plan comes off without a hitch."

Bors looked doubtfully at the task before them. Even with Leodegrance's ten thousand spears, it would not have been a walk in the park. Without them ... "Just checking, there's absolutely no way the solution here could be to give me a few minutes to visualise my wife and then to lie back and think of Britain?"

Uther grimaced. "We need to leave that young woman alone. She's had enough men in her life let her down without inflicting your unwelcome attentions on her." The King scanned the milling Saxons on the mainland and raised his voice. "No, we will not let anyone else detract from our glory. Think of the stories they will tell of this charge! With no Merlin, no Arthur, and no support from our allies, the British forces sallied forth from Tintagel and drove the Saxons into the sea. When we pull this off, our fame will be secure throughout all of history."

Bors cheered with the others but couldn't help muttering under his breath. "This is certainly going to be memorable. One way or another."

The Saxons had finally gathered the courage for another go at crossing and were edging their way onto the stone path leading to the castle. "Right, well, no point overplanning things." He clapped Uther on the shoulder and moved about halfway across the bridge to meet the attack. "Glad to have you with us, Your Majesty. Leave some for the rest of us, eh? As soon as they start to run away, we go all in. And the first person back here gets the water boiling, eh?"

***

Life comes at you fast.

One minute, we were fleeing a handful of Scottish claymores, and the next, we were slap-bang in the middle of the Saxon encampment. Hundreds of pairs of eyes turned to us in astonishment as we manifested out of thin air.

"What the fuck, Merlin!"

257

I did explain, my dear, that I had all sorts of safeguards in place to stop cultivators appearing in the middle of the castle. What did you expect?

I hit <Personal Space Invader> as hard as I could and was gratified at the size of the wide circle free of spears that sprang up around us. I was certainly getting my Qi's worth from that skill.

"I don't know, maybe a head's up we were leaving a tiny Scottish frying pan for a much bigger, much more intensive Saxon volcano. That sort of thing?"

"Follow me. We're not too far from the bridge!" Arthur, in a faintly masterful way that I did not find wholly unappealing, set off at a run. There was just enough residual confusion in the Saxon ranks that he appeared to have a fairly clear route through.

Having absolutely no better idea, I followed him.

***

Bors abandoned his spear in the guts of the man collapsed at his feet and drew his sword. Say what you like about Saxons, and he'd said plenty in his time, but they didn't break easy. The three left of the group that had dared the crossing still gave no sign of calling it a day.

He felt sure, though, that if he dropped one more, the others would retreat. There was something about two-on-one against a man his size that did not inspire confidence. Especially after eight-on-one (And seven. And six) hadn't worked out too happily.

He closed to the tallest of those remaining and, with no warning, stomped down on his foot. An outraged look, quickly replaced by agony, crossed the Saxon's tattooed face. Bors took advantage of the sudden loss of balance to cuff him roughly across the head, which tumbled him into the sea.

As the screams vanished below the bridge, the other two looked at each and, yes, he was right, turned and ran for home.

"And now it becomes interesting."

With a blood-curdling war cry, Bors - accompanied by thirty others, including Uther Pendragon, King of the Britons - followed in their wake.

***

I'd never enjoyed sports at school.

It had always struck me that any activity which formalised the role of a handsy sadist like Mr Gibbons would not be worth my time. Fortunately, by Year 8, we'd learned if you told him you were on your period, there'd be no follow-up questions as to why you were not taking part. I didn't get changed once in four years after discovering that. Even now, I still have moments when I wonder what on earth he thought was up with my reproductive system.

I mention this because the sort of helter-skelter, running gauntlet I was currently engaged in was somewhat beyond my day-to-day experience.

Nevertheless, between the two of us, me constantly triggering <Personal Space Invader> and Arthur being steel-death personified - **Seriously, you need to talk to him for me. I want in. The things we could achieve together!** - we'd not yet been cut into tiny pieces.

Obviously, surprise was the biggest factor in our survival, but I felt more than a little proud of how far I'd come since arriving in the Dark Ages. Not that long ago,

I was rolling on the floor wrestling with a wolf, and now I was blasting enemies out of my way like Obi Wan on speed.

There are other spells available, you know? Whilst effective, there's a significant lack of nuance to your current actions.

"Fuck nuance. I'm not the wizard you're looking for, motherfucker. Move along!"

In the near distance, I could make out a thin stone bridge which seemed to be Arthur's destination. Oddly, it looked like there was a handful of people coming the other way. A welcome home party? Well, wasn't that lovely.

"Wizard, can you see that structure?"

Turning, I looked to where Arthur was pointing, noticing lots and lots of what I presumed were cultivators pouring Qi into a giant bridge. It was to scale as if Thor ordered his own, portable Bifrost.

"They're going to use that to breach the walls. Can you do anything about it?"

"No idea. Merlin?"

They appear to be crafting it in its entirety from Wood Qi. It's quite an impressive working, actually. Although, of course, I would have been able to complete such a task on my own, whereas they need an entire team.

"Yes. All hail you. Can I do anything to disrupt it?"

I doubt any of your current spells would make much impact, my dear. The best bet would be to introduce some Fire Qi to proceedings.

'Say no more. Drynwyn, you want a chance to suck up to Arthur?"

***

After some initial success, the British charge had become bogged down. True, they'd pushed the Saxons further back than Bors had expected, but they were still well short of reaching the wizards and their huge bridge.

"Will you fucking get behind me, Your Majesty?" Bors once again dragged Uther back into formation. "This is hard enough without me needing to keep an eye on you too!"

Although all those who had begun the charge were still standing - more or less - they were increasingly in a beleaguered state. Now that their forward momentum had stalled, it was only a matter of time before the bodies began falling.

"You know the one thing I'd kill for right about now, Your Majesty?"

Uther slammed his shield into the face of a Saxon, the wood shattering into pieces. "Ten thousand spearmen?"

Bors moved closer to cover the King's exposed side. "Okay. Two things. Ten thousand spearmen and," he cursed as his sword was wrenched from his hand by a collapsing corpse, "a chance to say a proper goodbye to Arthur."

Uther threw him a hand axe, the last of the spare weapons he'd brought with him. Things were starting to look grim. "I share that sentiment, Sir Bors. What do you think he'd say if he saw the mess we'd got ourselves into without him?"

A bald man carrying a shield that appeared to be loudly critiquing his fighting technique suddenly leapt over the top of the Saxon press. He landed in front of the astonished Britons and smiled broadly.

"He'd say 'run, you fools.' That fire's no joke. Trust me!" And with that, he took off across the bridge towards Tintagel.

Bors and Uther just had time to exchange bemused looks when the Saxon line was pushed to the side as if by a massive blow of wind. A red-haired woman streaked through the gap, following the bald man.

"He's not joking. Drynwyn's about to show the Saxons something really special. Get moving!"

Needing no further incentive, Bors forced his men around, roughly pushing Uther in front of him. All the way back, the big man felt the searing heat of a chasing wave of fire scorch the flesh from his back.

As he ran, ignoring the pain, there was but one thought in his head. "That's for Isca, you bastards. Payback's a bitch."

CHAPTER 68 - IN WHICH IT CLEARLY DOES NOT PAY TO PLAY CASSANDRA AROUND CEDRIC

C edric's face did not change as the toll of the dead was outlined.
Although no one could explain the firestorm which had ravaged the army, the devastating outcome was more than evident. Fully half of the Saxons who had been preparing to assault the castle had been reduced to little more than ash. If the conflagration at Isca Dumnoniorum had crippled the defensive capabilities of the British, the same had been inflicted on the attacking forces before the walls of Tintagel. At both blazes, whole bloodlines of warriors had been snuffed out in moments: generations of spearmen gone in an instant. It would take decades for either side to recover from the devastation this invasion had wrought.

The West Saxon raised his hand to halt the seemingly interminable list of the fallen. "When can we expect reinforcements?"

The other remaining chieftains exchanged worried glances. While it was true that Cerdric did not often shoot the messenger, flaying them alive was very much his style.

"Is there a problem?" Cedric's face continued to hold its impassive mask.

Old Plegmund sighed and grasped the nettle. He'd lost both of his sons that morning and saw little joy remaining in his future. "We hear tell that the ships from Topsham have turned around and set sail for home. They will not be joining us."

Cedric's feral eyes fixed on Plegmund's. "And the reason for such cowardice?"

"Merlin."

The word travelled around the command tent in a ripple, dropping all eyes to the floor who muttered it.

For the first time, a crack appeared in Cedric's facade, his right eye twitching at the name. "It is held by you all that Merlin is responsible for this disaster?"

Plegmund looked around, seeing no one else willing to contribute. Cheers, guys. I'll remember this next time you appear at my hearth seeking favours. Although, as he reflected on the likely outcome of this meeting, most probably not. "It would seem that appropriate revenge has been taken for our actions at Isca."

"And you all think that Merlin did this, do you?"

The old Saxon spread his arms. "I tell you what the men are saying. But, yes, if you were to ask me, I would be seeking no other explanation. Our wizards burned their settlement to the ground, and their wizard has repaid us in kind."

"Did not the High King tell us that we would not need fear Merlin?"

"He did."

"Do the men think he was wrong?"

Plegmund opened his mouth the answer, then paused and shook his head. "I only know that when I hear hoofbeats, I think a horse is coming, not Sleipnir. Who else can wield that kind of power?"

Cedric smiled. That was more disconcerting to the audience than anything else. "It all becomes clearer. Our reinforcements are returning across the sea because they do not trust the High King's word. Do they believe he will welcome their mistrust? That he will listen to them confess their lack of faith and not seek recompense?"

"Begging your pardon, but I think, considering what has just happened, most would rather risk the High King's potential displeasure than the certainty of Merlin's."

"It sounds like you are advocating we retreat, Old Plegmund?"

Oh, fuck it. I never liked the way skin covered my bones anyway. "If you don't, Cedric, you are either madder than we all think or an utter fool. We've had a good run, and we're richer than we were before we crossed the border. But without our wizards, we're not taking Tintagel. There's one way in, and we've had no joy travelling it. We needed that magical bridge, and, in case you missed it, it's gone up in flames. Oh, and it took a good portion of our supplies with it as it burned. I guess if we're feeling all glass half-full this morning, the loss of so many spears probably means we can still feed the ones we have left, but we'll need all of them to cover a fighting retreat if the Britons decide to expel us. I don't think the question is whether we retreat or not, only why we are stood around talking about it?"

No one saw Cedric draw the hand-axe he embedded in Plegmund's forehead. Few missed its impact.

Oddly, the topic of retreat slipped down the agenda after that.

***

"If you keep killing the ones who tell you the truth, soon you'll only hear lies."

Cedric's lip wrinkled in distaste. He disliked communicating with the High King in this way. Everything about wizardry offended him. "You would have had him disrespect me like that? A wolf does not back down from a challenge."

"And that is your problem, Cedric. You forget you are a human, not a beast. That old man was no more challenging you than had he been a mouse in the field. You did not increase your glory in killing him; you simply showed yourself to be petty. Do you imagine anyone present will seek to tell you hard truths in the future?"

The West Saxon bared his teeth. "And what of your truth? You told us we would not need to fear Merlin!"

"And you do not. I do not know what caused the tragedy that befell our forces this day, but I can tell you it was not through the actions of Merlin."

Cedric was unsure, but he thought the image formed in the shadows before him shivered when saying that name. He would consider that reaction more deeply at another time. "Bretwalda, what would you have me do?"

The most powerful presence in the Saxon lands was softly spoken. When they had first met, Cedric had made the mistake of equating that quietness to weakness. His reeducation had been swift and not at all pleasant.

"What that old man said was not wholly incorrect. This invasion, whilst not succeeding in all our goals, has not been a failure. Isca has fallen, we have sown terror across Britain, and our warriors will come home laden with prizes."

"We are at the gates of Tintagel. I can smell Uther's fear! You would have me turn around and flee?"

A heaviness fell on Cedric, pressing him to the floor. "I think, rather, you smell the burning flesh of every cultivator I could press to your service. More can now rise, but it will take time before we are as strong again. Whilst you were not brought low by Merlin, we must consider the nature of those who oppose us. Yes, I would have you come home."

"With one more push -"

"With one more push, more of your spears will end up in the sea, and you will further erode the confidence of your men. We have achieved great things and laid the foundations for our victory, do not waste our gains on Tintagel's walls. Return to me with all haste."

The High King's shadow collapsed in on itself as Cedric began to snarl his response. To be so close to success and to be pulled back! Like a beaten dog straining at its leash.

What was worse was that the Bretwalda, and if he was being honest, the old man this morning, was correct. Without his cultivator's magical bridge, he could not bring enough men to bear to take Tintagel. Given enough time, he could probably order a conventional wooden bridge built, but with no prospect of reinforcements, that would be foolish. There was little benefit in taking a castle to be cut off, without supplies, so far into enemy lands.

Standing, and tapping his teeth with a thin knife, he began issuing commands for the warbands to prepare to retreat. Without cultivators to manage communication, this would be a thoroughly ill-disciplined thing. Released from his leadership, each chieftain would take his spears away piecemeal. Most would strike directly for the border, but many would linger and hope to find easy pickings on the way.

He would lay odds on a third of the numbers now with him making it back home intact.

"That sounded pretty humiliating."

Cedric did not turn to look at the cultivator hanging from the wooden frame at the corner of his tent. There was not much left of this man, but what remained seemed determined to irritate the West Saxon.

"Have a care, wizard. I took your eyes but left your tongue should you have anything useful to say. I can always change my mind."

"You do seem to do that a lot. Attack the castle. Run away from the castle. No one knows what to think. Is Cedric the West Saxon a voracious wolf or a beaten cur? I'm quite sure I have no idea."

Refusing to rise to the bait, the war chief stormed from the tent, leaving Melehan alone with his pain. Cedric had learned nothing from him during the days of torture. In truth, there was little physical that could be done to the cultivator that his spirit was not already suffering. In fact, every cut, slice, and burn seemed to chip away, somewhat, at that colossal sense of agony.

His channels had long since recovered from healing Arthur, and, should he wish, he knew he had the power to free himself from his bonds. However, for now, this situation suited him. They were returning to the Bretwalda. That pleased him. He had words to share with the High King.

Making himself as comfortable as he could, Melehan let his mind once more drift away.

CHAPTER 69 - IN WHICH WE BRING BOOK ONE TO A CLOSE

"They'll be back."

We were atop Tintagel's battlements, watching the remnants of the Saxon army pack up and wind their way back home, when Arthur gave it his best Arnie impression.

The blue-painted warriors were dispersing in dribs and drabs, and I knew that Bors was just itching to lead some of the boys over the bridge to speed them on their way. So far, Uther had forbidden any sorties until he properly understood what had occurred to cause the retreat.

I was looking forward to introducing him to Drynwyn.

The woods of the mainland were still smouldering with the aftermath of the unholy firestorm unleashed by that sword. It really had gone all out to make a good impression on the Prince of the Britons. I wasn't sure how I was going to break it to it that Arthur would rather lop off and eat his own dick than touch that sword again.

At some stage, I would have to wander over that side of the bridge and retrieve it. I figured I'd wait until my daily 'fuck' quotient ran low.

After everything I'd been through recently, though, I felt I deserved the indulgence of a game of duelling movie misquotes. "They may come back, but not soon. You know, once, I had that sword cook an entire army for half a day. When it was over, I walked up to see what was left. I didn't find one of them. Not one Saxon body."

The wind picked up and blew through our hair - well, my hair. Arthur was still channelling his inner Yul Brynner.

He looked at me sideways. "I don't understand what you just said."

"That doesn't matter. I was just explaining how much I loved the smell of napalm in the morning."

"You are very strange, my Lady. Even for a cultivator."

"Stop. You're making me blush."

Even to my jaded emotional senses, the reunion between Arthur and his parents had been rather touching. They had so clearly reconciled themselves to his loss that it took some time for it to sink in that he was still alive. When that dam of refusal broke and the cheering and hugging began, I appeared to get something in my eye.

I'd shared a flat with a Russian girl back in the day, and she'd kept leaving these giant, doorstop books around for me to read. She worried for my soul, apparently. I'd ignored most of them, but after a particularly rough breakup, I let the one about the girl who got hit by the train get under my skin.

There's a line in it that comes back to me now as I watch Arthur, face flushed with embarrassment, accept the outpouring of parental love that came his way. "Happy families are all alike; every unhappy family is unhappy in its own way."

I wondered how my sister was.

We had not spoken in years. My choice.

Of course, being a lovely person, Zizzie never stopped trying to reconnect. Birthday messages. Christmas cards. She even turned up at my work the day Mum died.

At some point in my downward spiral, I'd decided that her life would be so much brighter without me in it. I still think that was the right decision.

A wash of relief flooded me. I realised I was thinking about her properly. Not as a potential blackhole. Whatever we had done this day, in whatever small way, had solidified her existence again.

Are you okay, my dear?

I watched Arthur move to the back of the hall to awkwardly greet a willowy blonde in a striking green dress. The Princess Guinevere, I assumed. That 'welcome home' was a touch less effusive. She didn't quite spit on him, but she clearly considered it.

"Not really, Big M."

Is there anything I can do?

"Doubt it. How bad do you think the changes to the future will be?"

It is impossible to tell, I'm afraid. My only frame of reference is that you are still here. I am working on the assumption that if the Saxons had been able to cause a catastrophic break in the timeline, your existence would cease.

"And as the polaroid you have of me is still complete, we're good?"

What?

"Don't worry about it. Well, that's rather terrifying and somewhat puts the city of Exeter in its place. Obliterated from existence, and the world keeps turning. How about all the dead Knights of the Round Table? I'd have expected that to cause ructions?"

I assume, with the invasion repulsed, there will be time to find suitable replacements, and the timeline can continue largely unaltered.

"So, we won?"

The lengthy pause was hardly the sort of thing that presaged a victory lap. *Define 'won.'*

"Mate, everything we've been doing has been to keep this timeline rolling. You're saying - acknowledging Exeter as acceptable collateral damage - we've achieved that. So are we done?"

If I say 'yes,' what do you envisage happening next?

I went to answer and then stopped. If the imminent danger had now passed, what *did* I see as my next step? That Merlin would let me go back to being dead? Was that really what I wanted anymore? After everything I'd done over the last few weeks?

We have foiled this first attempt, but we need not be so naive as to think that the Saxons will now retreat behind their borders, never to be heard of again. My death has released a tidal wave of Qi in the world, and it is clear that there are innumerable cultivators now growing in the vacuum I have left behind. I do not seek to flatter, but you are currently the pre-eminent British wizard of the age. We have discussed the flaws in your foundations, and we will need to address those urgently, but Britain will not stand without your support.

"That's a lot of pressure, Big M."

I looked around the room.

At Arthur, now experiencing a thorough tongue-lashing from his wife. And not the good kind. At Uther and Igraine - I had not taken to the Queen of the Britons.

There was more than a touch of the White Witch from the Chronicles of Narnia about her. At giant Sir Bors and the handful of remaining Knights.

They didn't exactly need me, but me being around would certainly make their upcoming struggles easier. When was the last time I could say that about anyone?

And that was how, a few hours later, I found myself at the top of Tintagel, swapping movie quotes with the Once and Future King.

"Apparently, you have the voice of Merlin in your head?" Arthur's eyes were firmly fixed ahead on the retreating Saxons.

"I do. Is there something you want to ask him?"

He wet his lips nervously. "Not really. It's just... I cannot get used to living in a world without him. His prophecies have shaped my whole life, and I don't know what it means for his hope for the future if he is not around to make it happen."

"I think he'd say that his prophecies were very clear. They were not about the deeds and achievements of Merlin. They were focused on the time of peace and justice that King Arthur would bring about. Just because he's not here doesn't make much difference. You're the important one. That right, Big M?"

I couldn't have put it better myself, my dear.

There was suddenly an explosion of flame from within the centre of the Saxons. I assume some unfortunate spearman had thought to pick up the expensive-looking sword innocently lying around behind their lines. I was going to need to go and get it sooner or later.

When I looked back over at Arthur, he was staring at me intently.

"What?"

"Will you be sticking around to help that vision become a reality? There will be a need for a new Court Mage in the world that is to come."

Rather than answer, I took a breath and dropped into my artist's studio.

What I thought of as my 'water feature' core was rapidly filling up, and I could sense that whatever changes that would cause might well be worth sticking around for. In fact, watching my Qi flow around my channels was an incredibly relaxing pastime.

There were indeed worse places to spend some time.

Suddenly hearing Arthur swear, I was pulled back into reality. He was pointing to a solitary figure sitting astride a horse. The man was clad in wolf fur and was holding a spear in the air.

Cedric.

The last of the blue-skinned spearmen were swarming past him and away, leaving this lone man as the final Saxon before Tintagel.

Arthur raised his own spear in reply. I was told this was called Rhongomyniad, and while it didn't appear to speak, it was still a fuck-off deadly piece of wood and iron.

The two commanders held the pose for what felt like the length of the Bible. Eventually, the Saxon dipped his head in some sort of acknowledgement, then sharply turned his horse around to ride away.

"What was all that about?" I was somewhat unfamiliar with the etiquette of penis measuring.

"He was letting us know he would be seeing us soon. So?" He turned back to me. "Will you be here when he comes back?"

I could feel Merlin's intangible eyes turn on me as they both awaited my answer.

In response, I filled my hands with Qi and fired energy beams towards the disappearing Saxons. I didn't have the strength to do any damage at this range, but I certainly managed to cause some panic; I was especially pleased to see Cedric's horse rear and deposit him in the mud. As the retreat descended into chaos, I channelled some Qi to my voicebox and boomed a speech out over the mainland.

"I know who you are. I know what you wanted. You sought to conquer these lands, and I can tell you I don't have the patience for that. But what I do have are a very particular set of skills. Skills I have acquired over a very short period of time and in an entirely random way. Skills that make me a nightmare for ... well, anyone, basically. Ask Arthur where his hair went. If you leave Britain now, that'll be the end of it. I will not look for you, I will not pursue you. But if you don't, I will look for you, I will find you and I will kill you."

I held out my hand for Drynwyn and pulled at the thread that connected us. It rose in the air, and then Catherine-wheeled to me, spiralling flames as it came. Its hilt slapped into the palm of my hand and then fired out the most over-the-top beam of light into the sky since the last time Lion-O summoned the Thundercats.

I levelled the sword towards the Saxons. "Fly, you fools."

And reader, they did.

I turned back to the now gawping Prince of the Britons. "Arthur, I think this is the beginning of a beautiful friendship."

END OF BOOK ONE

THANK YOU

Hi everyone! First off, well done. You've survived Book One, which is no small feat. I hope you're still mostly intact. If not... well, Morgan would say you're finally starting to understand the vibe around here.

Morgan's very much not done yet, though. If you thought this book played fast and loose with the rules of Arthurian mythos, wait until a few more familiar faces show up in the next book. More mayhem, more bad ideas, and yes, even more dark age debauchery. I won't spoil anything, but suffice to say, things are going to get worse before they get... well, worse.

If you've enjoyed the ride so far, I'd love for you to leave a review or spread the word. It's one of the best ways to keep this circus rolling, and it means a lot. Plus, it lets me know you're out there, as unhinged as the rest of us.

Thanks again for sticking with it. There's plenty more madness where this came from, and I can't wait to share it.

Cheers,

Malory
20/12/2024

JOURNEY TO THE DARK TOWER

Nothing ruins your day like a quest with a ransom note.

Especially when you're a fake wizard with real problems.
I was supposed to be dead. Instead, I'm stumbling through medieval Britain
with Merlin's ghost backseat-driving my magical education.
And now? Princess Guinevere's gone missing, and everyone's looking at me like
I'm supposed to know what to do about it.

Fantastic.

Nothing says "qualified wizard" like leading a rescue party of misfits—a prince
with anger issues, a berserker who thinks diplomacy means hitting people slightly
less hard, and me, still trying to figure out which end of my sword shoots fire.

Between dodging Saxon war parties, navigating the Enchanted Forest, and
searching for a Dark Tower that's playing hard to get, I'm starting to think death
might have been the easier option.

**Welcome to the Dark Tower, where the quests are impossible, the magic
is unreliable, and historical accuracy is someone else's problem.**

Coming soon!

RISE OF MANKIND 6 : AGE OF GLASS

By Jez Cajiao

The Age of Glass dawns, a fragile era balanced on the edge of oblivion. Will it shatter beneath the relentless hammer of fate?

From the depths of despair to the pinnacle of power, Matt's ascension to Dungeon Lord has been a crucible of blood and terror. But the higher he climbs, the more precarious his perch becomes. As winter's icy fingers close around his hard-won domain, Matt and his beleaguered allies yearn for respite. Instead, they face a nightmare beyond imagining.

The Coronaught infection sweeps through the land like wildfire, twisting human flesh into abominations that defy sanity. Grotesque mutations stalk the shadows, their hunger insatiable. In this maelstrom of horror, Matt must be more than a leader – he must become a legend.

With each agonizing decision, the weight of command threatens to crush his spirit. Can he salvage the humanity of the infected, or will the price of compassion be too steep? Nuclear fire looms on the horizon, a cleansing inferno that promises annihilation. How much of his soul will Matt sacrifice to shield his people from the coming storm?

In the bowels of the earth, Matt labors to transform his dungeon into an impregnable fortress. But in a world where loyalty shatters like spun sugar, yesterday's allies may become tomorrow's executioners. Survival exacts a terrible toll, paid in blood and betrayal.

Step carefully into the Age of Glass, where every triumph balances on a knife's edge, and a single misstep can leave you bleeding in the dark.

Preorder Now!

THEFT OF DECKS

By Lars Machmuller

When the deck is stacked against you? Change the game!

In the frontier town of Isarn, Chase will never be more than the lowly Darkborn thief he is. Banned from training, banned from acquiring better cards, if the Lightborn had their way, he'd be banned from life itself.

He's not alone though, and the one thing he and his friends have is determination. Losing a hand to a brutal punishment only fueled his obsession to get access to his own amazing, reality-bending cards.

That is the path to power and a future for them all. Nobody cares where you came from when you're rich enough. For now, though, they're facing both established powers, churches and age-old prejudices. It's time to get to work, and if the Lightborn won't share and play nice?

Sometimes the only way to get dealt a better hand is to steal the whole damn deck!

Buy on Amazon

QUEST ACADEMY

By Brian J. Nordon

A world infested by demons.
An Academy designed to train Heroes to save humanity from annihilation.
A new student's power could make all the difference.

Humans have been pushed to the brink of extinction by an ever-evolving demonic threat. Portals are opening faster than ever, Towers bursting into the skies and Dungeons being mined below the last safe havens of society. The demons are winning.

Quest Academy stands defiantly against them, as a place to train the next generation of Heroes. The Guild Association is holding the line, but are in dire need of new blood and the powerful abilities they could bring to the battlefront. To be the saviors that humanity needs, they need to surpass the limits of those that came before them.

In a war with everything on the line, every power matters. With an adaptive enemy, comes the need for a constant shift in tactics. A new age of strategy is emerging, with even the unlikeliest of Heroes making an impact.

Salvatore Argento has never seen a demon.
He has never aspired to become a Hero.
Yet his power might be the one to tip the odds in humanity's favor.

Buy on Amazon

WANDERING WARRIOR

By Michael Head

A divine quest to deliver justice.
One year to accomplish his mission.
After nineteen planets, there's something different about this one.

James Holden has reached the maximum level there is for a human. That's perfect, since he's the only one of his kind. A wandering warrior, without control of his destination, tossed between universes by gods who've failed to tell him why. James is the lone Judge on a new world in need of someone to balance the scales. He isn't afraid to do so with extreme prejudice. As the Chief Justice, he has to right the wrongs the innocent can't fix themselves.

As James quickly discovers, the roots of corruption run deep. Guilds choose to protect themselves rather than the people. Monsters roam the wilderness unchecked. Judgment is usually a decision between right and wrong, but nothing is ever that simple. This time, being the strongest human won't be enough to punish the guilty. James might have to recruit some new blood, even if he prefers to work alone.

On his twentieth world, he is going to win, no matter the cost. James will have to find a way to break past the limits of the system if he's going to have a chance at making a difference.

Buy on Amazon

KNIGHTS OF ETERNITY

By Rachel Ní Chuirc

When Zara awoke in chains she thought she'd gone mad.

She was Zara the Fury - mistress of flame and fear. Her name was whispered across the land, from ramshackle taverns to the royal court. Even the heroic Gilded Knights thought twice before crossing her path.
She was feared—*respected.*
Now she was curled up on a dirt floor on her fiancé's orders. Valerius, leader of the Gilded, mocks her cries for help. And the kingdom is on the brink of war over the missing Lady Eternity…
But that wasn't why Zara thought she had gone mad.
The reason why is that the last thing she remembered was blood, an arcade screen, and the gun that changed everything.

But no chains can hold the Fury, and when she gets out?
The world is going to *burn.*

Buy on Amazon

SCARLET CITADEL

By Jack Fields

Gormon Hughes is 19, thin as a broom, and has—not for the first time in his life—been swept into the path of trouble. Poor, recently heartbroken, and indebted to the sort of people who file their teeth into needle points and devour wriggling bloated spiders for fun, Hughes sets his sights on salvation.

That salvation is the Scarlet Citadel, a wealthy organization of pageant fighters, monster hunters, and secret keepers. With the aid of strange oracles, rare good fortune, and a unique power that bubbles like champagne in the core of Hughes' being, he must join the Citadel and advance himself.

But the ladder of progression is harsh and dark. The rungs are slippery.

And falling means disaster…

Buy on Amazon

LITRPG!

To learn more about LitRPG, talk to other authors including myself, and to just have an awesome time, please join the LitRPG Group

www.facebook.com/groups/LitRPGGroup

FACEBOOK

There's also a few really active Facebook groups I'd recommend you join, as you'll get to hear about great new books, new releases and interact with all your (new) favorite authors! (I may also be there, skulking at the back and enjoying the memes…)

https://www.facebook.com/groups/LitRPGlegion/

https://www.facebook.com/groups/GamelitSociety

https://www.facebook.com/groups/LitRPG.books

https://www.facebook.com/groups/LitRPGforum/

MALORY

BV - #0014 - 070325 - C0 - 229/152/16 - PB - 9781916729353 - Gloss Lamination